Miss
Understanding

By Stephanie Lessing

Miss Understanding
She's Got Issues

Miss Understanding

Stephanie Lessing

AVON
TRADE

An Imprint of HarperCollins*Publishers*

MISS UNDERSTANDING. Copyright © 2006 by Stephanie Lessing. All rights reserved. Printed in the United States of America. No part of this book may be used or reproduced in any manner whatsoever without written permission except in the case of brief quotations embodied in critical articles and reviews. For information address HarperCollins Publishers Inc., 10 East 53rd Street, New York, NY 10022.

HarperCollins books may be purchased for educational, business, or sales promotional use. For information please write: Special Markets Department, HarperCollins Publishers Inc., 10 East 53rd Street, New York, NY 10022.

FIRST EDITION

Interior text designed by Elizabeth M. Glover

Library of Congress Cataloging-in-Publication Data

Lessing, Stephanie.
  Miss Understanding / by Stephanie Lessing.—1st ed.
     p. cm.
  ISBN-13: 978-0-06-113388-6
  ISBN-10: 0-06-113388-4
  1. Fashion editors—Fiction. 2. Women editors—Fiction. 3. Young women—Fiction.
  4. Periodicals—Publishing—Fiction. 5. New York (N.Y.)—Fiction.   I. Title.

PS3612.E8188M57 2006
813'.6—dc22   2006008995

06 07 08 09 10 JTC/RRD 10 9 8 7 6 5 4 3 2 1

For my mother and sister,
the first girls I ever loved.

And for my father,
who pretty much taught me everything.

Acknowledgments

I'd like to acknowledge my devastatingly handsome and supportive husband, Dan, and my two amazing children, Kim and Jesse, who are, hands down, the most inspiring and entertaining best friends anyone could ever ask for. I'm so grateful to have you in my life. You're everything to me and I love you so much.

I want to thank my devoted father for his never-ending love and devotion and my niece and nephew, Chelsea and Zack, for always cheering me on, all the way from Boston and Florida. And of course, M&M and her amazing e-mails, my Aunt Bert, my cousins, Randi and Scottie, and the newest member of the family, Paul, a.k.a. Charlie.

I'd also like to thank Carla Lessing for bringing Dan into this world (you too, Ed) and for being absolutely nothing like Anita.

And on the publishing end of things, I'd like to thank my editor, May Chen, for making me reach further and dig deeper; you made all the difference. I'd also like to thank my agent, Kate Garrick, for being so incredibly cool and talented and for knowing when to tell me something is a very bad idea. I'm lucky to have you. I'd also like to thank Fauzia and John Burke and Erin Bradshaw at FSB, Courtney Lukitsch at Gotham, Pamela Spengler-Jaffee and Kacey Barron, Adrienne DiPietro and Nicole Rosenblum, Rhonda Rose, and of course, Liate Stehlik and Carrie Feron, and last, but certainly not least, my candy-loving buddy, Rachel Bressler, and every single person who worked on this book. Even if I don't know who you are, I still appreciate everything you did to make this book happen.

Thank you everyone.

Mom, Dad, and Robin, this one is for you.

Chapter 1

I'm not sure if this qualifies as some sort of obsessive compulsion or just a simple fear of children, but I've just taken my third consecutive home pregnancy test and I'm about to reach for my fourth. One can never be too sure, that's why I've taken to buying these little sticks in bulk.

Of course the results are always negative, because the truth is I've only gotten my period maybe a handful of times in my entire life—and I'm about to turn thirty. There's obviously something wrong with me.

Something very unfemale.

And yet, I live in fear.

After twenty-six rings, I pick up the phone and then hang it back up. I like to think this is our little signal but in all likelihood Chloe isn't aware of the fact that I'm trying to avoid her, which I can only manage to do for so long—because she keeps calling back.

"Hello?"

"Hi, it's me."

"So I imagined."

"I was just wondering what you're planning to wear tomorrow."

"Shouldn't you be asleep? It's nine-thirty."

"I was asleep. I had a nightmare."

"About my clothes?"

"You were wearing a turban."

"Don't worry, I won't embarrass you."

"Just tell me so I can picture it."

"Either shorts or sweats, something nice, I'll see."

"I'm getting up and coming over to help you."

"No you're not. Go back to bed."

"Zoe, you have to make them think you're an ally. If you dress yourself, you'll show up looking like an angry, confrontational, anti-social freak, who came from left field. Let me help you at least appear to be one of them."

"I appreciate your faith in me, but the truth is I refuse to use some sort of wardrobing affectation as a tool to influence people. Either they'll like and accept my ideas for the magazine or they won't. I couldn't care less what they think of my appearance."

"So, really what you're saying is you have no idea what to wear."

"That too. But I'm on the verge of a breakthrough."

"I know that's not true and I know you're pretending not to care. You're the one who always says, 'clothes make the man because they can make a woman believe anything.' "

"When did I ever say that?"

"I don't know, but it got stuck in my head somehow. Even though I'm not even sure what it means."

"Me neither, but if I did say it, I'm sure it was in the context of not giving a shit. There's no sense in trying to hide what I am. I'm sure Dan's already explained to the editors that I intend to make changes in the magazine—changes that reflect my values. I don't think they're expecting someone to walk in there dressed like a model. But if you're *that* afraid, come over and do what you have to do. I'll wear whatever you want me to wear. I've got eight million other more important things to worry about and I'd like to get started obsessing on them right away. So let's get this over with."

When Chloe arrives at my apartment, she's wearing a velour sweat outfit with some kind of skirt over her pants, an abnormally long, skinny, knitted scarf around her neck—and a pair of well-oiled cowboy boots. All this and it's about eighty degrees outside.

"Is it cold in your apartment?" I ask.

"Don't worry, I won't pick out anything like this for you. I was half asleep when I got dressed."

"I'm not worried. I don't have any sort of ranch-wear or anything velour. In fact, I've got nothing. You were right in suspecting I was exaggerating when I hinted at a breakthrough. All I did was walk into my closet and then walk back out. I can't imagine how you're going to pass me off as Deputy Editor of anything, least of all a fashion magazine."

"I thought Michael finally threw that thing away," she says pointing to the "Save the Peregrine Falcon" T-shirt I'm wearing. I've had it since middle school and it still fits me. For some reason, I stopped growing in seventh grade.

"Nope. I still have it. He tries to hide it from me every now and then but I always find it." I look down at my T-shirt. The picture of the falcon is so hideous and frightening, no one would want to save it, and yet I can't part with it. I have a thing for unlovable birds.

My sister and I make small talk for about thirty seconds and then she heads off to my closet to do her job. I follow her into my room and sit on the bed facing the window, trying to make it clear that I'm ignoring her, but she doesn't notice things like being ignored and immediately tries to get me involved.

"How is this possible?" she calls out.

"How is *what* possible?" I call back.

"Everything in here is pea green."

"Pea green is my favorite color."

There's a few moments of blissful silence but then she starts in again. "You don't even own a belt or one pair of normal-looking shoes or any panty hose with feet and believe it or not, I just found your field hockey skirt from eighth grade." Suddenly the tone of her voice changes and she says, "Although we might actually be able to use this somehow."

I walk over and take a quick look at my sister who's sitting on the floor of my grossly oversized closet, looking up. She's always been the type of person who believes that if you pray very, very hard, things you really want will fall from the ceiling. She looks so hopeful in there despite the fact that the only thing my closet is really good for is hiding cartons of art supplies I have no intention of unpacking. I haven't painted anything in months. At this point it's healthier if I just forget I ever tried and use the cartons for additional seating—particularly since I'm not really into decorating with furniture in the traditional sense.

Chloe spots a bunch of copies of Michael's latest book hidden in the back of my closet. She digs one out and starts flipping through it.

"Is this the one he's traveling around to promote?" she asks. She reads the title with the same degree of enthusiasm Michael intended, *"The New Conservatism: It's All Right!"*

"I'm afraid so, and how embarrassing is that title?"

"You should be more supportive of the books he writes. He can't help it if they're boring."

"I am supportive, considering how I feel about them." I take the book out of her hand and glance over the back cover copy.

"It's not that I don't appreciate his long-winded, antiquated notions of the importance of American polemic supremacy. On the contrary, I find it very comforting to know that I live 'under the corpulent wing of the prodigious father of all other nations.' I just can't believe anyone would go around bragging about it. The fact that I am knowingly and willingly living and sleeping with a Republican makes me the biggest hypocrite I know."

"I wonder if Dan's a Republican," Chloe says biting her lip.

Everything about my relationship with Michael reminds me of the time Chloe gave a speech in front of the entire school on how high school students need to get more involved in the animal rights movement. The speech was surprisingly educational; unfortunately, Chloe wore a fur vest to school that day.

The truth is I'm in love with Michael for all the wrong reasons. And by reasons, I mean key body parts. I can't help myself. He's so long and lean and muscular, all of his clothes lie perfectly flat on him. His long body and long straight bangs are a killer combination for someone of my height and hair texture. Sometimes I think our whole relationship hinges on the fact that I admire him for never looking wrinkled. And like most couples whose relationships are based on purely external features, we've learned how to live with our differences simply by fighting.

"I need at least one shirt with buttons to create the illusion of professionalism," Chloe suddenly yells out again, out of nowhere, trying to sound authoritative. I almost forgot she was in there.

"Michael's closet has loads of shirts with buttons. Feel free to look in there. And check out how all his shirts face the same way."

While Chloe meanders back and forth between the two closets, I go back and sit on my bed and open my laptop. I still can't believe that in less than twenty-four hours I'll have access to the minds of literally millions of highly competitive, willingly objectified, brainwashed fashion and beauty addicts. Once I hold up a mirror to the inner workings of the self-destructive girlish psyche and show them how to stop physically and intellectually starving themselves to compete for male attention, they'll finally be empowered to redirect their collective energy toward competing *against* those very same men.

It's imperative that we get ourselves elected to positions of real power that will enable us to make the kinds of decisions that affect our minds, our bodies, and ultimately our collective fate on this planet. It's now or never. We've got to stop undermining one another and start building the bigger, better team. What if Oprah gets hit by car? Then what?

I glance at my headline ideas for tomorrow's editorial meeting, hoping I've chosen a voice that the readers of *Issues* will relate to and understand. I need to appeal to them on their level and then somehow lead them down a path they'd ordinarily ignore. It's very difficult for me to talk like them and think like them without sounding a little condescending or as though I'm just outright laughing at them. Some of them could be cheerleaders for all I know. The idea is to strike just the right chord, gain their trust, and then enlighten them with just the right dose of humor about the way girls of all ages think and behave. That's the first step toward recovery. I think these article ideas are a perfect vehicle for change:

Do You Despise Your Female Boss, Your Female Co-Workers, Most of Your Girlfriends and Pretty Much All of Your Female Relatives? If So, You're Not Alone!

Why Your Girl Boss Hates You Way More Than You Hate Any of Those Other People!

Why Your Girl Boss Is Mean to You When You Dress up for Work!

Why Girls Are Mean to Redheads, Fat Girls, Girls with Freakishly Large Breasts and Sluts!

Why Some Girls Eat Their Makeup!

Why Some Girls' Teeth Fall out When They Drive over Speed Bumps!

Why Your Mother-in-law Still Shops in the Junior Department!

I close my screen and try to hear what Chloe is saying. She sounds upset. I really can't blame her, but she brought this upon herself.

"You don't own one decent pair of black pants. What if somebody dies on short notice? I wish you had told me a few days ago."

"I wanted it to be a surprise."

"Well, I hate to tell you this, but your only real option is to wear one of Michael's shirts tomorrow. We'll just have to roll up the sleeves and cut about two feet off the bottom. You can wear it with your field hockey skirt. That's the best I can do."

"Fine. Now go home and get some sleep. You look exhausted."

"Are you kidding? That's one outfit. I want to set you up for at least a month."

"That's totally unnecessary. I'll be fine. I'm working on a plan."

"Me too! I can already see you in a tight little nineteen forties wool bouclé jacket with a peplum, a knee-length straight skirt, and some really pretty vintage jewelry, and pearls. It's a shame the stores are closed. I'd love to take care of this while the concept is fresh in my mind."

Somehow she got a second wind.

"Are you sure that's me you're seeing?" I ask.

"I'm positive, why?"

"Well, seeing as how I'm four eleven, I tend to look like a prison guard in knee-length skirts. And I don't think I should wear short, tight little jackets either," I say, pointing to my un-wieldy set of 36 double Ds.

"Okay, how about if we replace the jacket with a beaded sweater? You don't have to wear the sweater, of course. Just keep it hanging on the back of your chair."

"I have to dress my chair, too?"

"You don't *have to*. But I'm trying to help you blend in. Everyone at *Issues* dresses their chairs with either a sweater or a cute jacket or a really adorable handbag."

I'm already thinking my usual ugly, *unblendable* thoughts.

"I'm afraid dressing my chair simply isn't in the cards at this particular juncture in my life, and I'm pretty sure I'll never own any of the articles of clothing you just described either."

"Work with me, Zoe. Just do a little fill-in shopping first thing in the morning and then swing by the magazine. I'll just explain to Dan that you don't own any clothing so you weren't able to come in right at nine."

"I can't be late on my first day because I went shopping. That would be blatantly taking advantage of the fact that Dan is your husband."

"So?" she shrugs, her eyes still scanning my closet. "What's in that box over there?" She's pointing to a huge carton in the corner that I was hoping would eventually shrivel up and disappear if I ignored it long enough.

"I have no idea."

"I think there're clothes in there," she says.

"How can you tell?" I ask, squinting at it.

"I just have a feeling."

I begin to pry it open. Chloe could very well be sensing something I'm naturally ill equipped to detect.

As soon as I lift one corner, I spot a big ball of T-shirts. I rip off the rest of the tape and stare into the box.

"I think you're going to be a little disappointed," I announce once I've gotten a good look.

"There must be something interesting in there," Chloe says, gently nudging me aside. At first she doesn't comment on the fact that there's hardly anything in the box. Instead she starts pulling things out and throwing them on the floor. When the box is empty, we both stare at the wee little pile.

"How many outfits did you say you wanted to make? Because I'm thinking thirty is probably an unrealistic number at this point."

"What are we going to do?" Chloe asks. I think she might actually cry over this.

"I can always wash and repeat. I once wore the exact same

thing three days in a row when I worked for *The Radical Mind*. Actually, I was wearing a different pair of pants and shirt each of the three days, but they were triplicates of each other, so no one believed my clothes were clean by the third day. It was pretty amusing over there, but I doubt it would go over well at a place like *Issues*."

"Did you do it to be funny?"

"No. I thought I had a little look going."

"When you have *a little look* going, you still have to change something about the outfit every day. Do you even speak English?"

Odd as that question may sound, I can explain.

When Chloe was a little more than a year old, and I was three, she fell down a full flight of stairs while trying to balance in a pair of our mother's high heels. Ever since then, it's almost as though she has two brains. One normally functioning brain and one tiny, hard-of-hearing brain that doesn't realize the other brain just said something.

I'll never forget that day. She had just taken her very first steps only a few days before and, even without shoes, had yet to master the finer points of walking. Like most toddlers, she had a tendency to take a running start, flailing her arms around, drunk with power, unencumbered by any specific plan, time frame, or even a clearly defined destination. In an effort to steady herself, she was always grabbing on to objects that made no sense. Like she'd pick up the phone receiver or a candy dish or a bottle of wine. Things were always crashing to the floor as she walked by.

I remember when she first appeared at the top of the steps in those giant heels. I felt my heart skip a beat. My whole body went stiff. The next thing I knew, she was on her way down, headfirst.

I saw the whole thing from the bottom of the stairs where I was playing with a Tonka truck (a stinging detail that never fails to humiliate me).

She must have hit her head at least seventeen times. I was so scared; I started crying hysterically, but Chloe didn't even care. She just reached up to check that her little hair clip was still in place and then turned around and went right back up the steps. "Where are you going now?" I screamed, petrified to let her out of my sight.

"New shoes," she answered, and then returned moments later wearing the exact same lethal pumps in a different color. I should have recognized this as an early warning that my sister would one day assign shoes, in general, much more importance than they deserve, and that her goal in life would be to grow up and become shoe editor of a fashion magazine—which she did.

I've been watching Chloe like a hawk ever since, and I still hold that fall responsible for half the things she does and says.

Years later when I saw her line up her shoes and assign them various office jobs, I got a flashback of her flying down the steps and naturally assumed that she was suffering from some sort of post-traumatic schizophrenia caused by the repeated head bashings. And when I witnessed her dressing up in grown women's clothing and applying about twenty coats of lipstick so she could fire herself in the mirror for showing up to work ten hours late, I really started to get frightened. I spoke privately about it to our pediatrician, who explained that my sister was engaging in a common form of play that many normal little girls enjoy, known as "make-believe."

Peculiar as that seemed to me at the time, I was nevertheless relieved. But I kept my eye on her, just in case.

★   ★   ★

Chloe starts sorting through the little pile of clothes, shaking her head as though I'm the one with all the mental problems. And then she spots my black boots.

"What are those?"

"They're my boots, Chloe. You know that. You see me wear them every single day. I don't know what I would do without them. They go with *every*thing," I say as quickly as I can before she has a chance to criticize them.

"What's all over them?"

"I think it's mold."

She picks up a T-shirt and holds it between her thumb and index finger, keeping it as far away from her body as possible, as though it's infested with red ants.

"Where do people buy these Ramona T-shirts?" she asks.

"Look carefully, Chloe. It says Ramones."

"Oh right, like that old band. I almost forgot about your punk phase."

"Punk phase? I had one band shirt and it wasn't even mine. I would never let myself fall into the grips of any sort of pseudo counterculture club that enslaves its members by forcing them to adhere to some monotoned, graphically uninspired, formulaic dress code. That's why I refused to become a Brownie, remember?"

She's ignoring me now because she's preoccupied with separating my clothing into three distinct piles: Garbage, To Be Ironed, and Maybe. There is no "Yes" pile as of yet. For some reason, one of my favorite T-shirts is in the Garbage pile.

"Are you throwing that away?" I ask.

"Of course I'm throwing it away. It has a hole in it," she says, careful not to look me in the eye.

"No, it doesn't. I just wore that T-shirt the other day."

"I guess a moth ate it in the meantime," she answers, faking a bored yawn.

"That's impossible, Chloe. You ripped it. Didn't you?"

"Don't be silly. You've been standing right here this whole time."

"No, I was sitting over there going over my notes a few short minutes ago. Don't rip stuff you don't like. Just put it in the Maybe pile."

"Okay, fine," she says.

I can't believe her. Even I wouldn't rip an article of someone else's clothing just because I didn't like it. Actually, I would. But I'd be more likely to do it while it was still on them.

She looks around some more and lets out a big sigh. We both walk toward the living area and she sits down on the box I was just about to sit on. I could really use some more cartons in this room.

"We're going to be up all night. Call Dan and tell him I'm sleeping over," she says.

Chloe's husband, Dan, happens to be the editor in chief of *Issues* magazine, which is run by his father, his uncles, and to some degree his mother. Chloe had been working at the magazine for about a month or so when Dan discovered her locked in the magazine's shoe closet talking out loud to a pair of Mary Janes. He fell in love with her that same day. Then he met me and fell in love with my articles—on the politics of corporate prostitution, women who compete with one another in the workplace using skirt lengths and heel height as their weaponry, liposuction addicts, and girls who just go ahead and tweeze their eyebrows right off without any sort of a backup plan—and offered me a job.

I accepted the job Dan offered me under one condition. I

forced him to make Chloe shoe editor. It was something she's wanted her entire life and I wanted her to have it. It was a mortifying moment for everyone, but Dan, like most good husbands, proved he isn't opposed to humiliating himself to make his wife happy. Now that I'll be working with my sister, I'll be able to watch over her all the time.

"Are you going to keep that hat?" Chloe asks, pointing to my old beret, which landed in the Maybe pile.

"Yup."

"May I ask why you bought it?"

"It was an emergency. My hair puffed up out of nowhere and I had to give a presentation to the volunteers for my Women in Crisis group. I needed the hat so as not to make a mockery of the situation."

"Big hair is very *in* I'll have you know."

"Yeah, well, not for me it isn't."

I tug on the ends of my hair to make sure it still reaches my waist. I never cut it, but it's so incredibly stubborn, every now and then I find a slightly shorter, stray curl reaching for the sun. I guess for old time's sake.

My entire childhood was ruined because of my hair—that and my complete lack of any sort of social skills. In retrospect, the thing I found most perplexing about being a kid was that most of the girls in my class reminded me exactly of Chloe. They looked like Chloe, dressed like Chloe, talked like Chloe, and played like Chloe, though none of them had sustained multiple blows to the head at any time in their lives. Believe me, I asked. Not even a mild concussion.

It was almost as if my sister had been a member of this exclusive club I had no idea existed. They all seemed to know things instinctively that would take me years to figure out. They operated according to a completely different set of rules than the ones I had made up for myself. Almost like a secret code.

For instance, unlike the other girls, I thought that if I liked a boy, I should alert him immediately. How else was he supposed to know? Since I liked all the boys in the class, I just wrote one note that said "I like you!" and passed it around. The other girls wrote notes to boys that said "I don't like you." *A lot of good that will do them*, I thought.

Go figure.

That's the interesting thing about secret codes. You have to crack them.

Everything girls did and said was a mystery to me. On my very first day of school, my mom begged me to wear the little jean mini skirt she had just bought, but I insisted on dressing more conservatively. There was something freakishly adultlike about me and I wanted to make sure the teacher knew I was a serious student. So I wore brown shoes with a buckle, navy blue anklets, a sort of brownish, greenish, gray dress that was hemmed just below my knees, and what I thought was a very arresting red cardigan.

Although I'm still completely inept at dressing myself to create any sort of desirable effect, I do recall that outfit being particularly morbid. I'll never forget my first day of kindergarten.

"Well, how was it? Did you have a good day? Did you make any friends?" my mom asked. She was standing at the door with this huge, hopeful grin on her face. My heart went out to her, it really did, even at that age, but I had to tell her the truth.

"Well, mom, I'm not sure if it was a *good* day, but here's how it went: The teacher opened the door to greet us and then told us all to just walk around and introduce ourselves. I guess I didn't understand her because I walked right out the door. I wasn't sure what the walking-around-the-hall exercise was all about, but later realized I didn't hear her say the part about introducing ourselves.

"While I was walking around in circles in the hallway, I suddenly felt like running. I ran back and forth for a while, which made me feel better, until the fourth-grade science teacher found me. Once he brought me back to my classroom, I saw that everyone was sort of clumped together in the middle of the room. I walked right into the middle of the huddle and tried to shake hands with some of the girls, but no one really felt like shaking hands once they all knew each other. After a few minutes, I sat down on a chair next to the coat closet. Finally, a girl named Caren Westman came up to me and asked, 'Are you going to wear that wig all day?'

" 'What wig?' I asked her.

" 'The *Annie* wig,' she said, tapping her foot as though she thought I was pretending not to know.

" 'This is my regular hair,' I told her; and then a few minutes later, she told on me. Can you believe that?"

"She told on you? For doing what?"

"For not sharing. I guess it was impossible for her to believe that anyone was actually born with an orange wig as hair."

"You've got to be kidding," my mother said.

"Yeah, well, it would seem that way, but I'm not. And it gets worse. When the teacher asked us to find seats in the circle, I asked this girl, Emily Coddington, if I could sit in the empty seat next to her, but she said, no.

" 'Why not?' I asked her. 'Everyone else is already sitting down and there's no one in this chair.' But she said she was saving it, on the off chance someone else decided to sit there later. So I had to sort of kneel down next to the chair so the teacher wouldn't think I was standing."

At this point, my mom, who normally forbade my sister

and me to even smell sugar, took out all the cookies that my dad had hidden around the house and lined them up in front of me.

I took a bite of a Vanilla Wafer and said, "Oh yeah, and then this other girl, Ellen Clark, who I was eighty percent sure was going to be my best friend for the whole year, told the teacher I said she looked like a corpse . . . which was entirely untrue."

"Wait a minute. Who did you call a corpse? The teacher or Ellen?" my mom asked.

"Neither, but Ellen said I called *the teacher* a corpse.

"And then this girl Mary Alice colored in her upper lip with Magic Marker and when one of the boys told her it looked horrible, she wiped it off on my cardigan. Oh and then, by mistake, I ate Morgan Bogdanfy's lunch instead of mine. Morgan had two cupcakes in her lunch and a bag of real potato chips. I thought it was mine, sort of, otherwise I never would have eaten the entire thing, and when I offered her the lunch you packed for me, you know the one with the green tea-marinated tofu chunks and the unsalted organic soy chips, she put her head down and started crying uncontrollably. She cried for so long, I thought she was going to pass out, but then, out of nowhere, she stopped and looked up at me.

"She just sat there staring at me for the longest time, almost as though she thought she knew me from somewhere else. Her head was tilted and she had this really funny look on her face, so I thought she was going to say something like 'Wow, where did you buy that dress?' but she didn't say that. She just kept staring and slowly tilting her head from side to side, like something was confusing her, and then she said, 'Are you a clown?'

"Oh and just as I was getting on the bus, I peed in my pants a tiny bit by accident. So, how was your day mom? Make any new friends? Cause I'm pretty sure I didn't."

"Did you remember to bring home your cardigan?" she asked, reaching for the cake mix with one hand and stirring a vat of chocolate pudding with the other.

"Nope. I gave it to Caroline Prichard because she swore on a stack of invisible holy Bibles (that only she and five other girls could see) that it was hers."

"Why didn't you tell the teacher?" my mother asked. She was clearly distraught but trying to retain an air of subtlety.

"Why would I tell that corpse some girl took my cardigan? Anyway, I didn't want it anymore. It had Magic Marker and saliva all over it and besides, I've got her shoes," I answered, feeling justice had been somewhat served. My mom looked down at my feet, which were neatly tucked away in the toes of a brand-new pair of sneakers that were at least four sizes too big for me.

"How old is Caroline Prichard?" she asked, looking at the giant shoes engulfing my tiny feet and imagining I had given up my cardigan to a grown woman.

"She's my age, Mom," I said. "See how big her shoes are? That's how big her feet are and that's how big most of the kids in my class's feet are. Is there a reason why you never mentioned that I'm a midget?"

"You're not a midget! You're just small for your age. You'll grow. Everyone grows. And don't use that word," she said, trying to convince herself.

She immediately looked up Prichard in the school directory and marched over to the phone. As she was waiting for Mrs. Prichard to answer, she asked me, "How did Caroline Prichard fit into your shoes?"

"I have no idea. She's no Cinderella, I'll tell you that. My guess is that she bent the heels down and wore them as slip-ons. I can't be sure, though. I never actually saw her wearing them. Basically, she just said, 'That's my cardigan.' And I said, 'No, it's not.' And then she did that whole swearing on a stack of Bibles thing, surrounded by all of her friends, so I said, 'Yeah, well, those are my sneakers,' and she said, 'Here, take them. See what I care.' And then she took them off and threw them at my feet so I threw mine at her, too. And that was that. I didn't wait around to make sure she was comfortable with the fit."

I could tell my mom was a little nervous to talk to Caroline's mom, but the strangest thing happened. Something I never would've imagined in a thousand years. After only a few minutes on the phone, my mom started laughing. I mean, really laughing. At one point, I heard her say, "cute sneakers," and then I could swear I heard, "Touché!" And then, a few minutes later, she said, "Bloomingdale's." The only explanation I could come up with was that my mom was challenging Mrs. Prichard to some sort of a duel in a nearby department store. And then it dawned on me. My mother and Mrs. Prichard were becoming friends by way of (and here's the clincher) cracking jokes and pretending nothing mattered. I grabbed a pen and started taking notes.

As soon as I wrote, *How to Make Friends: A) Say something funny and B) Act like nothing matters,* I got an overwhelming sense that I was in serious trouble. How in the world would I be able to convince myself that nothing mattered when everything mattered so much to me?

The next day, I officially began my study of girls. I recorded the way they interacted with one another, entire conversations, word for word, what they wore, and how they did their hair. I was particularly interested in hair talk because my hair spoke volumes about me from every possible angle, and I was anxious to try my hand at figuring out what the other girls were trying to make their hair say when they experimented with different hairstyles. Day after day, they sauntered into class with their new headbands and up-dos.

"I'm a fun girl!" said Jennifer's high ponytail on Monday.

"Fun girl. Got it!" said Rachel's high ponytail on Tuesday.

"I'm trendy," said Andrea's hair clip with the dangling Lucite balls.

"I'm pretty no matter what I do," said Laura's defiant pigtail buns.

"Don't even think about coming near me," said Mary Alice's lice on Wednesday.

I tried to fashion my curly dome into some fun shapes too, you know, for the hell of it, but no matter what I did, it always popped back into a perfect semicircle by the end of the day. I even tried to Krazy Glue some of my curls directly on to my scalp, but my hair is immune to things like glue.

By the time seventh grade rolled around, I finally figured out that if you let curly hair grow long enough, it eventually keels right over. That was the same year I discovered that if you color your hair, it's no longer red. From the moment I saw myself with dark hair, I knew there was no turning back.

Coloring my hair is the only thing I do that falls under the category of careful grooming. That and the constant showering. The showering is more of a disorder, though. I think it stems from the fact that our mother bathed Chloe and me in Phisohex every night for the first three years of our lives. If we played with other children, we soaked in it for at least forty-five minutes. They eventually took Phisohex off the market—probably because they got wind of how our mother was using it. I recently found out it's back on the market and it's taking every ounce of my willpower not to run out and buy it. When you've been bathed exclusively in germicide for a number of years, regular soap is a pale substitute.

Chloe walks over to my bed and starts reading my notes.

"What is this stuff?" she asks.

"Those are just some headline ideas I was planning to present tomorrow when Dan introduces me to the other editors—just to sort of give them an idea of what direction I'd like to take the editorial. I think these ideas will really hit home. Look at all the exclamation marks I used!"

"You're kidding, right?"

"No, why?"

"These article ideas are totally sarcastic. What could you possibly be thinking?"

"I'm just trying to subtly engage them in a little self-deprecating humor."

"There is nothing subtle about any of this and I think you should know that the editors of *Issues* never engage in self-deprecating humor. They engage in hair and makeup. I know your intentions are to cure girls of their bad behavior so they can no longer be reduced to stereotypes, but in the end you're going to be the one accused of stereotyping. I promise you, Zoe, no one is going to get this bizarre method of rehabilitation you've cooked up." She scrolls down a little further, her eyes bulging, "And how could you possibly suggest putting Michael Moore on the cover of our fall fashion issue?"

"I'm only suggesting Michael because he embodies the spirit of the underdog and the infinite possibilities that are created when the oppressed band together. Women need a role model, Chloe."

"But he's not even a girl. And what does any of this have to do with updating your wardrobe?"

"Look, we've got to turn *Issues* into something that will empower and transform our readers into intelligent, civic-minded individuals. Once we get our audience to understand the importance of banding together as a collective force in both government and the corporate world—instead of encouraging them to sit around wallowing in who's wearing what or who's dating whom—the world, as we know it, will never be the same."

"But he doesn't even brush his hair."

"You're missing my point. Women need to form a coalition. In order to do that, they must first take a good long look at why they can't get their minds off their hair, their bodies, their clothes, and their obsession with undermining one another. Magazines have always pitted them against one another for the sake of their advertisers' profits. And they keep upping the ante, forcing girls to think they need more of this and more of that to outdo one another when there are a lot more important things we could be teaching them. But first they need to really look at themselves—and laugh—before they can change."

"Zoe, there are plenty of dull magazines out there for people who don't care what they look like and besides, girls need to undermine one another. That's how they make friends."

"There are other ways to make friends and there will still be plenty of fashion and beauty advice, but it will be health-conscious, self-esteem–building advice. Someone should at least tell our audience that it doesn't make sense to look at girls who are five foot nine and weigh ninety-eight pounds for outfits that will look good on them—considering that the majority of our readers are between five foot three and five foot six and weigh somewhere between one-thirty and one-sixty."

"I know our readers. They want fashion tips and beauty advice from tall, skinny girls, period," she says and slides off the bed. As she's walking back to my closet, she turns to look at me for a second. She looks incredibly sad.

"Chloe, I thought you were happy that I'm coming to work with you," I say, watching her sift through the little Maybe pile.

"I was happy because I thought we'd be able to go out to lunch. I understood your plan to incorporate girl relationships into the editorial, but I thought you were going to do it in a nice way."

"How could you think that? When was the last time I was nice to anyone?"

She's walking toward me with a pair of beige socks in her hand. She puts them on the bed.

"I know they're beige. They're dad's," I say before she has a chance to say anything.

"Personally, I blame your entire clothing situation on Sarah Lawrence. Mom should have put her foot down, but you were so adamant about going there. All they did was turn you into a slob. Now we have nothing to work with. What a waste of money that place was."

"Granted, I'm not the best-dressed girl in New York City, Chloe, but college opened my eyes."

"Opened your eyes to what? How ridiculous it is to be feminine? You should have gone to charm school, not Sarah Lawrence. Look, Zoe, I think it's great that you want girls to recognize the absurdity of their own behavior, but you have to admit, your sense of humor is a little off."

"I like that skirt you're wearing," I say, changing the subject.

"You do?"

"Yup," I say. It works every time.

"Do you want it?"

"Not really."

"Well, take it anyway. It's way too short on me. I wore it to work a few days ago and I think my underwear was showing all day. It'll be perfect on you."

"Look at that. Now I have two outfits. Maybe I'll wear it tomorrow instead of my hockey skirt."

"I just told you, I wore it the other day."

"So?"

"So, no. You can't wear it. That's a basic rule. You can't wear something right after I wore it. Everyone will know it's mine. How could you not know that?"

"No one will notice."

"Uh, that's all they'll notice."

"Fine, I'll wear it the next day."

"No, you have to wait at least a month, and even that's risky. But try it on anyway," she says.

"I hate trying on clothes."

"Then at least try on the outfit I picked out for you to wear tomorrow. If there's anything wrong with it, you need to know now. You don't want any surprises, and you're going to be late tomorrow morning as it is."

"Why am I going to be late?"

"Because you're going shopping, remember?"

Like that'll ever happen.

Chloe takes off the skirt and gives it to me. It's brown corduroy with a brown leather buckle on each side. I think it might look great with a subtle pea green T-shirt. As soon as she takes it off, I ask her if I can have her velour pants, too. She takes them off immediately and I tell her I was only kidding.

But then I have to turn around for a second because I don't

want to laugh at her underwear. They have a ruffle on each hip. Sometimes I think she might actually be a little retarded. I slip off my T-shirt and reach for my hockey skirt and the white shirt she found in Michael's closet. At that moment, Michael walks through the bedroom door. I'm wearing a bra and underpants and Chloe is wearing her velour sweatshirt jacket, those frilly underpants, and her boots. She lost the scarf in the meantime.

"I didn't hear you come in," I say, standing on the balls of my feet to reach him.

"I'm not complaining, but is there a reason you're hanging out in your underwear?" he asks, hugging me back.

"Chloe is outfitting me so we can fool everyone into thinking I'm one of the girls tomorrow."

"Really? Since when do you care about dressing like a girl?"

"I don't, but she seems to think it's important for me to look the part."

"As a ruse?"

"They'll have their guard up if she walks in there looking like some radical feminist."

"Good thinking, but what's going to happen when she opens her mouth? And cute underpants, by the way."

"You really like them?" she asks, ignoring his question.

"They're a little out-there for me, but you look nice in them," he says.

Chloe puts her pants on, and I put on the outfit she picked out for me. Once I'm dressed, he gives me the thumbs up and then squints a little and asks, "Is that my shirt?"

"I didn't have anything with buttons. What do you think?"

"I think you look a hell of a lot better in it than I do."

"Then you won't mind if I cut the bottom off of it?" I ask, slipping it off.

"You can do whatever you want," he says and kisses me on the head. We talk for a few more minutes and then Chloe hugs us both good night. As she's leaving, she turns around and looks at me.

"What are you looking at?" I ask.

"Did they get bigger?" she asks, pointing at my chest.

"I think so."

"Wow. That's truly amazing."

"I think they get a tiny bit bigger every year."

"I always forget how big your chest is compared to the rest of you. It's uncanny, if you really think about it."

"I'd rather not."

"Which reminds me, we need to go bra shopping, too."

"Why, what's wrong with my bra?" I ask, while quickly slipping Michael's shirt back on and wrapping it around me.

"It doesn't fit you and it makes your breasts look like torpedoes."

"In a bad way?" I ask, without looking in their direction. I typically avoid looking down at them unless they've caught on fire or something. They do look a bit more obtrusive than usual.

About three seconds after Chloe's gone, Michael and I have sex. I should have taken the shirt off first, but I couldn't wait. I really missed him. It's looking a little rumpled at this point and now the collar won't seem to stay down on one side. I guess it'll be fine if I smooth it out a bit.

While we're having sex for the second time, I look down and notice that two of the buttons are now dangling by a thread and it's significantly more wrinkled. It occurs to me that I should try to take it off, but Michael won't stop moving.

When it's all over, I take the shirt off and lay it down on the floor. I vigorously rub my palms back and forth on my thighs to heat them up so I can flatten out some of the deeper creases. I can see now why irons are so popular. Next I take off the hockey skirt and lay it down neatly next to the shirt.

After I shower, I quickly take another pregnancy test and get back into bed, while Michael goes into a long, elaborate description of the discussion he had defending our current administration with the poor guy who was unlucky enough to sit next to him on the plane. As he's talking, I get up and pick up my black combat boots and put them down next to my skirt and Michael's shirt. I think they look pretty good together—all things considered. Besides, no one will notice.

Chapter 2

I realize that five-thirty A.M. is entirely too early to call someone. It's just that I need to tell Chloe about my decision to forgo shopping this morning, which means I'm now available to commute with her and I'd much prefer to get an early start. I'm so anxious to get there my whole scalp feels tight. Actually, my scalp has been feeling tight a lot lately.

I'm thinking that if I shoot uptown to get Chloe right now, we'll be able to completely avoid rush hour, be in midtown by six-thirty, have time for a quick breakfast, and still arrive at work by seven-fifteen.

I go back to the living room, sit on the nearest carton and stare at the wall. What do people do in the morning that makes them late? I've already retyped all of my notes and taken two more pregnancy tests. What else is there? I even had time to locate two tiny safety pins in lieu of shirt buttons.

I get up and go back into the bedroom where Michael is sleeping in another time zone. He won't be available to keep me company for at least another six hours. He's lying on his stomach with his arm hanging over the side of the bed. He has the most sculpted arms of any man I've ever known.

Everyone in Michael's family is blond and blue-eyed except for him. He has dark hair and brown eyes. Like me, he often wonders where he came from.

And, also like me, he harbors a suspicion that it's not the same place his siblings came from. This feeling of being different from our families is pretty much the only thing that Michael and I have in common. So far it's enough.

I sit down next to him and watch him sleep. There's no question that he's beautiful. Every strand of hair on his head is perfectly straight and exactly the same as every other. I could look at his hair for hours, contemplating its sheer dependability. No matter what happens, he knows exactly what to expect every time he looks in the mirror. He never has to wonder if it's defying gravity while he's just sitting there talking to someone. As much as I hate to admit it, I would do anything for that hair.

I lift up the blanket to look at his body. Still perfect. I keep expecting to wake up one morning only to discover that he's sprouted a patch of hair on his lower back. I expect this because that's the part of his body that I love the most and I'm certain God is planning to ruin it for me. I kiss Michael on the head and stand up to leave the room but he grabs my arm.

"Are you finished checking me out?" he asks.

"I thought you were sleeping."

"I know," he says, pulling me down on the bed. "I thought so too."

There goes another button. I make yet another mental note never to have sex in my clothes right before work ever again.

I take everything off, get back in the shower, and go through my routine all over again. Once my body is dry and my hair is reconditioned, I slip on my underpants, skirt, socks and boots, and survey my bra. I knew I heard something crack when Michael pulled me on the bed. This is the third bra I've lost to a faulty clasp. This is why I hate plastic. Anything that cracks under extreme pressure is useless as far as I'm concerned. And now I'm getting a sore throat and a headache. I hope my throat isn't sore because I inadvertently swallowed a little piece of the clasp? I could just see myself on the news as the first person ever to die from her bra.

Now what the hell am I supposed to do? That was my last goddamn bra. How could I possibly walk out of here braless? I haven't been outdoors without a bra since third grade. Maybe Chloe has one I can borrow. What's even more upsetting is that Michael's shirt is now missing three buttons and there's a little rip under the arm. Overall it sort of resembles a crumpled-up piece of paper. But I'd hate to cut off the bottom of another one, considering I haven't even worn this one outside yet.

I search around the apartment for another safety pin. No luck, but this bread twist-tie might work. I take a steak knife and make a little slit where the third button used to be. I slip the wire through both holes and twist the two ends together. This actually doesn't look too bad. I probably invented a whole new thing here, twist-tie buttons.

I call Chloe to tell her it's almost eight o'clock and to meet me at the subway on the north corner of Seventy-seventh Street in twenty-five minutes and to bring me the biggest bra she can find.

I grab the long scarf she left here last night, drape it across my chest, and run out.

As soon as I see Chloe walking toward me, I realize she's having a problem negotiating her way from one end of the block to the other. She can't see me yet because she's totally fixated on her feet. It looks like she's trying to ice skate for the first time—uphill. She's not even attempting to lift her feet off the ground. This is how she always walks when her shoes are too big. She must have made a particularly absurd purchase this time because she's taking millions of tiny steps instead of the standard thirty that it takes to walk one city block. Chloe will buy pretty much any size shoe if they don't have one of her top three favorite sizes.

As soon as she's close enough, she grabs on to me as though I'm the nearest railing. I'm about to suggest that we take a taxi the rest of the way when she says, "Damn! I have to go back."

"Why? Did you forget something?" I ask.

"I think I left my blow dryer and oven on and the shower running," she lies, still looking down at her feet.

"I'll just go ahead without you then," I say, pretending to believe her.

"Are you sure you don't mind?"

"Yeah, I'm sure. Do you want me to spin you or can you turn around on your own?" I ask.

"I think I can do it. I'll see you there," she says. She carefully navigates a 180-degree turn and begins awkwardly skate-walking back to her apartment. I try to estimate what time she'll get to work at her current speed. I'm thinking somewhere between eleven and eleven-thirty, if there's no traffic and a taxi happens to be waiting at her front door.

As soon as she's gone I break into a sweat realizing I'm still not wearing a bra. I quickly feel around to make sure my safety pins are secured and adjust my scarf. The good news is that she didn't even notice my boots, which means they probably look even better than I thought. Although she didn't really have an opportunity to adequately assess my appearance, what with trying to lie and keep her shoes on at the same time.

It must be such a great feeling to aimlessly bumble along without a care in the world. I always try to imagine I'm Chloe when I'm panicking about something.

This morning was a perfect example. Just as I was about to walk out my door, I started imagining all these bizarre little scenarios that might cause me to be late until I actually had myself totally convinced that I was late, despite the fact that my watch showed otherwise. And the whole time I was panicking about being late, I kept getting these little stomach jabs every time I remembered that I washed my hair twice this morning, which on more than one occasion has produced horrifying results. And then just as I was rounding the corner to the subway, I spotted a little girl who looked exactly like me when I was a little girl. At which point I had this uncontrollable urge to kneel down and tell her not to go to school, which is exactly when I started feeling my all too familiar flu symptoms coming on. All of this, coupled with the realization that I knowingly and deliberately took a job at a fashion magazine and my creeping suspicion that I'm a hypochondriac, nearly put me over the edge. But then, as soon as I saw my sister happily toddling along the sidewalk in a pair of shoes that appeared to be at least a size fifteen, looking utterly ridiculous and yet completely unaffected, it all just fell away as though nothing mattered. Human Valium.

I am now walking down the subway steps, rejuvenated, carefree, and ready to face the world with open arms. I take a deep, cleansing breath and cheerfully look around at my fellow subway users.

I'm trying to feel good about these people but everyone always looks so swollen and unhealthy in the morning. Almost like they all have a cold. And they're always looking at each other. There's a woman standing a few yards away who's staring right at me. I can't stand that. I reposition my shoulder bag, which is so huge and stuffed with notebooks and papers it covers more than half my body. I turn my back to her and wait a few seconds. Then I slowly turn my head around and sure enough, she's still staring. She's wearing a flannel shirt and a pair of pants that look like they might be part of a policeman's uniform.

As soon as the subway door opens, I slip in and rush to get a seat, but the woman in blue pants beats me to it. Now I have to figure out a way to hold on to the pole without actually touching it. Poles are notorious for banking E coli bacteria. I reach into my bag, rip out a piece of paper from my notebook, wrap it around the pole and hold on. Naturally, in doing so, I feel uncomfortable calling so much attention to myself, but it's better than grabbing on to the back of someone else's shirt.

I hate standing here trying not to make eye contact with anyone the whole time. It's so much work. Everywhere you turn, there's another face. Life would be so much easier if our heads were designed to perpetually swivel. That way it wouldn't be considered insulting to look away every couple of seconds.

I close my eyes for a second thinking about how Chloe just flat out lied to me back there. She lies about everything, so it's not as though I was caught by surprise or anything. Unfortunately, there's nothing she can do about it. Lying is genetic and Chloe got a mad dose of the pathological liar gene. She got this from our mother's side of the family. I once tried to count how many times our mother lies in a day. I came up with an average of eighty. My personal favorite is the one about the special pill—the special pill that will prevent her from ever dying. That particular lie was a huge mistake because Chloe still believes her. At least my mother was smart enough to tell Chloe to keep it a secret.

As soon as I get out of the subway, my scalp starts tingling again, but this time I know it's because I got a little freaked out there for a second when I was stepping off the platform and I got a whiff of the guy's breath who was standing next to me. It smelled like ketchup, which is usually an indication of strep throat. I'm pretty sure I held my breath in time to avoid picking up the germ but you never know.

The subway station is only two blocks away from *Issues,* so I sprint the last block. I always feel like running in the morning. I pull open the door, rush through the lobby, and pass right through security with my temporary ID. I dash by the elevators and head toward the stairway door. I can run pretty fast in these boots.

Seven flights of stairs shouldn't be a problem. I've been to *Issues* several times to visit Chloe, so I know my way around. As soon as I get to the seventh floor, I whip the door open and bound in.

I'm a little out of breath but I manage to introduce myself to the receptionist, who nervously looks me over from head to toe. I look back at her but then she looks away. She's a little preoccupied because she's wrapping the ends of her hair around her arm. She's having so much fun, she's actually making herself laugh.

"Are you looking for the art department?" she asks.

"No, I'm looking for Dan Princely. Is he in?"

"Dan Princely, the editor-in-chief?" she asks.

"Yes, *that* Dan Princely," I say, biting my tongue. I don't want to unintentionally call her an imbecile.

"Oh, sure, he's in. Wait. Let me look at my list. Are you Zoe Rose?"

I nod.

She's giggling again.

Hair *is* fun.

"His office is right over there. I'll buzz you through those doors and I'll let him know you're here."

As I'm walking away, I turn around to ask her if Dan is alone in his office. She doesn't hear me at first because she's too busy trying to get her arm out of her hair, so I repeat the question.

"No, he's not alone. Mrs. Princely is in there with him," she says.

Chloe won't be in for another three hours. What is wrong with this girl?

"Are you going to be okay?" I ask.

"Yeah, it's not really stuck. I'm just playin' around."

"Okay, well, have a good time." I wave and walk through the double doors. As soon as I spot Dan's office, I barge in.

Dan immediately stands up to greet me with a big smile.

"Hey, there you are! Right on time. Oh wow. What happened?" he asks, looking in the general direction of my chin.

"What do you mean?"

"You're um . . . it's just that you've got . . . never mind."

"No seriously, what?" I ask.

"No, nothing."

I rub my chin a few times in case I accidentally drew on it or something. The woman sitting across from Dan turns her chair around just enough to show her face, but not enough to actually make eye contact with me.

It never occurred to me that Dan's mother would be sitting in his office at eight-thirty in the morning, and I would never have recognized her from the back anyway. She must be wearing some sort of fake hair.

Of course Anita doesn't bother to get up. Why would she? I'm only her daughter-in-law's sister. How could I possibly be of any value to her? Dan tilts his head in her direction, letting me know there's a third person in the room. Little does he know I would rather spend the whole day riding back and forth on the subway seated next to a kid with mono than give her the satisfaction of saying hello first.

There's an awkward silence as I plunge the better part of my upper body into my bag and pretend to root around for some sort of hidden treasure, while Anita immediately engages herself in pulling invisible fuzz off her sweater.

"Mom, you remember Chloe's sister, Zoe, from the rehearsal dinner? Why don't you officially welcome her aboard?"

"Well, well, well," Anita says, forcing herself to look me in the eye.

Well, well, well? What the hell is "well, well, well"?

"You're looking smart this morning, Zoe. I see you've decided to dress with your usual casual flair for your first day of work."

"Thank you, Anita. Nice hairpiece," I say with my head still in my bag.

"Oh! You noticed! You're very observant. Isn't it fun? I have one in every length. If I had half the hair you do, I wouldn't need this silly thing, would I?"

She reaches over to touch my hair, but I flinch so vehemently she quickly pulls her hand back. I don't know what she's so worried about. I would never hit her in front of Dan.

"Well, welcome aboard. I hope you find your office and co-workers satisfactory and I'm looking forward to seeing what you can do. Dan raves about you. You can't imagine how curious I am to see what all the fuss is about."

"I guess time will tell," I say, smoothing my hair with one hand as though I'm consoling a rabid dog.

Anita gets up to leave and I can't help but notice what a nice figure she has for such a wicked, old woman. She's tall and very thin and she has beautiful legs. Her posture is absolutely perfect. She has the body of an aging, starved ballerina—magnificent and tortured.

I'm sure Anita would still be very pretty had she let herself grow old gracefully, but her face has been stretched and tucked so many times, it looks as though she's peering out from behind a mask of Saran Wrap. Every feature on her face is slightly askew and yet there is beauty coming from somewhere. I just can't figure out where exactly.

Everything she's wearing fits her perfectly except for her pearl earrings, which are much too big for her tiny earlobes. I can't help remembering bits and pieces of an article I once wrote about a certain arriviste countess who was known for her audacious gems back in the nineties.

Everything about her screams ambition rather than good breeding. She reeks of that overly perfumed pungency unique to climbers. Stand close enough and you can smell her working. Nothing came easy to this woman; that much is clear. All one has to do is look into those piercing, bloodshot blue eyes to see her ferocious will. She clawed her way to the top and she is determined to stay there.

I should really dig that article out in case I decide to do a feature on Anita one of these days. The whole thing is already written. All I have to do is change the name. I'd probably start off with a description of her clothes. After all, this is a fashion magazine.

I can hear Dan talking to me but I'm too engrossed in trying to imagine how I'd best describe Anita's attire for my new fantasy fashion column: *Anita Princely is wearing a simple, pale salmon cashmere sweater and a gorgeous heather gray herringbone skirt. Just below the neckline of her sweater, she has strategically placed a colossal canary diamond and pink sapphire pin that could easily double as a machete—*

"Zoe!"

From a distance, Anita would appear to be the perfect new mother-in-law for my sister. She certainly loves to shop, but when I think of the way she talks down to Chloe and the way Chloe is completely unaware of Anita's resentment toward her, it breaks my heart. My sister deserves so much more. She has no idea that Anita has it in for her. But I do.

"Zoe!"

"What! Oh, I'm sorry. Were you talking to me? I was just thinking about something."

"My mother was just saying goodbye to you," Dan says.

Anita is halfway to the door when she realizes that she forgot her purse. She walks over to her chair and bends ever so slightly at the waist as she reaches for the tiny brown clutch lodged between the cushions. But I quickly reach in and pull it out before she has a chance.

"Looking for your colostomy bag?" I ask, holding her purse up in the air.

"Oh for heaven's sake, Zoe. What a perfectly wretched thing to say. That happens to be a very fine alligator skin," she says, taking it from me.

"Wow."

Anita says something to Dan under her breath, gives me the slightest hint of a nod, and walks out.

As soon as she leaves, Dan gives me a look.

"What?" I ask.

"I know she can be penetrating, but try not to totally ignore her and then insult her, okay?"

"I wasn't ignoring her. I was just thinking about something I'd like to write about her someday. You don't think I was being nice to her?"

"You can do better."

I try to look surprised but he's not buying it.

He takes me to my office, which is just around the corner from his, and right next to Chloe's.

"Chloe sits right over there, doesn't she?" I ask, pointing to her office.

"That's right," he says with a big smile. The man is a saint.

"Take a look around. Get yourself settled and, um, you might want to wash up in the ladies room or something."

I bet I look sick. I'm probably anemic again.

"You have plenty of time to prepare your notes for the editorial meeting so try to relax. Your assistant should be here at nine o'clock. Her name is Amanda. She's very good. I had her transferred from the publicity department where she was very much in demand by all three publicists, but this new position is a promotion for her and she's very excited about it."

After Dan leaves, I take a look around my new office, which is surprisingly large and bare. Other than the hideous vintage *Issues* covers that someone wasted their time framing and hanging all over the walls, it's not bad. Not bad at all. I have a desk, a chair, and there are two other chairs neatly arranged on the other side of my desk. Pretty standard. Nothing fancy.

It's almost calming in a way. There are some nice cabinets above my desk, and with a few candles I could transform this place into a tranquil writing den.

I pull a pile of notes out of my bag and arrange them on my desk. Now all I need is a stapler and I'll be just fine.

There's got to be one in here somewhere.

I staple things all the time. Granted, I sometimes find myself banging on it incessantly for no reason, but I still have to have one. As a matter of fact, I often keep two staplers on my desk, so that if one runs out of staples, I have a backup just in case I don't have time to reload. I slowly begin opening and closing a few drawers in my desk, but as it becomes more and more apparent that there's no stapler, I begin frantically opening and slamming every drawer and cabinet in the office. I can't work without a stapler. This is ridiculous!

Calm down.

Breathe.

Breathe without holding your breath this time.

Here comes the sweat.

And the nausea.

In the midst of my angst, a guy with long blond hair appears at my door wearing all black. He's pretty enough to be a girl, but there isn't anything particularly feminine about him—besides his coat, which is a little on the girly side, even for a girl, and the way he keeps putting his hair behind his ears, and his nail polish. And the fact that we're both wearing the same boots. Actually the boots aren't girly at all. I look down at my feet. I never noticed how incredibly masculine these boots are. They're not even tomboyish, they're out and out mannish. I never should have worn them, and I can't believe the way he just meandered in here as though I've known him all my life.

I've got to calm down.

"Hey," he says without looking at me.

"Who are you?" I ask.

"I'm Trai. I work in the art department. And you're Zoe, right? I used to work with your sister . . . until she married the Prince . . . and got promoted. I assume she's back from her little honeymoon?"

"That's right. Her new office is right next door. And you must be the guy who used to eat her lunch all the time."

"Yup," he says proudly, working the hair.

"Yeah, well, those days are over. Who told you to come in here?" I ask, as I resume opening and slamming drawers. Normally I would resent that remark about Chloe marrying the prince and getting promoted, but he's clearly torn up about it. He looks like a lost cocker spaniel with that blond, floppy hair.

"No one. I just wanted to meet you and see if, um, you need anything." His eyes are starting to wander in that downward direction. I'm assuming they will land . . . right . . . about . . . now.

"I need a stapler," I say to interrupt his visual tour of my chest. The more I look at him, the younger he gets.

"No problem. I'll get you one. I'm a stapler guy myself. You can't really rely on anything else if you want to keep things together, can you?" he says, with a little laugh.

"That is *so* funny. So, can you get it for me now?" I ask. I can't stand the staring for another second. As soon as he leaves I try distracting myself by imagining Michael wearing nail polish and then I adjust my safety pins, which were clearly not doing their job. I pull my shirt tighter and refasten everything and flatten the sides of the scarf over each breast. Then I continue searching my drawers.

There's an astonishing amount of supplies in here. Not that I don't love office supplies. I do. I take great comfort in large quantities of anything. As a child, I lived in constant fear of running out of things. When I was eleven, I had a shoe box filled with lip balms. By the time I was twelve, I'd discovered a certain type of hair band that actually went all the way around my ponytail. Every time we passed a drugstore, I'd make my mom pull over so I could run in and buy a few more packages. I also had a fear of running out of tampons (in case I ever got my period again), a certain type of notebook divider, and I had several bouts with different types of granola bars.

There must be fifty packs of Post-its in this drawer. I get up and walk over to the little closet behind my desk and pull open the door. There are stacks and stacks of printer paper, toner, pens, pencils, notepads, spiral notebooks, scissors, Magic Markers—there's even a whole box of self-addressed stamped envelopes, a carton of staples, and two packs of hair rubber bands in every color! I don't believe this. These people think of everything. There's also an entire shelf devoted to beauty-product samples. I've never seen so many tiny bottles of hair conditioner. I grab a few and throw them in my bag.

I pull down a big box of slides and bring them over to my desk. Most of them are blank, but there's a smaller box in here with duplicates of old *Issues* covers. There's a loop on my desk so I pick it up to get a closer look. One of the girls looks very familiar. It takes me a few seconds to realize she looks exactly like Dan. Wait a minute. This is Anita. She can't be more than fifteen or sixteen years old in this picture. And she couldn't have weighed more than eighty pounds back then. Talk about skeletons in your closet. She looks so delicate and sweet and vulnerable and pretty. What the hell happened to her?

I'd hate to think it was Dan and Chloe's wedding that did her in. Talk about the best-laid plans backfiring. Anita planned things for that wedding that no one would ever dream of. My personal favorite was the receiving line *rehearsal* videotaping session. The objective here was for the videographer to record funny things Anita was planning to say on the actual wedding-day video. In the event that she never got the opportunity to deliver her lines, he was instructed to splice them in. And then, of course, there was the pre-wedding hair and makeup consultation, the hair and makeup rehearsal luncheon, and the pre-wedding cocktail party for "who's who in the publishing industry." After the wedding-dress-fabric consultation break-fast, Dan got fed up and cancelled everything. Chloe was devastated and Anita was furious.

"What's wrong with picking out fabrics?" Chloe protested, but Dan put his foot down and they eloped. To this day Chloe still doesn't understand what turned Dan off to the idea of a wedding with a guest list of nearly five hundred *presents*.

My sister loves presents almost as much as Anita loves guests, but Dan assured Chloe that she could still wear her wedding dress, and so she agreed to run away with him.

Anita didn't take the news of their decision to elope very well. She promptly checked herself into the Betty Ford clinic, where she remained until precisely the day Dan and Chloe returned from their honeymoon.

Chloe was horrified to learn that Anita had gone on a drinking binge. Dan was neither horrified nor surprised. He could have predicted it. "It's her way of saying, 'Congratulations, you win,' " Dan explained.

"What did we win?" Chloe asked, hoping for something from Tiffany.

Chloe never pays attention to Dan's issues with Anita and

her desire to control their lives. If you ask her what she thinks of Anita, she'll say, "I think she's pretty."

I'm just about to take another look at Anita's picture when Trai comes back in.

"Here's your stapler," he says and puts it on my desk.

"Thanks," I say, reaching over to grab it.

"So, where's your sister?"

"Don't you have any work to do?"

"Not really. Where's your sister?"

"She's on her way. Do you want me to give her a message or perhaps your lunch order?"

At this point, he's staring point blank at my breasts even though they're completely covered. I'm tempted to let him know that I'm aware of what he's doing and that I'm contemplating calling security, but he's so obviously in love with Chloe, I feel sorry for him. I tilt my chin up, just as I always do when I sense someone is checking out my chest. It's an acquired body language that all big-breasted women learn. It's our way of leading the viewer away from the boob area and up toward the face area. If you're looking at someone and they start looking up, you will too. Except this guy. He refuses to let his eyes be led.

"So, what's the age difference between you two?" he asks my left breast.

"They're twins," I answer on behalf of both of them, "but Chloe and I are two years apart. I'm older."

"Oh," he answers. He's totally distracted. I wish I could make one of them talk.

"Neither of them understands English, so if you have any more questions, you should direct them up here, at my head," I finally suggest.

He laughs for a second and then announces that he has to go. No apology.

Nothing.

On the way out, he runs into Dan, who is on his way into my office. I can hear them talking in the hall.

"Hey, Mr. Princely, how's it goin'?"

"It's going well. But I've told you many times, call me Dan."

"Cool. How's Chloe, by the way?"

"She's good. She's great actually. Thanks for asking."

"Yeah. Her sister is really hot, too. Excellent call."

"I'm glad you approve."

There's a little laughter out there and I feel my face heat up. Then Dan walks in and announces that the meeting is about to begin in the conference room and that he'd be happy to escort me.

As soon as we're in the hallway, I can't help but notice that Dan is finding it difficult to look at me.

I'm getting the idea that my hair is doing that thing where it keeps expanding until it looks like I'm using it to hide a second head.

"So, have you been to the ladies room yet?" he asks.

"No, but I think I'll stop in on the way."

"Oh good! It's right over there," he says and points to a door right next to the conference room. "And feel free to visit the fashion closet if you're in a bind with that shirt. See you at the meeting," he says with a little sigh of relief.

I walk into the ladies room and check my safety pins. I can see why he felt uncomfortable. I lost a pin and that's a sickening amount of cleavage I've got going here. I take the other pin and sort of move it up and gather the fabric together, which looks sort of interesting, if I must say so myself. Almost like smocking. I rewrap the scarf so that it's tucked into the open areas of my shirt and head over to the wall mirror above the sink. Unfortunately it's too high for me to see anything except the very tip of my head. I try to stand on my toes to see some more of my hair but it's almost impossible. I jump up a few times, which helps, but I still can't see much, even when I back up a few steps and take a little running start. I glance down at my boots for a second to see if they're tied properly. For some reason I can't get as much air as I usually can. I used to be able to jump twice as high in these boots. I also can't help noticing how old and dirty they look. Maybe it's the lighting in here.

I grab a paper towel to turn on the faucet and let the water soak the paper towel. I can't wring it out because the paper towel touched the faucet so I pick it up and hold it over my boots, letting the water drip onto the lighter areas of the leather so they'll blend in with the darker areas. I'm trying to create the illusion that the boots are all one color and give them a gentle cleaning at the same time. That's the best I can do without a can of spray paint. I drop the paper towel in the sink, check out the top of my head one more time, and then I reach for another paper towel so I can wash my hands before I leave. I use this second paper towel as a little barrier between my hand and the soap dispenser and push it a few times, letting the soap fall into my hands. I use the same paper towel to turn on the faucet. I let the water run for a few seconds and then carefully position both of my hands under the water so they don't accidentally touch the faucet or the sink, and then I slowly lather up.

Once my hands are clean—more or less—I grab another paper towel. The purpose of the third paper towel is twofold. I will use it to dry my hands as well as to pick up the other two paper towels lying in the sink. Once I'm finished and ready to leave, I push the door open with one foot and hold it there while I look for a garbage can. Unfortunately, the garbage bin is too far to reach from the door, so I have to let the door slam shut. I'd rather repeat this entire process all over again than touch anything with my bare hands in a public bathroom.

I'm just about to take a step toward the garbage when I hear someone in one of the stalls.

"So, where was I?"

"You were talking about Chloe."

"Oh right. Can you believe how much weight she gained on her honeymoon?"

"Are you sure we're alone in here?"

"Of course. You heard the door close, didn't you?"

"Yeah, but I'm always so paranoid around here."

"Well, stop worrying. There's no one in here. The meeting's going to start in a little while. They're probably all downstairs getting coffee."

"I still can't believe Dan made Chloe's sister deputy editor. According to Anita, she's like three feet tall with the most enormous implants on the planet."

What!

"And don't expect another Miss Sweet-and-Innocent like her sister. Anita said she's a total bitch."

"More importantly, I'd say Chloe easily gained eight, maybe even nine pounds since their honeymoon. What's your guess?"

"At first I thought eight, but I'm leaning toward nine as of yesterday. Dan is totally not into fat chicks. She's so done."

"He'd probably be sick of her by now anyway. She's so dumb it's unbearable."

"How amazing does he look with that tan? What a waste."

"Where did they go on their honeymoon?"

"Some island that he, like, bought for her so she could get her fat ass tan without anyone seeing her."

There's a part of me that wants to tiptoe out of here and think this through. But then there's that other part of me.

First I knock on one stall and then the other.

"Um, excuse me. I hope you don't mind, but I'd like to introduce myself to both of you. Perhaps you've already heard of me. I'm Zoe. Zoe Rose."

Chapter 3

It's been at least five minutes and neither one of them has said a word or hinted at any signs of caving. And I'm sure as hell not going anywhere until they both show their faces.

It's amazing how much time girls spend in the common areas of public bathrooms. I can't think of anything even remotely entertaining to do in here. I guess it's a lot more fun if you can see yourself in the mirror.

I should at least turn the water on and off a few times to make it seem as though I'm still in here for a reason, but I don't want to waste it, and it's not like I'd be fooling either of them. We all know why we're in here. It's just a question of endurance at this point.

I'm this close to flinging myself under one of their stalls.

I walk over, squat down, and tilt my head so I can see if their feet are moving under there. Unbelievable. It's like they've both turned to stone. I squat down a little more to get a better look. I wish Chloe were in here with me. She'd probably get a real kick out of looking at people's shoes without them knowing. One of them is wearing a pair of silver ballet slippers and the other one is wearing the exact same slippers in gold.

I wouldn't mind getting the silver pair—for Chloe. I know she'd love them. They've got to be at least a size eight, but Chloe could probably make them work.

I put my ear up to her stall to see if I can hear breathing, but there's absolutely nothing coming out of this one. I put my ear up to the other stall—nothing there either. They can't possibly be holding their breath this long. I hope I didn't scare them to death.

The meeting is going to start any minute now. I walk over to the main bathroom door, kick it open as hard as I can and then stand aside to let it slam shut again.

Neither of them fell for it but what the hell.

I am now leaning against the wall across from their stalls, examining my scalp for tumors when Courtney walks in.

"Oh my God, hi!" she says, throwing her arms around me. I wasn't expecting that. I've only met her a couple of times and I don't recall being particularly friendly to her on either one of those occasions.

"Oh my God, yes, hello there to you too," I say, trying to be equally cheerful while stiffly patting her on the back.

"I just came in to tell everyone that the meeting is starting. Dan said to check the girl's room. Who else is in here?" she asks.

"I'm not sure. Maybe you can recognize them by their shoes," I suggest tilting my head toward the stalls.

Courtney bends down to look and says, "Blaire and Sloane, the meeting is starting." I look down at Courtney's shoes. She's wearing a pair of bronze stilettos with silver flowers embroidered all over them. What is it with this place and metallic shoes?

As soon as Courtney stands back up, I can't help but notice that her pants don't fit her at all. I always thought it was standard procedure to hide one's vagina at work. *Wait a minute. Blaire and Sloane. Blaire and Sloane. Where have I heard those names before?*

Oh right! Now I remember. Blaire and Sloane were the two editors who collaborated on that infantile attempt at a scathing expose starring Chloe as the evil assistant. Chloe sent me a copy of it last year. It was so poorly written, we hung it up at *The Radical Mind* for a few laughs, but deep down, I didn't really think it was that funny. In fact I had a nightmare about it. I don't want to repeat what I did to Sloane and Blaire in my dream, but suffice to say the police got involved.

Courtney and I walk into the conference room together and find Dan seated at the head of the oval table. As soon as we come in, he puts his face in one hand and starts tapping a pencil with the other.

"Is everything okay?" I ask, but then it occurs to me that Courtney is standing right next to him and he probably can't bear to see a vagina choking to death any more than the next guy.

"Nothing. I was just thinking about something," he says without looking up.

"Can I get you some more water or how about a little shoulder rub?" Courtney asks with a little giggle and then sits down right next to him.

"No thanks, Court, I'm fine."

I must have heard that wrong. No one would ask her boss if he wanted a little shoulder rub, especially with her boss's sister-in-law standing right there. I'm about to sit down and contemplate what she *really* said, when I spot Rhonda, the recently appointed art director from the promotion department.

Rhonda walks into the meeting with a sugar-glazed cheese Danish in one hand and an enormous paper cup of coffee in the other, as though she just happened to be walking by and spotted a group of old friends. I can't help but love Rhonda. She's always been incredibly loyal to Chloe. I guess, in a way, she's like family.

Rhonda and I give each other a quick kiss and I try not to laugh at her hair. For some reason, she has it all teased up, like she's impersonating a country western singer or something.

"How are you? How've you been?" I ask, trying to mask my smile as something joyful and warm as opposed to a childish and immature reaction to a comical hairstyle. I must be staring, though, because the next thing she says is, "How do you like my hair? I know it's ridiculous, but what can you do? This is the style now." She's puffing it up even more by pulling on it from every possible angle. She's also wearing a poncho that comes down to her knees, and I could swear she just mumbled something under her breath that sounded like, "Fix yourself up a little, honey." I smooth my hair down a bit but I'm more concerned about where I should sit, which is never an easy decision for me. I'd like to sit near Dan, but I want to leave a seat or two open for Chloe on either side of me.

I hover behind my two best options, while trying to anticipate who will sit where, and how many people are likely to arrive before Chloe. After a few nerve-racking moments of hemming and hawing, I finally sit one seat away from Dan, but then Rhonda immediately sits down next to me on the other side. I feel a little flutter of panic but it quickly subsides.

Rhonda says hello to Dan and then to Courtney, who's sitting up so straight her chest is pointing toward the ceiling. She

carefully tucks two little pieces of her scorched blond hair behind her ears and says, "Hiya Rhonda." She then reaches for
the entire stack of magazines in the middle of the table and
neatly arranges them in front of her in a little fan. She picks
one up and starts reading it as if she's sitting in her living
room. I wonder if I'll ever feel that relaxed here; although I'm
really never even that comfortable in my own living room, so
I doubt it.

I look over at Rhonda to see if she's going to try to start up
a little conversation with me, but as soon as I turn toward her,
she takes a huge bite out of her Danish. She then begins
chewing so haphazardly, it looks as though she might spit
everything right back out. I've never seen anything like this.
There is cheese and hardened sugar all over her mouth and
chin and she's just leaving it there.

Before she even has a chance to swallow and have her teeth
professionally cleaned, she takes another reckless bite and
says, "This is out of this world, want some?" I don't know
what to do. I can't possibly answer her without activating my
gag reflex, so I just shake my head no.

My stomach is turning so fast, I have to press on it to make
it slow down.

I've always had a bit of a problem understanding my emotions, but I'm almost positive I was jumping the gun when I
said I loved Rhonda. I look at Dan to see if he's going to perhaps fire her, but he is so deep in thought, he doesn't see a
thing. Just then her cell phone rings and I nearly jump out of
my skin. Her ring tone is "Piano Man" by Billy Joel. Again, I
look at Dan to see if he's reached his breaking point, but he
barely lifts his head.

Other people's chewed food is not something I tend to handle well under any circumstances, but I'm especially squeamish

today for some reason. If she doesn't stop chewing this instant, there's almost no way I can continue to sit next to her. Despite her history of protecting my sister from virtually everyone and everything in this place, I just can't get past the smacking sound of her tongue trying to pry itself off the roof of her mouth.

I'm about to get up and change my seat when Ruth walks in with two strikingly beautiful models.

Ruth is Chloe's ex-boss, who somehow managed to get a pass from the underworld to torture Chloe for a full year, while my sister did everything in her power to please her. Once Chloe was promoted, she was nice enough to then have Ruth promoted. Chloe, in her mind-boggling innocence was convinced that a promotion was all Ruth needed to become a better person. Now Ruth is the creative services director of the promotion department, but I seriously doubt the new title had any kind of remedial effect on her. Her mental state is so far from what one would consider normal that she often spends the better part of her day sitting in her office making phony phone calls. I'll never understand why companies keep people like Ruth on staff. It just doesn't make any sense.

Even more puzzling is why Dan invited models to this meeting. Maybe he thinks they're people too. One of them is the color of whole-wheat bread with long, honey brown hair and green eyes and the other one is a buttery blonde with blue eyes and a peaches-and-cream complexion. Bread is wearing extremely low-cut jeans and a few layered T-shirts, each of which would barely fit a newborn.

Butter is wearing a bright-colored flowery dress that sort of looks like curtains. Rhonda snaps her cell phone shut and whispers, "Here come the dynamic duo."

Actually, three people entered the room, but Ruth hardly qualifies as one of *them*. For one thing, she is easily in her sixties. And for another, she only dresses in costume and can hardly walk because she is riddled with bunions.

I can only get a glimpse of little bits and pieces of the three of them because Rhonda's hair is in the way and everyone here is so tall.

Ruth and the classic-breakfast-combination sit down next to Courtney. All three of them ignore Courtney, but Bread and Butter make it a point to give Dan a warm, friendly hello.

No one goes so far as to acknowledge Rhonda or me. In fact, no one will even look at me. I try to make small talk with Rhonda, who has finished mauling her Danish, but then I immediately regret it. You cannot imagine how many leftovers are on her face.

As soon as Rhonda makes a move to throw away her napkin, I get a full view of Ruth, who is examining herself in a compact mirror that says, "Girls Just Want to Have Fun." I've got to assume she's checking to see if there is lipstick on her teeth, which is not a bad idea. She must have applied it using a pair of tongs. Besides the lipstick smeared all over her teeth, she's got some under her eye and a few little dabs on her forehead. She keeps scraping at the lipstick on her forehead with her nail, which is starting to bend backwards a little. Chloe used to buy those same press-on nails all the time when she was a little kid, and then she'd beg me to polish them. I found the whole idea of three-inch, plastic nails a little spooky, but Chloe had so much fun picking things up and pointing to objects around the room with her fake nails, I always gave in. I can see Ruth has as much talent for nail polishing as I do. It's all over her cuticles.

Ruth is probably the only person in this whole building who's dressed worse than I am. She's wearing a pink satiny blouse with a gigantic ruffle around the collar and a white terry-cloth skirt. You'd think they'd put an age limit on ruffles.

I always feel a little sorry for Ruth whenever I see her walking around in one of her atrocious outfits. I know how hard it is to get dressed when you have no idea what you're doing. God knows what a challenge it must be for a person who imagines herself forty years younger than she actually is.

I'm a little worried that Chloe is going to miss this meeting and I'm also concerned about the lack of ventilation in this room. It's very constricting, and lately I've been experiencing the telltale signs of adult asthma. I put my hand to my forehead to see if I've been walking around with a low-grade fever. It's hard to tell, though, because my hands are freezing from nerves. I already want to get out of here and the meeting hasn't even started. I hardly know these people and yet I already can't stand half of them, and I'm pretty sure the feeling is mutual.

Another abnormally tall girl with long, straight black hair and no makeup, except for expertly applied bright red lipstick, walks in and over to Dan. She boldly shakes his hand and says, "Sorry I'm late, I was filling out forms in human resources." She looks a little like a young Cher but only from the neck up. From the neck down she is dressed impeccably. She's wearing a gray-and-white flannel pinstriped jacket with gray cuffed trousers and black patent leather pumps. She has on a dainty little pearl-and-crystal necklace and a perfectly pressed white button-down blouse. That's exactly how I would dress if I knew how. I watch her look around the table, nodding and smiling.

She's extremely confident and yet not overbearing. That's an art in itself—the ability to take control of a situation without pissing people off.

"Not your fault, don't be sorry," Dan says. Then he looks over at me and says, "This is Amanda." *My assistant? That's not what I was expecting!*

I say hello and Amanda says, "It's a pleasure to meet you." She motions to the chair next to me and asks, "May I?" I want to tell her that I've been saving this seat for my sister, but, because I am a grown woman, I say, "of course." She walks over to me and puts her hand out to shake mine. She's staring right into my eyes.

I stand up to greet her and immediately feel deformed. She's got to be at least six two. If she so much as lifts her heels off the ground to get something on a high shelf, and I happen to be sitting next to her, I'll be looking directly into her crotch.

I sit back down and try to forget about Amanda, but she's one of those people who's impossible to ignore. Her perfume, although not overpowering, is everywhere, and she has very large hands. I feel like she should be my babysitter, not my assistant. Hopefully Dan will be able to find another job for her in the building—perhaps on a floor with higher ceilings. I'm sure she doesn't want a boss who comes up to her private parts either. She's probably thinking the same thing I'm thinking.

Dan looks at his watch and clears his throat. "I guess we can't wait much longer, so let's get started," he says. He folds his hands and begins thanking everyone for coming. This is obviously going to be a very informal meeting. Courtney is reading a magazine. The perfect girls are talking to each other using their hair as privacy curtains. Rhonda is picking food out of her teeth with a credit card. Amanda is sitting with her hands folded in her lap, and Ruth is examining her clothing for what appears to be small insects. She's picking off little bits of something, squashing them with her fingers and then flicking her hallucinations across the room. Her seat isn't even pushed in. She's sitting in the aisle. I'm tempted to get up and push her chair in, but I'm afraid she'll think I'm giving her a ride.

"Before we get started I want to make one point very clear.

Some of you will undoubtedly find yourselves questioning our new editorial plans and that's to be expected. We're certainly going out on a limb here, but as long as we're in this together, and our collective goal is that of editorial enhancement and growth, we'll be able to rise above whatever minor disagreements come up. I think you all know how much your support means to me, and now more than ever, we're going to really have to pull together.

"Since we've already had a number of discussions regarding the key objectives of the new editorial, I'd like to get right down to business and tell you a little bit about our new deputy editor, Zoe Rose.

"As many of you know, Zoe had a very popular column at *The Radical Mind,* a business and news magazine most known for its liberal, outspoken political commentary, which won several highly coveted awards over the past few years. Many of those awards were directly linked to Zoe's extraordinary work exposing countless cases of corruption in some of our country's most high-profile corporations—particularly in regard to discrimination against women—and in many cases, discrimination against women by other women.

"A lifelong student of human behavior, Zoe is anxious to leave the world of hard news and investigative reporting and begin enlightening a different kind of audience—our readers.

"Although *The Radical Mind* has lost a valuable contributor, the world of fashion and beauty has gained an inspiring new voice. We will soon be the first fashion-and-beauty magazine in history to give primary focus to the issues women have with one another and how those issues hold them back professionally, politically, and most importantly, personally. Our editorial will now be geared toward improving how women look on the inside as well as on the outside. And of course, we will be disseminating that information through the eyes of Zoe's unique, comedic, and very entertaining perspective."

My cheeks, eyes, and neck are burning up from the combination of fever and my overwhelming sense that everyone in this room is already sick of hearing about me.

If he doesn't stop talking, there's an excellent chance that I will have cooked myself into a pile of ash before I even have a chance to say a single word about what I have planned for the magazine.

Dan continues talking as a trickle of sweat meanders its way down my right sideburn, and then, as if an angel has answered my prayers, there is a sudden commotion just outside the door, which forces Dan to stop talking. After a few seconds, a woman walks in the room who makes every head turn. She's that alarming. Her shampoo commercial, bouncy hair, her flawless skin, her power suit and her legs all come together in a way that makes everyone else in the room look like a whimpering housfrau. Something about the way she walks sets the whole mood in slow motion. She's in her early to mid thirties with enormous brown eyes, long chestnut hair, and not one split end. As beautiful as she is, everything about her is strictly business—right down to her brown briefcase. She is not attempting in any way to reflect the style of the magazine or to express her creativity. She's not trying to appear whimsical, intellectual, preppy, funky, sporty, trendy, waspy or anything else that clothes are used for around here. She is simply a woman who, on this day, has chosen to wear brown. She also has a good size slit on the side of that skirt, which can only mean one thing. She's in sales, and I would venture to say she's the advertising director.

The woman in brown shuts the door behind her and walks over to Dan to shake his hand.

She apologizes for being late and explains that she just flew in from the London office where she was giving the overseas sales team a heads-up about upcoming editorial changes. Then she sits down in the chair next to Dan—the one I was saving for Chloe. Her BlackBerry is out of her bag and on the table in a matter of seconds and she's ready to go.

Dan asks her if she would like him to repeat what he's said so far.

"That won't be necessary," she says, "I caught a bit of it out in the hall. Feel free to pick up where you left off."

Our seats are somewhat far apart so I have to lean all the way over to get a good look at her. She gives me an abrupt smile and a quick nod and then pulls the tiniest sliver of a lap-top out of her bag.

She looks at Dan as if to confirm that he should get on with it, but there is still a little excitement out in the hall. Dan excuses himself and gets up to open the door. And in walks Chloe.

"Ah, you made it!" he says.

She walks in smiling and gives him a quick kiss on the cheek. I'm so happy to see her, I nearly jump out of my seat, but as soon as she sees me, her face goes blank.

Since I last saw her, she's changed into a pink-and-cream tweed suit with a little scarf knotted at her neck. But for some reason, she's still hobbling around in those gigantic shoes. I can't see her feet from where I'm sitting, but there's no way in hell that she could possibly have more than one pair of shoes that cause her to walk like she's chained to a cinderblock. Why didn't she change her shoes when she changed her outfit? She had all the time in the world to find a pair of shoes that fit her because she obviously had time to go shopping; she's carrying about nine shopping bags.

She shuffles over to me with her packages, completely oblivious to the fact that everyone now knows she went shopping when she should have been at this meeting. I feel my pulse quicken as I try to imagine what everyone is thinking. I close my eyes for a second and try to get a grip.

I hear Chloe dragging a chair from up against the wall to the narrow space behind me. I quickly check her out as she maneuvers herself toward me. She doesn't look fat at all!

If she gained even a single pound on her honeymoon, I sure can't see it. What could Blaire and Sloane possibly have meant? She looks perfect! Nervous and pale, but perfect. I hope she doesn't have a fever too.

"Are you feeling okay?" I ask her. But she can't even answer me. It's almost as though she's in shock or on the verge of collapsing. I wonder if a salesperson was rude to her this morning. So help me if . . .

"Hi, I'm Chloe," she says to Amanda, trying to force a smile. "Do you mind if I squeeze in between you two? I really want to sit next to my sister. It's her first day." Poor Chloe. She can't even control the volume of her own voice. She said that so loud, everyone turned to look at her.

"Oh! Of course!" Amanda says, while Chloe makes a huge racket with her chair and packages, trying to reposition herself so that the legs of her chair are now entwined with mine. I never dreamed she'd be even more insecure than I am in this meeting. She's practically in my lap.

"Sorry, Dan, go ahead," Chloe says, once she is comfortably seated.

Dan picks up where he left off about how we're all going to re-create the term "women's magazine."

As he's speaking, Chloe puts her hand up to my ear and starts whispering something I can't possibly decipher. All I can hear is the sound of her lips popping against one another.

I look over at Dan who has every right to be annoyed that Chloe is whispering in my ear like a fourteen-year-old, but he shows no signs of disapproval—so I whisper back, "I can't understand what you're saying." Chloe asks Amanda if she can borrow a piece of paper. Amanda rips out a piece from her planner without taking her eyes off Dan and slides it over to Chloe. A few seconds later, Chloe asks her if she can borrow a pen. Amanda hands her a pen, once again, without moving her head while Dan says something about how we should all be willing to embrace change.

I'm trying to stay focused on Dan and read what Chloe is writing at the same time, but it's almost impossible because she's holding the paper so far away.

"Zoe has a very clear vision of how *Issues* can become a vehicle for readers to explore the inner workings of their own minds as well as the minds of all the other girls in their lives—particularly the ones they can't seem to get along with no matter how hard they try."

I slowly manage to look down as I hear Dan say, "Women need to come to terms with what it is about other women that causes them to experience such strong, visceral emotions." And then I catch a glimpse of Chloe's note, which says, "One of your breasts got out." I take the pen and paper from her and write back, "What does that mean?"

She takes the pen and paper back and writes, "It means your shirt popped open and one of them escaped."

"Are you sure?" I write back.

"Look down," she whispers. And so I do. And there it is, poking out of my shirt like a freakishly large, bald head. You'd think I would have felt something like that. Both safety pins are dangling helplessly on either side of my shirt.

Unbelievable.

"How could you possibly show up here without a bra?" she whispers.

"I broke my last one. And I distinctly asked you if I could borrow one of yours, but you forgot to bring me one. Unlike you, I didn't have time to go shopping. These safety pins were holding up fine until you walked in." I don't know why I'm taking this out on her.

"I can't believe you. No one breaks a bra!"

I twist my body toward Chloe as she slips off her jacket and holds it in front of me while I try to reattach the safety pins. Unfortunately, they're both shot. The good news is that when I turned toward Chloe, my breast went right back in my shirt. That means that it probably only pops out when I'm sitting at a certain angle! It's entirely possible that it just snuck out when Chloe walked in. Whether or not that's true, I will go to my grave believing it.

Where the hell is my scarf?

The only thing that held up was the twist tie.

I slip Chloe's jacket on, but it doesn't even come close to buttoning, so I take it off and put it on backward. Fortunately no one seems to notice because all of their eyes are on Dan, who has raised his voice so dramatically over the course of the last ten seconds, he is now virtually yelling at them. This is his way of distracting them from the horror show that is my breast and he's doing an excellent job.

I look over at Chloe. She's sweating so profusely, her hair is soaking wet. I feel so sorry for her.

We've only been working together for two and a half minutes and I've already completely dehydrated her. She picks up the scarf I was wearing off the floor and hands it to me.

"How did I lose that?" I ask.

"I lose this thing all the time. It slides right off for some reason," she answers. "Maybe it got caught under the wheel of your chair when you sat down. Just try to forget about it," she says.

That should be no problem.

Seeing that I am now completely clothed, Dan abruptly wraps up his speech with, "So, in conclusion, I'd like you all to give Zoe a warm welcome by going around the table and introducing yourselves and then Zoe, I'd like you to take the floor."

There's a light applause while I stand up to face my audience on my first day as deputy editor, wearing my sister's jacket backward. I thank them all for coming and look around to see who will be the first to introduce herself. Chloe is busy organizing packages. The businesswoman is typing word for word what Dan has just said; Bread and Butter are deeply involved in a conversation behind their hair wall; Rhonda fell asleep, perhaps from insulin shock; Ruth is smiling at the ceiling; and Courtney, oddly enough, is still reading her magazine.

I look around the table once more, hoping that someone will gain consciousness. After a few seconds, the businesswoman looks up and begins speaking.

"Zoe, I'd like to be the first to welcome you to *Issues*. I'm Alex Daniels. I'm the advertising director, and I'm very much looking forward to working with you." I nod my head and say thank you, but for some reason we're still staring at each other and I'm getting a very uncomfortable, tight feeling in my chest. I hope someone in this room is carrying an inhaler.

Before I have a chance to turn to the next person, Court-ney says, "I'm Courtney, as you know, and I'm the mental health editor, as you know. I write the column 'Don't Be Afraid to Ask Courtney,' as you know. And well, I'm just thrilled to have you here!"

"I'm thrilled to be here too," I say, trying to come across as a person who knows what it feels like to be thrilled. Then I turn to look at the model sitting next to her.

"I'm Sloane Worthington. I'm the beauty editor," Butter says, avoiding eye contact with me.

Butter is Sloane? "But of course," I say, trying not to swal-low my own tongue. I feel a surge of rage expanding my con-stricted airways. I might even be breathing normally again. I had no idea anger cures asthma, but just to be sure, I turn to Chloe and ask her if my face is blue. She assures me that it isn't and so I turn back toward the other model-like creature.

"And don't tell me. You must be Blaire. Well, I can't tell you how great it is to finally put names with faces. Gosh, I've heard so much about you two." I'd like to go on, but I can al-ready feel Chloe stepping on my toe. You'd think she'd realize that I can't feel a thing in these boots.

"And you are?" I say, turning to face Ruth.

"I'm Ruth Davis. We've met several times. Your sister used to work for me in the promotion department," she spits.

"Really? Oh! Wait a minute! Now I remember. You're the one who likes her coffee camel-colored. Not brown, not tan, but camel. Isn't that right?" Ruth lets out a loud, hearty laugh in celebration of being singled out for being quirky. She looks around the room for friends to share in the festivity of hear-ing stories about herself, but no one is paying any attention to either of us.

Next is Rhonda.

"I'm Rhonda Gold, *as you know,* and let's just say I think you're going to fit in just fine around here," she says, and slaps the table. A few little crumbs pop up. Rhonda is the kind of person who is always there when you need her. I make a silent vow never to be in the same room with her while she's eating, to keep things in perspective.

Last in line is Amanda, who I just met, and already mentally fired, so it's easy for me to be nice to her. It's my way of apologizing.

"I'm Amanda Cummings."

We shake hands again for some reason. I guess to show the rest of the people in the room what professionals we both are. And then she gives me this incredibly warm smile as if to acknowledge how formal we're being. *Goddamn it; tall as she is, she's obviously a very good person. Now what am I going to do?*

There are a few weak claps as I sit down and gather my notes.

"Well, now that I know who all of you are, I'll tell you a little bit about myself—but not too much, because Dan pretty much told you everything there is to know already." Little nervous chuckles all around.

"As Dan said, I wrote for *The Radical Mind* for seven years, but my focus has always been the people behind the politics. And since I am *'a girl'*—as you all bore witness to—I am particularly interested in the criteria we use to judge one another and how those criteria prevent us from getting along and getting ahead in the world.

"What I plan to do, and this is a phrase I often use, is raid the locker room of the female psyche and rip open the frilly facade of femininity once and for all with satirical articles aimed specifically at how girls really think, how they unfairly ostracize one another, and most importantly, why we can't go on like this.

"Once girls learn to accept the fact that we aren't going to get anywhere in this world without one another, we can begin to explore ways to retrain our thinking, embrace one another, and gain our rightful place in business, politics and society, as a cohesive, unified, supportive and well-functioning team."

Courtney's hand shoots up.

"I don't get it."

"What don't you get?"

"Are we going to be making fun of girls and are we allowed to do that?"

Chloe shrinks down in her seat about eight inches.

"One of the main purposes of satire, particularly with respect to social commentary, although often misunderstood, is to promote change. Our objective is to give women the chance to see the humor in what motivates them to want to annihilate one another, instead of help one another. Once I open our readers' eyes to the fact that it's the men out there, not each other, who we need to overcome, I think we'll all be able to sit back, have a good laugh, and get down to business. There's not a person in this room who doesn't know what I'm talking about because every single one of us is guilty of this, myself included."

I try not to look at Amanda.

"That's very big of you to include yourself. And I was just wondering; do you have any specific article ideas that you can share with us?" Sloane asks.

"Particularly ones that tie into fashion and beauty?" Blaire adds.

"As a matter of fact, most of my article ideas tie into fashion and beauty, because after all, that's what *Issues* is all about. We're not planning to change that. We're simply going to add a little insight into how girls *use* fashion and beauty to formulate opinions about one another.

"I'm very anxious to show you a few of my article ideas, but first I'd like to quickly pass around copies of this 'Letter from an Editor' that I'd like to use for our first issue." I hand the stack of letters to Amanda who seems slightly taken aback.

"As you'll see, the letter is about my first best friend and how all the other girls made fun of her because she wore a dirty, pink party dress on the first day of school. She was the kind of person who would give you the shirt off her back, but because she was ugly and dressed so foolishly, no one would even talk to her. I'd be happy to read it aloud. It's a lot of fun."

Dan thumbs through the letter and begins rubbing his temples. "Zoe, 'A Letter from an Editor' is supposed to be a paragraph or two. There are too many pages here."

"I realize it's lengthy but I think it sets the tone for the whole magazine."

"Exactly what tone were you going for?" Sloane asks with a look of horror on her face.

"Young and fun," I say.

"This is the most depressing thing I've ever read in my life," Rhonda says, flipping through the pages.

"True, but it's depressing in a young, fun way. Here, let me read it aloud—the way it's meant to be read.

Dear Reader,

My first best friend had only one dress. I know. But, it's true. It was a big pink party dress with white polka dots all over it and she wore it the first day she came to our school. Her family had just moved to New Jersey from Oregon. As you can well imagine, we were all totally mesmerized by the fact that the new girl showed up to school in eveningwear. Besides falling way out of bounds of the *appropriate for school* clothing and accessories list most of our moms carried around in their purses, the dress was, well, quite frankly, it was filthy. And even more noteworthy was the fact that the dirt was old.

The dress consisted of a thin sheath of pink, polka-dotted tulle, layered over a pink polyester lining. There was an enormous limp bow safety-pinned to the back of the dress and the lining was hanging out an inch or two longer than the top layer of the dress. There was also a little hole right next to the zipper going up her back and the dress was sleeveless. It was early January when she came to our school and all she had to wear was her sleeveless dress. No coat, no scarf, no gloves, no sweater, nothing. Her arms and legs were so skinny they looked like they could easily crack right off. It hurt to look at her.

As I'm reading, a thought occurs to Courtney and so she half raises her hand.

"Do you have something to say?" I ask her.

"Well, I was just guessing about this, but does she turn out to be really pretty in the end? Because I think I've read something like this before. Anyway, go on. I think it's really good so far, and totally related to fashion!"

At recess, I noticed her run by me toward the swings. Her face was flushed and sweaty and she had gotten herself even dirtier than when she first arrived at school. I imagined she was the bravest person I'd ever known. I was even considering trying the swings. I usually avoided them because I had a tendency to pump myself into such a frenzy my hair often got caught in the chains. But she had a way of making everything look a lot more fun than it actually was.

When we got inside, the teacher called the new girl to the front of the classroom to introduce her. She stood there with her hands folded behind her, swaying back and forth so her dress could swish from side to side. I was enjoying the dress swishing show, but I was concerned about the fact that her skeletal legs were covered in cuts and bruises. I made a note to myself to offer her some Neosporin after class because, at that particular time in my life, I was obsessed with skin infections.

"I'd like to introduce you to a new member of our class, who traveled all the way from Oregon," said Miss Whitmore.

"I bet she wore that dress the whole way, too," Caren Westman said.

Our teacher, Miss Whitmore, told Caren not to say things like that, but anyone could see she was trying not to laugh herself.

I'm just about to continue reading when Chloe whispers in my ear, "Is it possible that you've confused your 'Letter from an Editor' with your autobiography?"

The next day at recess, the new girl and I were on the swings when one of her brothers walked over to us. When she introduced me, I immediately fell in love and I'm pretty sure that's when I had my first panic attack. Fearing I would faint, fall off my swing, and crack my head open on the pavement, I began alternately pumping my legs with the wild, reckless abandon you usually see when a cartoon character is being chased by a bear. All I could see was the blur of her brother's bony knees through his jeans as my blood flooded my veins.

After about two or three minutes of agonizing, heart-wrenching pumping, her brother finally grabbed both of our swings and told us to "get off." And so we did. As we were walking away, I couldn't help noticing that he was giving us the finger. I looked at the new girl to see if she was as upset as I was that her brother bullied us into giving up our swings, but then she whispered something in my ear that assured me she was fine with it.

"Don't worry, I peed all over that swing as soon as I saw him coming," she said. I was, of course, completely sickened by this at the time, but looking back, I think she did the right thing.

The next morning, I saw the new girl walking toward the school wearing only the pink lining of her dress. I also noticed that she had taken the bow off her actual dress and attached it to the front of the lining. I asked her what happened to the rest of her dress. She said she was saving it.

I looked at her very carefully to see if she was ashamed to be wearing only the inside of her dress, which, to me, bore a striking resemblance to a nightgown, but she didn't care. She wasn't thinking about it at all.

When we got into class, I was overjoyed to see that we had a substitute teacher, Mrs. Desmond. But as soon as she told us to take out our markers and I dropped mine all over the floor, she suggested I leave the room. I asked the teacher if I could go to the nurse instead of just standing out in the hall and the new girl offered to escort me, which I thought was not only kind and considerate, but a wise safety measure. I was feeling a little wobbly after being yelled at. It would have been nice to have had someone nearby in case I accidentally fell down a flight of stairs. Unfortunately, she was told to sit down and mind her own business. On the way to her seat, she took a little something out of the garbage can that appeared to be a huge wad of gum and put it on Mrs. Desmond's seat.

We spent that entire night on the phone making plans to run over Mrs. Desmond as soon as we learned to drive. The new girl was opening up a whole new world for me.

When my alarm went off the next morning, I jumped out of bed. I was ready to go back to school. I knew there was something unfair about teachers who picked on little kids, but I figured it wasn't any more unfair than the wardrobe God gave the new girl.

One afternoon after school, while I was waiting for the bus, I saw my new friend and her brothers leaving together to walk home. As she was walking away, Caren yelled to her, "Your underwear is showing. Oh, never mind. I forgot. That's your dress."

My friend's three brothers ran over to Caren and within seconds they had her pinned to a tree. I started crying because I thought I was about to witness a murder and also because I saw the new girl in the background twisting her dress around so she could get the bow off. I watched her unhook the safety pin and quickly pin the bow to the front of her dress so it would look less like a slip. Something about seeing her do that just tore me apart.

"I think I'm going to cry," Courtney interrupts.

Toward the end of that year, my best friend told me that she was moving back to Oregon because her dad lost his job again. On the last day of school, she wore a pair of pants for the first time. The pants were at least three sizes too big and they looked an awful lot like the pants one of her brothers always wore. When she turned around to talk to me, I noticed that she had tried to sew a little patch in the shape of a pocket over one of the holes by her knee.

It took me a long time to figure out why girls treat the girls who don't fit in as if they did something wrong. I had to do quite a bit of research, but I understand now and I'm going to pass on everything I've learned about girls over the years to my readers.

Hopefully, our new magazine, *Miss Understanding: A Girl's Guide to Girls*, will help us all see each other differently—enough so that when another little girl shows up to class wearing the lining of her one and only dress on the second day at a new school, we'll have all taught our daughters how that must feel and how wrong it is to want to hurt someone's feelings for being poor and different and dirty. Well, I hope that explains what I've come here to do! Have a great day!

Sincerely,
Your New Deputy Editor, Zoe Rose

I can't help but sense a heavy, stillness in the air. Almost as though I just announced that all of us have only a few seconds left to live.

"I don't mean to sound stupid, but I've never heard 'A Letter from an Editor' like that," Courtney says, wiping a tear from her eye.

"Maybe we can use it for something else," Blaire suggests. "Perhaps our farewell letter to the industry."

"It's a good letter, Zoe. We can definitely work with it. We'll just need to cut it down a bit. Like I said, to about a paragraph," Dan says. He's massaging his temples again.

"I was going to field some questions, but since there don't appear to be any, I'll just go ahead and read off some of the fashion- and beauty-related article ideas I'd like to use for our first issue.

Now, in keeping with the whole "judging people by their appearance" theme, I've got:

What Dirty, Stained Clothing Really Says About You as a Person and a Potential Friend!

Understanding Girls with Moustaches!

Why Girls Are Mean to Overweight Girls Who Want to Borrow Their Clothes!

Understanding Ugly Girls!

Why Models Are Such Assholes!

I look around the room. Blaire and Sloane are frozen stiff. Rhonda gives me the thumbs-up and I thumb her right back. The advertising director, Alex, is frantically typing and trying not to smile; Courtney is waving her hand in the air, and Amanda has her head down, all the way down. Ruth has inadvertently turned her chair all the way around, and she is now facing the door. Sadly, she is unaware of this and just sits there continuing to pull imaginary objects off of her clothing. Chloe is slouched so far down in her chair, her head is now just below the table, and Dan looks like he just saw a ghost. I should have warned him that I rewrote some of the headlines we'd selected for me to present today.

I point to Courtney who says, "I have two questions. The first one is more of a suggestion. If we go with the article about the overweight girl, I was thinking that we should start featuring some more carb-free products as part of our editorial." She looks around the room, smiling and hopeful, but gets very little in return.

"My second question is, I mean, even though that one wasn't really a question per se is, are these article ideas supposed to be a little mean? Because on the one hand we're telling girls not to make fun of each other, but on the other hand, that's sort of what we're doing."

"I understand your confusion but our goal here is to magnify these behaviors by exaggerating what they look like on paper. These article ideas are intended to represent the absurd criteria girls use to judge and alienate one another. That's why they, themselves, sound absurd."

"How about doing an issue on how we judge girls who wear rotting, old boots to work?" Sloane suggests.

I hear a little thump and realize that Chloe just bumped her head on the table.

"Absolutely," I answer Sloane. "Now you're catching on. It's funny, though, isn't it? You'd think when we were sitting there in fifth grade with our neat little notebooks and matching highlighter pens that we would be the ones to grow up and become the decision makers for this country. But somehow those little slobs who never handed in their homework and refused to brush their teeth ended up ruling the world. Do you ever ask yourselves how we ended up being their secretaries instead of their bosses, or their president?

"It's because instead of eliminating the talented players because they were afraid of being shown up or worse yet, afraid to be seen with a guy who might have something really great to bring to the table, but was unfortunately wearing *the wrong boots,* the boys were out there patting each other on the back—on the field—and then inviting one another into their offices. They figured out long ago that by building hugely successful teams they could run the world.

"And while they were out there collecting each other's talent, we were cleverly disinviting one another to our parties.

"I'm not saying all women judge each other by their shoes or the size of their asses. There are plenty of educated, evolved women out there who get it, but you can be sure that the millions of girls who read *Issues* are exactly the girls we need to reach."

"Don't you think our readers will feel betrayed when they pick up their favorite magazine only to find out it's been infiltrated by some hostile militant feminist?" Blaire asks.

"I think rescued is a better word."

"In your letter, you spoke about a name change. Is that definite?" Alex asks.

"That's entirely up to Dan. I do think the name *Issues* is more fitting than ever, but I also love the name, *Miss Understanding: A Girl's Guide to Girls,* because I think it's more feminine, more descriptive, and more fun. I want the magazine to be a best friend to all types of girls."

"That's sweet," Blaire says as sarcastically as she can, although I could've said it so much better had I been the one answering me.

"That's enough," Alex says and turns her chair toward Blaire. "This meeting has been called so that Zoe can explain her vision for the magazine. We'll have plenty of opportunities to express our opinions after she's finished speaking. In the meantime, if you can't control yourself, perhaps Dan will agree with me that you should probably leave."

"I think Alex is right. Let's hold off on expressing our concerns until we're fully acquainted with the material Zoe is presenting," Dan says.

"Let me put it to you another way," Sloane interrupts. "We're going to turn this magazine into a rant fest for intellectual frumps who think ugly, overweight girls who don't know enough to wash their clothes are better than the rest of us simply because they're unattractive. And Zoe is going to speak on their behalf so the rest of us feel like shallow, looks-obsessed dumb blondes."

"Why? Why would we want to do that? I'm so not getting this. What about our readers? What if they hate this new idea? Shouldn't we have asked them first?" Courtney asks, folding down the page of her magazine.

"Hold on a minute, Courtney," Alex interjects, and then quickly turns her attention to Sloane, "If you're honestly incapable of grasping this new editorial concept, and I'm beginning to think you are, we can certainly ask Dan to hire you a private tutor. But for now, I'd like to ask you to keep your negative comments to yourself for the remainder of the meeting so as not to confuse Courtney.

"And to answer your question, Courtney; the reason I assume Dan and Zoe have decided to make an editorial change is that they believe they are doing the right thing. Sometimes people make a moral decision that has very little to do with dollars and cents. Perhaps our readers will love our new editorial and perhaps they won't. That's the chance Dan is willing to take and it's our job to make sure he succeeds, whether we agree with it or not. We are taking a risk for *a cause*. Does that make sense?"

"Yes, thank you. And despite my concerns, I still think this all sounds very electrifying."

"I'm very interested to see how this is going to play out as well," says Amanda, whose words I can't help noticing are remarkably carefully chosen.

"Well, I'm sure our new editorial will cover some fascinating aspects of female behavior and relationships, and rest assured we'll get plenty of press. I will tell you this, however: Satire is typically unsavory bait for advertisers, but I support you one hundred percent, and I will do everything I can to sell this idea to every advertiser I can get my hands on. It's not often that a salesperson is privileged enough to sell a product she truly believes in."

Alex looks at Dan and then at me and says, "Thank you both." I'm assuming the meeting is now over but just then Alex turns to look at Ruth, who is still facing the door, and proceeds to talk to her back.

"Ruth, I'd like to meet with you later to discuss some ideas for selling pieces. In the meantime, I'm also going to need you to contact the research department and get me some hard-hitting numbers with regards to the buying habits of the type of reader Zoe is trying to reach. Go with the following demographics: eighteen to forty-five, nothing less than a four-year college degree, and likely to have a graduate degree or perhaps some graduate work. Income somewhere between thirty to a hundred thousand dollars a year max.

"Next, we'll need some figures on highly educated, avid readers. As far as their music preferences, plug in: alternative, classic rock, classical, and jazz. For shopping venues, plug in: vintage, boutique, Internet, and bulk. For car preferences, plug in: Hybrid, Volkswagen, Mini Cooper, Volvo, Subaru, Honda, and Audi. I'll get you some more target words as soon as I get a minute to think. Also, since our age group just expanded considerably, plug in: one or more children and all child-related product-buying habits.

"Although I firmly believe that we're going to lose a large chunk of our twenty-something and single readership, I will do my best to keep our current advertisers. Somehow we'll have to convince these guys that we're going to convert our readers into people who think below the surface without influencing their buying habits. It's a long shot but, as I said, it's for a good cause. I'll talk to Rob about splitting up the sales team into two groups: Those who will spend all of their time trying to keep our current advertisers and those whose job it will be to go after advertisers who appeal to the practical-minded academic, the intellectual set, and women over thirty, who may have a couple of kids, a minivan, and a mortgage competing with their discretionary income.

"I commend you, Dan and Zoe. You both have great courage."

Alex looks over at Ruth again and without missing a beat continues talking to the back of her head, "I'll send you a memo this afternoon. We're going to need some support material *immediately*. Ladies, Dan, have a good day."

I can't lie. I worship her.

Alex collects her things and gets up to leave. She has my "Letter from an Editor" on top of her pile. She glances at it and lingers at the door for a moment while she reads. Dan addresses the group and asks if anyone has anything to add before we adjourn. There are a few minor questions, all of which

Dan answers. After a couple of minutes, Alex, who is still standing at the door, lifts her head from the letter and says, "I have a question, Dan. It's actually a question for Zoe." She turns to look at me and asks, "Did you by any chance grow up in New Jersey?"

"Yes, why?" I ask.

"No, it's just that. . . No, it couldn't be."

"What?" I ask.

"For a second I thought this letter was about me. But my best friend in second grade was a redhead, so never mind," she says and walks out the door.

Chapter 4

By the time I get back to my office I'm already completely inundated with e-mails and Amanda keeps walking in with more and more messages. I've asked her to hold my calls while I try to pull myself together.

First of all, my best friend's name in second grade was Ali and her family moved back to Oregon. And she was nothing at all like Alex. It's just not possible. Although I guess it's not entirely out of the question that she moved back to the East Coast, changed her look, and picked up a new nickname over the course of the last twenty-three years. These things happen.

Part of me wants to go flying down to her office, but I don't even know her. If it is her, the thing I'm most surprised about is that she even remembers me. I'm sure I couldn't possibly have had the same impact on her life that she had on mine. Aside from Chloe, I haven't had too many best friends since Ali. I've always had a lot more in common with boys. That's probably why I remember Ali so well. I wonder if it was the same for her. Nevertheless, I should at least find her and apologize for telling the staff she peed on a swing—just in case it is her.

As I stand up to stretch my legs, Chloe pops her head into my office.

"I brought you a sweater and some shoes," she says. "And don't worry. I have an idea to get you out of this mess."

"What mess?"

"The whole *Girl's Guide* thing."

"What are you talking about?"

"Zoe, you totally bombed in that meeting. No one understood what you were trying to say. Least of all poor Courtney. But everyone will be going to lunch in a little while. And it's pouring outside so they'll all be going down to the cafeteria. While everyone's sitting around, I'll just casually mention another idea, as though you and I had been working on it all along, and before you know it, no one will even remember today's meeting ever happened. You'll see; everything will be fine." As she's talking she's taking one shoe box after another out of her shopping bags.

"Chloe, please understand that I don't need your help with the *Girl's Guide,* and what are those?" I ask

"Ballet slippers."

"Are you taking ballet lessons?"

"I bought them for you."

"Why?"

"I went shoe shopping this morning so you could change out of your boots."

"Ah, so that's how 'I left the oven and my blow dryer on' translates."

"I thought that was understood."

"I didn't think you even noticed my boots, and why didn't you just tell me you were going shopping? Why do you have to lie all the time?"

"I don't know. I sort of thought you knew and at the same

time I didn't want you to try to talk me out of it." She takes another pair of slippers out of their box.

"Those are silver, Chloe! They're the same shoes Blaire is wearing."

"I know. Aren't they adorable?" she asks, taking out the gold pair.

"Are you crazy? Isn't there some rule about me copying Blaire and Sloane?"

"Actually no. You're allowed to do that, and besides everyone in this whole building wears these slippers. I got this suit on sale today too and that sweater I just gave you. I would have given it to you during the meeting, but I didn't want anyone to know I went shopping."

"Are you joking? You walked into that meeting with fifty bags."

"So? I could have just been carrying them around for all they know. What do you think of my suit?" she asks, petting the lapel.

"It looks great, but why didn't you get yourself a pair of shoes that fit you while you were out shopping?" I ask, putting the ballet slippers back in their boxes.

"What's wrong with these?" she asks, turning her foot from side to side.

"Nothing. They're beautiful, but you can't walk in them."

"Sure I can, which is amazing because they're a nine and a half."

"Chloe, you wear a size six."

"I know, that's what's so amazing about them."

I'm about to explain to my sister why it doesn't make sense to buy shoes that are three sizes too big when Ruth tears into my office with Amanda running right behind her. Amanda is asking Ruth if she can help her with something in an attempt to stop Ruth from barging in, but she just ignores her and walks right up to me. Amanda steps in front of her but Ruth pushes her aside.

"Let me put it to you this way, Zoe, what we have here is a rant fest for intellectual frumps who think ugly, overweight girls with stained clothes, who don't know enough to get their moustaches waxed are better than the rest of us!"

The room is silent. No one knows what to say. She just wigged out in front of everyone. Rhonda must have heard Ruth ranting out in the hall because suddenly she's in my office too.

I can already see there's very little privacy in this place.

"Don't worry," Rhonda chimes in. "She's been doing stuff like this all the time lately. She'll be fine."

"We are young, sexy, and hot," Ruth bellows. "We're not a bunch of intelligent moustaches who can't even . . . who can't even. Think straight."

"Ruth, I think perhaps you've misunderstood something," Amanda begins.

"Save your breath," Rhonda whispers to her.

"We don't need to sit on the sidelines booing the winners because we can't measure up. We are the yardstick of what is hip and what is now. We're not afraid to swim with the sharks because we *are* the sharks. I mean, look at me for example. Look at what I've accomplished in my career, simply because I've been able to stay on top of trends."

"This from a woman who wears orthopedic Keds," Rhonda adds, a little insensitively. Even for my taste. Ruth walks out of my office as though she just came in to tell me she was leaving for lunch.

"What the hell was that?" I ask, looking at everyone.

"I think she might be very ill," Amanda whispers sympathetically. "Would you like me to call someone?"

"Don't be ridiculous. This is nothing. She once called our publisher and told him to come down to her office immediately because she'd just received a threatening e-mail from one of our advertisers and she wanted to discuss it with him in person. When he walked into her office, she was lying on her desk with her shirt unbuttoned and her skirt hiked up around her waist. Her door was wide open. I saw the whole thing. The poor guy. I've never seen him so shook up. When everyone else came back from lunch, she was still lying there on her desk," Rhonda explains.

"Oh my goodness, that's terrible," says Amanda.

"What's so terrible about it? She fell asleep. She falls asleep all the time," Rhonda continues. "She probably just went back to her office to take a little nap right now."

"Well, she's obviously suffering from a mental illness of some kind. It's almost as if she was talking in her sleep. She has no idea what she was even saying and yet she was trying to repeat what Sloane said in the meeting. This is very scary," Amanda says.

"Nah, she's just a drunk. Personally, I think she's having the time of her life. It's hard for you to understand how happy she is because you didn't know her before. But this is the best she's ever been. She finally has the job she's wanted for seven years, and she's wearing a new blouse. If we call someone to *help* her, she'll spend the rest of her life under strict psychiatric care. The humanitarian thing to do, in my opinion, is ignore her. Besides the Princelys will never fire her. She's always threatening to sue and she's been trying to build a case against them for years."

"That's true," Chloe says. "I saw her files."

"Well, I guess as long as she can function," Amanda says, trying to consider Rhonda's point.

"She can function, all right. And she can make your life miserable—when she's sober. Just be grateful that they transferred you from publicity to editorial instead of the promotion department. Chloe had to suffer with Ruth as her boss for an entire year, and all because she pressed the wrong button on the elevator when she came for her interview. The poor kid got off on the wrong floor, stumbled into the wrong office, and ended up getting the wrong job," Rhonda explains.

"That's true too; I did press the wrong button," Chloe says.

This conversation continues as Amanda, Rhonda, and I head downstairs to the cafeteria. Chloe says she's going to find Dan and that she'll meet us down there.

As soon as I have my tray of food, I look around for a place to sit. I'm ravenous, to say the least, and since I was the first one to get on and off the lunch line, it's up to me to pick a spot. I can see that Anita is lunching with Blaire, Courtney, and Sloane at a table in the corner, but I'd rather share a trough with a family of lepers than eat with Anita; and look at that—here comes Ruth. Somehow she managed to pull herself together. She's heading over to Anita's table with a tray filled with desserts.

I find a seat at an empty table just as Chloe and Dan walk into the cafeteria. I motion to Chloe and she holds up a finger. She cuts in front of the line, puts the money for a brownie on the counter, and comes and sits down.

Dan, Rhonda, and Amanda join us as I dive into my vegetarian chili. It's not very good but I wouldn't care if there were a big hunk of meat sitting right on the top of it. I've never been so hungry in my entire life.

As soon as everyone's comfortable and settled, Anita walks right over to our table and sits herself down as if she's been invited. I can't help noticing that she carelessly left her empty

tray for someone else to take care of, nor the fact that Courtney, Blaire, and Sloane followed her lead without a moment's
hesitation. Remarkably, Courtney is still reading the same
magazine she had at the meeting and her head is still buried
in it while she follows the three of them over to our table. She
sits down without ever once lifting up her head. I had no idea
she was such a voracious reader. Ruth doesn't notice that they
all got up so she just sits there staring at the wall. I think she
might still be a little drunk.

"You forgot to bus your trays," I tell them as they're walking over.

"We never do," Blaire says.

"That's very thoughtful of you," I say, somewhat under my
breath.

"Dan," Anita cuts in, ignoring me, "I'd like to say something
if I may. The girls were just filling me in on how the editorial
meeting went today and I'm more than a little concerned. I'm
sure you've taken into consideration the fact that we don't intend to swim in waters that may very well be over our heads.
Although brainstorming sessions are always fun and entertaining, we are nevertheless committed to who we are and what the
purpose of this magazine has always been. Are we not?"

"On the contrary. Our intention is to start giving the magazine some character and integrity," Dan says.

Way to contraire.

Anita begins to speak again, but Dan gives her a look, and
she instantly shuts up.

Damn! I'd love to be able to make people stop talking like that.

I hear Courtney whisper to Blaire, "This article I'm reading totally reminds me of my first boss when I worked as a
makeup assistant at Bloomingdale's. She was so mean to me
and I could never figure out why. I thought it was because I

was very naive and inexperienced at the time, but then later I found out that she had irritable bowel syndrome, which made perfect sense! If only I'd known."

"If only you'd known *what?*" Blaire asks.

"That she was suffering from bowel-related irritability."

At that moment, Chloe clears her throat to begin speaking. I hope she's not about to try to *save* me. I'm almost tempted to jump her and cover her mouth, but I don't want to make a scene.

I look at my sister sitting there in her little pink-and-cream suit and I can't help but remember her as a little girl pretending to be a fashion editor. She looks almost exactly the same—except she's not wearing the shower cap. She looks at me and gives me a little wink and a smile as if to say, "Don't you worry. I have everything under control."

"Well, I hate to disagree with you, Anita, but I absolutely love Zoe's new editorial idea. But I was just this second remembering another idea that I think is equally philosophical and psychological, but a little more on the fashiony side.

"This particular idea is one that Zoe and I talked about a few weeks ago—so, in a way, it's as much Zoe's idea as it is mine. So if you all like it, you can thank her just as much as you can thank me." Amanda leans over to me and says, "She's very sweet, isn't she?" I can't even answer her. I'm too busy praying for a fire drill.

Anita has her hands folded on the table and the same expression on her face that she always has when Chloe is talking. She looks like a cat who just ate a mouse.

And the mouse is still alive.

And the cat's trying to hide how much she's enjoying it.

"Okay, here I go," Chloe says and looks right at me. She said her idea was both philosophical and psychological, two words that should never be used in the same sentence, but maybe she's on to something. It's possible that she figured out a way to package all the pieces of the *Girl's Guide to Girls* in a way that will finally resonate with them.

"Okay, my idea can be summed up in only five words.

" 'SHOES! . . . A METAPHOR FOR LIFE!' "

Courtney stands up and starts clapping as though Chloe announced that she's just discovered a cure for wrinkles.

"Are you serious?" Sloane asks.

"Why wouldn't she be?" I say, hoping and praying she's not.

"Well, it's just sort of like we went from one extreme to the other," Blaire says.

Suddenly Ruth turns around and says, "Well, that's a novel idea, isn't it?" —and then proceeds to roll off her chair and onto the floor.

"I knew that was coming," Rhonda says.

Amanda rushes over to help her off the floor and Ruth tells her to get her filthy hands off her before she calls the cops. She's now flat on her back with her arms and legs spread eagle. Dan gets up and walks behind the food counter to call security, while Ruth tries to roll herself over.

Everyone is frozen in their seat, except Chloe, who stands up and walks over to Ruth. She leans over her and reaches out to put her hand on Ruth's forehead when Anita rushes over. "Do not touch her," she says, grabbing Chloe's wrist as though she's afraid Ruth might spontaneously combust.

"Why shouldn't she touch her?" I ask, even though I would much prefer if she didn't. Ruth could be harboring any number of diseases.

"Just do as I say," Anita demands.

I'm so tempted to tell her to go fuck herself, but instead I use Anita's command as an excuse to keep my sister away from the festering lunatic lying on the floor.

"Just get away from her, like Hitler said," I sort of whisper and sort of say really loudly as I pull Chloe away.

"Hold on, Ruth, help is on the way," Chloe calls to her as I usher her back to her seat.

"Don't anyone touch me! You people are going to find yourself with a big, fat lawsuit on your hands," Ruth says. I feel Anita's eyes penetrating me, as if to say "See? I know exactly what I'm doing at all times. Never question my authority and always do as I say," as two security guards walk in, pick Ruth up under her arms, and escort her out.

"I hate to report something like this, but I think you're right about her Rhonda, I definitely detected alcohol on her breath," Amanda says regretfully.

"Well if you hate to report something like that, then keep it to yourself," Anita says, and sits back down. "I'd like you all to forget what just happened. We can't afford to get sidetracked by our employees' personal problems. I'll make sure Ruth gets the medical attention she needs. In the meantime, Chloe, permit me to save time by letting you know that we won't be using shoes as a metaphor for life in any Princely magazine, so there's no need to waste any more of this lunch on such a thing."

Dan looks at his mother and tries not to react, but he's obviously lost his patience.

"Chloe, please continue with what you were saying," he says, looking at Chloe encouragingly, despite the vein bulging out of Anita's forehead.

"But, she just said . . ."

"I said continue."

Poor Chloe doesn't know whom to obey. Dan nods and tells her again that it's okay to continue.

"As I was saying, the reason I chose 'Shoes! A Metaphor for Life' is because, if you think about it, they really are! It's the way they look and everything and the way, as you get older, you want different things out of life and out of your shoes, and the way you always remember what shoes you were wearing on the occasions that mark the big milestones in your life, and there are all those sayings that you wouldn't have without shoes, such as: Don't judge someone until you've walked a mile in their shoes, which is sort of what Zoe has been saying from the beginning; and also the one about not wanting to be in someone else's shoes, and of course there's 'look before you leap,' but I guess that's not directly related to shoes—"

"I know exactly what you mean," I interrupt. "It's almost as if shoes are designed to be perfect little models of who we wish we were. They're like our little spokespeople. Take running shoes for example. When we choose the hottest new sneaker, for example—sure, we're buying athletic footwear, but we're also buying into a lifestyle. Running shoes say we're living on the edge, cool and fast, and that we're free to dress down. And then, when we put on those running shoes, we actually believe that's who we are, and we walk around hoping to project that image."

"Yes! Yes! Yes!" Chloe says. "And when we choose a high-heeled simple pump, we feel grown-up, important, ladylike, and in control; and hopefully, if we can walk in them, we can project that sort of image as well."

I knew she'd catch on to what she was trying to say.

"For instance, take my boots," I say, lifting my foot above the table and holding it in the air.

"When other people look at these boots, they might see a lame attempt to hold on to a youthful, rebellious persona and perhaps some unsightly discoloration. They might also notice that they are a boys' size three, which translates into a girls' size five. However, since I think a little differently than the average girl, I see comfort, independence, and power because they say, 'I'm not like you. I don't want to be like you, and you can't make me be like you.' They also make my feet look a lot larger than they really are, which makes me feel as though I'm the same age as everyone else, which I rarely do, because I have a height complex.

"So, in a way, these shoes are a metaphor for my life." I look over at Blaire and ask her if she's taking notes. "They prove that I'm not like other girls and that I'm fine with it. And that is why I see them as one thing and other girls see them as something else."

"You forgot to say holes," Blaire says.

"Excuse me?"

"We see holes. There's a hole in the toe."

"That must have just happened. It wasn't there before."

"Okay great," Dan interrupts. "That's certainly an interesting concept, Chloe. And you reiterated it very well, Zoe. I will definitely give it some more thought. I know how important shoes are to you, Chloe, and you've done some fabulous promotions using shoes in the past. I'm sure you'll continue to find ways to spice up our *Girl's Guide* with some interesting articles about shoes as well."

"You don't like my idea at all, do you?" Chloe mumbles.

"Of course he doesn't. It's preposterous," Anita says.

"Of course he does, Chloe. He loves it. He wants to use it. He just said so," I disagree.

"No, he said he wants me to spice up the *Guide* with some

interesting shoe articles, which is a nice way of saying he's heard just about enough of shoes."

"Don't be ridiculous. It's a great idea," I say.

"So can we use it instead of this whole *Girl's Guide* thing?" she asks, as though she's suggesting soup instead of salad.

"Chloe, we can't just bag a whole concept in exchange for articles about old shoe sayings," Dan says impatiently. I can't blame him for being annoyed. This lunch has somehow turned into a continuation of the same grueling editorial meeting we just ended, he has the most horrible mother in the world, and this shoe thing has got to be the worst idea anyone has ever had.

"Well, you have to admit it's a lot less risky than printing articles about girls who are mean to each other because they're fat and hairy. What if no one gets that we're on the ugly girls' side?" Courtney asks.

Oh my God.

"That's right, Courtney. But, if we go with my 'Shoes! A Metaphor for Life' theme, we'll not only be providing our readers with thought-provoking editorial, we'll be making our advertisers happy by helping them sell more shoes. According to our research, we are down close to eleven percent in shoe advertising dollars. Does anyone realize what that means for our economy? Women typically spend more money on shoes than any other item in their wardrobe, and shoe sales are down all over America.

"Somewhere along the line, we've lost communication with our readers. We're not teaching them what they need to know. We're not even showcasing our shoe advertisers' products properly. In fact, the whole shoe market is at risk."

I can't hold it in anymore. This is going too far.

"Chloe, you're talking about the shoe market as though it's

something worth giving a shit about! We're trying to reform a nation of women here."

"Zoe, you may be right about a lot of things, but we can't turn our backs on the entire shoe industry, and therefore, the economy at large."

"Chloe, please listen to me. This could be a very exciting time in history if we take advantage of the fact that we have a magazine with a huge readership at our disposal. We have an amazing opportunity here to really make a difference for women. I'm afraid the shoe thing might be a tad limiting in light of what's at stake here."

"I know you think my idea is dumb but I can't let you do the *Girl's Guide*. It's a mistake. Please believe me. They already tried this whole womany thing in the sixties, or maybe it was the fifties; I can't remember anymore—whenever that *Feminine Mystique* book came out that we all had to read in eleventh grade."

"Perhaps the two of you can resolve your editorial differences elsewhere, on your own time, because I for one do not think either of your ideas warrant further discussion. Zoe is obviously some sort of misogynist. I can't imagine who you think you're fooling, throwing around insults in the name of social consciousness, and, Chloe, your idea is so shortsighted, I hardly see the point in me being here another minute," says Anita.

"Then go," I say.

"Dan, I'd like to see you in my office as soon as you're finished with this nonsense," she says and walks out.

As soon as Anita is safely down the hall, Dan says, "I'd like to explore your idea further, Chloe. I think it has tremendous potential. But my gut is telling me that the time is right for the *Guide,* and although we may have to refine our approach—

tone it down a bit, and try to make it more user friendly—I think it's a very powerful concept and we should at least give it a try."

He looks at her with so much love and sympathy, if you couldn't hear what he was saying, you'd think he was telling her that her dog died.

There's some shuffling around and mumbling as everyone gathers their trays to leave.

"I'm afraid it's time, then," Chloe says.

"Time for what?" Dan asks, holding his tray in one hand and pushing his chair in with the other. He picks up his bag and turns to walk away.

"Time for me to take a sabbatical from my position as shoe editor."

"Chloe, you've only been shoe editor for a few hours," he says without looking at her. "That's too soon to take a sabbatical." He dumps the remains of his tray into the garbage can and places it on top of the pile, completely unmoved.

"Under normal circumstances, yes, I would agree with you. A few hours is not a very long time, but under these conditions, I simply can't go on."

"If you'll excuse us," Dan says, realizing that Chloe is serious and that they will have to leave the cafeteria if they want any privacy. No one else seems to be moving away from the table just yet.

He puts his bag back down on the table and lifts Chloe out of her chair by her arm. They walk out of the cafeteria while everyone else lingers for a while, hoping to catch a word or two of their conversation. As soon as it becomes clear that they're out of earshot, one by one, everyone leaves. Except for me. I know for a fact that Chloe can't get very far in her shoes and that they're most likely going to use the empty office next door to continue their conversation. I take Dan's bag and get back on line to get myself an iced tea, and then I take a seat at a table next to the wall.

After a few seconds, I hear muffled voices. It's like listening to a play on an old radio.

"Chloe, you can't walk out of here like this. You'd be setting a very poor example for the rest of the staff, not to mention that you'd be taking unfair advantage of the fact that you're my wife. It's going to take time to work through all of our editorial differences, but success hinges on compromise. We can't all go around quitting when we don't get our way."

"First of all, success does not hinge on compromise. It hinges on not making stupid decisions and secondly, I'm not quitting. I'm taking a sabbatical, and not because I didn't get my way. I'm leaving, *temporarily,* because I refuse to stand by and watch my sister go down. I know all too well what those editors are going to do to her, not to mention what our advertisers and readers are going to do to our numbers when this ludicrous idea for a fashion and beauty magazine hits the stands.

"My sister has been trying to force the truth down people's throats her entire life and let me tell you something, nobody wants it. Least of all girls who read fashion magazines. Why do people need to know the truth, Dan? Answer me that. Zoe isn't going to change the way girls *are,* simply by *telling* them the way they are. Do midgets need to know that they always look a little fat? Of course not, because there is nothing they can do about it and there's nothing girls can do about the way they are either. We are what we are. Maybe we weren't meant to form these amazing teams that men form. Maybe we're meant to operate on our own, or in pairs, or small groups of three, where one girl is always left out. And maybe there's a good reason why we're different than men. And if our differences, and our inability to get along and form *great teams,* is what causes men to have all the power, then that's a shame, I agree. I just don't think announcing every single thing we do wrong is going to make a bit of difference. It's just going to ruin a perfectly good magazine.

"Sure, we can try to change for a while, but we'll always go back to being exactly what we've always been, which is more interested in fashion and beauty than forming a coalition. Most girls don't want to run the world, Dan. They want to have fun. And if being mean to each other is the way they have fun, right or wrong, no magazine in the world will be able to convince them to stop doing it."

"Chloe, that's a ridiculous argument. I can't even believe you could be satisfied with it."

"Well, I'm sorry. It may sound narrow-minded but that's the way I feel. But more importantly, if I quit, I mean, take a sabbatical, then Zoe will too, and that's exactly what I'm hoping she'll do. It will save us all a lot of embarrassment, and hopefully it will save my sister a lot of unnecessary pain."

"Your sister is not going to quit. She's committed to her cause and I'm sure that she is more than a little disappointed that you totally contradicted her in that meeting after the way she stuck up for you. She needs your support now more than ever, and you completely let her down."

"No, Dan, she needs me to get her out of this mess before she destroys everything and that's why I have to go. I obviously can't convince you that I'm right and I can't bear to witness what I know is going to happen. I'm just not strong enough and that's why I have to leave immediately. I need to begin preparing myself for the fight of my life. It's time for me to venture out into the real world and become the strongest, most capable woman I can possibly be, because that's the kind of woman you're going to need to bring this magazine back to life when this is all over."

"Chloe, what are you talking about?"

"It's time for me to find my inner strength, to conquer my fears, become the person I need to become, and then, when you call me back, I'll be fit for the job."

"What job?"

"The job where I save the magazine."

"Oh. That job."

"I realized something today. I'm only half a woman. That's why you don't take me seriously and that's why I can't convince you that I'm right."

"Are you being serious right now? Because it's really hard to tell. But I will tell you this. You're everything to me and I need you here now, not later, now."

"I'll still be here in spirit and I'll be in touch."

"You'll be in touch? Chloe, you're my wife. We live together, remember?"

"I mean, I'll be in touch throughout the day, silly, on and off. I'll send you ideas periodically and try to help you in times of trouble, but I can't physically be here. Not even for another minute. I love this magazine too much to watch it go down, but more importantly, I love my sister way too much to live through what I know is inequitable."

"I think you mean inevitable."

"Well, perhaps now I'll have time to brush up on my vocabulary, as well."

"Chloe, do not walk out of here."

"Think about it, Dan. You want me to stay for all the wrong reasons. You don't want me to quit on my first day because you think I'm proving to Anita and the whole staff that I'm unprofessional, but I don't care about being professional and you should know that by now. I don't have anything to contribute to *A Girl's Guide to Girls*. I'm not a psychologist and I don't pretend to be one."

"Chloe, don't leave."

"What can I possibly do for you as shoe editor of a satirical, femininitism literary magazine?"

I don't know how much longer I can sit here and listen to Chloe butcher the English language. I was hoping to hear a real play, not one about grammatical errors and how I'm about to make an ass of myself.

"Okay Chloe, go ahead then, if you're so sure this is the right thing to do. We'll just have to do without a shoe editor for now, either that or I'll have to find someone else for the job."

"Don't be ridiculous, Dan, you'll never be able to find anyone who can fill my shoes. But you're welcome to try," and then all I can hear is her heels scraping down the hall, then a little crash, and then the pitter patter of stocking feet. Dan comes back into the cafeteria to get his bag. He's holding Chloe's shoes, one in each hand.

"I was hoping you'd still be here," he says.

"What happened?" I ask, pointing to her shoes.

"She walked right out of them on her way out," he says, shaking his head.

I get up to pat Dan on the back and we walk out together while I try to convince him that she'll be back. Dan walks back to his office, and as I'm heading toward mine, I spot Blaire and Sloane walking by in the hall.

"She's gone for good," Blaire says, and they give each other a little high five. They must have seen Chloe leave and that pretty much clinches it for me. I'm not going to let anyone get in my way—even though I know I'm in for the fight of my life. If I have to take on every single girl in this building, I will. And if I open the eyes of only one reader in the process, I will have accomplished something. Everyone deserves to know the truth, and I've got to tell it, once and for all. Besides, after all these years, I may have actually found a best friend again. I'm not going anywhere.

Chapter 5

I've seen Alex in the hallway a few times, rushing around with her head down, completely absorbed in her own little world. She's always all dressed up, on her way somewhere important. She's impossible to approach.

Whenever I see her whizzing by, I walk a little faster, but most of the time I'm just on my way to the bathroom or the cafeteria. Lately I need to eat every three hours or my hands start shaking. This is something new. My symptoms are very similar to that of a rare neurological disorder that's been linked to pressure on the pre-frontal cortex. Although, it's probably just my hypoglycemia acting up again. Either that or a mild vitamin deficiency of some sort.

Or severe diabetes.

Either way I've got to stop spending so much time on WebMD. It's making me insane.

Alex and I have so much to talk about. I don't know where to begin. I guess it's silly to go over every single thing that happened to me since the day she left our school in second grade, but for some reason I want to tell her everything. I made sure I got to her office early this morning so we'll have a chance to talk before she's off and running.

I knock on her door a few times.

No answer.

I knock a little louder, until I hear a faint, "Who is it?"

"Oh! You're there? I was just walking by and thought I'd say hi," I call to her.

"Good morning!" she calls back.

I guess she'll open the door any second now.

I knock again.

"Who's there?"

"It's Zoe Rose," I yell. I hear the doorknob turn and then Alex pokes her head out.

"How are you, Zoe? What can I do for you?" she asks, her neck straining between the door and the jam.

"I was just walking by and thought we could, you know, catch up a little before the day begins."

"Oh, I'm sorry. Can you give me until the end of the week to get my thoughts together?"

"Of course, absolutely, the end of the week is great, but I was hoping maybe *you and I* could catch up a bit."

Doesn't she want to throw her arms around me and tell me she's been searching for me for years on findaclassmate.com? "It's just that it's been so long."

"Zoe, I just saw you yesterday."

"I don't think you understand, Alex. Remember when you asked me if I grew up in New Jersey at the editorial meeting last week? Well, I did. I'm the same Zoe you thought I was. I was your best friend in second grade. The one with the red afro who was the same size as the pre-schoolers. You were right about the letter. It was about you and me. I just never dreamed in a million years I'd ever see you again, never mind that I'd end up working with you. This whole thing is so bizarre."

"You can't be serious," she says, staring directly at my head.

"I'm totally serious. Believe me, this is not my natural color," I say, holding up a big chunk of my hair.

"This is unbelievable. I can't possibly describe how I felt when you were reading that letter. Part of me knew it was about me. How could it not be? But I honestly wouldn't recognize you in a million years. I just had to assume there was some other little girl out there with the same crappy childhood . . . and dress."

"Alex, I'm so sorry."

"Don't be sorry. It's just that you brought back so many memories. That dress! You have no idea how badly I wanted that dress. I thought it was so beautiful. My mother did too. And she wanted me to have it more than anything. She saved up for so long. The day she bought it for me, I just sat on my bed and stared at it. I'm pretty sure I slept in it that night. I never would have dreamed it would turn out to be such an embarrassment. Once they started making fun of me, I hated it. But there was nothing I could do. It was all I had."

I can just picture her falling asleep that first night with her new dress, trying not to move, thanking God for her one chance to feel like a princess. That overly pink, hopeful dress with its loose threads and limp bow and the lining that was sewn too long. How clueless she was standing there in front of the whole class, thinking she was being admired, not knowing how well those little girls could spot a cheap dress a mile away, and how badly it incriminated her. She was so innocent. That's what made them so cruel.

"I never would have read that letter in a million years if I thought you'd see it. I was writing about a memory, not a person. That was more than twenty years ago. I'd do anything not to have read it—especially to *them*."

"I'm glad you read it. Obviously your point was to defend me, even after all these years. We were always looking out for one another. I can't believe I'm admitting this, but I still see those girls in my dreams. I fought so hard not to let them destroy me, and they didn't. But they certainly left their mark.

"Everything I am is because of them. I was determined to have everything they had. I hated being poor but I pretended I didn't care. I wanted them to think I felt better than them, but I felt like a nothing. I don't feel that way anymore, though. I guess I owe them a thank-you, if you really think about it. They forced me to see myself for what I really was. They gave me the willpower to rise above it. It would have been so easy to just give up, but I worked my ass off to get where I am."

"They're all probably a bunch of country club housewife whores by now."

"Oh, I'm sure they are."

"I can't believe we're even talking about them," I say.

She laughs and rubs her eye with her palm.

"Believe it or not, you were probably the best friend I ever had—to this day. How pathetic is that? I've never been great with girls, ever since then."

"Me neither. If I didn't have my sister—"

"Yeah, you have Chloe. You're very fortunate."

I hear a loud thump in her office and then Alex closes the door a little tighter against her neck. "Listen, Zoe, I'm sort of in the middle of something right now. But I really want to talk some more. I'll call you, okay?"

"Sure, go ahead. I just wanted to apologize and tell you that I'll pull the letter out of the issue if you want me to."

"Absolutely not. It's a perfect letter for our launch. I want it to stay in."

"Okay then. Oh, and whenever you're ready, I have some ideas for the launch cover. If you want to go out to lunch or something, I can show them to you," I say, bending my knees a little. I've been standing in the same spot for so long I'm afraid the blood pooling in my ankles is going to cause permanent swelling.

"Lunch sounds good," she says.

"Are you free today?" I ask.

"Today? I'm afraid not. I'm not free at all this week. I have back-to-back lunch appointments straight through Friday. Two a day. Lunch is the most important sales event of the day. You should know that." She's practically choking herself with the door. It's like she's hiding a dead body in there.

"You eat lunch twice a day?"

"Sometimes three times."

"That whole *sales* thing; wow!"

"Yup. It's quite a challenge trying to get advertisers to commit to our launch issue. I got the memo that you want to use the headline 'The New Feminism.' "

"That's another thing I wanted to talk about," I say, thinking it might not be a bad idea to switch over to sales until my appetite settles down.

"Don't worry. I can sell it. I just need a little more time. It's so damn competitive out there. Our editorial used to give us an edge because it was so blatantly sales driven. Now we're getting a reputation as the magazine that cut its nose off to spite its face. Still, I intend to give this my all. I'm reorienting my sales pitch to attract a different kind of advertiser. I'll be calling on Timberland, Nike, Adidas, Aerosoles, Talbots, and Eileen Fisher this week. I'll let you know how it goes."

"We lost all of our big, high-fashion accounts for the first issue, didn't we?"

"No, not all. We still have Hanes."

"I don't know what to say."

"Just get out there and fight for what you believe in. There's nothing else we can do. We're trying to reform a nation of women here, right? Isn't that what you said? So, let's do it. It's just a shame we can't start with the little girls," she winks.

I can tell she wants to get back to work, but as she's talking I can almost remember her—she still moves her mouth the same way. And she still makes me feel like we're partners and that together we can conquer the world. Something about her tone makes me want to finally open up about how difficult things have been for me lately.

"I'm trying to put up a fight but I'm just so tired all the time. The stress is really starting to take a toll on me physically. I've always been prone to mood swings, and I had a very serious case of walking pneumonia in sixth grade. I diagnosed myself so I'm not one hundred percent sure it was pneumonia, but it sure felt like it."

"Even walking pneumonia can be very serious," she says.

"Anyway, lately all I can do to ease the tension is eat incessantly and I'm so bloated, I can't even button my pants; I mean look at me. I must have gained ten pounds. And I'm so itchy, it's driving me crazy."

"I've heard that stress can do that," she says.

"Lately I've been pouring pancake syrup on everything. It's hard to believe I was once responsible for single-handedly blowing the lid off the refined-sugar industry. And all that sugar has totally messed up my memory. My bill situation is completely out of control, and I never used to be like this—"

"I hate to interrupt you, Zoe, and I'd love to hear more

about your bills and everything, but I really have to get back to work. I realize you need to talk and we will, I promise. We have a ton of stuff to catch up on, but I was just finishing something when you came by. I'm so sorry. Actually, wait just a moment and I'll jot something down for you." She steps away from the door for a second and comes back with a pen and a small pad. She writes down a few numbers and hands me the piece of paper.

"Here are the names and phone numbers of the top psychiatrists, nutritionists, and personal trainers in the city. You need to get yourself under control immediately. This is no time to wallow in self-pity. You're eating to medicate yourself and that's a very dangerous thing to do. Let me know how it all works out, okay?" she says with a tight little smile and a quick nod, indicating that she'd like me to go away.

I went too far.

"Sure, okay. Thanks a lot," I wave as she's closing the door.

Well, I guess it's safe to say we're no longer inseparable.

Chapter 6

"What is wrong with you?"

"Me? Nothing's wrong with me? I think the real question here is what's wrong with you?"

"I just miss you because you've been traveling so much," I answer.

"No, you don't. You just want to have sex all the time. And I have to be honest, it's really starting to get on my nerves."

"Well then stop going along with it," I say accusingly.

"I can't help it once you get me started."

"Then don't complain."

"I'm not complaining. I just need a break. My back hurts."

"Sorry."

"Don't be sorry. Just go and do something else for a while. Take a walk or start a painting or something."

"I don't feel like taking a walk and I can't just start a painting before work. And besides, I don't paint anymore. You know that. How about if we just hold hands?"

"Nice try, Zoe. I'm not falling for that one again."

"Fine. I have to work on these photographs for the launch cover anyway. My favorite so far is a shot of a group of women—all different ages—holding hands in such a way that they form a peace sign. I think it pretty much says it all."

"It sounds a little dull to me."

"It may sound dull, but wait until you see how it looks under a bright pink headline that says, 'The New Feminism.'" I'm sitting as close to him as possible, hoping he'll change his mind and go for one more round, but I can feel him pulling away. I imagine he's in a great deal of pain with the amount of sex I've been forcing on him lately. It's almost mean.

"Well, as long as you're not going to take a walk, I think we should use this time to talk about us for a minute, instead of the magazine, for a change."

"Sure."

"I want to move forward, Zoe. And I want you to start thinking about a time frame."

"A time frame? You can't just pick a date and hope I'll be ready to take the next step on that very day. It has to come naturally."

"Actually, in your case, I think we should pin down a date. Otherwise, the day may never come."

"Well, then, that should tell you something."

"What should it tell me?"

"Exactly what you just said—that the possibility exists that I might never be ready."

"Don't say things like that, Zoe."

"Why not? *You* just said it."

"I said that I want to pin down a date and I still do."

"A date for what exactly? Let's stop beating around the bush."

"A date to start making some serious plans, about our future. I want to start a family, Zoe. You know that."

"Okay, fine. But not right now. I really don't feel well and I have to take a shower."

"Fine, go take a shower. We'll talk when you get out."

I really do feel a little light-headed and not only because of the conversation. It's because I'm not sleeping well lately. I'm so worried about the launch issue, it's been keeping me up at night.

Michael gets up and walks away without saying anything. I try to ignore him but he makes a lot of subtle noise when he's upset.

I e-mail the shot of the women holding hands to my office computer and go to the bathroom to turn the water on. Instinctively I reach for one of my tester sticks.

I don't believe it. I used up over one hundred and fifty of those things in less than a month? How is that even possible? *Poor Michael.*

"Is there any way you feel like going to the drugstore?" I yell out.

"For what?" he asks, but I don't bother to answer him because the phone is ringing and now might not be the best time to ask for anything that has to do with me being deathly afraid of getting pregnant. He picks up the phone, and yells, "It's for you; it's Chloe."

"Hey."

"Hi."

"What's up?" I ask, anxious to get in the shower.

"Just calling to see how things are going?"

"Well, let's see. I ran out of home pregnancy tests. Michael is pressuring me to 'take the next step; everyone at the magazine is pretty much against all of my ideas, and I just weighed myself and I've gained seven pounds. What else do you want to know?"

"Actually, I was really calling to see how the new ballet slippers were working out for you. But as long as you brought up the pregnancy test thing, I was thinking you might want to try a different form of birth control. Perhaps something that's used either before or during sex."

"I can't. I'm allergic to condoms and I can't function on birth control pills. I become bipolar."

"You just get a little moody. That doesn't mean you're bipolar."

"Whatever. I don't need birth control. Only normal girls, who actually menstruate, need it. And as far as my slippers go, they don't fit me anymore, but I wear them everyday anyway."

"You're not wearing them with sweat socks are you?"

"Of course not," I say, thinking I need new socks.

As soon as we hang up, I realize that Chloe called me from her cell phone and it's not even seven o'clock in the morning. I call her back and she answers after one ring.

"Where are you, by the way?" I ask.

"I thought you'd never ask! Last night I packed up Dan's car and drove to New Hampshire. I'm going to climb Mt. Washington today!"

"You're in New Hampshire?"

"Isn't it amazing? I'm like a different person already. I mean, when was the last time I made a long distance phone call?"

"Are you out of your mind? You're going to drive up Mt. Washington in Dan's tiny convertible?"

"No, I'm going to climb it."

"With your feet? What shoes are you wearing?"

"Only like the most adorable hiking boots ever! They're pink suede! And I'm wearing my new pink-and-gray Burberry plaid parka, and I've got a new backpack."

"Is there a water bottle in your new backpack?"

"Unfortunately, no. I couldn't fit anything in here like that, which is a shame really, because I'll probably want a drink of water during my ascent. That's what they call it, you know, *my ascent*."

"Well I suggest you bring a bigger backpack and a few bottles of water and something to eat and sunscreen and make sure your cell is charged."

"Don't worry. I have a list of everything I'll need. I'm not stupid enough to bring this tiny backpack and nothing else."

"What else are you bringing?"

"A suitcase."

Colossal beads of sweat are beginning to form on my upper lip. "You're going to climb Mt. Washington carrying a suitcase?" I ask.

"It's Louis Vuitton!"

"Oh good. Then you won't look like an idiot carrying it up a mountain."

"So, anyway, we're all hanging out in the cafeteria waiting for the group leader to take us up. Stay on the phone with me until he comes out, okay?"

"Who else is climbing with you?"

"A bunch of old ladies and a group of stoned high school kids on a class trip."

She's got no backup!

"I don't feel good about this," I tell her as calmly as I possibly can. "In fact, I feel really queasy."

"Please don't make me nervous. I'm not afraid of anything anymore and you shouldn't be either."

"Why are you suddenly so brave?"

"It's sort of a secret."

"I promise I won't tell anyone."

"Okay, Mom gave me these amazing pills and now I'm totally fearless. I was telling her about how I'm on sabbatical to try to become a stronger, more adventurous person. And then we got to talking about how I never try anything new because I'm afraid of falling, so she suggested pills!"

"Well, at least that confirms my suspicion that she's completely out of her mind."

"Oh! The instructor is here. I'll call you from the top of the mountain!"

"Okay. Bye."

She hangs up. This is terrible. Chloe should not be climbing mountains. She can't even get off an escalator without stumbling and knocking everyone over.

On the way to work, I keep checking my watch. I want to make sure I get there early to get my final cover choice down to production in time. I went back and forth so many times deciding between covers, but I'm sure this is the one.

The right cover will make all the difference in the world. It has to set the precedent for everything we're trying to do and I know this one will send just the right message.

When I get to my office and open the door, I get hit with a blast of heat. It feels like it's about two hundred degrees in here. It can't have anything to do with the way I'm dressed. I'm only wearing a T-shirt and Chloe's corduroy skirt over a pair of long underwear—which double as underpants—and of course my slippers. It's hot as hell in here. I sit down at my desk and slip off my slippers and sweat socks, and fan myself for a few seconds with my socks but after a while I can't take it anymore. I take my leggings off, which is fine, really, because my skirt covers everything and I really shouldn't have worn long underwear to work anyway. It's just that none of my regular underwear fit me anymore. I didn't think it was possible to grow out of one's underpants.

I feel a little better now, but it's really unbearable in here. You'd think whoever equipped this office with hair accessories and office supplies would at least have left me a few hand towels or something, but there's nothing at all in the linen category, so I have to use my socks to mop up the back of my neck. I walk out of my office in my bare feet to see if it's as hot in the hall as it is in my office, and surprisingly it's about twenty degrees cooler out here. I tiptoe by the fashion and beauty departments. The air temperature is fine around here too.

I go back to my office and call down to maintenance to have them check if there's a problem with my heat and if they happen to have any type of industrial-strength antibacterial cleanser handy for my bare feet, but the line is busy. I call back a few minutes later and it's still busy. The air is really getting thick in here. I don't know how much longer I can take this.

I try to create some ventilation by vigorously opening and closing the door to my supply closet, but it's like trying to cool down a sauna. I don't know what else to do. I try to ignore the situation because I have to get down to production, but as soon as I turn on my computer, I can see that it's dead.

I call downstairs to tell them I'll be there in a minute, but their line is busy too. That's strange. I call Dan, and again I get a busy signal. It's too early for him to be calling anyone. Maybe he's calling maintenance about something, too. I crawl under my desk to see if everything is plugged in.

What the hell is going on here?

Every single plug is in the wrong place, and I might not be seeing straight but this doesn't even look like my hard drive. How could this be happening? I crawl around to the other side and begin switching the plugs. I'm sweating like crazy under here. I get up and retry my computer. It goes on this time, but my screen is blinking. The whole thing must have crashed. If this is my hard drive, everything I've been working on is gone! I don't believe this. I don't have my cover shot. Maybe something happened to my hard drive and the maintenance people put in a temporary one. Regardless, I have to go home and get the cover, otherwise I'll miss this morning's deadline and they'll go with the shot I gave them as a backup. I knew I shouldn't have waited until the last minute, but I wanted to be absolutely sure I had the right choice. Now I have nothing.

I walk back out into the hall in search of help but of course it's still too early for anyone except Dan and me, and the maintenance and production people to be here.

I can't very well walk around in a soaking wet T-shirt. I'll get sick. I go into the ladies' room to try to dry myself off under the hand dryer. I take a quick look in the mirror. The tip of my forehead is bright red! I jump up a few times to see if the rest of my face is flushed. Something is very wrong with me. I hope I'm not having a stroke. Not here please, not now. I always pictured myself having a stroke at home. This is awful. I'll never make it home and back in time with my laptop. I can't even think clearly. I'll just have to go down to production and tell them they'll have to wait. I'll take a cab home and back. That's what I'll do. I'll just get my shoes and socks and leggings and go home.

I go back to my office and sit down for a second, but I can't even keep my head up. After a second or two, I let myself fall to my knees. I realize it's probably not a good idea to try to work in here, nor would it be appropriate for me to take off any more clothing. I'm too weak and dizzy to fully stand up, so I sort of stagger, hunched over, out into the hall.

*   *   *

"Zoe, what's the matter?" I hear Dan's voice but I can't open my eyes.

"Is that you, Dan?" I ask.

"Yes, of course it's me. What happened to you? Have you been drinking?"

I can hardly get the words out but I manage to say, "My office is very hot. I think I'm fainting and I need to go home to get my cover art. I need to submit it right away."

"Don't worry about that, Zoe. Just tell me what's wrong. Did you take something?"

"No, it's just that it's about a hundred and twenty degrees in my office, and I'm so weak I can't see straight. Please help me get my cover art from home. I e-mailed it to myself but my computer crashed."

"Zoe, stop worrying about the cover. We'll get it in on time. You're panicking for no reason. Sloane and Blaire just came in and I can send one of them to deliver it."

"But they'll never find it. It's at home. Unless you can get my computer to work. I e-mailed it to myself."

"I'll take care of everything. I'm sure we can get your computer up and running."

He takes me by my wrists and pulls me up off the floor. We walk over to a cubicle and I fall back into a chair. As soon as I hit the chair, I hear my wet thighs slap against the leather. I'm not sure what position I landed in or how far apart my legs are, but the next thing Dan says is, "Look, Zoe, I'm not asking you to go out and buy a new wardrobe for this job, but you've got to start wearing underwear and shoes." I'm so humiliated, I may even be crying, but it's hard to tell. There's entirely too much perspiration in my eyes to determine what sort of liquid is pouring down my face. *I can't hear him anymore. God I hope I'm not dying.*

★　　★　　★

"Zoe. It's me. Try to sit up. Your eyes are opening. You're going to be okay."

I open my eyes and see Michael sitting on the bed next to me. I turn my head to look at the clock.

"What happened to me?" I ask.

"You passed out and Dan brought you home."

"You've been asleep for almost fifteen hours."

"What?"

"Your body must be completely dehydrated. I made you an appointment to see a doctor this afternoon."

"Are you out of your mind? There's nothing wrong with me. My office was hot, that's all. I don't need a doctor for that."

"Zoe, you passed out cold."

"So? Anyone would have fainted. Believe me, if I thought there was something wrong with me I'd be worried, but this was different. It was like I was being cooked to death. Oh no. I missed the deadline! My computer crashed so I had nothing to give them."

"I heard all about it and it's fine. Dan told me to tell you that everything was taken care of. Apparently they found what they needed on your desk."

"But I didn't have it on my desk."

"Well, somehow they managed to find everything and it's all straightened out."

"It can't be straightened out. You don't understand. I'm the only one who has the art. Unless my computer suddenly started working."

"You're overreacting again, over nothing. This is not the end of the world."

"It is to me. I'm responsible for this. If the cover is wrong, it will ruin everything."

"Zoe, you can't allow yourself to get so emotional over this. You're making yourself sick. Things happen in business all the time. You deal with it and you get through it. This isn't your life, Zoe. It's your job."

"But it's everything to me right now. I have to make this work. I have to succeed at this."

"Of course you want it to work and you have every right to succeed, but not at the cost of your health. Think about what you're doing. Is proving some point about girls worth running yourself into the ground? It's a good point, don't get me wrong, but you've got way too much invested in it. If you're thinking this new magazine is going to somehow erase all the wrongs that you and every other little girl ever suffered, you're going to be very disappointed. You're doing a great thing and I'm proud of you—but no amount of education will ever—"

"Will ever what?"

"Will ever make girls like them understand girls like you."

"God, Michael, you think I'm doing this for myself?"

"A little bit."

"Well then you're reading way too much into it. I'm just doing it because it's something that needs to be done."

"Fine. But you can't let it get to this point anymore. From now on, you'll work normal hours and get on with your life. You're just getting started at that place. You can't possibly keep this up without falling apart. And as far as the cover is concerned, you need to stop thinking about it. You can't do anything about it now anyway. The art was submitted and the magazine went to press. You'll be able to see it in the morning. Just relax and try not to think about it."

"Okay, sure," I say and run to the bathroom. I must have some sort of stomach flu. That's probably what it was all along.

Chapter 7

It's seven-thirty. I'm just about to leave for work when
the phone rings.

"Zoe, this is Alex."

"What's the matter? You sound terrible."

"Are you coming into the office soon?"

"I'm on my way right now. Why? Did you want to see me
about something?"

"Yes, as a matter of fact. I'll be in your office when you get
there."

"Do you want to tell me what this is about?"

"It's about the cover of the magazine."

When I get to my office, Alex is sitting across from my desk
with a pile of magazines facedown on her lap.

"Let me see it," I say, standing in front of her.

"First sit down."

"I can't sit down. I fully expected something to go wrong.
Just show it to me."

"Well, I'm sure you weren't expecting this," she says, and
holds up a copy of the magazine.

It says "The New Feminism" right across the top, in bright

pink letters, just the way I wanted it, and right below the headline is a photograph of a woman with long dark curly hair, topless, raising her arms up to the sky revealing two of the hairiest underarms I've ever seen in my entire life. Michael doesn't even have that much hair under his arms. No man does. Fortunately, you can't see her chest because the photo stops just below her armpits. But her cleavage is about eight inches long. All in all, it's one of the most revolting sights I've ever seen in my life.

"I'm gonna be sick again," I say, and run to the bathroom. When I get back. Alex is still sitting in the exact same position I left her. She might very well be in shock.

"Is it safe to say I've ruined any chances of us selling even one copy of this issue?"

"Please tell me you're not planning on taking responsibility for this?"

"Why shouldn't I? It's my fault. I missed the deadline and somehow Blaire and Sloane got their hands on the wrong cover. I knew something like this would happen and it did."

"Are you out of your mind?"

"I'm pretty sure I am, yes. But what are you getting at?"

"Zoe, you were sabotaged. This was deliberate. Blaire and Sloane were making a point. I just can't believe they were given permission to turn in the artwork for this. Tell me everything that happened yesterday."

I go through the entire scenario, beginning with me walking into my sweltering office, discovering that my computer had crashed, and that I'd been given a new hard drive and then passing out—right before Dan asked me to start wearing underwear—and then, finally, waking up at home, in the middle of the night.

"Well, it's pretty clear to me what went on here and I'm not going to sit back and let them get away with this." She calls everyone to a meeting and within about fifteen minutes everyone is assembled in Dan's office, including Anita, who looks like she's just about ready to murder someone. I can't blame her. I want to kill me, too.

"Dan, if I may, I'd like to begin this meeting by asking Blaire and Sloane what the hell they were thinking when they submitted this cover to production," Alex says, holding the cover up to their faces.

Sloane speaks first, looking as innocent as a baby lamb.

"Dan asked us to go to Zoe's office and find the cover art and bring it downstairs right away. At first we couldn't find anything so we tried to open her e-mail because Dan told us Zoe had sent herself an e-mail from home which contained the art. But her computer wasn't working so we looked around her office some more and there on her desk was this photo with the title, 'The New Feminism,' so we just assumed this was it."

"And now, in retrospect, can you think of any reason why this might not be the type of cover Zoe would have wanted? And did it occur to you, at any point, that this is not a pretty picture?"

"I did think that," Blaire says. "But I thought that's what Zoe wanted. I thought she was putting a girl on the cover, who looked like her, to say that she is the new face of feminism."

"Really? You thought that? Because Zoe doesn't strike me as the type of person who would try to turn people off to her cause before she even had a chance to get started. At least not deliberately. And this girl does not look anything at all like Zoe!"

"You can't possibly blame Blaire and Sloane for this!" Anita breaks in with a high-pitched squeal.

"Right now I would blame them for the color of my skin. They obviously replaced Zoe's hard drive with whatever piece of garbage they could find and somehow managed to get maintenance to turn her heat up so high she was forced to leave her office with nothing to show for any of the work she's been doing, and then, if that wasn't enough, they managed to make themselves available just in time to bring the cover art downstairs. Have you ever known Blaire or Sloane to get to this office before nine-thirty in the morning? Because this certainly is a first for me. The only thing I'm not sure of is where they got this photograph, but I can assure you of two things. They sure as hell didn't find it on Zoe's desk and I will, without question, get to the bottom of this."

"You can't prove anything, Alex. We did what we were told and we used what we thought we were supposed to use."

"Well, that's just fine. And now I'm telling you something else to do. Get on the phone with every single advertiser in this magazine and apologize for your little misunderstanding. This is not the message we are trying to convey and whether our advertisers are comfortable with her underarms or not, there's something about this girl's face that is so angry and disturbing, I'd be surprised if the newsstands don't send it back."

"We didn't like it either, Alex. I can assure you."

"Don't play innocent with me, Blaire. I see right through you, whether Dan does or not. Now I'd like you both to leave so you can get started on your phone calls."

"Just a minute, Alex. I'm just as upset as you are, but I don't want my editorial people interfacing with our advertisers under any circumstances."

"Well, then you call them, Anita," Alex says and turns to Dan.

"Is there any way we can print a new cover before the shipment date?" she asks.

"It'll cost a fortune but I'll look into it."

Anita ushers Blaire and Sloane out of the room, muttering under her breath, but Ruth apparently didn't notice because she's still sitting here and smiling. Eventually she looks around and gets up and leaves without even saying goodbye.

Once everyone is out of the room, except for Alex and me, Dan finally speaks.

"Well, this is obviously a terrible blow and we're going to pay for it big-time, but the last thing we can afford at this point is dissension. We're in for a rocky period and I need my staff to stick together as much as possible. I realize the brunt of this is going to fall on you, Alex, but I'm sure you can imagine the shape we'd be in right now without Blaire or Sloane. I'm not one hundred percent sure they were deliberately trying to sabotage Zoe's efforts, but I think it's safe to say that their judgment is not what I thought it was. Regardless, we need them to keep the fashion and beauty pages on target while we iron this all out. We can't start firing people during our relaunch."

"I understand what you're saying, but please understand that they are going to do everything in their power to destroy Zoe's plans, and you're the one who's ultimately going to pay for their mistakes. Whether or not you choose to believe they were being malicious, the fact remains that they were. Understand that they have no interest in the magazine aside from getting their way. You're only going to hurt yourself more by keeping them on board."

"I'm trying to maintain some order here, Alex. I need my staff. But I am going to talk to them and I'll have my eye on them at all times. Right now I need to believe that they thought they were doing what Zoe wanted. After all, I gave them full responsibility, with very little direction, to get that cover delivered."

"Dan, you have to understand, I've never even seen that photograph before. They had to have gotten it from somewhere and it sure as hell wasn't from my desk or even my computer."

"Listen to me, both of you. I'm not stupid. I know something devious went on here, but I think they were put up to it, and that's what's disturbing me more than anything. But I'm not going to turn this place into a detective agency, and I can't start training a new beauty editor and a new fashion editor overnight. They're good at what they do. You are both going to have to work around them until I figure something out. Just keep in mind that I'm aware of everything.

"I hate to admit this, but my mother didn't really seem that surprised when I showed her the cover. There's a lot I wouldn't put past her, but she would never ever do anything to directly jeopardize the success of this magazine. It just doesn't make any sense. For now, just keep working on the next issue and we'll have to eat this one. If we can go back to press, which I doubt, we'll have to do a black-and-white cover to save money. It's a shame, I know how hard you worked on this, Zoe, but we'll get through it."

As I walk through the halls, I can hear the phones ringing like crazy in everyone's offices. I can't imagine what the ramifications of this are going to be. One thing is for sure; we're definitely going to get noticed.

Chapter 8

Ever since we started getting feedback from our readers and advertisers about the new editorial, there's this perpetual buzz that permeates the building. By midday the buzz has sort of a jackhammer quality to it, and by two o'clock everyone just walks around yelling. We've gotten more media attention this month than in the last fifteen years combined. We've gone where no publisher has ever dared to go. It's no wonder the reaction from our advertisers has been unprecedented. So far we've lost Gucci, Yves Saint Laurent, Chanel, Diane von Furstenberg, Donna Karan, Revlon, Clinique and Estée Lauder, and we've received at least twenty bales of letters from our readers that essentially all say the same thing, "What the fuck?"

Although the launch issue ran with a revised cover, someone leaked the hairy underarm version and the media industry had a field day with it. The tension has been unbearable ever since. Anita refuses to acknowledge me and therefore, everyone else around here is afraid to talk to me as well. The whole situation is completely unnerving; it's like I'm back in school, pissing off the teacher for disrupting the class, and making a spectacle of myself in front of all the other students.

At least this time around I understand what I've done wrong, which is comforting in some small way.

We've all been working ungodly hours. No one leaves at five o'clock anymore. Some of the editors have even given up their weekly hair and nail appointments.

Seriously. It's that intense.

Despite the overwhelming hysteria, I have almost no energy at all. The faster the world spins, the slower I react—mostly because I can't help but overthink everything to the point where I'm finding it increasingly difficult to make even the simplest decisions, and also because I've developed hives up and down my legs, which makes it very difficult for me to walk.

Fortunately, our second issue, which focused on best friends, did a little better in terms of newsstand sales, and we did get a slight increase in ad pages, but the mail still keeps coming. The articles were meant to show the power of female bonding in the face of adversity, but somehow our article on *"Why You Find Yourself Strangely Attracted to Your Best Friend's Bald, Fat, Fiancé,"* got misconstrued. It included a very compelling interview with a bridesmaid who did everything in her power to run off with the groom, and the maid of honor who saved the day by letting the groom know, in no uncertain terms, that the bridesmaid in question had a very debilitating case of herpes—just in case he was considering her offer.

Alex and I worked on all of the articles together and we oversaw the layout from beginning to end. We worked day and night on that issue, and personally hand-delivered everything to production. We watch each other's backs at all times now and leave nothing to chance. My whole heart is in this thing and despite the failing numbers, I still feel as though I'm somehow being heard by the girls who need me most.

And on a more fashionable note, I was reading an article

about the environmental benefits of using naturally dyed organic hemp instead of cotton and discovered a new designer. He was mentioned in the article because a major Japanese clothing manufacturer has picked up his line. We're meeting with the designer this morning to take some shots of the clothes. We'll be the first American fashion magazine ever to showcase this revolutionary new fabric. Alex sees the designer as a very strong potential advertiser and I see his natural, alternative fabric as the perfect fashion statement for our new editorial. It will give our readers a completely different perspective on clothing. The spring fashion issue is critical to our overall bottom line and this designer might just be the answer to our prayers. I can't believe it; for the first time in my life, I'm actually enjoying thinking about clothes.

I've invited Blaire, Sloane, and Courtney to the meeting because I want all of them to stretch their imaginations to the limit to highlight the beauty and versatility of this new fabric and make it come alive on our pages. I was thinking they might be able to design some sort of hemp dollhouse using the fabric for everything: the walls, the furniture, the floor coverings, even little lamp shades and accessories, and have all the little dolls wearing tiny, organic hemp clothes. I've also invited Ruth and Rhonda because I'm going to need some unique selling pieces to start promoting this issue right away.

Alex and I had planned to get to the meeting early, but as soon as I arrive at the showroom, I can sense something is wrong. The door is ajar and I can hear voices. I walk in, half expecting to see the designers sitting and waiting for me, but instead I see Blaire and Sloane.

"Why are you here so early?" I ask.

"We're not early. You're late," Blaire says.

"The meeting was set for nine," I say, looking at my watch.

"Actually, it was for eight. Didn't you get the e-mail? Amanda sent it."

"No, I didn't get the e-mail. Did the designer change the time or did you?"

"I can't remember. Can you?" she asks Sloane.

"Not really."

"So you set the meeting for eight o'clock and made sure the rest of us weren't here to meet the designer. Lovely. How'd it go?"

"Not very well, I'm afraid," Sloane says.

"Really? And why is that?"

"Well, for one thing, he came with a design team and they were all Japanese. They didn't speak any English whatsoever, and my Japanese, I'm sorry to say, isn't very good."

"And, aside from that, the clothes were hideous. So we pretty much told them we weren't interested."

I feel all the muscles in my neck tightening, rendering me completely immobile. We continue discussing the matter for quite some time as civilly as possible because I don't want them to know how much I had my hopes pinned on this concept that they just destroyed. It would be far too enjoyable for them. So now we're just sitting here chatting away as though this was just another unfortunate mishap that couldn't be helped. I'm about to mention to them that I had scheduled an interpreter to join us at nine o'clock, when Alex walks in. I try to turn my head to greet her, but I have to turn my whole body.

"Am I late?" she asks, looking at her watch, wondering what Blaire and Sloane are doing here at eight-thirty.

"No, Alex, you're not late. Technically you're a half hour early but the meeting got rescheduled. For eight o'clock. Unfortunately you and I missed it, because I neglected to triple confirm, but not to worry because Blaire and Sloane took it upon themselves to tell our *almost* new clients that they weren't interested. Apparently they didn't like the clothes."

"You're joking, right?"

"No, we're perfectly serious," Blaire says, with a little smirk, as if to say, *and there's not a damn thing you can do about it.*

"Are you both aware that the designer flew in from Japan to meet with all the major magazines this week, and that we were their first appointment and that we were going to try to negotiate an exclusive editorial for this issue? Their company is enormously funded, and I was counting on getting a ten-page, four-color insert from them."

"Nobody told us," Sloane shrugs.

"Sorry," Blaire says, "But you do realize we see dozens of designers every week and only a fraction of them make it into the magazine. I mean, what were their chances?"

"Their chances were one hundred percent. We wanted this account."

"The clothes were awful, Alex."

"This designer is going to be huge. You should have at least kept him here until Zoe and I had a chance to see the line."

"But neither of you are fashion editors and you shouldn't be using the promise of editorial coverage to get ads. That's not ethical. Editorial and advertising are supposed to function independently of one another, you know that. Technically, this meeting should have never been scheduled," Blaire says.

Alex explains to them that we're trying to keep this magazine from going under and that this would have been an enormous score for us both in terms of revenue and editorial forecasting. And that she's sure corporate would have shown leniency at a time like this. And that in the future, she foresees no reason for them to suddenly take on something as weighty as ethics on her behalf.

"Advertorials are a perfectly legitimate way to do business so there's no need to worry that we'd be compromising our integrity in any way," Alex continues.

"For some magazines, yes, but Anita doesn't like them, and you know that, Alex," Sloane says.

I'm watching Alex's every move, expecting her to go ballistic on them, but she's staying as cool as humanly possible. She ignores their comment about Anita and focuses instead on the cancelled meeting. She tells them both not to give it another thought and that it was just a simple misunderstanding that could have happened to anyone. I realize that Alex is walking a fine line and that I put her in this position. She's doing things she's never done before to get ads, and Blaire and Sloane know they have the power not to help her.

An entire breakfast is in front of us, which Amanda had ordered for the meeting. Alex makes a polite gesture toward one of the plates encouraging everyone to eat.

I try not to load up my plate too high, as Courtney, Rhonda, Ruth, and the Japanese interpreter enter the room. Courtney is wearing six-inch high heels that appear to be covered in glitter, and as usual, she has a few choice magazines in her arms.

Alex invites everyone in for breakfast and explains that the meeting has been postponed, but that we should instead take this opportunity to go over some of our other ideas for the fashion issue. She gives me a look as if to say "Think fast," and then she takes the interpreter aside and quietly explains to him what happened. He immediately calls the designer on his cell phone and leaves a message in his voicemail. She invites him to have breakfast to make up for the fact that his time has been wasted, but he politely declines her offer. He assures her that he'll organize a conference call as soon as possible and then he leaves.

Alex calmly walks back to the group and asks me to lead the discussion. She reiterates that our Japanese designer was just a small part of our plans and that we have a lot of other interesting ideas to share. Something about the way she just repeated herself makes it obvious to everyone that we're in trouble. She reaches for a coffee cup and I can see that her hands aren't steady. I hope no one else happened to see it. The fact that we lost this designer and his account is going to cost us everything, and everyone in this room knows it.

"Although I was hoping this issue would give our readers an entirely new perspective about the purpose of clothing and the many ways we can use it to express ourselves creatively and politically, there are certainly plenty of other ways to use our biggest issue of the year to influence our readers thinking when it comes to dressing themselves.

"I think the first thing we need to do is educate our readers about the language of clothing and how girls speak to one another, without saying a word, simply by letting their clothing do all the talking. We especially want to teach the girls who have no idea what sort of signals they're sending out how to hear what others *hear* when they walk into a room. I've written a feature article called, 'Are Your Clothes Talking About You Behind Your Back?' that proves how clothing is manufactured and marketed to reach girls by selling the 'message' that girls have been trained to buy into.

"What I'd like to do in this issue is focus on how our readers consciously use clothing to attract the opposite sex, even after they've come to the realization that it works against them in the workplace. I want to show them how they can stop falling into this self-defeating trap and show them how to start thinking about the purpose of clothing in a whole new way."

I look over at Alex to see if she's comfortable with all of this but she's still staring into space. So I just keep talking.

"At the same time we want to discourage the practice of making assumptions about girls simply because of the way they dress, especially since half the girls out there have no idea what their clothes are saying. So in other words, we want to tackle this issue from both ends."

"You mean like 'Dress for Success'? Because there was a book about that once," Courtney asks.

"Yes, exactly. Sometimes women are ostracized and ridiculed in the workplace and they have no idea why. We want to show those women how their clothing choices keep them from getting ahead, and, at the same time, how it can prevent them from making friends."

"Was this editorial idea inspired by the pink school dress, by any chance?" Blaire asks.

"In some ways, I guess it was. Thank you for noticing," I answer sweetly, while trying to will the chandelier above her head to dislodge itself from the ceiling.

"You know, I was just thinking about how often I catch girls laughing at me behind my back. I mean, sometimes I'm saying something funny on purpose, but sometimes I could be just standing on line at the bank or something. It doesn't make any sense and I've had this problem for years. Maybe I'm missing something." Courtney looks down at her body and then right at me.

"Well, in keeping with what Zoe was saying about the way girls react to one another, Court, perhaps other girls feel nervous and threatened around you because you're not afraid to express your sexuality," Rhonda says. "Most girls aren't comfortable walking around the office with bare thighs. But hey, if you've got 'em, flaunt 'em. That's what I always say."

"I'm sorry, but it's not your thighs, Courtney. It's because your thong is always showing," Sloane says.

"What's so funny about that?" Courtney asks.

"It's only funny when half your ass is hanging out, too," Blaire says.

"Don't listen to them, Courtney. It's because you're misunderstood," Rhonda interrupts. "I've known you for a long time and you happen to be a wonderful person. When I first met you, I have to admit, I thought you were a little slu-uh-—flirty. But then I realized that you're just unusually friendly. It's possible, though, and I'm only guessing here, that you may have been absentmindedly flirting with someone on line at the bank that day or wearing something people don't often expect to see at the bank."

"Courtney is a perfect example of a person who doesn't hear what her clothing says about her, as well as a person who is being wrongly judged because of her clothing choices. Ultimately, it's her decision. She has the right to dress however she pleases, but she should at least be given the opportunity to see how she's perceived and how those perceptions will affect her ability to move up in this predominately female workplace," I explain.

"I think Zoe's forgetting that the person who promotes people around here is a man, and this seems like an awful lot of trouble to go through to get people to stop making fun of *certain other peoples'* clothes, don't you think?" Blaire asks Sloane.

"Hold on," Courtney interjects, "I totally get this. You're saying that if a girl dresses up for work, other girls will unfairly assume she's promiscuous, and treat her like she's some kind of criminal, which is totally unfair. Promiscuity is not a crime and it's time we put a stop to the ill treatment of sluts everywhere!"

"I don't think she quite gets it yet," Rhonda says. "But she's getting warm."

"Would you like to be a contributing editor if we do an issue on sluts?" Blaire asks.

"I'm already an editor," Courtney says, not quite feeling the sting. "Actually, it's a big coincidence that we got on the topic of this whole slut thing because one of my readers sent in a question, and I've been sort of wrestling with my answer because I wasn't sure if our new editorial was going to be pro-slut or anti-slut."

"We won't be pro-slut, I can assure you, but we will make a definitive statement discouraging our readers from condemning women based on their level of sexual activity as well as their attire. But I really didn't mean to turn this into a discussion solely on sexual behavior. That's really only a very small aspect of the point I'm trying to make about the language of clothing and how it defines us professionally and culturally. There are many other characteristics that our clothing assigns to us and many other labels that we may be unknowingly carrying around."

"So are we going to tell our readers it's wrong to have a lot of sexual partners or are we going to tell them *how* to have a lot of sexual partners?" Courtney asks.

"Again, I don't want to spend too much time on this, but to answer your question, I'd say, neither one. There are enough magazines out there that teach women how to have a lot of sexual partners. We have so many other issues to explore I don't think we need to give our readers advice about their sex lives one way or the other. However, I do think it's important for us to take a stand against the denigration of women who are victims of promiscuity."

"You think sluts are victims?" Courtney asks with a pained, thoughtful expression.

"I think there's something about sexual addiction that reeks of self-loathing. I also think self-esteem can be taught and that once we enable our readers to reach a higher level of self-satisfaction, I think they'll begin to see that they have more to offer than their bodies and their looks. And equally as important, I think those among us who resent sexually active women will be less apt to jump to conclusions when it's revealed that promiscuity is often the result of a pitifully poor self-image. But, like I said, I really don't want to make this the focus of our discussion."

"That's so weird. I always thought sluts were just really horny," Courtney says.

"Why don't you read your column and perhaps we can jump off from there," I suggest, trying to move things along.

Courtney clears her throat and holds her paper up in the air to read.

Dear Courtney,

I give my boyfriend and two of his really good friends blow jobs almost every weekend. It's not that I mind or anything, it's just that sometimes I feel like it's not that fair. I know it's wrong to expect something in return every single time you do some-one a favor but I was thinking that if I asked for, say, five dol-lars a head (ha! I totally didn't even say that on purpose), I could make twenty-five bucks every weekend and I could really use the money. Do you think I'm being greedy?

Love,
L. J.

P.S. I'm kind of on a diet. Do you also by any chance know how many calories are in three blow jobs?

"What's so funny?" Courtney asks, looking around the table.

"Is that a real letter?" I ask.

"Yes."

"Can you please read us what you have so far, in terms of an answer?" I ask.

"Sure, um. Let's see. Oh, here it is. I keep getting this one confused with the girl who eats paper. She's on a diet as well."

Dear Def Not Greedy,

First things first, one hundred and ten. Now, as far as greediness is concerned, you don't sound like a greedy person to me. Not at all. In fact, you sound almost too generous. I mean you're totally going off your diet, and for what? Instead of asking them for money, why not hint around that you wouldn't mind a nice bottle of perfume or something. I wouldn't come right out and ask but you might want to say something like, 'You boys are as sweet as _____. Just fill in the blank with your favorite scent! If they're nice boys, they'll get the hint and you'll get what you deserve. Then you can decide if you want to return the perfume and make a little money or simply keep the perfume as a momentum.

And always remember . . . I love you.

Forever Yours,
Courtney

I'm not sure what to say. I can never tell if she's kidding.

"That's really great, Courtney. I never would've thought of suggesting to ask for presents before moving on to hard cash," Sloane says. "I guess that's why you're the mental health editor."

"It's a good thing she didn't write that letter to me," Rhonda says, "because I would have told her that her boyfriend is an abusive little prick and the next time he wants a blow job, she should tell his two really good friends to help him out."

"I don't think they're homosexuals," Courtney says.

"Regardless of their sexual preferences, they should not be using that poor girl. Don't you see that?" Rhonda asks.

"Actually, I think she's doing exactly what she feels like doing. She just thinks the arrangement is sort of one-sided. And anyway, I thought you just said we're going to be non-judgmental. If we show our disapproval of sluttery, then we're no different than the very girls we're trying to teach. If we tell her how she can and can't use her body, then how are we em-powering her?

"We're simply manipulating her to adhere to an archaic moral standard a *liberal* magazine like *Miss Understanding* should be trying to erase. I mean who's to say whether a cer-tain behavior, any behavior, is right or wrong, unless it's hurt-ing another person? And who's to really say why someone is doing what she chooses to do? Can you actually prove that someone who likes to give a lot of blow jobs has low self-esteem or that the act itself, no matter how many people she performs it on, is damaging to her self-esteem? How could anyone prove anything like that, ever? I mean it's not like any-one's going to believe us anyway, unless we were, like, Freud or something.

"I'm just trying to give her the information she asked for, which is a calorie count and whether or not I think she's greedy."

"That's very existential of you, Courtney," I say, fearing that I actually agree with her on this.

"The reason my column is so popular—" she continues.

"Is because it's so dumb?" Blaire interrupts.

"No, it's because I answer people's questions, as best I can, without telling them how they should *really* be thinking or living. I give them answers, not a psychological evaluation. Since when did we decide to become moral dictators?"

"Ever since whores started writing to us," Sloane says. "And since when did you start using terms like *moral dictators* and *archaic moral standards* in every other sentence?"

"I got it off the cover of this magazine Zoe used to write for. See? It says it right here, 'The New Moral Dictatorship.' I just sort of used it in a different context. Why? Did I use it wrong?"

"No, you actually sounded smart there for a second. I was just wondering how it happened," Sloane says.

"You make a strong point, Courtney. And you're absolutely right. We have no right to pass moral judgments or perform psychiatric evaluations on our readers. It's just that prostitution is illegal. That's the only thing I can say without bringing my personal feelings into play." For some reason, I'm sort of flattered that she's reading my old magazine. I'm not sure why, though. I'm pretty sure she wasn't our target audience.

"Also, I think you're way off on your calorie count," Rhonda says.

"Seriously? That's what someone told me! Do you think it's more or less?"

"I think it's more. The girl who sits next to me at my Weight Watchers meetings counts it as a three-pointer."

Somehow I never thought I'd end up in a meeting discussing the nutritional facts of sperm.

"The last thing I want to do is give out incorrect information. I probably shouldn't use that letter at all. Luckily I have another one with me that's sort of similar. Should I read it?" she asks.

"We'd be insulted if you didn't," Blaire says.

"Okay, this one is sort of weird because it's about a girl who's been having sex with two of her relatives and now the poor thing thinks she has acne down there. So the first thing I told her was to go see her pediatrician.

"This particular letter really touched me because I had a step-uncle who used to flirt with me all the time and my aunt used to get mad at me, like it was my fault. I was just about the same age as this girl, too. It's probably not her fault that her relatives keep falling for her. I never slept with my uncle, though. He was so fat."

"I never realized what a great example you are of someone who's constantly being misjudged because of her looks," Sloane says.

"I know. I'm like the poster girl for misunderstanding," Courtney says, twirling her hair. "I wish I could do something about it, but it just seems hopeless."

"I hope you won't think I'm overstepping my bounds here, but I don't think your biggest problem with women is your clothes," Sloane says.

"You don't?" Courtney asks.

"No, I think it's partially your clothes, but mostly your hair—"

"And your shoes," Blaire interrupts.

"My hair?" she asks, feeling her head with both hands.

"Yes, you see girls have a tendency to equate three-inch black roots with poor grooming. And since girls equate poor grooming with poor decision-making skills, that puts you at a significant disadvantage before you even open your mouth," Sloane says.

"Exactly," Blaire takes over, "And we all know that in the world of *archaic, judgmental girls*, things like: overgrown roots, incest, and multiple blow jobs are considered immoral."

"And since most girls equate sparkly stilettos with strip clubs," Blaire continues, pointing to Courtney's shoes, "what it comes down to is that girls treat you unfairly because you have the words, *Fuck me. I'm immoral,* written all over you."

"It's also a style," Courtney says, without flinching. As she's talking, something in her reading material catches her eye. She puts her finger on the page, so she can stay somewhat focused on the conversation, but she keeps glancing back at the article.

"What's a style?" Rhonda asks, touching her own hair and wondering if she might have missed something.

"Black roots and sparkly stilettos. It's very L.A." Courtney says halfheartedly. She's totally distracted by the article at this point. A cow could walk in here and she wouldn't bat an eye.

"L.A. Hooker?" Blaire adds.

"Well, anyway, I didn't really want to know why those girls were laughing at me at the bank. I was just sort of noting something that I thought went along with what you all were saying." She lifts her finger on the page to make sure she didn't lose her spot.

"Courtney, there's no reason why anyone should feel singled out here. Although you are an excellent example of how some girls are unfairly treated by other girls, the purpose here is to reveal *why* it happens so we can prevent it and get on with business."

"What? Oh, I'm sorry. I was just reading this article on fiber."

"Courtney, you can stop reading that magazine now. No one here really thinks you're enjoying it," Blaire says.

I take that as my final clue that we're not getting anywhere with this. I make a few more lame attempts to introduce some other ways in which our clothing defines us: culturally, socially, intellectually, etc., but clearly the burning issue here is simply how clothes define Courtney. We've made absolutely no progress today, and I can't watch Courtney suffer at the hands of Sloane and Blaire for another minute. Clearly, our big fashion issue has already come apart at the seams.

I let the discussion dwindle down to nothing and eventually announce that it's time to take a break. I ask everyone to e-mail me with any other ideas by the end of the week. There're a few marginally enthusiastic responses, but for the most part, everyone already knows we've got nothing and that we're just going through the motions at this point. We slowly filter out of the room as I catch Alex out of the corner of my eye dashing away.

I spend the next week trying to get another appointment with the hemp people, but it's impossible to get them on the phone. They were probably scooped up immediately.

I reach out to some other less exciting but equally ecologically aware designers, but none of them are big enough to become potential advertisers, nor do they feel they have enough designs for the enormous space I've allocated in the magazine for a fashion spread. As the deadline for this issue comes closer, I realize I've wasted so much time chasing down designers that don't want to be in the magazine, the only material I have is my notes from the showroom meeting. In order to make deadline, I rename my feature article *"Are Your Clothes Calling You a Slut Behind Your Back?"* and use it as the main focus of our most important issue of the year. I tell Alex and she proceeds to go after every lingerie and sex shop in the city for advertising. That's how desperate we are.

We manage to scrape by with a serious commitment from Victoria's Secret and my slut article as our feature story. I had to stretch that article out to twenty pages. It might just be the worst thing I've ever read.

I submit it to the copy editor at five o'clock Friday afternoon. She hands it back to me an hour later and I hand deliver it to the typesetter. The important thing at this point is that we closed another issue without folding.

By the time I get home Friday night, my back is in a spasm and I literally cannot get out of bed Saturday morning. Michael has been back and forth to the drugstore at least five times with every pain remedy on the market, but I can't move. I'm completely falling apart. I can't even eat solid food without getting heartburn, and so I drink milkshakes all weekend, which isn't helping with the sudden weight gain. I finally find a comfortable position and then proceed to sleep the entire weekend away.

By Monday morning I'm so rested, I'm actually pleasant to Michael. He's so grateful; he brings me breakfast in bed, which consists of oatmeal, a milkshake, a banana, and a huge bowl of applesauce.

"I brought you a few things because I wasn't sure what you'd be in the mood for," he says and puts the tray down in front of me. I smile at him and he looks at me suspiciously and leaves the room.

"Why'd you leave?" I yell to him. By the time he comes back the tray is half empty.

"I don't know. You're acting kind of weird."

"What do you mean?"

"I thought I saw you smile."

Chapter 9

When I get to my office bright and early Monday morning, I almost feel like my old self again. I already have some ideas brewing for the summer issues and I think, despite my all-liquid, mostly sugar and dairy diet of late, I've actually begun losing some of the weight I've put on.

I sit down at my desk and check my e-mails. There's one from Alex that says, "URGENT!!"

I open the attachment and begin reading what is clearly a revision of the slut article that I handed in Friday night. In this version my point about girls being judged by their clothing is replaced with an expose of girls who have slept their way to the top. To prove my point, I name the people in this very company who have done exactly that. I also name the men they've slept with and where they slept with them. Among my victims are: Chloe, Courtney, Alex, and Rhonda. According to this, Chloe slept with Dan in the shoe closet. Alex slept with the publisher in London. Rhonda slept with the previous art director in Southhampton, and Courtney slept with everyone including a bunch of guys from other magazines, pretty much all over town. I can't even believe this.

I call Alex hoping this isn't the end of our friendship.

As soon as she hears my voice, she says, "Well, I thought we had every base covered, but they nailed you again somehow, didn't they? I've had it, Zoe, they're dead."

"It's impossible, Alex. I literally handed the proofs to the typesetter on Friday. No one else was even here."

"Well, apparently someone else *was* here. And she handed in a revision. You neglected to do your research, Zoe. Otherwise you would have also mentioned in your article that Blaire sleeps with one of the typesetters. Admittedly, he's the better looking of the two. Had you known that, you would have handed your proofs to the ugly typesetter."

"Why didn't you tell me?"

"I just found out myself, but I can assure you, nothing like this will ever happen again. I've instituted a new policy. Either you or I have to sign off on every word and photograph that goes into the magazine, in front of the ugly typesetter, whom I just promoted to type director, or nothing goes in the magazine. It's going to be a pain in the ass but we have no other choice."

"This article is actually worse than the one I wrote," I say, as I quickly skim through the pages. "Is any of this true?" I ask.

"I don't know. I can't speak for anyone but myself. I certainly never slept with Rob. And I doubt Rhonda slept with the former gay art director, and Courtney couldn't possibly have slept with this many people in one lifetime. Although I think it's safe to assume that your sister slept with Dan."

"In the shoe closet?"

"She did hang out there a lot."

"I really need to talk to her."

"I wouldn't worry about it too much. Things worked out pretty well for her. And, fortunately, this article won't hurt us with our advertisers or our readers, and that's all I really care about. In fact, they love this sort of thing."

Alex and I pass by Dan's office and see that Anita, Ruth, Blaire, Courtney, Sloane, and Rhonda are all standing in front of his desk. I poke my head into the office and announce that Alex and I would like to have a word with everyone.

Before we're even inside the door, Anita holds out a hand to Alex.

"You, of all people, must be devastated by this, Alex. Here you must have thought Zoe was your good friend, the way you two have been spending so much time together. And honestly, Zoe, to point the finger at your own sister. You must be ashamed of yourself."

"Nice try, Anita. But Alex already spoke to the typesetter and he told us what happened. You and one of your little puppets—the one who has a thing for cute typesetters— added all that stuff about who slept their way to the top.

"Alex knows I didn't write any of this, and yes, we are good friends, because we trust one another. And I don't even have to check with my sister," I say, throwing the magazine on Dan's desk. "You didn't honestly think you could turn my sister and my best friend against me, did you? I think they know me a little better than that, Anita, but I admire your effort, and at least this little trick didn't cost us any money. So, honestly, I can't really say I care." There's a dead silence. Finally Rhonda speaks.

"Which one of you sleeps with the typesetter?" she asks.

Blaire is turning bright red. She is about to spew any minute.

"But you said you thought he was ugly!" Courtney says.

"I think she might have been referring to the other typesetter," I cut in.

"I don't think that should be your main concern right now. Aren't you even a little upset about what was written about you?" Blaire asks.

"Not really. You've said this stuff about me before. It's not really news. And I knew you wrote it the second I read it. What kind of a person are you?"

"I'm afraid she's a very sick person," Rhonda says. "And what do you have to say for yourself, Sloane? Because I know you had to be in on this somehow."

"I had nothing to do with this," Sloane says, giving Blaire a cold look. I guess she sleeps with Anthony, too. He wasn't *that* cute.

Anita leaves in a hurry as soon as she comes to the realization that no one cares about the article. I thank everyone for trusting me, and Alex and I stay and talk to Dan about what we need to do to stop all of this nonsense. Dan says he's been giving it a lot of thought and he realizes he has to make a move soon. He tells us to watch out for one another while he comes up with a plan to resolve the situation. I'm beginning to feel very sorry for him. The only way to resolve this is to get rid of me and he knows it.

On the way out, I turn to Alex and ask, "How did you get the typesetter to tell you what happened?"

"This is a very complicated place, Zoe. Anita has her people and I have mine."

"Seriously? You have *people?* Who?"

"All in good time."

Chapter 10

On my way to the subway, I realize that I've left all of my notes at home and that my slippers are ripping. I've finally gained so much weight that my shoes are too small. I've never even heard of that. I walk back home as delicately as possible so as not to tear them in half. And for some reason, I feel like crying the whole way. I never cry. Never. Ever.

When I get back into my building the doorman hands me a bouquet of flowers and tells me they were just delivered a few minutes ago. He asks me why I'm crying and I tell him it's because my shoes ripped. I guess he's used to seeing people cry over their shoes because all he does is nod.

I bring the flowers upstairs and read the card. They're from Michael, of course, who's doing another mini book tour. I read the card, "I miss you and I'll be home this afternoon. I hate being away from you. Love, Michael." I try not to start crying again, but here it comes. He knows how stressed out I've been lately and even though pretty much all of my symptoms come and go, making them suspect, there's no denying that even if I am a hypochondriac, I'm looking pretty bad these days. How could he still love me? I put the flowers in water, I change into my other slippers, and pray that they're magically bigger than my other pair, despite the fact that they're the same size. I collect my papers and head back out. I still can't believe I ever succumbed to wearing these little ballerina shoes in the first place.

I look down at my notes for today's meeting. Somehow I still managed to leave half of them at home, but I think I can wing this with what I have. I keep thinking that each next issue will be the one that turns everything around.

Dan and Alex have been a little less nervous lately because our slut issue actually did pretty well, all things considered. But we're still in serious financial trouble and I need a very strong editorial statement this month to pull us out of this mess I've created. That's why I've decided to focus on my *"Why Girls Get Mad When Overweight Girls Want to Borrow Their Clothes"* article. I spent a great deal of time researching eating disorders in college and I think our readers will find my perspective on this topic quite intriguing. And, of course, Alex will have every advertiser at her feet. Just say the word fat, and they all come running.

I take a hair clip from my top drawer. I rip open the plastic wrapper and clip all my hair on top of my head and gather my notes for the meeting. I'm as ready as I'll ever be. I head to the conference room secure in the fact that I've finally chosen a subject that will garner the support of all the editors. This topic is so universal, I know it's going to be the one that finally saves me—I mean, us.

Blaire and Sloane are already here and ready to walk down the runway. Blaire is wearing some kind of long, flowy shirt/dress/nightgown thing over jeans with the highest heels I've ever seen. It's almost like she's balancing on two pencils.

I hope she doesn't accidentally trip over a huge pile of animal waste once she steps outside into the real world where people don't wear pencils. God, I hate her. Sloane is wearing a beautiful creamy-colored skirt suit. The skirt is sort of longish with wide pleats and it flares out. She's wearing crocodile shoes and a matching handbag with a clasp that may very well be the Hope Diamond. If you look very closely, you can see that her white wool skirt has little white flowers embroidered all over it. When she takes off her jacket, the lining is embroidered with those same tiny flowers.

I try to imagine myself in that suit. It looks pretty good on me—except for the skirt's way too long. I actually look ridiculous in it the more I think about it. Her panty hose have a little design on them too. I wonder if they came with the suit.

Ruth isn't here today but Amanda just got here and she looks absolutely perfect, as usual. She's dressed in a black sleeveless turtleneck, a black wool pleated skirt, black tights, black patent leather sling-backs, and a black-and-white houndstooth blazer with pearls.

Oh, and here comes Courtney. And she's practically naked! She's wearing two large breasts with a small peasant shirt under them, a jean skirt that could easily be worn as a belt, her legs are totally bare, and she's wearing her hot pink high heels again. Her hair is wavy and messy and she's wearing lipstick that matches her shoes. Amazing. Blaire and Sloane's comments about her hair, shoes, and clothes had absolutely no effect on her whatsoever.

I look down at what I'm wearing.

I'm so sick of these overalls.

Dan and Alex walk in together. Alex looks like she's entering the courtroom of the biggest case of the decade. Maybe it's the hair. It always looks like it's being televised. She takes out her laptop and her slew of other electronic devices and begins plugging herself in. I always forget how impressive she is when she first walks into a room.

Instead of magazines, Courtney is using a hot pink nail file to occupy herself today. It has little red hearts all over it. I'm sitting here mesmerized by the fact that she's not the least bit embarrassed, when Rhonda walks in wearing colossal Jackie O sunglasses and what appears to be a remake of the *Hairspray* hairdo. Her whole outfit is silver, and by that I mean the lipstick, the jumpsuit, the belted trench coat, the pocketbook, *and* the platform shoes!

"Cosmic" is the first thing that comes to mind and then out of my mouth.

"Oh stop it. I look terrible," she says, fluffing up her hair even more while running her tongue along her upper teeth.

"No, you don't," I say, searching for something a person who cares about clothes would say. "That whole astronaut thing is so happening right this second."

"Please, I look like the Tin Man," she says, untying her belt, "but, what the hell, I got this whole outfit on sale. Forty off. I'll probably only wear it once so I figured, why not? Right?"

I guess forty off of anything is a good deal, even a cleverly configured roll of Reynolds Wrap. The truth of the matter is that someone should have been making clothes out of tinfoil a long time ago. That's the whole problem with clothes in my opinion. They should be more versatile. The only article of clothing I ever owned that made perfect sense was my paper smock. It had a waterproof underside. You could write, paint, glue, or spill your juice all over it and no one said a word because it was disposable. God I miss that smock.

Dan stands up to begin the meeting and quickly gives me the floor.

"I've spent the last couple of weeks trying to come up with a more palatable approach to our editorial. I realize we're skating on thin ice with our readers as well as our advertisers and we can't afford to ignore their reaction, but that doesn't mean we have to abandon our cause or suddenly turn timid. We simply have to find a way to repackage our message with even greater enthusiasm, and I think I've found the perfect hook for our next issue."

I look over at Alex. I can tell she approves of the way I'm handling this.

"Let's start with the weakest link in the female chain. Who can tell me what type of girl gets the least respect from other girls and why?"

Courtney's hand shoots up. She's practically jumping out of her seat. "I totally know this!"

"Great, let's hear it," I say.

"Fat girls!"

Like a moth to a flame.

There is a moment of silence. Everyone in the room shifts uncomfortably in their seats or tucks their hands under their thighs almost as though they're doing an imaginary weight check. Every girl in this room would qualify as skinny by anyone's standards, but they all feel a little stab of recognition at the sound of those two words. Either they've been fat, hated someone because she was fat, or simply live in fear of being fat, but no matter what they're thinking, they all agree that the union of the words *fat* and *girl* is the most feared adjective–noun combination in the English language. All I want them to know is why.

"Excellent, Courtney! I couldn't agree more. Girls typically alienate overweight girls, and they do so for one reason and one reason only, fear. It's just that simple."

"You mean, you think deep down girls think fat is contagious? Because that's a medical impossibility; I happen to know that for a fact," Courtney says while licking the dust off of her pinky nail.

"No, I don't think they're afraid of *catching* fatness," I explain. "I think it's more a case of being afraid to face their fears. If a girl is afraid of dying, she will most likely avoid people who are very old or very ill. By the same token, girls who are afraid of being fat feel uncomfortable around overweight girls, or pregnant girls." I choke on those last two words.

"That's so sad for both the elderly and the fat," Courtney says while cheerily tilting her head and speeding up her nail-filing technique. *I'm trying to envision what her life story would sound like if she ever decided to write it down. I imagine it would be something like, "So far nothing bad happened. Phew! The End."*

I'm trying to stay focused on what I'm saying, but for some reason I can't get the words out anymore. It's like my mind suddenly went completely blank. I hadn't meant to bring up the topic of pregnancy and that's the last thing I want to discuss. And now I'm sure someone's going to bring it up again. I'd love to change the subject altogether but I don't have anything else prepared.

My chest starts to tighten up and I can already tell I'm going to have an anxiety attack right here, right now, in front of everyone. I try to control my breathing but it's coming in fast little spurts, and I can already feel the sweat bursting from my pores. What's even worse than my fear of discussing pregnant girls is the disturbingly loud fan overhead and the fact that my stomach is growling, and the fax machine is pumping out page after page and no one is responding. What if it's an emergency fax? And what if the ceiling fan spins out of control and starts flying around the room? Of course the likelihood of such a thing is very small and yet I feel I need to pre-pare for it somehow.

I hold my arm above my head, as though it will somehow protect me from a fifty-pound spinning blade, and try to count every time I inhale, but I'm pretty sure I've stopped breathing altogether. I have to get up and walk around or I might not make it through this meeting. Why the hell do I have to live like this? There's got to be a way to control these feelings.

I push my chair away from the table and slowly stand up. I hope no one can tell what's happening to me. I need to find something to do to get my mind off myself. I walk over to the fax machine and pretend I'm only mildly curious about the incoming fax and not that I'm one hundred percent certain it's from the President of the United States announcing that we're under attack. I quickly pull it out and read it. Dan asks me if the fax is important and I tell him it's from Chloe.

"Really? I thought she was out bear hunting today," some-one says. It could have been anyone. Normally I would care, but I'm too busy trying not to run out of the room.

"Would you like me to read this out loud?" I ask, trying to steady my voice. "It's addressed to the editorial department."

"Sure," Dan says, "go right ahead."

I take a deep breath and as soon as I begin reading, I can hear Chloe's voice and I feel myself calming down.

Hi Everyone!

I have a very exciting concept to share with you. I've been working on it for months. The idea came to me a while back, when I was just about to climb Mt. Washington for the very first time. Unfortunately, I never actually made it to the top of the mountain because I got a huge blister walking from the car to the mountain base. There was nothing I could do about it except wait for the rest of the group with fresh muffins.

Thank God for pink suede hiking boots.

Anyway, while I was hiking back to the car, I suddenly got this amazing idea for an article that I believe will give us a whole new identity. It's all about how I wore the wrong boots to go hiking and how that made me feel as both a person and a mountain climber. All the other climbers had boots that were specially designed to prevent them from getting an injury such as mine. Suddenly I got to thinking: *Why Not Let Performance Footwear Be Your Life Coach?*

I mean think about it. When you're outfitted in the right footwear, you suddenly feel empowered in a way that you could never be in a pair of high heels. Suddenly your fear of toppling over is completely gone and you no longer have to live in pain.

The right pair of hiking boots can take you places you've never dreamed of going before. The article possibilities are endless, *"Finding Your Inner Sole," "How Gore-Tex Changed My Life," "One Woman's Journey: One Sensible Step at a Time."* I could go on forever but I think you know what I'm saying. Let me know if you want me to go ahead and write one of these articles because I think any of them would really give us a leg up on the competition. That was a play on words! Speak to you soon.

Love,
Chloe

While I'm reading, I can sense that my heat rate has slowed down considerably. I take another deep breath and notice Anita has slipped into the conference room. She sits down, listening intently. When I finish, she asks, "Is that it?"

"That's it," I answer.

"Well, that's just fine, then. Can I have that fax, please?" she asks. I hand it to her and she crumbles it up before I even have a chance to let go.

"I can't think of anything less feminine or less inspiring than a girl in hiking books. The last thing we need is to lose ourselves in the *great outdoors*. I'll be back later to check on the progress of this meeting. I've got an appointment," she says and storms out.

I look at Dan and he shakes his head. I sit down without saying anything but as soon as I hit the chair, it feels like I either sat on something or I suddenly grew another vagina. There's something between my legs that was never there before. That much I know. I try to ignore it but it feels like a pair of socks.

"Should we continue where we left off because I have something to say?" Sloane asks.

"Go right ahead," I say nonchalantly, as though there's nothing unusual going on between my legs.

"Well, what I was about to say before the fax came in was that I hate to disagree with you, but I'm pretty sure that girls are not *afraid* of fat girls. They simply refuse to associate with fat girls the same way they refuse to associate with girls who smell. As a rule, girls tend to avoid things that disgust them."

"I completely disagree with that," Blaire says with her chin up. "Big women can be incredibly beautiful."

Another moment of silence.

No one knows what to say.

It's almost as if Blaire suddenly sprouted a soul. She holds her breath for a few seconds and then cracks up. She cackles and coughs, straining to catch her breath until Sloane joins in with her own brand of hysterical, uncontrollable laughter. I just realized that I've never seen Sloane with her mouth wide open before. I can't believe those are her real teeth. Some of them are extremely pointy. It's all making sense now. Sloane and Blaire are vampires. Blaire smacks Sloane on the knee to get her to stop laughing and then puts her hand over Sloane's mouth to control her.

"I think girls don't like fat girls because fat girls repel men and girls don't like to get too close to things that repel men. Isn't that right?" Courtney asks. Everyone ignores her because Blaire and Sloane are so entertaining. It's hard for anyone to take their eyes off of two such pretty girls laughing themselves sick over other people's figure problems. They look so happy.

"Perhaps, and I'm certainly not claiming to be an expert by any means, but it might just be that people tend to equate certain physical characteristics with personality or character traits," Amanda says, putting her hair neatly behind her ears with both hands. She's used to girls like Blaire and Sloane. She's equally pretty and notably smarter, so it only takes her a few seconds to pull her attention away from them. The rest of us reluctantly follow her lead.

"I'm not sure about this, but I would venture to say that it's not entirely out of the question that some people, or some girls rather, perceive *fat girls,* as you call them, as weak or perhaps lazy. Of course, that's completely unfair, but I'm not so sure that it's not true."

Way to speculate. I spread my fingers across the width of my thighs.

"I think it's because thin girls just assume they have more in common with other thin girls. Like for instance they probably both use Pam," Courtney says.

"And when you say 'Pam,' you're referring to the cooking spray; are you not?" I ask.

"Yes!"

"So, to sort of pull it all together, what you're saying is that thin girls are more attractive because they represent more desirable character traits?"

"Pretty much."

"So, in effect, self-control is a magnet for positive reinforcement from other people?"

"Or you could just use the word love instead of positive reinforcement," Courtney suggests.

"So, in other words, not eating equals love and acceptance?" I ask, leading the witness.

"Sometimes I wonder, though, because recently I saw a really cute guy holding hands with a fat girl. At first I thought 'That's so weird,' and then I thought, 'Maybe he only has one leg or something,' but then I noticed that he had both legs, so who knows?"

"Maybe she wasn't fat when he first met her. Sometimes skinny women let themselves go when they feel comfortable and in love, and we all know what happens then," Blaire says.

"You mean when they let themselves get pregnant?" Courtney asks with a little giggle.

My forehead is perspiring again. I think I need some water or perhaps a cot.

"Pregnant or not, we can't always be in control of what we eat. I mean there have been plenty of times when I've eaten something that just makes me hate myself and there's nothing I can do about it, except—"

I look over at Sloane, who looks worse than I feel. It's almost like she might be having some sort of an allergic reaction to something. Her eyes are watering and her hair suddenly looks dark and greasy. It could be sweat. It's hard to tell with blondes. Her face is turning red and she's clenching her fists and holding them down at her sides almost as if she's trying to stop herself from gnawing on them. I'm about to scream "Does anyone have an EpiPen?" when suddenly Sloane interrupts Courtney.

"Last night I was starving to death and really irritable and my roommate's dog was barking like crazy, but I didn't want to take her out because I knew I would get something to eat and I knew my roommate was thinking the exact same thing, so she totally scammed me. She was, like, 'If you take her out now, I'll take her out at eleven. And if you do go out, will you pick me up some spareribs?' And I was like, 'Are you serious?' "

"I'm afraid I don't understand," Amanda says, leaning on the table with her hands neatly folded.

"Me neither," says Courtney. "Why doesn't she just walk her own dog?"

"Sloane's roommate is a total bitch," Blaire says, patting Sloane on the leg. "I knew it the minute I met her."

"So, are you saying that your roommate was manipulating you into walking the dog?" Amanda asks.

"No! She was trying to get me to eat! My roommate's on Atkins', so she can eat spareribs, but I can't eat anything or I gain like a hundred pounds."

Sloane is breathing funny, but I have to get to the bottom of this. I thought I knew everything about this eating disorder thing, and then along comes Sloane's roommate and I'm stumped all over again.

"Why?" I ask.

"Because they like the same guy and Sloane's roommate is the most competitive girl on the planet. All she wants is to get Sloane fat."

Blaire spit the word planet. Granted, it's a hard word to say without spitting, even when you're not foaming at the mouth.

"I never should have moved in with her. I knew she was out of her mind. She's constantly weighing that poor dog," Sloane says.

"How exactly was she trying to get you to eat?" I ask.

"She totally knew I would buy something and eat it when I bought her spareribs."

"Obviously," confirms Blaire.

"So what *did* you do?" I ask.

"What did I do? I'll tell you exactly what I did. I bought a whole fucking quart of chicken fried rice, a quart of chow fun, and two quarts of lo mein, and ate it all standing up. Then I bought my roommate her precious spareribs and then I walked out of the goddamn door, walked two blocks, and stuck my finger down my fucking throat."

Silence.

I admit I forced the eating disorder thing to come up, so to speak. I mean, one couldn't help but assume that at least someone in this room might serve as an excellent working model of how an eating disorder works. But somehow I didn't really expect anyone in particular, let alone Sloane, to really admit they throw up their food. And now I can't stop picturing her vomiting up chicken fried rice, and I hate vomit more than anything.

It makes me . . . vomit.

And I don't feel particularly well to begin with.

"You threw up chow fun?" Courtney asks.

Sloane's face is drenched. She's totally enraged, seething with some sort of vampiric girly venom that I can only assume is exactly the same substance that causes acid reflux. She pushes her hair back and leans in toward the table addressing Courtney, "Yeah, I did. Okay? Like you never threw up your food?"

"No, it's just that, I mean, maybe once or twice I did, way, way back, when I was, like, in high school; but, as a rule, I always avoid noodles, to this day," Courtney says, blowing a little dust off the table.

"Italian food is ten times worse," Blaire says and then looks around as if to say, "So shoot me."

I actually like her a little better now.

"You throw up?" Sloane asks Blaire as though she just discovered they're both from the same little town in Kentucky.

"No. I mean, I've done it, but I don't do it regularly."

"Well, I do," Amanda says standing up. "And I'm not afraid to admit it. I throw up every day and I hope by admitting it, this is the first step toward recovery and by that I mean, for all of us."

"I don't believe what's going on here. This is absolutely insane. Do you realize what you people sound like?" Rhonda asks.

Sloane stands up, sorely in need of an exorcism at this point, and turns to look at Rhonda, "I don't care what I *sound* like. Do you realize what you *look* like? Why the hell would I want to recover from the only thing that ever made me feel good about myself? You think I'd rather look like you?"

"Sloane, pull yourself together! I understand that you've all decided to come clean on this eating disorder thing and I think that's very admirable, but it's not going to happen at the expense of another person's feelings. Is that understood?" Alex is standing up now.

"Thank you, Alex," Dan says. I'm surprised he managed to get the words out. He looks a little disoriented.

"I'm not trying to insult anyone. I'm being honest. That's what Zoe asked us to do and I'm doing it. Rhonda isn't helping herself by keeping the extra weight on. You think she enjoys being overweight? All the poor girl wants is a husband, and every time she goes on one of her JDates she comes back depressed. If we're supposed to be so helpful and honest, why can't any of us tell her why she's not finding the man of her dreams. It's because men don't like big hips. There! Now she knows what every single guy who never called her back was really thinking, and now she can do something about it. Is that so mean?"

"I'm five pounds away from becoming a lifetime Weight Watchers member! What the hell are you talking about? I may not have a perfect figure but according to the charts, I'm already in my ideal weight range. You're the one who's not helping herself because you should have had your head examined a long time ago," Rhonda says. Except for the silver jumpsuit, Rhonda might just be my new idol.

"Oh, please. Those weight charts are a joke. I'm five foot eight. According to those charts, I'd still be considered normal at one hundred and fifty pounds. I look like a cow at one-twenty. I need to be thin otherwise I feel self-conscious all the time and weak and unattractive. Honestly, Rhonda, I'm not saying that you're any of those things. I'm just saying that *I* would feel that way if I looked like you."

"Thanks, I can't tell you how much this means to me," Rhonda says.

"Can you please stop using Rhonda as an example?" Amanda says, practically in tears. "You're hurting her feelings and she doesn't deserve this kind of treatment. Honesty is one thing, but I'm finding this intolerable. Rhonda, I just want to say that I've never even noticed your hips."

"Well, I'm having a little exhibition later. Remind me to put you on the guest list. In the meantime, don't worry about hurting my feelings. I don't have to look perfect to be happy.

I have a life. I have friends. I don't have a boyfriend at the moment, but I go out and have fun every weekend. People don't *only* love perfect people. In fact, I bet if someone did a study, they'd find that people who try to be perfect are very unlovable because all they think about is themselves.

"I think that's where the confusion lies. If you're wondering why I'm not horrified by the fact that you think my hips are too big, it's because I don't measure my overall worth by any one particular part of my body. My body is my body. Some parts are better than others and I accept that. I always have. I don't want a guy who wants a girl with a perfect body. I would hate a guy like that.

"The reason it's taking me so long to find the right guy is because I'm searching for a human being. I'm not looking for an ass man or a leg man or a breast man. I'm looking for someone who finds me attractive but who is also interested in me as a person. I'm looking for someone who is interested in how I like to spend my day, my relationships, my family, my music, my recipe for kugel, and my collection of antique Raggedy Ann dolls."

"Good luck with that," Blaire says.

"One day I'll meet a guy who loves me for who I am, and what I am and that includes my hips and my thighs. Trust me on this. Relationships based on measurements don't last very long."

"The funny thing is," Courtney interrupts, "I was just thinking to myself that you should wear jumpsuits more often. They're very flattering."

"Thank you, Courtney. You're a wonderful person. I mean that," Rhonda says.

Dan opens his mouth to speak. It takes a few seconds, but eventually he whispers something that resembles a word. I think it was either "so" or "sod." After a few more seconds, he manages to piece together a real sentence, but the guy is truly taken aback by the fact that his staff is so heavily populated with bulimics.

"Well, I've certainly gotten an education here today, and for the record, Rhonda, I just want to say that I think you look great, but we seemed to have veered off track again."

I look over at Sloane who's mumbling to Blaire, "If I go over five hundred calories a day, I blow up like a balloon. Rick hates having sex when I'm fat and he notices immediately. He's like a human scale. He's always slapping my hips saying, 'If you keep it up, we're going to have to get you a new saddle for those bags.'"

Rhonda leans forward and says to Sloane, "If I were you, honey, I wouldn't be so worried about me not finding the right guy. I'd be much more concerned about the fact that your boyfriend sounds like he'd have a lot more fun riding a different kind of horse altogether. The kind with balls. From my experience, men who hate hips typically don't like girls."

I wish I had met Rhonda in kindergarten. I could have used a friend who wasn't afraid to say balls in front of a group of people. But right now I really need to get out of this room and pull myself together. I don't feel well at all. I attempt to wrap things up by making it clear that I don't intend to touch this eating disorder thing without the advice of a professional.

"Bulimia is a very serious disease and although it's been beaten to death by virtually every magazine in America, I think if we handle it properly, we may be able to encourage our readers to face up to what they've been doing to their bodies and to get proper help. Of course, I'm a big believer in the healing power of humor, but we need to tread very carefully here." Dan looks over at both Sloane and Amanda with sincere concern.

"Zoe, can you give us a quick list of headlines before we break?"

"Okay, sure," I say, wondering if perhaps I should rethink a few of these.

"But I might not use all of these in light of what we've learned here today. Suddenly this topic seems a lot more frightening to me than it did a few minutes ago. But, so far I have the article on why girls get mad when overweight girls want to borrow their clothes. I've wanted to use that one for a while, and then I have the one about why some girls eat their makeup, and the one about how you can be sitting in the car with a friend, when suddenly you hit a bump, and one of her teeth falls out. And with the help of today's discussion, I'm toying with the idea of adding another one: *'Are You Starving Yourself Because Your Boyfriend Wishes You Were a Boy?'* "

"Oh my God!" Courtney throws down her nail file, "What a great idea for my column. *Homosexuality: Getting to the Bottom of Bulimia.* I love it! It's even got, like, a huge pun in it!" She's so excited I think she might scream.

"But I don't get the one about the teeth," Courtney adds.

"Sometimes, when a girl has been throwing up for a while, her teeth rot. And as gross as that sounds, it's a lot grosser if it happens to a friend and you don't know why—that's called ignorance. And although humor is sometimes offensive, it works. Humor forces people to sit up and take notice of the things they need to face before it's too late. It's just as therapeutic to laugh at a problem, as it is to cry about it."

"I agree with you. But we have to face up to the fact that not all of our readers have a sense of humor. I think we've pretty much established that," Rhonda says.

"That's because we're still not reaching the audience I'm targeting. I'm going after a highly educated demographic—readers who are able to look below the surface. And besides, I'm not going to write articles on girls who are starving themselves to the point of death. That's not what I'm talking about here and I wouldn't touch that with a ten-foot pole. I'm talking about the girls who occasionally vomit, the ones who aren't even necessarily thin, but they use vomiting as an emergency dieting technique. They need to stop too."

"That's true, Zoe, and I agree with you about all of this. Humor is therapeutic and a great way to approach this topic. But I think the focus of any article on eating disorders should include the importance of eating three meals a day and exercising at least five times a week. That's what I do and I've never had a weight problem. But I agree with you that we have to get the word out that binging and purging, even on special occasions, is obviously not an option," Alex says, looking around the table.

"Well, based on Zoe's description of your childhood, if that was, in fact, you she wrote about in her 'Letter from an Editor,' you don't exactly qualify as the norm, given that you most likely suffered from malnutrition in your formative years. It's a well-known fact that the total loss of body fat for any length of time permanently alters your metabolism so you have an unfair advantage over the rest of us," Blaire says.

I look over at Alex hoping she's not thinking that had I not written that letter, Blaire wouldn't have that information, but as usual, she looks completely unmoved.

"You're right, Blaire. I did have a tremendous advantage over all of you, so you'll have to forgive me."

"I hate to change the subject, and believe me, I understand perfectly why girls get mad when fat girls want to borrow their clothes, but what makes you think some girls eat their makeup?" Sloane asks.

"Because it tastes like candy and it's got, like, zero calories and it's fat free. At least that's what somebody told me," Courtney says and then covers her mouth. There's a long silence.

"I used to eat Play-doh," Blaire says.

"Oh my God. I used to eat Silly Putty," Sloane jumps in.

"Look at that. They're practically sisters," Rhonda says.

After a second or two, Sloane ventures to speak again.

"The truth of the matter is that weight is not really a health issue at all. It's a jealousy issue. Women get angry when they see a friend or a celebrity get thin. Instantly the successfully thin girl is accused of being too thin or dangerously anorexic. Meanwhile the girls who are so 'concerned' are paying a fortune for gym memberships and food-delivered-to-your-door diets because they will pay anything to look like the girls they are suddenly so worried about. If only someone would tell them the truth about the one little finger diet, we could blow up the whole billion-dollar-diet rip-off industry once and for all. If you want to do something good for women, and you want to tell them the truth, teach them how to vomit instead of all this bullshit about so-called eating disorders.

"I've been throwing up since ninth grade and I've never had a problem with it. I'm certainly a lot healthier than some girl who's walking around with a load of fat choking her heart.

"And once more, for the record," Sloane continues, "diets don't work because no one can control what they eat for any length of time. Eventually it all backfires and every person making money in the diet industry knows it."

"Yeah, like anyone in this building doesn't throw up their food on occasion. I mean, come on. I've yet to walk into a bathroom, at least once a day, without hearing someone retching in the stall next to me," Blaire says.

Every time one of them says, "throw up," I feel a little pinch in the back of my throat and my mouth fills up with saliva. *Please God, don't let her say it again.*

"We should get this over with right now. Amanda, Blaire, and I have all admitted that we throw up. Rhonda admitted that she doesn't throw up, but we all know she should. So, how about you, Alex? Tell the truth, you mean to tell me that the thought has never even crossed your mind if you happen to miss your daily run?"

"Not only have I never deliberately vomited but the more I sit here, the more this meeting proves how very desperately we need to expose how dangerously far some girls will go to stay thin. And although I agree with Zoe that none of you are severely bulimic, it's still a disease no matter how often you do it. And although I usually like the idea of healing through humor, I am very nervous about this. If we do decide to cover this topic in our editorial, and I think we should, I suggest we treat it with the utmost tact and delicacy. And how dare you ask me that question?"

"Okay, fine. That's one *no* so far. How about you, Zoe? Are you brave enough to admit it? Have you ever vomited to lose weight?"

Please don't say that word again, please!

"Just answer me, Zoe. There's nothing to be ashamed of. Do you vomit up your food?" Sloane repeats. "It's a simple question, Zoe. We've pretty much all admitted it. You'll feel a lot better once you get it out. Do you or do you not vomit?"

"No! I manage to yell as I grab the garbage can under the conference table and launch into a lengthy audio-visual presentation of the contents of my stomach. As soon as I lift my head from the garbage, Blaire takes a picture of me with her cell phone. I immediately get a vision of that shot gracing the cover of our *Are You Ready for Summer?* issue, but as I stand up to leave, still holding the garbage can, I see Alex grab the phone out of Blaire's hand and delete the shot.

I'm deciding whether to run to the bathroom, or all the way home, when I spot Anita walking toward me in the hall. Somehow, in the time that she left and came back, she managed to change into a floor-length python coat and matching boots. All that dead skin is giving me the chills and I'm pretty sure I have to throw up again. And just as I suspected, out it comes again, right in front of her. It's a good thing I brought the garbage can with me. Before I even have a chance to duck into the bathroom, I see Anita glance at her watch.

"My goodness! Isn't it a little early in the day for that sort of thing?"

Chapter 11

The last time I was this sick was when our Aunt Dottie slept over and made her famous onion burgers. I wanted her to love me so I ate eleven of them, despite the fact that my whole family warned me that they weren't digestible.

I try to stand up but I'm much too weak. I think I might have to sleep here tonight. I attempt to lift my head up off the roll of toilet paper I'm using as a pillow, on the toilet-paper-lined toilet seat, when I hear the bathroom door swing open.

"Zoe, are you still in here?"

I manage a barely audible grunt and within a second or two Alex has crawled under the stall door and is sitting right next to me on the floor.

"Alex, what are you doing?"

"I'm sitting next to you while you throw up."

"You're going to get all dirty."

"What the hell do I care? And how many seat covers did you layer on that toilet seat?"

"About eleven."

"You should be okay, then."

"Unless I missed a spot."

"It looks pretty well covered to me."

"You know what I was just thinking?"

"No, what?"

"Remember that first time I came to visit you after I had just read the letter about your pink dress?"

"Yeah."

"Why didn't you invite me in to talk? You wouldn't even open your door."

"I was trying to get rid of you. I had someone in my office."

"Really? I thought you just didn't feel like hearing about all my problems."

"Well, that too."

"So, was it a guy?"

"Yup."

"Anyone I know?"

"Sort of."

"Are you going to tell me who it was?"

"Yes, but now really isn't the time to talk about it."

"Fine. Let's go back to the meeting. I'm finished throwing up," I say.

"We can go to my office," Alex says. "You absolutely cannot go back into a meeting after you vomit in it."

"Is that your motto?"

"It is now."

She's definitely the same old Ali.

As soon as we enter Alex's office, I can think of a few more reasons, besides hiding a man, why she might not want to let just anyone in here. The place looks like a bomb hit it. For someone who keeps herself looking so immaculate, Alex is quite the slob.

There are food cartons everywhere and banana peels and spilled coffee cups, about a dozen sweaters, piles of magazines

and letters and phone books, and some old food-delivery
bags. Her garbage can is so full; it fell over and there's another
pile of garbage on top of it. The place is a dump. No wonder
we always work in my office. It's a shame too, because this is
a really cool office. She's got an enormous window with an
amazing view of the park.

"I like what you've done with the place," I say.

"It's pretty disgusting, isn't it? I never let anyone in here—
especially not the maintenance people. They're notorious
snoops. I'm planning to clean it up very soon, though. Just
make yourself at home. I have to make a few phone calls. Feel
free to look through my stuff."

"I sit down on Alex's leather couch and pick up a magazine
while Alex starts making phone calls. I should probably call
Chloe and tell her what happened or maybe Michael. Or I
could just sit here and doze off for a minute. I've never been
so exhausted in my life.

When I wake up, Alex is still on the phone and she's eating
a banana. She puts up one finger and mouths, "one minute."
As soon as she hangs up I ask her how long I slept.

"About an hour," she says.

"Seriously? I never fall asleep."

"I know, I know, but lately you've been so tired," she says,
mimicking my voice. "And your thighs itch and you're gaining weight and you can't remember anything and you've been
late paying your bills for the first time in—" she suddenly
stops mimicking me as she stands up and begins slowly walking toward me. When she's standing right next to me she
stares directly at the top of my head. I can only assume she's
looking for signs of redheadedness but then, out of nowhere,
she yells, "OH NO, WHERE DID YOU GET THAT HAIR
CLIP?"

"WHY?" I yell back, assuming there's something crawling on it, as I rip it out of my head. But then I understand her concern. As soon as the hair clip falls to the floor, I see that all of my hair is still stuck in it.

"WHAT THE HELL JUST HAPPENED?" I scream.

"That hair clip has a razor in it. Someone was circulating a bunch of those hair clips around here last year and there was massive hysteria until a memo went around warning everyone to report it immediately if they found one on their desk. Someone must have hidden one in your desk! When you first clip it in your hair, nothing happens, but when you take it out, the opening mechanism releases the razor."

"What are you saying?"

"I'm saying that there's a very sick person among us, and whoever she is, she's back in action."

"No, I mean about my hair. Is that really my hair in that clip or does it just look like my hair? Because if it is my hair, I'm going to go into shock now so please call an ambulance before I'm no longer conscious," I say, and close my eyes.

"Zoe, try to control yourself."

"I can only control myself if you tell me you're lying. Please tell me you're lying."

"Zoe, it's not what you think."

"You mean I still have my hair?" I ask, afraid to touch my head.

"A lot of your hair is in the clip but your hair still looks long."

"It's not an afro?"

"No, definitely not."

"Swear to God?"

"Your God or mine?"

"You don't want to swear. That means you're lying."

"It's not that bad, I promise. You just need to get used to it. And I need to make another phone call so just calm down."

Alex is whispering into her cell phone just outside her office. I can only assume she's talking to her mystery man. I quickly put both of my hands on my head and feel my eyes fill up. I can't believe I'm going to have to relive my childhood before I even had a chance to recover from it the first time.

Chapter 12

Alex has agreed to let me stay in her office for the rest of my life and also to let me sterilize it for her so I can live here comfortably. I sent her to Duane Reade to get me some supplies so I can get started cleaning right away. I didn't expect her to agree to go so easily, but I think she was happy to get a break from me. I've been ranting and raving about my hair and falling asleep on and off in between each little fit for two hours. I have no idea what to do with myself and I'm already getting claustrophobic in this office. I'll have to get some sort of air purifier if I'm going to stay here for any length of time.

Alex wasn't lying about my hair being longer than it was in second grade, but it is definitely sticking up in some key areas and therein lies the crux of ninety percent of all my insecurities. I attribute the other ten percent to the fact that I read far too many medical journals as a child.

The good news is that it's almost five o'clock. Everyone will be cleared out of here soon, so I can walk freely around the building and get a change of scenery. I have the rest of the evening planned out perfectly. I'm going to call Michael and tell him I'm working late, and then I'll call him in the morning and tell him I fell asleep at work. No one will notice me—except for the fact that someone is now knocking on Alex's door.

I can't answer it, but I can't ignore it either.

Whoever it is really wants to see her. The knocking is getting incredibly loud.

There's only one solution. I scramble into position against the wall and yell, "Come in" as casually as possible.

In walks Ruth holding hands with what appears to be a man. It's hard for me to see exactly who he is and what he looks like because I'm standing on my head. The only thing I'm one hundred percent certain of is that Ruth is wearing a tube top. They should really institute a dress code in this place. There are two rolls of fat hanging over the waistband of her polka dot miniskirt, and it seems as though one of her knee socks has fallen to her ankle. I'm hoping this is all an optical illusion.

"Oh, excuse us," Ruth says. "Are we interrupting something?"

"Not at all, I'm just doing a little yoga."

"Where's Alex?" she asks abruptly.

"She's shopping for cleaning supplies. Can I help you with something?"

Ruth's companion is half in and half out the door until she gives him a hard yank, reeling him into the office. He stumbles a bit but then he gets his balance, and from where I'm standing, he's the handsomest man ever to walk the face of the earth. He's got to be at least six-two with piercing blue eyes and long sandy blond bangs that cover half his face. The sleeves of his jacket are a bit short on him, which adds to his overall disheveled adorableness. I wonder if he's her grandson.

"I'd like you to meet my new beau," Ruth says.

My feet fall to the floor, but I make no attempt to lift up my head. Basically I'm facing them through my legs, which means they're both forced to talk to my ass. But there's no way I'm standing up without a hat. I move my arms around as best I can to mimic a flying motion as if this is all part of my regular yoga routine.

The handsome one is doing that twitching thing people with long bangs do, and he's got sort of a crooked smile—the sort of crooked smile that gives me chest pains. I immediately recognize these as the same chest pains I got the first time I was kissed and find comfort in that memory because it enables me to forgo my fear that I'm having a heart attack.

Ruth gives him another yank and for some reason that makes him smile. It's kind of an *isn't-it-ridiculous-that-I'm-this-good-looking?* smile. He's obviously a model that she picked up somewhere in the building, but she never mentioned him before and he's definitely the sort of thing one would mention. I'm just about to ask them how they possibly could've met and if this is some sort of a joke, when he reaches around Ruth's waist with both arms and starts making out with her. I feel a rush of bile instantly flood my throat. I walk stiff-legged, with my head still down by my ankles, over to the garbage can—just in case.

His hands are all over her, and Ruth is having a hell of a time standing up. Both of her knees have collapsed in toward one another. This is obviously the most exciting moment of her life. I just wish I didn't have to witness it.

They're so into each other, I doubt either of them would even notice if I stood up, but as soon as I start to straighten up, Courtney walks in, so I stay put.

"So this is the handsome devil you've been bringing

around for show-and-tell," she says to Ruth while looking right into the handsome one's eyes.

"It's strictly show," I say. "So far there's been no telling."

Ruth's face turns bright red as soon as her boyfriend returns Courtney's gaze. I must say Courtney looks particularly sex-kittenish today, what with her hardly wearing any clothes and all.

"Oh, I didn't realize you were there, Zoe. Are you feeling better?" Courtney asks me.

"Oh much better," I say. "That's why I've decided to stand on my head. It prevents me from throwing up."

"Where's Alex?" she asks, as though she understands.

"She's out getting cleaning supplies," I say.

"Oh, can you tell her I came by?" she asks and then turns her attention to the model. "So, anyway, it was nice meeting you," she says with a faraway look, as she reaches out to shake his hand. He's all misty-eyed too. He's probably kicking himself. Had he the foresight to wait just a few more minutes before committing himself to the first person who grabbed him out in the hall, he would have had the opportunity to meet the girl of his dreams. Timing is everything.

It seems Ruth senses that her new boyfriend already found a new love interest, so she grabs him and tells him a little secret, all the while licking his ear until he shivers.

I can't look anymore so I turn myself around by taking tiny little steps until I'm facing the wall. Courtney and the male party doll are obviously meant for each other. Anyone could see it.

Ruth quickly drags her man out of the office and Courtney sits down.

"He was gorgeous," she sighs.

"I know," I say to the wall.

"I mean he was absolutely perfect."

"I agree," I say, "and dumb."

"I know," she says wistfully.

"Where do you think she met him?" she asks.

"I can only assume she picked him up in the hall. In case you haven't noticed, there are guys who look like him walking around all over this place. They're called models. All you have to do is stand outside one of the studios and just grab one of them as they're walking by."

"But I only want *him*."

"That's ridiculous, Courtney. They're all the same. You know that. Just go down to the fifth floor and take one."

"That's not very romantic. And besides, there was something special about him. I felt a connection."

"That's just because you both have the same highlights."

"No, it's because I've seen him before and we've made eye contact. I know we could have had something."

"Stop thinking about him. He looked like a scarecrow."

"You really think so?"

"Absolutely, and for all we know, he might not even be able to speak. He didn't say one word the entire time he was in here."

"I thought it was because he was shy or a foreigner. And besides, I'd be willing to teach him."

"He might not have any capacity for learning at all."

"So?"

I can't help remembering the time Courtney recommended a glycolic peel for a woman who had written in to confess that she'd been stealing money from her housekeeper's purse for three years.

"How much longer do you think Ruth has to live?" she asks me.

"Probably not that much longer."

"Then I'll wait for him."

"Suit yourself," I say and change positions so I'm sort of resting in a fetal ball with my hands covering my head.

"You know a lot of cool moves," Courtney says.

"Yes, well, I've been doing yoga for years and years."

"Do you mind if I read you the letter I came here to discuss with Alex?"

"Not at all, go right ahead."

"Okay, here it is."

Dear Courtney,

Lately I've been waking up in the middle of the night drenched in sweat. I have joint pain, sores in my mouth, and a rash that spreads all the way across my nose to my cheeks in the shape of a butterfly. Also, I'm Jewish and my boyfriend doesn't know. My question is: should I tell him?

Your friend,
Marsha Lowenstein

She looks at me, waiting for some kind of feedback.

"So far so good. Read me your answer," I say.

Dear Marcia,

Shalom!

Well, the first thing you should do is get yourself a good pair of cotton-crotch panties. If you're sweating like that, you could easily develop a yeast infection and what with all your other ailments, you really need to be comfortable in that arena.

Now, as far as your other symptoms, I suggest a good moisturizer without heavy perfumes for your rash and Anbesol for those painful mouth sores.

As far as your boyfriend is concerned, first find out if he's *anti*-Semitic. That means someone who *doesn't* like Jews. And always remember . . . I love you.

Forever Yours,
Courtney

"Can I ask why you wanted to discuss this letter with Alex?"

"Well, I did recommend cotton-crotch panties and a moisturizer, so I just wanted to see if Alex wanted me to specifically mention one of our advertisers' brands."

"Courtney, that woman has lupus. I recognize all the symptoms. She needs immediate medical attention, not crotchless panties."

"I said, *'cotton crotch'* panties."

"Whatever! She doesn't need new panties, she needs to see a rheumatologist."

Poor Courtney runs out of the office practically in tears.

By the time Alex comes back with the bag of supplies, I'm so nervous and worked up over Marcia Lowenstein's health, I can't even think about cleaning. I explain this to Alex and she immediately shoves all the cleaning fluids under her desk.

"Thank God, I didn't feel like watching you clean anyway," she admits.

"Well, I just want you to know that you had a couple of visitors while you were gone. Ruth came by with her new boyfriend, and then Courtney came by to discuss panties and moisturizer."

"I was expecting Ruth."

"Were you expecting her to show up with a boyfriend?"

"Yup."

"You mean, you know about him?"

"Uh-huh."

"Is that not the oddest couple you've ever seen in your entire life?"

"No, not really."

"Why not?"

"Because her boyfriend works for me."

"You own an escort service?"

"No, don't be ridiculous."

"Then explain what you mean by *works for me*."

"He does favors for me, that's all."

"What type of favors?"

"Well, for example, today he's going to get Ruth to take him back to her apartment and have sex with her. *That* type of favor." Alex is transferring the contents of her desk into neat piles on the floor.

"What are you doing?" I ask her.

"I'm organizing myself for tomorrow."

"Well, that's good. It's always nice to meet an organized pimp."

"I'm not a pimp. Well, I guess, technically, today I am, but mostly I use him for spying. He doesn't have to sleep with her as long as he gets the information from her apartment that I'm looking for. But he probably will. He'll sleep with anything."

"Ah, now I remember you telling me that you had someone who does this sort of thing for you. Where did you find him and what type of information are you looking for?"

"He doesn't look familiar to you?" she asks.

"I guess so. I'm sure I've seen his picture in *Issues*. Has he been modeling for a long time?"

"He started a few years ago, but he was in demand almost immediately. Before becoming a model, he was a bartender and before that, he was in jail. Of the three careers, I'd say the modeling is the most lucrative, but of course he spends everything he makes. How about his bony knees? Did they look familiar to you?" she asks, and then takes a bite out of a candy bar on her desk that looks like it's been sitting around for weeks.

"His knees? How would I know what his knees look like? Oh, wait a minute. Hold on. Don't tell me. He's your brother! Is he the one who pushed us on the swings?"

"It's hard to say. My memory isn't as good as yours."

"I can't believe it. That's amazing, Alex. He's still gorgeous."

"He's an idiot," she says and throws the rest of the candy in the garbage.

What a waste. I totally would have eaten that.

"No, I realize that, it's just that he's so cute. How did you possibly set him up with Ruth? And why?"

"I've actually been preparing him for this particular assignment for a while. Basically, I hired him to help me untangle some of the more subtle alliances in this terrorist network we call an office. Obviously, Sloane and Blaire have always been Anita's little helper, but I'm still not sure exactly who does what around here. And we need to figure out how Ruth fits into the picture, once and for all, to get a clearer understanding of how their whole system operates. It's the only way we can protect ourselves more efficiently."

"Have you always been this investigative, or just since I started working here?"

"You just pulled a clip out of your hair that had a razor in it. Aren't you a little curious as to how it got in your office?"

"Honestly, I just want my hair back. As far as I'm concerned, they're all guilty and I don't really care which one of them is responsible for each and every one of their little schemes. However, I do appreciate the fact that you went to the trouble of hiring someone to help me. How did you know you'd be able to get them together as a couple? And I thought you ate three meals a day and nothing more."

"That was only partially true. I also eat junk food and bananas all day. I think Blaire was right about my metabolism. The truth is I eat like a pig and I can't gain an ounce. As far as my brother and Ruth, all he had to do was stand next to her. The rest was easy. By the way, he was the guy I was hiding in my office the first time you came to see me. I still don't want anyone to know he's my brother, so please don't mention it to anyone."

"Who would I possibly tell?"

"And that was him on my cell phone before. I didn't want to tell you about him until my plan was underway. I had a feeling you'd try to talk me out of it and I didn't want you interfering."

"You kept him a secret for a very long time."

"I'm not used to confiding in people. Especially when I'm doing something I'm pretty sure is illegal."

"What makes you suddenly think Ruth has a bigger role in all of this?"

"I still think she's mostly a secondary player, but, lately, she just seems to be more visible, which doesn't really make any sense. She's at every single meeting and I've caught her walking around the editorial floor at very odd hours. She never used to come down here.

"You don't pose a direct threat to her, and you're the only thing that's new around here. That's why I'm curious about her sudden interest in what's happening on our floor. Anyway, her apartment is a great place to look for clues."

"Maybe she's coming down here more often because she got promoted and she wants to get more involved."

"She hardly even works. The promotion is just a title change."

"You're right, though. She does come down here a lot. But what'll you do if he can't get himself into her apartment?"

"Are you serious?"

She's right. All he'd have to do is visualize asking her and he'd be in the door.

"So what kind of arrangement do you have with him? He just does whatever you want him to do?"

"Let's just say he owes me a lot of money. He's working it off slowly."

"Wow, I'd love to have a boy slave too. What are your other brothers up to these days?"

"The youngest is in rehab. The oldest is *on the road*. Things turned out for them exactly the way everyone predicted. I could have been just like them, believe me. The instincts are there, but I fight them every day. When I first got out of high school, I worked three jobs. And then I started taking college courses so I was only able to work two jobs, but as soon as I graduated, I started working here full-time. Dan hired me after a three-minute interview. He basically asked, 'What are your qualifications?' And I said, 'My mother is a drunk, my brother is in jail, my father ran away when I was eleven, my other brother is on drugs, and I'd like to be rich.'"

"I forgot to tell you, while Courtney was here, I think she fell in love with your brother too. It was incredible in a way. She went down almost immediately."

"That's pretty funny."

"I bet they'd make a fascinating couple," I say.

"Has she heard him speak yet?"

"No, why?"

"He gets *me* and *I* confused."

"I don't think that type of thing bothers her very much."

Just then Alex's cell rings. It's her brother.

They talk for a few minutes and then Alex sort of snorts and tosses her phone down on her desk.

"My brother liked you."

"That's so sweet. Did he mention my hair?"

"No, not a word. He just wanted to know if, by any chance, I needed him to sleep with you too."

"What did you tell him?"

"I told him, no, because you have a boyfriend . . . remember?"

"Oh right."

Chapter 13

It was only a matter of time before I had to finally leave Alex's office. It smelled like rotten bananas and it was making me sick. I couldn't think of any other place to go so I decided to go home and face Michael.

I'm about to open the front door to my apartment but something's holding me back. It's not that I'm afraid for him to see my hair. It's just that I'm already anticipating that he's going to say, "It looks fine," which will set off a whole chain of events that will inevitably turn into a fight, and I'm too tired to fight. Even though I know I'm the one who's going to start it.

I open the door and yell out, "Welcome home," and head directly to the bathroom and shut the door. A few minutes later, he knocks on the door.

"Hi!"

"Hello," I answer.

"Are you okay in there?"

"Fine, thank you."

"Aren't you even going to kiss me hello?"

"Of course I am. I'll be right out."

★　　★　　★

A half hour later, he knocks again.

"Are you all right in there?"

"Yes, I'm fine. I just need a little more time."

"What's going on, Zoe? Are you sick or something?"

"No. I mean I might be, but I don't think so."

"Do you need help? Do you want me to come in and get you?"

"God no."

"Are you upset about something?"

"Yes, very."

"So open the door."

"I'm afraid that's not possible. I lost the majority of my hair today. I'm just trying to get reacquainted with my old self. The one I wished was never born. So I'm going to need just a bit more time."

"Zoe, what are you talking about?"

"Somebody put a hair clip in my drawer and I used it, and it had a razor in it. It's sort of a sick joke somebody played on me and it cut off all my hair."

"Are you fucking kidding me? Which one of them did it?"

"What difference does it make? I have an Afro. That's all there is to know."

"I don't care what sort of hairstyle you have, Zoe. I care that this happened to you."

"You don't care about my hair?"

"Not particularly. I'm not a hair man. I never was. Now let me in."

I'm not even answering him anymore. I'm too busy staring at myself in the mirror.

"Do you want me to break the door down? Because I've always wanted to try something like that."

"If you do, I'll jump out the window."

"No, you won't. You can't possibly care about your hair that much. And since when do you put other people's clips in your hair? Weren't you afraid of catching some kind of scalp disease or something?"

"It was in its original wrapper!"

"Well, if you won't open the door, I'm going out to get something to eat. Do you want anything?"

"No, thank you."

"Are you sure? I was thinking Chinese."

As soon as he says, "Chinese," I feel sick again.

"I don't want anything. Just get something for yourself."

I can't believe what I look like. I'm not upset about it anymore. I'm thinking of it more from a sociological standpoint. I find it fascinating that I am once again a victim of circumstance, and people's perceptions of me will be based on the fact that they think I've chosen to wear my hair like this on purpose. And because of that, they will assume a whole host of personality traits that I don't actually have and treat me accordingly. For example, they will think everything I say is meant to be funny and that I'm so comfortable with my God-given hair that I'm not trying to hide the fact that it looks ridiculous.

They'll think I'm this incredibly evolved, carefree person who's totally comfortable in her own skin, and then they will tell me things about themselves that are far too personal and I won't have the faintest idea how to respond.

I sit on the edge of the tub and turn the water on. I thought I'd come so far defying my maker with my long, not-funny-anymore hair, but once again, he gets the last laugh.

I hear the doorbell ring but I don't care who it is. I'm not coming out for anyone. I put my feet in the tub and run the water, but as soon as I move around a little on the hard ledge, I notice that thing between my legs again. What the hell is happening to me? Even my vagina is falling apart. Is nothing sacred anymore? I take the hand mirror off the shelf. I'm scared but I've got to see what's going on down there. I force myself to look and then, I try not to scream.

"Your sister's here!" Michael yells, while I sit here trying not to react. "And she has a present for you."

I open the door and stick my face out, careful to keep the bulk of my head out of sight and order Chloe to come into the bathroom immediately. She's carrying a large package wrapped in brown paper. She leans it against the wall and slips into the bathroom. I slam the door and tell her to turn around and face the wall. She immediately obeys.

"Now, turn around slowly but don't open your eyes yet. I have two things to show you and you need to brace yourself. One of them is my hair and the other one is my vagina. No matter what you think of either of them, do not react.

"Okay," she says.

"Now, close your eyes and turn around." Chloe has her eyes closed like a little kid watching a horror film.

"You don't have to hold your breath just because your eyes are closed," I say. She exhales and says, "Thank you."

"Okay. Ready? First look at my hair, but don't say anything."

She opens her eyes and yells, "Oh my God! What did you do!"

"I told you not to react!" I yell back, "Is it that bad? I didn't think it was that bad."

She's covering her whole face with her hands and then she mumbles, "No, I really like it."

"See!" Michael says from outside the bathroom door, "She likes it."

"I thought you were going out to get something to eat."

"I just said that to get you to come out."

"Well, get away from the door," I call to him, and then I turn to Chloe and take her hands in mine. "Listen, you're going to have to mentally prepare yourself a little better for this next one, okay?"

"Okay, I'm totally ready."

"You promise you won't scream because I think I've either grown a second *you know*, or something is terribly wrong with my original one," I say, pointing in the general vicinity of whatever's hiding between my legs.

"Please don't make me look down there," Chloe begs.

"Aren't you even a little curious as to what's wrong with me?"

"No."

"But what if it's serious?"

"I think Michael would have noticed if there was something suddenly abnormal about it, don't you?"

"Not necessarily, it seems to come and go."

"Well, you should have it checked by a professional. I don't know the first thing about vaginas and I wouldn't look at it even if it fell on the floor. I can hardly stand to look at my own. And more importantly, why did you cut your hair? I mean I love it. I'm just wondering what you were thinking."

"I put a clip in my hair that I found in my drawer at work. It had a razor in it and it cut off all my hair."

"I heard about those clips! They were all over the news or at least they were in the *Fashion Daily*. I can't believe you put someone else's clip in your hair in the first place."

"It was in its original wrapper!"

*   *   *

We've been in the bathroom for quite a while now, experimenting with different hairstyles on my large sphere, and I can tell Chloe is getting bored. But I don't want to be alone.

"What's all that stuff behind the toilet?" she asks.

"Bills," I say.

"How come you keep them behind the toilet?" she asks.

"I'm hiding them. Some of them have definitely been sent to me in error and I've made several irate phone calls explaining the situation, but now I can't remember which ones I'm supposed to pay and which ones I'm disputing and the whole situation has gotten so out of hand, every time I sit down to sort it out, I get so worked up, I'm pretty much waiting for the situation to work itself out at this point. I don't want Michael to know because I can tell he thinks I've been acting strange lately. I just hope they don't turn off our phone."

"Yeah, that would really mess things up for you. I can't believe it, Zoe. This isn't like you at all."

"I know. I'm not thinking clearly at all lately. Sometimes I honestly think I've lost my mind. She looks at me in the mirror a little more intently for a second and says, "Turn toward me." I turn my head toward her and she says, "Come closer, I mean right up to my face and tilt your head back."

"Why, do I have a bloody nose?" I ask.

"No, worse."

"What? Tell me."

"You have a moustache."

"I do not!!"

"Zoe, you do. Look closely. We have to get rid of it."

"How?"

"We'll go for laser treatments, but in the meantime you have to shave it off."

"I can't shave my face. It will grow back nubby."

"Exactly and then we'll go for the laser treatments." Before I have a chance to argue, she's already located the shaving cream and she's lathering up my upper lip.

"I think we're making a terrible mistake here," I mumble. "Maybe I should bleach it."

"That never looks right. We have to shave it."

She reaches in the cabinet above the sink and pulls out one of Michael's razors.

"Wow, he keeps this nice," she says tilting it back and forth. "Now hold still." She's gently shaving off half my moustache when the doorknob turns and in walks Michael.

"What the hell are you doing?" he yells and Chloe drops the razor in the sink.

"Nothing!" I scream and slam the door shut.

"That was a terrible answer," Chloe whispers. "Now he knows."

"You're both sick," Michael says.

"Chloe, I can't believe you. You didn't even lock the door."

"Neither did you."

"Well, now what am I going to do?"

"We're going to shave the other side."

"No, we're not! And I meant, what am I supposed to do about Michael?"

"What do you mean?"

"Chloe, he saw you shaving it!"

"So?"

"Forget it. This is ridiculous. I can't believe you. You were supposed to come in here and fix my hair not shave my moustache."

"Well, it had to be done," she says eyeing the razor.

"Put it away. I'm not letting you finish. And can you tell Michael to leave so we can get out of this bathroom?"

"Where would you like me to tell him to go?" she asks.

"I have no idea. Tell him to pack himself a duffle bag and find himself a room somewhere until I can face him again. I have too many things to work out right now to deal with him."

"Okay," Chloe says.

When she comes back to the bathroom, she says, "You can come out. He's gone."

"He really left?"

"Yeah, he said to call him when you're normal again, and I see you shaved the other side in the meantime."

"I couldn't leave it like that. And I can't believe he actually left."

"I think he was on his way out anyway."

"For good?"

"No! Of course not."

We leave the bathroom and go and sit on my bed to try to figure out what to do about my bulbous head. Chloe agrees with me that the only viable solution is to find my ski hat.

We search through a bunch of cartons, but the ski hat is nowhere to be found. We do, however, find a photo album of our family on the Disney cruise. I'm standing with my back to Minnie Mouse in every picture while Chloe hugs her, wearing a wide toothy grin as though they're long lost friends.

"Why were you so mean to Minnie?" Chloe asks, studying the pictures with her head tilted.

"I knew she was a fraud. I remember telling her so, and she didn't even have the decency to answer me."

"She wasn't allowed to talk," Chloe says. "They get fired for talking."

"Yeah, well, I still think she was very rude to me the entire cruise."

"What's this?" Chloe asks, holding up an old, beat-up spiral notebook.

"I think it's my old diary," I say lifting it right out of her hand.

"That's so cute. You recorded your entire childhood. Can we read it?" she asks.

Normally I would refuse, but Chloe was there for the whole humiliating ordeal, so there's no reason to hide it from her. We sit side by side while I read.

Dear Diary,

As it turns out, my mother has been lying to me about absolutely everything. For starters, remember that whole Santa Claus thing? Turns out he's not even *half* Jewish. Trust me. I made a lot of calls. And you know those chocolate circles she gives out on Hanukkah? The ones that look like money—well, you're not going to believe this, but they're counterfeit. The woman belongs in jail.

Sometimes I wonder if any of these people are even my real relatives. How could I be the only redhead in an entire family? Every night I go to bed and pray that I will wake up with a different hairstyle, but every morning I wake up and there it is, just sitting there, straight up, exactly the way I left it. The good thing about it is that I don't have to comb it or anything. It hardly moves.

Tuesday

I called Town Hall again today, but they still refuse to give me any information about my real family. I know they're in cahoots with my mom. I just know it.

Yesterday I asked her about a million questions the second she woke up, to see if I could catch her off guard. I climbed up onto her bed and waited silently in the space between her and my dad. I must have sat staring at her for over an hour. As soon as I saw one of her eyelashes flutter, BAM! I started right in. "How long have you and Dad been married? Were you ever married before? What time was I born? What did I look like the second I came out? How much blood was on me? Did you ever kiss another man besides daddy?"

I thought this rapid-fire method would surely trip her up and that a few morsels of valuable information would soon be mine. But, as usual, she kept her cool and continued spitting out lies. She's the kind of liar who can look you right in the eye and just belt one out like she's the most innocent thing in the world. She doesn't even crack a smile or try to cover her face up.

For instance she told me there was no blood on me at all and that I was the most perfect baby she'd ever seen in her entire life. She said my lips were like tiny cherry blossoms and that my skin looked like I had been bathed in a river of pearls and my eyes were like two little emerald dewdrops.

"I guess my hair hadn't come in yet," I said.

The whole time she was lying, she was holding me in her arms and it was hard for me not to cry. She's so beautiful and she smells exactly like baked apples. And I swear, you've never felt anything as smooth and silky as my mom's cheeks unless you've felt the skin on a dead butterfly's wings, which I have personally. As I was lying there thinking how much I wished I could believe her, she hit me with another one.

"You know, in my beauty parlor, women pay a fortune to have their hair permed to look exactly like the hair you have naturally. Curly hair is so much more interesting," she lied.

I will never lie to my little girl the way that woman lies to me. It's too confusing. I don't want my daughter to spend her whole life wondering why people don't treat her like the adorable person her mother pretends she is.

Your friend,
Zoe Rose

We skip a few blank pages and find my elementary school field work, all of which is incredibly depressing.

Teacher: Mrs. Desmond
Specimens: Eliza Martins & Caren Westman

October 10, 1980

Eliza Martins has long blond hair. Today she is wearing leg warmers even though it's about 78 degrees out. She must be very sensitive to weather.

October 18, 1980

Caren Westman pulled Eliza's hair 118 times today. They are best friends. At recess, they pretend that they are twin sisters and that their mother (the tree) is always yelling at them and then they gang up on the mother (the tree) and then they run away to another tree. They seem to enjoy this.

October 20, 1980

Caren and Eliza trade snacks every day. Today Eliza got two chocolate chip cookies and Caren got a bag of Doritos. They are both wearing something pink and something purple, exactly the way Chloe mixes those two colors. I always thought pink and purple were an either/or type of thing.

I checked my lunch bag to see if I had anything good in case someone wanted to trade snacks with me. As it turns out, freeze-dried yams aren't equivalent to anything.

October 22, 1980

I told every single girl in the whole class that I think I might be a genius but I still can't get any of them to be my friend. How is this possible?

Who wouldn't want to befriend a young genius?

October 23, 1980

Caren put Jell-O in Eliza's blond hair today and so I told on Caren, hoping that Eliza would like me better, but she told Caren that I was a tattletale and now they both hate me. Why God Why?

October 26, 1980

Eliza was sick today with an ear infection. Caren and I are now officially best friends forever. My life is finally turning out right.

October 27, 1980

Eliza is back in school today. It's almost like Caren forgot all about yesterday. I wrote her a note to remind her but she definitely forgot. I guess memory loss can strike at any age.

October 28,1980

Today all the girls were telling secrets and I admitted that I still play with Legos, and on occasion, very small cars. Turns out I'm the only one. What's the point of living anyway?

October 31, 1980 Halloween

Today I learned that secrets are supposed to be lies. I also learned that you are not supposed to tell girls that you don't have any friends as a way of making new friends. No one liked my Florence Henderson costume.

November 1, 1980

I saw Caren write a note and leave it on Eliza's desk. I picked it up before Eliza turned around to read it. It said, "Dear Eliza, Every won hates you. Yor Enemee, Annonimouse." I quickly threw it on the floor. It was loaded with spelling errors and I wanted no part of it. Eliza turned around just as I was throwing it. She picked it up and read it. Caren told Eliza that she saw me write the note. At lunch, Eliza and Caren held hands and told secrets the entire time. I think I'm the only kid in the whole school who eats lentils.

November 2, 1980

Today I won the spelling bee! I offered to give Eliza my certificate. It has a bright yellow smiling bee on the top, right next to my name. I didn't want to give it away but I would do anything to make Eliza like me. She didn't want it though.
Caren said she would take it but I offered to give her complimentary spelling lessons instead.

By the time I finish reading, Chloe is fast asleep. I tuck the diary under my bed and wake her up. She mumbles something about the present that she forgot to give me.

"I can't believe you brought me a present for no reason. That's so nice of you," I say, feeling guilty. I already know it can't possibly be something I'll enjoy in my current state of mind.

"Is it fuzzy?" I ask.

"No, it's not fuzzy. Why would I surprise you with something fuzzy?"

"Well it's important that I rule out certain categories altogether. I was just picturing one of those furry phones. I thought you might be disguising it in that enormous flat box."

"You're not even close," she says and walks over to get the present. "What I have here is a work of art that I want to share with you."

"Really? I never would have guessed that. I hope you didn't waste a lot of money on it because, if you did, I don't even want to open it."

"Zoe, I brought you a present. You have to open it. Why do you have to make such a big deal over everything?"

"Well, to be honest, I've been thinking a lot about artists lately and how much I resent them, as a people."

"You're against artists now too?"

"No, of course not. I'm not against artists in and of themselves. I'm against the worship of artists."

Chloe turns her head. I can't blame her. Sometimes I can't stand to hear what I have to say either. It's bad enough listening to myself think.

"It just bothers me when people think the simple act of putting a brush to a canvas is something worth celebrating."

"Zoe, what's happened to you? You were an art history major! People rarely celebrate an artist's character. They celebrate his genius."

"Most people mistake the two."

"You're just frustrated because you never make time to paint anymore." I get up and walk toward the kitchen to get a drink, but lately my refrigerator isn't cold enough so everything tastes bad. I think refrigeration in general isn't what it used to be.

"It's almost like you're against everything," she complains.

"No, just art."

"How could anyone be against art? That's like being against trees."

"Actually it's nothing at all like being against trees, but I just feel as though people only look at a work of art in search of something that reminds them of themselves and when they find it, they think, 'Hey! There I am! Therefore that artist must be a genius.' It's the emotional equivalent of seeing oneself on TV or staring at oneself in the mirror. It just doesn't seem worth it to me anymore. It hasn't for a long time."

"Did this anti-art thing, by any chance, start up when you got turned down to have your work exhibited in that Contemporary Young American Artists and Photographers Showcase Photography Show Thing, or whatever the hell that was called?"

"I almost forgot about that exhibit. Thanks for reminding me."

"And as usual, you've turned the rejection into a cause."

"Gee, when you put it that way, it makes me feel so much better. You just saved me thousands of dollars worth of therapy I was planning on never having."

"Zoe, you submitted a painting of a dead bird. What did you expect?"

"I was trying to make a statement."

"And you're still not over it?"

"Not really."

"Well, maybe this will help."

She hands me the painting and walks over to my mirror and starts brushing her hair. That mirror is the only thing I've hung up since we moved in, but in light of what happened today, I'm thinking of taking it down.

"You used to stare at your art books for hours," she says absentmindedly.

"I know. You're right," I say. "I just can't enjoy them anymore." I can feel my eyes burning.

"And can you believe I cried this morning, for no reason at

all? I never cry. Everything just seems off lately. And this has nothing to do with my hair. I cried on my way to work, before any of this happened. Everything suddenly seems so hopeless. I can't get anywhere at the magazine and I feel like it's because all anybody wants is lies. The reason my dead bird was rejected was because nobody can face the truth anymore."

"I'm pretty sure that's not why it was rejected."

"Why do you think it was rejected?" I ask, cringing at the thought that she might actually know and that I might not be able to handle the truth any better than anyone else.

"It's because there were bugs crawling all over it. It was rejected because it was gross."

"Gross and real," I say in my own defense. "That's why I will never acquire another piece of art for as long as I live. If I want to experience lies, I'll just read the newspaper. It's much cheaper. I prefer to remain completely unconnected to art in every way. That way, if I do happen to stumble upon something 'real,' there's no risk of falling in love with myself."

"Well, whatever, I still want you to have this, because despite everything you've just said, I think you're going to like it. Please open it; it's getting late and I have to go home."

In an impulsive attempt to get her to stay, I take the package from her and start ripping off the paper. I breathe in, puff up my cheeks, and blow out. I'm prepared for the worst. I try not to look at it but a shot of color jumps out at me. I numbly continue to rip and unravel long strips as the paper drops to the floor, curling by my feet.

"What is this?" I ask. "Is it titled?"

"Yup. It's called 'Three Happy Daisies.' "

Hold on a minute. I've seen this painting before. I know I have. I remember the colors—layers and layers of pinks and reds and cranberry and fuchsia all fighting against one another. I can almost smell the petals, and feel the drops of water falling off the canvas. I can hear the stems brushing up against one another, chafing to come together to form one big, enormous flower. I have to take in each flower separately, over and over again. I take another deep breath, and let all the anger rush out with a long, satisfying exhale—"I love this," I whisper, "I love the way this makes me feel."

"Who are you talking to?" Chloe asks. "Me or the painting?"

I can't answer her because there's a pounding in my chest. I'm just sitting there listening to myself looking at this painting. I can actually hear my own body responding to it.

"There it is," I finally manage to say. "I have that feeling that I haven't felt in so long. I was wondering if I would ever feel it again. It's the feeling I used to get when I saw something so beautiful, I wanted to consume it, to keep it inside of me forever."

"See? I knew you'd like it."

"It's true. I feel almost reborn. I'm not angry anymore. It's been so long since I felt this excited about something."

"See? And all it took was three, honest happy daisies."

"You're right, Chloe. This might just be the most honest piece of work I've ever seen."

"Well, I'm glad you like it, because it's yours," Chloe says, putting her hands together.

"Absolutely not, I couldn't take this from you. You have to keep it," I say.

"No, I insist, because truthfully, it's yours."

"Don't be ridiculous. I'm glad you showed it to me, but you should keep something like this."

"It's not mine. It's yours. You painted it."

"What are you talking about?" I ask, unable to take my eyes off of it.

"Mom gave it to me when I went by to pick up some of my old stuff. You painted this in sixth grade. You gave it to me for my birthday, but now I want to give it to you."

"I painted this? I can feel it somehow but I don't remember it the way I remember my other paintings. And yet, I do remember something, a feeling, but I don't know what it is exactly.

"I really don't remember painting this. I don't remember ever being this happy."

"Maybe you were lying."

"I could never lie this well."

Chloe sits down next to me. We're both staring. I'm staring at the painting and she's staring at me. After a long silence, Chloe leans over and says, "The important thing is that it's not like you're sitting here and staring at yourself in the mirror."

I put the painting down for a second, but then I pick it up again. I realize how this must look to her, after everything I've just said. But, she's my sister. She's seen me do a lot worse.

As soon as Chloe leaves, I dig out my old diary and read it for a while longer until I can't take it anymore. I slip the notebook back under my mattress and try to put that little girl out of my mind. I hate knowing what she looked like, how she spoke, how ridiculous her hair and clothes and shoes were. She was so odd, and so much older than she was supposed to be—completely incapable of fitting in. I actually hate her. I hate her for ruining everything for me.

Why couldn't she be like everyone else? I wish I'd never found my old diary. I hate facing her, and here I am, right back where I started.

I walk back into the living area and rip open a few more

boxes to get my mind off my old diary. After sifting through a few cartons of books and canvases, I discover my ski hat sitting right on top of my old gas mask in a carton marked ACCESSORIES. I slip the hat on and it's just perfect. It looks almost as though I chose to wear it on purpose.

And I can't believe I totally forgot about this crazy old mask! I used to wear this thing everywhere during the anthrax scare. I get such an overwhelming sense of security just looking at it. I'm always surprised more people don't purchase gas masks—especially for traveling. They're so practical. Nothing could go wrong when you're wearing one of these babies. I try it on over my ski hat and lean back against the carton, remembering all the good times I had wearing it around the city, not a care in the world, totally safe and protected from everyone and their germs.

Chapter 14

By the time Michael comes home I've fallen into a deep peaceful sleep, perhaps for the first time in months, but his screaming wakes me up.

"What the fuck are you wearing?" he yells.

"What??? Oh this? It's just my gas mask. You scared me." I almost forgot I had it on. It's surprisingly comfortable.

"Well, take it off!" he yells.

"Fine, fine, fine," I say and slip it off.

"I'm not going to even ask you why you're wearing it. I'm just going to ask you to please put it away immediately. I don't know what's gotten into you lately, Zoe," he says, as he carries a couple of deli bags into the kitchen.

"I was just trying it on. What did you get to eat?" I ask.

"I ate at the diner, but I picked up a few essentials for you around the corner."

"Any cereal?"

"Yeah, I got you four boxes of Captain Crunch."

"Oh."

"What's the matter?"

"Nothing."

"I got you Cocoa Puffs too," he says.

"How did you know I switched to Cocoa Puffs? I only eat them at work."

"I noticed that you keep a box of them in your pocketbook lately."

"Well, it's nice of you to notice." I'm suddenly so grateful to have a boyfriend, after reading my diary, I'm being a lot nicer to him. If he ever knew me as a child, I doubt we'd be living together. I walk over and kiss him and then he asks me to please put the mask away by the time he comes out of the kitchen.

While I'm deciding what cereal to have, the phone rings. It's Chloe.

"Are you feeling better?" she asks.

"Yes, much better. I'm in love with my painting."

"Good! I wish you could see me right now," she says.

"Why?"

"I'm trying on the cutest skydiving clothes! I got them at Paragon."

"Any particular reason?"

"I forgot to tell you, I'm going skydiving."

"In the sky?"

"Of course in the sky!"

"Who is that?" Michael asks.

"It's Chloe. She's going skydiving."

"In the sky?" he asks.

"Yup."

"Can we discuss this later?" I ask. "I'm about to have some cereal."

"Okay, sorry. But I just want you to know how excited I am to be finally going skydiving after all these years."

"When are you going?" I ask.

"I don't have any definite plans but now that I have the

clothes, it's just a matter of time." We hang up and I try to remember a time when Chloe said she wanted to go skydiving.
As far as I can remember, she's never mentioned it. Except
once, when we were playing that game where you have to
choose between the two worst things you can possibly imagine. I asked her whether she would rather be forced to jump
out of a plane or get raped and Chloe said, "I'd so rather get
raped."

Michael comes into the bedroom as I'm shoving my mask
into a carton in my closet. "And take that ridiculous hat off
while you're at it. Your hair is fine. I can see it sticking out a
little and I think it looks very cute that way."

"Trust me, it doesn't, but I'm only wearing the hat because
I'm cold."

"How long are you planning on wearing it, then?"

"I'd say roughly two years."

Chapter 15

Michael is away again for phase two of his book tour. I called in sick today, and yesterday, because I have some sort of virus. I've never called in sick before. At first it felt sort of freeing because everyone at work seemed so understanding when I listed all of my symptoms: stomach cramps, blurred vision, arthritis, insomnia, TMJ, excessive fluid retention, gum sensitivity, and general malaise. But then I started to panic about the fact that they seemed almost too understanding. It sounded like they were treating me like someone who was having a nervous breakdown.

Of all the things that are bothering me, my gums are the worst. I have to eat gallons and gallons of ice cream to numb them.

I flip through the channels looking for a decent morning news program but the only thing that holds my attention is "Mary Ellen's Tip of the Day." Mary Ellen is exactly the kind of grandmother I always wanted. Today she's using a potato to take out juice stains from what looks like an old napkin. I love this show.

As soon as it's over, I try to roll myself onto my side but for some reason my hip is bothering me. It's too soon for me to have bedsores. Although I haven't really been moving very much, unless I have to answer the door or go to the bathroom. I'd like to get up more often but it's just not worth it. I've never been overweight before; it's incredibly exhausting. Although, it's sort of interesting to see how my body has responded to the incredible amounts of food I've been shoveling into it.

It's not surprising to me that people find themselves inching toward the thousand-pound mark once they take to their beds. I'd hate for something like that to happen to me, but if that's the price I have to pay for lying around all day and ordering in, then so be it.

One thing I was surprised to find out is that you can get a pizza delivered as early as nine-thirty in the morning. Most people aren't aware of that. As soon as I'm back on my feet, I'm going to spread the word.

I'm about to dial for my first pie of the day when my phone rings. My caller ID indicates that it's my mom.

"Hi, Mom."

"How'd you know it was me?"

"I have caller ID, remember? I tell you that every day."

"Oh right. Sorry. So, how are you feeling today? Any better?"

"The bloating is out of control. It's more like elephantiasis at this point, and my rash has flared up considerably since we last spoke, and my vision is definitely still blurry, and my hip is sore, but other than that, everything is fine. You were right to suggest that I stay home for a few days. I'm definitely contagious, and besides, the air quality in that place was just horrendous."

"So have you been to the doctor yet?"

"Nope."

"You need to see a doctor, Zoe. You do realize you're pregnant, don't you?"

"No, I wasn't aware of that, but, thank you."

"I'm serious, Zoe. I've been trying to keep my mouth shut about this, but you have to face up to this."

"Mom, I think I would know if I was pregnant. I'm just fat. Michael has been gone for two weeks. It's impossible."

"Zoe, please, you're much farther along than two weeks."

"Mom, stop. This kind of thing doesn't work on me. It never did. You should know that by now. You can't scare me into going to the doctor by picking random illnesses out of a hat."

"Pregnancy is not an illness."

"It's not?"

"No, of course not."

"Well, anyway, I'm not pregnant. I've taken enough home pregnancy tests to prove it."

"I think you need to take one more."

"I'm all out."

"You're joking."

"Why would I joke about a thing like that?"

"Suddenly you're all out? This is called denial, Zoe. You know you're pregnant and you're afraid to face it."

"I can't get pregnant. I only take those tests because I like to prove it to myself every now and then. I've gotten two periods in the last ten years, or something like that. I'm not exactly fertile. I'm probably not even a woman."

"Of course you're a woman."

"Then why do I feel so unfeminine?"

"It's because of the way you dress. Chloe and I have been telling you that for years."

"Whatever, but as long as we're on the subject of Chloe,

I've been meaning to tell you that I think you stepped way over the line when you told her that whopper you still consider a little white lie."

"Which whopper?"

"Remember when you told her that you're never going to die because you took a special pill? Well, guess what. She still believes you. Just the other day she was saying how lucky we are that you found out about the special pill before anyone else."

"The reason I told Chloe that I wasn't going to die was because she was up every night for two months with nightmares about me dying. When you give birth to your baby, then talk to me about how it's wrong to lie to a suffering child."

"I understand why you lied to her, Mom. I just think you should tell her the truth before she turns thirty. And I also don't think you should be giving her pills without a prescription. That's very dangerous. I know your intentions were good, but giving someone drugs is actually considered a crime in this country."

"I didn't give her drugs."

"I'm pretty sure 'anti-fear' pills, as Chloe calls them, qualify as drugs."

"Well, in this case, I can assure you, they don't."

"And why is that?" I ask.

"I gave her Tums."

"You gave her Tums and told her they were anti-fear pills?"

"I gave them to her because she was petrified of doing the type of things that she thought she needed to do to become the person she's always wanted to be. All she needed was a little courage and Chloe responds well to placebos."

"Don't you feel guilty manipulating her like that? She's a grown woman. She has a right to understand the world be-

yond the one you've so craftily redesigned for her. Don't you
think she's entitled to know the truth? Besides, now she's
threatening to go skydiving."

"Of course I think she's entitled to know the truth. But I
think she's more entitled to be happy."

"You treat her like she's . . . like she's . . ."

"Like she's my child?"

"Exactly! That's why she's so childlike. I never realized that
before."

"Is that such a terrible thing?"

"Well, it can be embarrassing at times."

"Chloe seems to be doing very well in my opinion. She has
parents and a sister and a husband who love her. She's out
there in the world trying to conquer her fears. She makes
everyone she meets smile, and she will soon be back at work
doing what she loves to do. I don't think she turned out so
badly, do you?"

"No, actually, she turned out pretty well, come to think of
it. What do you suppose you did differently with me?"

"Nothing, why?"

"Oh, I don't know. I seem to be just a tad off."

"Zoe, you're wonderful!"

"Face it, Mom, I'm a mess. Maybe you should have lied to
me more often."

"I lied to you plenty. And I'm very proud of you, Zoe. I'm
proud of you exactly the way you are.

"Your sister adores you. I adore you. Your father adores
you, and you have the most wonderful boyfriend. It's like I
handpicked him for you myself. You're a writer and therefore
you're free to do and say as you please and that's all you've
ever wanted. And soon you'll be a mother, and then you'll
know love like you've never imagined it could be. The mo-

ment that child looks up at you with that questioning look in her eye, asking you what it's all about and what's going to happen next, you'll forget every ugly truth you've ever known and you'll want to rewrite the entire world to keep that baby safe and happy. So don't talk to me about the truth, and don't talk to me about how messed up you are until you're a mother. Then, and only then, will you understand the miracle of who you are and what you have to offer another person."

I hang up and call my gynecologist.

Although I seriously doubt I'm pregnant, I wouldn't mind getting to the bottom of that thing between my legs. I think that's important.

Chapter 16

"Hi!"

"Hi," I yawn.

"What are you doing now?"

"Same thing I was doing the last time you called."

"You're still in bed?"

"Yes, but I've turned it into a little makeshift office. So technically you're calling me at work, so I can't really talk. Call me tomorrow."

"Don't hang up. I need to talk to you."

"Michael, it's nine-forty in the morning and you've already called me six times. Nothing new happened since nine-twenty and I can't get any work done if you keep interrupting me," I say, clicking off the TV.

"Zoe, you're obviously suffering from depression and exercise is the best thing for you. I want you to get up and take a walk. I mean it; you'll feel better."

"How do you expect me to do something like that? I don't own any walking shoes, and besides, I have a virus. I don't want to infect the other pedestrians."

"If you can get up to answer the door for food deliveries,

you can put on any pair of shoes and take a walk. It's a beautiful day. It's going to be in the seventies."

"How would you know? You're miles away."

"I read the paper, which gives me all kinds of global information."

"Don't believe everything you read. It looks like rain."

"Zoe, I mean it. If you don't get out of that bed I'm going to call someone to come over and physically take you outside. Is that what you want?"

"What I want is to watch TV and for you to stop bothering me every five minutes. Besides, there's no way you can find someone who can lift me."

"You're watching TV on a Friday morning? Look, Zoe, you need to see a doctor and you need to get up and move. Are you listening to me?"

"For your information, I have a doctor's appointment all set up for this Tuesday."

"Seriously?"

"Yep."

"Wow! That's great! I'm so proud of you."

"All I did was make a phone call. It's not that big of a deal. People call people all the time. I'll speak to you tonight, okay?"

"It was an important phone call and I'm glad you made it. I'll call you in a few hours to see how you're doing."

No kidding.

What's he so worried about? That I'll fall asleep, roll off the bed, out the door, down ten flights of stairs and into a busy intersection? I haven't moved more than three inches in the last two hours. Oh good, *Teletubbies* is on!

As soon as I hear the doorbell, I instinctively jump out of

bed, although I don't remember ordering anything as yet. Maybe they just come automatically after awhile.

I look through the peephole and see that it's Alex and open the door. She looks beautiful as usual. Hair in a high, bouncy ponytail, bony wrists with her tiny gold watch, perfumed sweater with a tiny white camisole underneath, which shows her collarbones; she's femininity personified. It's a wonder her true self never seeps out. I feel around for my collarbones but they're completely submerged.

"Hey! What a nice surprise. What brings you here on a Friday?" I ask. I'm so happy to see her. She's never even been to my apartment. I wish I'd known she was coming, though. I would have straightened up and adjusted my hat.

"What's that thing on your head?" she asks.

"It's what keeps me from offing myself."

"Fine, but just so you know, it looks ridiculous and I can't believe how fat you're getting!"

"Thanks, but you just saw me a few days ago. I couldn't have gained that much weight in a few days. What's in the garbage bag?"

"Well, truth be told, Ruth wasn't so quick to let my brother in her apartment after all, but he finally got himself in last night—after agreeing to respect her in the morning."

"So, I guess it's safe to assume she's no longer a virgin."

"And the good news is," she says, while taking everything out of the bag, "I have the contents of your hard drive on a disc, and a whole bunch of sweat socks that he assumed were yours because they have your name in them. There are about twenty pairs here. Why someone would keep twenty pairs of sweat socks in her office is a puzzle in itself, especially these socks. Why Ruth chose to steal them is anyone's guess as well."

"My socks! I've been looking all over for them. I've had these since camp. I keep a lot of them in my office because I have a fear of running out. I realize it's an irrational fear—"

"And he found these really weird photos of Chloe," she continues with a little shrug.

I take the photos from Alex and turn them right-side up. There are five photographs here of Chloe in bed with a man. Oddly enough the man is wearing a suit and it looks like he's sort of lying down, but if you turn the photo sideways, he's actually reclining in a standing position. Chloe's head is right next to his except she's staring into space as if there's nobody there.

In another one of the photos she's jumping on the bed with her arms and legs out and the guy is in the exact same position, lying on the bed next to her, with his suit still on.

"What the hell are these?" I ask.

"It's hard to say, but I think we should find out, and is that a cartoon I hear coming from the bedroom?"

Damn! I thought I turned that off.

"Why would Ruth, or anyone for that matter, go to all this trouble to make it look like Chloe and this person are in bed together?"

"I can think of a number of reasons why someone would want to get your sister in trouble, but whoever retouched these photos needs to brush up on her Photoshop skills. The only thing someone might surmise by looking at these is that Chloe and this man weren't even in the same room when they were taken."

"I just can't picture Ruth having the wherewithal to coordinate a project where there was cutting and pasting involved. What else did he find?"

"Nothing really," she says. "Aside from these." She casually hands me another manila envelope as she heads toward the bedroom. "Oh, and he said her apartment was actually pretty nice. Is this the show where the giant fur babies talk to each other? I thought they took this off the air," she asks, sitting on my bed.

"Ruth has a nice apartment? I pictured it covered in leopard with lipstick smeared all over the walls."

"It probably was. You just described my brother's taste perfectly. So, I hate to ask you this, but don't you think it's a little creepy that you're sitting here watching kids' shows all day in that hat?"

"Creepy how?" I ask, as I slide out the contents of the envelope onto my bed revealing four eight-by-ten glossy versions of the same hairy girl who appeared on our launch cover and two copies of my original slut article.

"Wait a minute. This is a little over my head. Ruth, the woman we have all seen fall flat on her face in the cafeteria, had my hard drive and these cover photos and my original article and those ridiculously retouched photos of Chloe—not to mention my socks? How could she possibly even get her hands on this stuff? The woman is half plastered ninety percent of the time."

"I have no idea, but check these out," she says, pulling a handful of hair clips out of her handbag.

As soon as I see the hairclips, I feel my eyes filling up again.

"I'm as confused as you are. I never expected him to find this much stuff. It would be absolutely impossible for her to have pulled off every single one of these stunts alone."

"Maybe she just goes around everyone's offices collecting things for her scrapbook."

"Here's what I think: There's a definite possibility that she may be at least partially responsible for the photos of Chloe.

She's always hated Chloe and no one else could possibly edit photos this poorly unless they were drunk. Although I still can't see why she'd bother. I'm pretty sure she's completely over Chloe.

"I also think she may have something to do with the hair clips because she's always complaining about her hair, and I think it bothers her that no one else's falls out in clumps the way hers does. And these were planted all over the building a few years ago. She was a lot peppier back then, so who knows. On the other hand, I don't really see you as a direct threat to her either, so why would she care what you look like or how long you'd stay away from work if your hair got cut off?"

"I'm not staying home because my hair got cut off. I have a virus! A very serious virus," I say, pulling my hat down on the sides.

"Whatever, but I don't think she's responsible for the cover shots either, because that sort of thing is way over her head. And I'm pretty sure she had nothing to do with the slut article revision because she can't write in full sentences. I think Blaire is the culprit in both of those cases, and she's very close with Ruth, always has been, so there's an excellent chance that she asked Ruth to either hide or destroy the article and covers for her.

"Of course Anita is an even more likely suspect for all of these crimes because she's been out to get you and Chloe from the start, and she has a few hair issues of her own. But I can't imagine her being stupid enough to trust Ruth to hide her evidence, nor, as Dan pointed out, would she ever do anything to hurt her profits. Therefore Anita couldn't possibly have anything to do with that cover.

"And then there's always Amanda, who has full access to your office at all times, and who has recently become Anita's new best friend. They're together constantly lately. And since she's smarter than all of them put together, we have to take her into consideration."

"Wow, you've really thought this through."

"However, something like adding the names of girls who slept their way to the top is something Anita's been known to orchestrate in the past. And even though it was obvious that Blaire was responsible for that one, lately I've been thinking that Anita might have put her up to it."

"Really?"

"Oh yeah. She loves gossip. She's been trying to turn *Issues* into a gossip magazine for years, but Dan won't let her. Every now and then she manages to slip in a little dirt and then they have a huge fight about it. That article has her name all over it. I'm surprised I didn't realize it sooner."

"I'm with you, detective, but what about my socks?"

"That's a tough one, I agree. But Ruth's been known to swipe other people's shoes in the past. I guess she decided to move on to socks."

"I think I remember Chloe telling me she once caught Ruth trying on an extra pair of shoes that Chloe had left in her drawer."

"Now, the hard drive was definitely a joint effort," Alex continues, without missing a beat, "because Ruth isn't particularly technologically inclined, but, as we know, Blaire and Sloane could easily have gotten maintenance to do the job for them, and Amanda could have easily helped them with that one. My instincts tell me that was a three-person job and they decided to hide the evidence in Ruth's apartment for now."

"You're good."

"I'm pretty good, but not good enough. I still can't figure out why Ruth had *all* the loot."

"Okay, please don't say loot ever again."

"Sorry. It's so hard not to use the right lingo."

"My headache is coming back. Do you want to watch *Family Guy*? I taped it. It's really funny. The baby's a snob."

"So I've heard. Maybe we need to get you out of this room for a little while."

"That would be good but I can't go anywhere. I think this virus made me agoraphobic. Although, Michael thinks it's depression and I can't even repeat what my mother thinks."

"I doubt you have anything."

"Are you kidding? Do you have any idea how many things are wrong with me? I can't even think straight," I say, while thumbing through the photographs of the launch cover and the ones of Chloe lying next to the man in the suit.

"No one would believe this stuff," Alex says, picking up the first page of my original slut article.

"I know. And the thing that bothers me even more than the fact that the entire editorial department is working against me, full-time, is how my sister got saddled with the absolute worst mother-in-law on the planet," I say, holding up the photograph of Chloe jumping on the bed. "Somehow I think Anita had something to do with these photos, don't you?"

"She does hate your sister, but it seems like such a waste of her time."

"As soon as I'm better, I'm going to write an article on mother-in-laws. I want to open up that bag of worms right away, before Anita has a chance to get her claws any deeper into my poor sister's skin."

"I think you should be worrying more about your own problems with Anita at the moment."

"I can take care of Anita. She doesn't scare me. But I might not always be around to take care of Chloe, and I need to nip this in the bud for her before I totally fall apart and become useless to everyone."

"You're not going to fall apart. You're going to get better. You just need some vitamins or something. And maybe a personal trainer. And who's sending you all these packages?" she asks, pointing to a little collection of small, brown, unopened boxes crammed into a corner behind the TV.

"Infomercials."

"Seriously? You didn't by any chance buy the ultimate chopper?"

"I did. I also got Proactiv and bareMinerals."

"I've wanted bareMinerals for so long! Let's open it."

"I don't want to. I'm returning it."

"Why? It blends in naturally with your own skin."

"I heard it's really messy."

"From who? Who do you even talk to? And what's the point of buying this stuff if you're not going to try it? Let's open it. If you don't like it, we'll return it. We'll just mark the reason for the return as 'too messy.' "

I finally give in and let her try it because she's so desperate. I always picture her on Christmas morning as a kid with no presents. I'm this close to giving her my ultimate chopper but I really want it. In case I ever learn to cook.

Alex rips open the box and neatly stacks all the little tubs and tubes until she comes across the video. She's really enjoying herself.

"Can we watch the video?" she asks, organizing the little towers of blushes and powders. She's totally in awe of the packaging. It's breaking my heart.

"You can if you want to," I say, hoping she'll lose interest.

"You don't want to watch it? Don't you want to learn the proper way to 'dip, tap, and swipe?' "

"Not really. I'm missing *The Simpsons*. Is there any way you'd want to watch that instead?"

"Definitely not," she says. She walks over to my closet and comes out with a small standing mirror that I didn't even know I had. She puts in the DVD and sits down on the bed cross-legged with all her minerals lined up inside the box top, which she's using as a little tray. Then she turns to look at me. "Now, pay attention. I'm going to press Play."

"I can't believe you're falling for this," I say.

"You bought it!" she answers. Which is true. But at least I knew enough to want to return it as soon as it came.

"If you're not interested, why don't you go run around the block or something? You're so out of shape, Zoe, really. Go."

"You just want me to leave so I won't see how bad you are at putting on makeup."

"You can watch if you want. But I think you should spend this time more productively. Go take a shower or do some sit-ups."

As soon as the DVD starts playing, the phone rings and Ali turns it off. It's Michael.

"Listen, I was thinking, let's get married," he says, before I even have a chance to say my usual, "Who is this?"

"If it's that important to you, I promise I'll take a walk first thing tomorrow morning. You don't have to go to the trouble of marrying me just so I'll have to make my way down the aisle."

"Zoe, I want to get married."

"So, get married."

"I want to marry *you*. And I want to do it right away. I think it's crazy to wait."

"Why all of a sudden?" I ask.

"Is that Michael?" Alex asks.

"Is someone with you?" Michael asks.

"Yes, Alex is here. She came over to harass me."

"Zoe, I want you to think about this," Michael says.

"I have thought about it. You know how I feel about marriage. It's just a fascist form of crowd control designed to cut the population in half and rob individuals of their ability to think for themselves."

"We can create whatever kind of marriage we want."

"What's he saying?" Alex asks. I hold the phone out so she can hear.

"Zoe, you know it's the right thing to do. We have to face it sooner or later."

"Hold on a minute. I know what this is about. You think I'm pregnant too. I can't believe this."

"Oh my God, he's right. That's why you're so bloated!" Alex says. I continue holding the phone out so she can hear.

"I never said I thought you were pregnant, but if you are, or even if you aren't, I think it's time we start creating some sort of structured home life. We can't go on living without any sort of plans for the future."

"Or furniture," Alex whispers.

Alex picks up a picture of Michael that's leaning up against the wall. It's a black-and-white photo taken of him at the beach. No shirt, just the body with the ripped abs and the perfect face with the windswept hair. He's very tan and there's a tiny bit of sand on his arm. His face is turned to the camera with an expression that says, "I don't feel like having my picture taken, but for you, anything." It's an amazing shot of him. I can't even look at it.

"This is Michael?" Alex asks, tilting the photograph and her head.

"He doesn't really look like that," I whisper with my hand over the phone.

"Michael, we've been over this a million times. You can't expect me to just marry you out of the blue because you're wording it differently. We hardly know each other and you travel all the time. You've never even met Alex."

"Zoe, I've known you for five years and we've lived together for over a year. Believe me, I know you."

"Trust me, you don't."

The conversation goes around in circles until we finally hang up with nothing resolved.

When I put the phone down, Alex says, "I forgot to tell you. You made the worst dressed list in the magazine."

"Seriously? Who else made it?"

"Just you and Trai."

"Trai? Are you kidding? He's the best dresser in that whole magazine."

"When you're on the worst dressed list, that's your first clue that you're probably not the best judge."

"But he had those amazing boots I wanted so badly and that black jacket with the hairy buttons."

"True, the buttons fashioned from human hair were somewhat of a novelty, but the last few weeks he's taken to wearing a kilt and a mink stole."

"Guys look great in skirts!"

"Again, not your call."

"I actually miss him. I bet he misses me too. I should call him one of these days."

"Don't bother, he's in the midst of coming out and probably wants to be left alone."

"Trai is gay now? I've only been gone a couple of days! And I thought he was in love with Chloe."

"People change."

"Just like that?"

"Apparently," she says, looking at me accusingly.

"Whatever. I can't think about this stuff anymore. Are you sure you don't want to watch something with me? How about Suze Orman?"

"Is she on now?"

"No, I bought the tapes. How do they come up with the worst-dressed list anyway?"

"Blaire and Sloane put a suggestion box under the receptionist's desk to keep the voting anonymous and to keep Dan from finding out. They do it behind his back every year and every year he freaks out when he realizes they did it again. It's amazing what you can get done around here if you know the right people."

"So, what you're saying is that they managed to slip by the type director that you personally appointed."

"The ex-type director. He's since been replaced."

"Impressive."

"That's nothing compared to what else I have to tell you."

"Does it involve me winning any more awards?"

"Nope. It involves a plan that I've devised to finally repay Blaire and Sloane for all of this," she says, pointing to the stuff strewn all over my bed.

"What about Ruth and Anita?"

"I can't be bothered with Ruth. She hardly has any fight left in her. And there's nothing I can do about Anita; it's her magazine. It's Blaire and Sloane I'm after at the moment.

"I realize Dan was right when he said that firing them during our relaunch is probably not in our best interest, and as much as I've spent my whole life trying to rise above girls like Blaire and Sloane, it's time for them to get a taste of their own medicine."

"I'm not sure I want to hear this."

"Don't worry. I'm not going to hurt them. I simply arranged a little double-dating assignment for my brother, that's all."

"He really comes in handy, doesn't he?" I say, looking down at myself to see what I'm wearing. "So what's your plan?"

"Well, his first assignment is to go out on a date with Blaire. He'll take her to this really cool restaurant downtown where he knows everyone, and he'll introduce her to all his friends as 'someone special.' Then he'll take her to his friend's loft, where a bunch of models will be hanging out, and when all the girls start hitting on him, he'll walk over to Blaire and put his arms around her. Then he'll helicopter her over to my beach house, which he'll pretend is his, and in the morning they'll have the mandatory champagne and chocolate-covered strawberries and sex on the beach.

"Sadly, their date will end there because that's when he'll tell her that he has to meet his investment banker for lunch because he's planning to buy the Chrylser Building and he doesn't want to hold up the deal simply because he might be falling in love. Then he'll helicopter her back, deliver her to her door, and go get Sloane, who he'll have met two days before, while accidentally bumping into her in the cafeteria."

"You have a beach house?"

"Yeah, but I never use it. It's just an investment property."

"So then what?"

"So then he'll knock on Sloane's door and tell her he's been thinking about her nonstop, ever since he bumped into her, and can he take her out for brunch. She'll agree and off they'll go to the airport. They'll fly to L.A., stay in the Beverly Hills Hotel, and have brunch at the Ivy the next day. They'll spend the rest of the day out by the pool. He'll have bought her a new bikini at the gift shop, and he'll arrange for her to get a pedicure out by the pool. When they fly back home, it will be because he's meeting Donald Trump to discuss building a promenade from Manhattan to New Jersey, with shops and restaurants, that he's seriously thinking of naming 'Sloane's Way.'

"He'll drop her off at home, tell her he's fallen madly in love, and then he'll probably go home and sleep for twenty-four hours because he gets the worst jet lag of anyone I've ever known.

"When he finally wakes up, he's going to send them both flowers, but he'll put the wrong name on each card. At that point, I've instructed him to go find Courtney. He's agreed to reduce his debt by fifteen percent simply by maintaining some sort of relationship with Courtney for at least three months, which should be no problem because he pretty much fell in love with her when he met her in my office with Ruth that day.

"You're sick. You worked this whole thing out all because of the way they've been treating me? Really, Alex, you didn't have to do this."

"It was the least I could do. And truthfully, I did it for my-self too. Somehow, all of this is such a painful reminder of what I went through as a kid. Seeing you go through it as an adult is just too much for me. I can only sit back for so long. I'm still the same girl I always was, except now I have the means to even the score. I tried to outthink the girls who were mean to me when I was little, but for some reason they were always way ahead of me. I couldn't think like them so I couldn't defend myself. But now I can.

"But after this assignment, I have to get my brother another job. He's having way too much sex and it's getting on my nerves."

By now she's opened all the little tubs of makeup and she's absentmindedly brushing them all over her face and legs. She knows less about makeup than I do.

"That's not for your legs," I tell her.

"So when are you going to agree to marry Michael?" she asks, as she continues to color in her knees.

"You can't tell from that picture, but he's a Republican," I say.

"You're right, you can't tell at all," she says, dipping the contouring brush into "the glow" bronzer and brushing it on the top of her shoes.

"You're getting that brush dirty!" I say.

"So? You're not going to use it."

"But now I can't even return it."

"So, I'll just keep it, then." She looks up at me. It looks like she rubbed mud all over her chin.

"That's not the right color for you."

"Too dark?" she asks.

"Go look in the mirror, and you tell me."

While she's in the bathroom, she yells out to me, "You know, I hate to bring this up, but I can't start targeting any potential advertisers for the July issue until I know what we're doing. Were you serious about that mother-in-law idea?"

"Absolutely, but I'd like to save that one. I think we should lighten things up a bit for the next couple of months. I've been working on some ideas the last few days, but I haven't come up with anything really special. I know something will come to me, but so far everything I write sounds so blah. Maybe I'm just being too hard on myself."

"Without even seeing anything you've written, I'm sure that's exactly what's happening. You're *always* too hard on yourself. Let me hear some of your ideas. I bet they're great."

I hesitate for a minute because I really don't think they're that good. I'm always so distracted by TV lately, it's so hard for me to concentrate on anything else. I open my laptop and force myself to call them out to her.

"Okay ready?"

"Yup."

"Okay, the first few are somewhat of a departure from my usual stuff, but I guess they're still empowering on some level."

"Just read them already!"

"Okay, here we go.

Fun and Easy Recipes for a Rainy Day Using Bread

How to Make a Decorative Placemat Using Unusual and Unique Items Commonly Found Around the Home, such as: Pieces of Cloth from Your Discards, Old Playing Cards, Molted Feathers (if you have a bird, that is) and Colorful Pencil Shavings. All You Need is a Laminator and Your Imagination!

How to Get Started Buying Stocks

"They're not good, are they?" I call out.

"Read me a few more," she says.

"Okay. *How to Make Millions in Real Estate with No Money Down.*

I give them a toll free number with this one, but I won't bother to read it now."

"Thanks."

"What?"

"Nothing. Keep reading."

"Really? Okay, let's see. This one is pretty good, *How to Learn a Foreign Language in Ten Days and Land Your Dream Job as an Interpreter or a Legal Aid or Another Job of Your Choice.*"

Alex isn't saying anything so I walk over to the bathroom and open the door. She's still washing her face.

"What's the matter?" I ask.

"Nothing, why?"

"I was expecting you to say something."

"Like what?"

"Like whether you like them or not. Never mind. I knew they weren't good."

"They're not bad. The one about making a placemat out of a bird was my favorite."

"I knew they were terrible."

"Read me the one about the bird again."

When she comes out of the bathroom, her face is all blotchy from scrubbing it and from trying not to laugh. She packs up the bareMinerals and goes into the kitchen to look for something to eat.

"If you want to eat something we have to order in," I say, avoiding any discussion about the fact that she thought my ideas were comical enough to cause her face to discolor.

"It's almost as though you had a lobotomy," she says.

"I'm pretty sure they stopped giving those."

We sit down and try to think of some article ideas that are more in keeping with the theme of the magazine, but I can't concentrate. I'm too hungry. We order a pizza, even though I thought I already ordered one this morning. Within fifteen minutes my new friend Harold shows up with a large pie and a big, friendly smile on his face.

"Hey, Harold," I say. "How's it going?"

"Not bad. How's my girl today?"

"Good, good. Did you miss me?"

Alex looks at me as though I've just said something very stupid. Little does she know, Harold and I have a little system.

"So, Harold, how many deliveries do you have after mine?" I ask, leaning against the door jam and unbuttoning the top few buttons of my flannel shirt, revealing my dark cleavage, which, as I gaze down, is starting to look more and more like an ass.

"Not that many," he says, all drooly and nineteen.

Alex walks over to stand between us. I never realized how annoying she is. Between this and that overblown dating scam, I'm starting to think she's a little overly protective.

"Alex, can you excuse us, please?"

"What the hell are you doing?" she whispers.

"I'm getting us more pizzas, now leave me alone," I say, stamping my foot with the fake smile still plastered neatly on my face.

"So, Harold, would you say you have somewhere in the vicinity of two or even three pizzas to spare?"

"That depends, how many do you want?" he asks.

"All of them," I say, touching his nose with one dainty out-stretched finger.

"You're sick," Alex says.

He does have a lot of pimples, I must admit, but I'm starving lately.

As soon as he steps away to go get the pizzas, Alex makes some remark about how she can't believe I didn't at least throw the Proactiv into the deal. Obviously she has no experience seducing pizza-delivery boys.

Harold comes back up with three pizzas! I pay him lovingly

and he leaves. We sit down on the floor and I take a slice out of the first box and hand it to Alex; I stack the rest of the boxes on my lap.

"One of these days Harold is going to get the wrong idea, don't you think?"

"Michael's coming home in a few days. From then on, whenever I order a pizza, I'll just hide in the bathroom or something."

"You're disgusting. I can't believe you would flirt with some pimply kid for a free pizza when you have a guy who looks like that begging you to marry him," she says, pointing at Michael's picture.

"I know but I couldn't live with myself if I actually ordered three pizzas, and Michael isn't as great as you think he is. He's getting more and more conservative by the minute. I can already picture my life if I marry him. Kids, a minivan, nosy neighbors, pie-eating contests—"

"I think you might want to hurry up and get used to the idea of having kids." She tries to take the top box away from me, but I hold on tight. Somehow she manages to slip her hand in and takes another piece.

"I'm not pregnant! What's wrong with everyone lately? Haven't any of you ever seen a fat person before? If I were pregnant, my stomach would be bigger than the rest of me, don't you think?"

"Not necessarily. Some women carry in the back."

"Ah, so that explains why so many babies are delivered by liposuction these days."

"I'm just saying there's an excellent chance that you're pregnant even though you don't actually look pregnant in the traditional sense."

"Believe me. I'm not the type. I just can't stop eating. Everyone looks a little pregnant when they're fat."

"That's true, especially pregnant people."

"I can't believe we're even having this conversation. It's absolutely ridiculous. And besides, I have a million other things to worry about."

"Like the fact that you need to come back to work?" Alex asks.

"Alex, you know I can't come back. Look at me."

"Plenty of fat people work, Zoe."

"I mean, look how sick I am!"

"Well, it just so happens I think I found a way to make you feel better," she says, trying to get comfortable with her back against the wall. I should really buy a chair.

She reaches into her pocket and pulls out a little business card. "I found *the* best place for extensions. The guy is supposedly a genius—the hair guru for ladies who lunch," she says, tightening her pin-straight, I don't have a Semitic bone in my body, ponytail.

"Blaire was telling everyone about him the other day. Apparently they all got themselves appointments already."

She hands me a card that says *Leonardo & You* in curly gold script.

"Would you stop referring to my sickness as my hair, and what exactly about this place made you think I would ever go there?" I ask, turning the frou frou card over in my hand and flicking it across the room.

"I don't know. Maybe the fact that you can walk in wearing a ski cap and walk out with perfectly straight hair down to your waist."

I get up to get the card I so recklessly flung across the room and sprint to the phone.

Chapter 17

"I'm so sorry, Ms. Rose, but I don't have you in the book."

"Then look in another book because my appointment is definitely for today."

"We only have one appointment book and you're not in it. Is it possible that you're scheduled for *next* Tuesday?"

"Yes, it's possible—if the receptionist wrote it down wrong. Can I see that book?" I ask, and grab it off her desk.

That's funny. I'm not in here. I toss the book back on her desk and go and sit down.

"Excuse me, would you like to reschedule because I'd be more than hap—"

"What for?" I ask.

I'm in a really bad mood. I hope it doesn't show.

"Well, it's just that, if you'd like an actual appointment, you're going to need to schedule one."

"I *have* an appointment. Someone just neglected to write it down. But don't worry, I'm not mad or anything and I won't tell the doctor—if that's what you're worried about. Just squeeze me in whenever there's a little lull. I'll just be over here napping." I look around. There are about thirty pregnant

women staring at me. Most of them are scratching themselves. I can't look. So I close my eyes.

The receptionist wakes me up by whispering my name over
and over again until I can't take it anymore.

"What? What?"

"The doctor will see you now," she says.

"I'm sorry, but can you wake me up in like fifteen
minutes?"

"Ms. Rose, the doctor was kind enough to squeeze you in.
You might as well take the appointment or you're going to
lose it."

"How long was I sleeping?" I ask.

"Three and a half hours."

"You made me wait three and a half hours?"

My gynecologist, Dr. Stacy Luden, is an obese woman with a
big sloppy smile, short greasy hair, and a little moustache just
around the corners of her mouth. The only reason I go to her
is because she's so physically unappealing, I'm not embarrassed to show her my vagina.

"So, Zoe, how are you?"

"Do you really want to know?"

"I really want to know," she says smiling. You'd think God
would have made her beautiful, but oh no. He decided to design the most hideous face he could think of for the nicest person in the world.

"Well, for starters, I'm a little itchy," I say, revealing the
scabs on my thighs, "And I think I'm losing my memory and
a good deal of my mind as well. My vision is sort of blurry,
my gums hurt, I'm also very tired and irritable and lately
everything sort of smells funny, particularly certain people.

I'm also under a tremendous amount of stress at work. In fact, I didn't even go the last couple of days. I just stayed home and ate. Oh, and I need to have sex at least three or four times a day."

"Let's get a urine sample and then why don't you come back in here and step on the scale so we can get a weight on you? In the meantime, when was your last period?"

I wasn't even halfway through my list of symptoms. I could have anything, for all she knows.

"I have no idea. I stopped keeping track a long time ago. It's always been so erratic. The last time I came to see you was because I hadn't had my period for more than a day or two in years, and then I stopped getting it altogether."

"I remember," she says looking at my chart. "So have you had a period since you came to see me last?"

"I can't remember. How long ago was I here?"

"Let's see, your last visit was January twenty-seventh, two thousand one."

"And what month are we in now, if you don't mind me asking?"

She hands me the cup with a sympathetic smile and I go to the bathroom to pee in it. I try to pee as daintily as possible, but within two seconds the cup overflows and I have to spill some out so the nurse won't think I'm manly.

I hand over my urine sample and lie down on the table for my exam.

After what feels like a minute or two, my own snoring and the sound of Dr. Luden's voice wakes me up.

"Zoe, Zoe, you need to wake up now."

"Dr. Luden, what are you doing here?" I ask, looking around.

"I work here," she says good humoredly, "and you and I

need to have a little talk. Get dressed and meet me in my office."

"What about my exam?"

"You slept through it and passed with flying colors."

On the way home in the cab, I call Michael, and then Chloe, and then my mom, and then Alex, and then just before my battery runs out, I call Harold. But then I call back and cancel my order. I don't feel very well.

Chapter 18

"How can this be happening? Kids hate me!" I say, waking myself up. I can't believe how loud I must have said that. I look over at Michael pretending to be asleep with a big grin on his face.

"Stop looking so happy," I say and punch his arm. He pretends I really hurt him and jumps all over me.

"I'm sorry, Zoe, but I *am* happy. This is great news. We're going to be a family," he takes my face in his hands and kisses me.

"How could you kiss me at a time like this? You're so insensitive."

"I love you and we're going to have a baby."

"What about me? What about the fact that I didn't plan this or even *want* this? I feel like you tricked me into it."

"I don't think so. You're the one who wants to have sex constantly. I just go along with it to keep you quiet." He turns on his side and leans on his elbow to face me, but I refuse to look at him.

"Zoe, listen, I think you did want this. Otherwise you would have prevented it from happening. He puts his hand on my stomach and I bat it off. Then he puts it right back in the same exact spot. I let him leave it there this time, only because his hand is warm and who knows, maybe the baby likes him.

"I just thought since my periods were messed up, I wasn't really a candidate for this sort of thing."

"Really? You thought that? Then why did you keep a case of pregnancy tests in the bathroom?"

"I wanted to be sure. But then I ran out of them and I just, I don't know—did you discuss this with my mother, by any chance?"

"No, why?"

"You ask a lot of the same questions."

"That's because it's obvious what happened here, Zoe. You never used birth control. That was your choice."

"I'm allergic to latex, you know that."

"There are many other forms of birth control."

"I know, but they don't agree with me. Nothing does. I just didn't think it was possible. I really didn't. Whatever. What's done is done. Hopefully it won't affect my life that much. But what if the baby comes out like you?"

"You keep forgetting that you love me. And, yes, there's an excellent chance that the baby will come out like me and maybe even a little like you. Is that so bad? I mean, it's a risk, but I'm willing to take it."

"What if it comes out anti-gay marriage and pro-war?"

"All babies are anti-war and pro-gay marriage. So you have nothing to worry about."

"But what if it's anti-abortion?"

"Zoe!"

"Okay, I shouldn't have said that, but this whole thing isn't right. We're too different. We're going to confuse her. And I'm not prepared to give up my life for someone who, in fifteen years, is going to call me a square."

"No one uses that word anymore."

"That's what I thought too, but then I heard some kid say it, like, two days ago."

"Our kid won't talk to us like that, I can assure you."

"And if she does?"

"I'll tell him we don't allow that kind of language in our house."

"I already can't stand the way you're raising her."

"If it will make you happy, I won't talk to him at all, okay?"

"That *is* what I want, and that's why this is so wrong. I'm so afraid you're going to influence her."

"That's it. I've had it," he says, getting up. "I think it's time you put this in perspective so you can start enjoying it. Let me tell you what your problem is, okay? Your biggest fear is that this poor kid is going to one day grow up and think for himself. You're not worried that he'll think like me. You're worried that he won't think exactly like you."

"Her. I'm pretty sure it's a girl."

"Okay fine, her."

"The idea is to expose her to everything and let her decide. I exist and I'm not going anywhere, and my ideas exist and there are plenty of people out there who agree with me and you can't protect her from every single political viewpoint other than your own. Just accept that there is a person in there, not a magazine.

"You can't impose your viewpoints on her anymore than I can, because the first thing we're going to teach her is how to think for herself. And, at the same time, I'm going to teach you both how to be tolerant.

"Believe it or not, there's more to raising a baby than politics. It's about how she'll feel when she comes home from school and someone made fun of her hair and how we get her through that. And that she knows she can call us at any time of the night when she's out with some guy who ran out of gas and she has no money because she spent it all on pot and has no way home. That's what it's all about, Zoe."

"You read my diary!"

"I did not. I would never do that. You talk in your sleep all goddamn night. That's how I knew about the bills behind the toilet too. That was an excellent system you had going, by the way."

"I never knew that about myself. I wonder if our baby will talk in her sleep."

"I hope so. I hope she's exactly like you. I can't imagine anything better than living my life with you all over again, starting with the day you were born.

"That's how much I love you and that's what matters. It's not about who we voted for or anything I wrote in those books. It's about us. And her. And that's it."

"Promise you didn't read it?"

"I promise. And I know you believe me. And that's why we're going to get married. Because you know you can trust me. And because you love me. But mostly because you can trust me. So that's settled. We're getting married whether you like it or not."

"Isn't there anything you wish you could change about me before she's born?"

"I wish you weren't such a pain in the ass. Other than that, no."

As soon as he gets up to go in the shower, I reach under the bed and check my diary for clues. There are no mysterious fingerprints anywhere so I put it back under the mattress and resolve to find a better hiding place as soon as I can get up.

After his shower, Michael gets back into bed and props

himself up as if he's going to read. Then he reaches under his side of the mattress and pulls out a book.

"What are you reading?" I ask.

" *'What to Expect When You're Expecting.'* "

"How long have you been reading it?"

"I started it a few months ago."

"You knew I was pregnant a few months ago?"

"Not necessarily. You just asked me when I started reading the book and I told you."

"Michael, why would you be reading a pregnancy book unless you thought I was pregnant?"

"The truth is I was hoping you were."

"But you never actually said that you thought I might be pregnant."

"I honestly assumed you knew you were pregnant, but that you were just being weird about it. You're weird about everything. I just thought, 'So this is what she's like pregnant.' "

"So you went out and bought this, this *book*?" I pull it out of his hands and toss it out of his reach.

"I wanted to be prepared," he says and holds me back so he can reach in front of me to get his little girly book.

"*You* wanted to be prepared? What about me?" I grab the book out of his hand and randomly open to page 119 and begin reading aloud. " 'What you may be feeling physically: fatigue and sleepiness, a need to urinate frequently, nausea with or without vomiting, faintness and dizziness, heartburn, flatulence, bloating, food aversions and cravings, breast changes, clothes begin to feel tight, increased appetite' . . . I don't believe it, I'm a walking cliché."

"I wouldn't exactly call you a walking anything. Skip to the part where you get a dark line that starts at your belly button."

"No, thank you."

"No, seriously, just do it."

"Please. I want to die right now. Can you get me a book on what to expect when you're dying?"

"Stop it, Zoe, you should be reading this every month."

"You read it and fill me in on the good parts."

"Okay, fine with me. I love this book."

"Good. At least I don't have to worry about our baby being gay."

"I'm not gay! Not that there's anything wrong with it."

"Right now you look so gay, it's not even funny."

"Oh yeah, well at least I'm not the one with a moustache."

Believe it or not, this comment turns into a ridiculously careful wrestling match that culminates in the most amazing sex ever. I guess we're making enough love for three now. Sick as that sounds.

Chapter 19

Being pregnant at work is something I need to remind myself never to do again. Every time I get up from a meeting to walk to the bathroom, which is every couple of minutes, I can feel the editors laughing at me. I know I look comical waddling around here like this, but I would never laugh at someone in my condition.

"You left your feed bag," Sloane says as I get up and push my chair in for the tenth time during this meeting.

"Thanks," I say, grabbing it from her on my way out.

Alex has called an emergency damage-control meeting while Dan is out of the office. Apparently we didn't get a very good response from our advertisers to our "Wiccans in the Workplace" issue. In retrospect, I want to kick myself for not following through with my home-crafts idea.

I thought the wiccan theme would grab the attention of an edgier audience and give us a sort of cult following, which would have opened up a whole new world of potential advertisers, but all it did was scare the hell out of everyone and run us even farther into the ground. As soon as we started working on the issue, Blaire and Sloane started leaving me little presents in my office, such as the horrible little monkey claw

I flushed down the toilet and the little vile of blood they purchased on eBay.

When I get back from the ladies' room, everyone is staring at Alex as though she's lost her mind. She's trying so hard to put a positive spin on the mess I've made, I can't even look at her. Everything I've tried at this magazine has been a miserable failure—and I think I smell spaghetti and meatballs, if I'm not mistaken.

"While I was in the ladies' room, I had an idea," I say.

"That's really great? Can we go now?" Blaire asks Alex, ignoring me.

"What's your idea, Zoe?" Alex asks, ignoring Blaire.

"I was just thinking that it might be interesting if we take a more psychological approach to our ongoing discussion of girl behavior. Perhaps we could interview some psychologists and lay off the humor for a while. We could focus on a different type of behavior each month and get some real professional opinions on why girls do what they do to one another." The tone of my voice is so tense, I have to stop talking before I even finish my thought.

"Um, I think *Psychology Today* already tried this brilliant idea," Sloane says.

"Well, I wasn't suggesting that we copy *Psychology Today*. My idea was to focus exclusively on girl behavior, as we've been doing all along."

"Oh, I'm sorry. I must have misunderstood. So what you're saying is that, as a last resort, you'd like to try boring our readers to death. Is that right?" Blaire asks. Sloane gives her a high five and I can see Alex is reaching her breaking point. Blaire and Sloane are a lot meaner when Dan's not around.

The meeting drags on until Courtney raises her hand and offers to read all of our palms. At that point, pretty much everyone excuses themselves and heads back to their respective offices. I would get up too, but I don't really feel like it. As soon as everyone leaves, Alex helps me out of my chair and I slowly make my way back to my office after another quick stop in the ladies' room. The days are getting longer and more depressing with every failed issue. I just wish I could think of something.

My phone is ringing. There's no doubt about it, but it's impossible for me to answer it. I'm wedged in so tight behind my desk I might have cut off my circulation. I try to push myself free with my feet but they're both asleep. Somehow I manage to inch my fingers across the desk and pick up the phone. Another little miracle.

"It's me," Chloe murmurs into the phone.

"Why are you murmuring?" I ask.

"Please don't tell anyone but I think I broke both my legs."

"Okay, I won't tell anyone but should I call an ambulance?"

"No, I'm fine. I can still walk. It's just very painful."

"If you can walk, then I'm pretty sure your legs aren't broken. You weren't skydiving, by any chance, were you?"

"Of course not. I gave that up months ago."

"You didn't like it?"

"Not so much, no."

"Did you ever try it?"

"Not really."

"Where are you now?"

"I'm in Colorado. I flew out here to learn how to snowboard, and then Dan just showed up out of nowhere last night to surprise me."

"Snowboarding is a very dangerous sport, especially if you're totally uncoordinated. Exactly where are you right now and where's Dan?"

"He's out on the slopes. He picked up the snowboarding thing right away. He's a skier so I guess he had somewhat of an advantage over me."

"That and the fact that he can stand up straight without holding on to anything. Are there patrol guys out there? Has anyone been notified of your condition and whereabouts?"

"What do you mean?"

"Chloe, someone has to get you off that mountain and get you immediate medical attention. You should be on the phone with ski patrol, not me."

"Zoe, I'm in the gift shop."

"You're not stranded on the mountain in the middle of nowhere?"

"No, of course not. I never even made it to the mountain. It's freezing out."

"So then how did you break your legs?"

"Buckling my boots. As soon as I had them buckled the guy told me to bend my knees and lean all the way forward. So I leaned forward, but I forgot to bend my knees, so I basically fell head first and then I remembered to bend my knees, so they hit the ground first and I literally heard them both crack."

"So, what you're saying is that you broke both your knees?"

"Oh, hold on just a minute. That's better. I just straightened them both out. They probably just stiffened up for a few minutes. They hardly hurt at all anymore. That's a relief. I really scared myself for a second there."

"Are you still wearing the boots?"

"Yeah, I think I might get them."

"What for?"

"For when I go snowboarding. I should probably get a pair of après-ski boots too. Of all the ski shops I've been to in the last few months, this one has *the* best merchandise. I really had to do a lot of research for the performance-footwear series I'm working on, but after today, I think I have enough to finish the whole thing."

"What's the latest article about?"

"How Gore-Tex changed my life."

"Shouldn't it be, 'How Gore-Tex Almost Maimed Me?' "

"No, absolutely not. The leg-breaking incident was totally my fault. But you just gave me another article idea. It will be all about how it's important to take responsibility for your own mistakes—when it comes to purchasing boots. Remind me to write that down.

"Anyway, the article isn't really about me. It's about this woman who thinks she's too short so she walks around in really uncomfortable high heels all the time, even at home. But then she signs up for this hiking-skiing-snowboarding vacation weekend to meet new and interesting people, even though she's not that athletic. After purchasing her first pair of Gore-Tex boots, she suddenly feels as though anything is possible because she's no longer in pain or wasting all of her mental and physical energy on trying to balance and stay dry. And surprisingly enough, the boots give her just a little bit of height too. The next thing she knows, she's trying things she's been rejecting all her life—because she's always been afraid of how she looks in flats—like snowshoeing for example. Anyway, one day she's outside hiking up a small hill in her backyard, in her new all-terrain mountain-climbing boots and she just keeps walking, right through her yard, and then right through her neighbor's yard, and to make a long story short, she never comes back."

"How does it end?"

"She opens up her own stationery store."

"I knew you were going to say that."

"Really? Dan thought it was a total surprise. Anyway, I think he really likes it. He said if we don't nail anything down for September, he might run it!"

"That's great, Chloe. It sounds very inspiring."

As much as I can't believe Dan is willing to publish something like that, I'm still happy for her. I know how much this means to her and my ideas aren't exactly winning us any awards.

"He wants you to read it first, though, because it's very different than the articles we've been printing lately. I was hoping to bring it over tomorrow night, if that's okay. We're heading out of here in a few hours. I can't wait to get home.

"We're both dying to see the baby . . . and your new extensions."

"I don't have either of those things yet."

"I know you don't have the baby. I want to see you *carrying* the baby. I haven't seen you in so long."

"It's not really a baby yet, Chloe. It's still just a bloody wad."

"See how maternal you're becoming? You don't call it mucous anymore. You definitely have a confirmed hair appointment, though, right?"

"I think so. I mean, of course I do. I'm just not sure exactly when it is."

"I think you said it was this Saturday."

"I said it was Saturday?"

"I think so, but you should call to make sure. I'll see you tomorrow night."

As soon as I hang up, I dig out the pregnancy book and look up "memory loss." And sure enough, here it is on page 187: "Continued Absentmindedness." I can't believe how well

I'm sticking to the book. It's almost like I'm normal for the first time in my life. Wait, what's this? It says, "Colostrums leaking and swollen labia."

Well, at least that explains the sensation of sitting on a pair of socks, and I'm certainly looking forward to the day my breasts begin spewing. This is all very pretty.

I'm trying to figure out what I should wear to go see Leonardo when there's a knock on my door and Alex yells, "Let me in." When I open the door she's all pulled together and ready to go.

"You're not ready? Your appointment is in a half hour."

"You're coming with me?"

"I'm not letting you go to that place alone."

"Can we stop off and eat first?"

"I brought snacks," she says, taking a bag of donuts out of her purse.

"I wonder if I should get dressed up for this place," I say, trying to estimate how many donuts are in the bag.

"Yeah, you should wear a dress or something."

"I'm the shape of an egg and you're telling me to put on a dress? I can't even picture that."

"That's because you neglected to buy any maternity clothes. They specifically make clothes in the shape of an egg for people in your condition."

"Well, for your information, they don't make maternity clothes in a children's size twelve."

"Just wear what you're wearing."

"I'm in my underwear."

"Oh, I thought you were wearing some sort of pregnancy exercise clothes."

"I don't exercise. I just happen to be wearing support hose and a sports bra. Two sports bras to be exact."

"Well then put on a big T-shirt over all that and let's go," she says with her mouth full.

She's already eating one of the donuts and I'm starting to feel uncomfortably possessive of the ones that are left. If she eats another one, there's an excellent chance I might start crying.

"How many donuts are left in there?"

"A ton. Get dressed."

I'm not sure if I look okay or not. Alex isn't really very helpful in the clothing department. She wears pretty much the same thing every day to work, and on the weekends she only wears jeans and a white T-shirt. She has six pairs of the same jeans and about a million white T-shirts. Sometimes she alternates with a gray T-shirt, but that's it in terms of variety. I should really develop a foolproof system like that.

I can't stand the way she's rushing me so I tell her to go downstairs and get us a cab while I finish getting ready.

I have no idea what to put on here, so I throw on one of Michael's button-downs over my support hose and top it all off with my ballet slippers and hat. I guess this is good enough.

When I get downstairs, she's already waiting for me in the taxi with the door open. It takes me a few minutes to get situated. Once I'm in, I can't reach the door so she has to lean all the way over to close it for me. The whole situation makes me feel like a big fat baby. As soon as the cab starts moving, Alex says, "You're not wearing any pants."

"I know. That's what I was trying to tell you. You're the one who said to just put a shirt over what I was wearing."

"I thought that putting on pants was a given."

"Well, it's too late now. Doesn't this big shirt make it look like I'm wearing a dress?"

"No, it looks like you're not wearing pants."

"Who cares? No one will notice."

As soon as we enter the doors of *Leonardo and You,* I notice that everyone here looks like they're dressed for a dinner party.

"Can I help choo ladies, my name eees Eduardo?"

Eduardo looks like a bullfighter in those white pants.

"This is Zoe Rose. She's here to see Leonardo," Alex says. "She's getting fusion extensions and she accidentally left her pants at home. We're both terribly sorry," she says, trying to sound like we belong here.

"Don't gworry about eenythink. You are both lava-ly." Eduardo says, dipping at the knee and offering me his sweaty, perfumed palm to shake. "Please, come and seet down. Leonardo wheel be here soon." As we're following Eduardo, I can't help noticing that Alex is walking like she has two wooden legs.

"Why are you marching?"

"Stop talking!" she whispers back."

"Alex, we're not in school."

"Shhh!"

"Can I get choo sometheeng to dreenk?" Eduardo asks, rolling his *r.* I can already tell he thinks Alex and I are here by mistake and he's just playing along.

"Nothing for me, thank you," Alex says.

"You wouldn't happen to have a milkshake back there by any chance, would you?" I ask.

"A meelkshake? But, of course. Eats no trrrouble at tall. Just geeve me a moment," he says and swishes away with his shiny black hair swinging all over the place.

"How could you ask him to get you a milkshake? He meant a soda. Now he has to order it."

"So? It's just a milkshake. It's not like I asked him to go slaughter a cow."

"Asking for a milkshake is almost as ridiculous. What's wrong with you?"

"What's wrong with *me*? You're the one who's a nervous wreck. I'm just trying to enjoy myself."

"Since when do you enjoy yourself?"

I look around the place. It's exactly what I was expecting. Lavish décor, classical music, and every single person here has blond hair. What a freak show. Chloe always wonders how she'd look as a blonde. I think her coloring isn't quite right, but mine is perfect. I've never admitted that to myself before, but it's true. I see it so clearly now as I gaze in the mirror, tilting my hat to the side.

"Stop staring at yourself!" Alex whispers in my ear.

"I'm looking in the mirror! That's what it's here for."

"But you're staring," she whispers.

"What the hell is the matter with you? Haven't you ever been to a hair salon before?"

"Of course I have. Not like this, though."

"Well, hello, you must be Zoe Rose. It's wonderful to meet you."

"And you must be Leonardo," I say.

Leonardo is wearing black leather pants, a loosely unbuttoned silk shirt, false teeth, and several layers of self-tanner. He has shoulder-length blond hair, which he has pulled straight back into a little ponytail, and he's obviously had lip implants, a face lift, and all of his body hair, freckles, and accent removed.

"I must tell you something, Zoe. Your appointment was for last week. We tried several times to reach you but we never leave a voice mail because we value our clients' privacy more than our appointment book."

"Is this place a secret or something?"

"No, it's just that some women are very private about their hair."

"Why?" I ask, as yet another tall, thin, attractive homosexual carrying a wig in each hand whizzes over to a little old lady with a fifty-pound diamond on her finger.

"Oh, I see," I say.

"Exactly," he says, with a mischievous little grin.

"Oh, wait a minute! Now I see what happened! My gynecologist appointment was today! I can't get anything straight anymore. I'm pregnant by the way, in case you were wondering why I'm dressed so inappropriately," I explain.

"Oh congratulations, my dear! This is the perfect time for you to get extensions. You shouldn't have to bother with your hair. You should spend all your time celebrating," he says, nonchalantly slipping off my hat.

I can just imagine Leonardo and Eduardo on the Italian Riveria with their tiny bikinis and shaven legs celebrating absolutely everything.

"Leonardo, come queeckly. I just woke up."

"Oh! Congratulations, Eduardo. This calls for a toast."

"Oh! Look at that! I just lost an eyelash."

"Ah! Let's toast again!"

Everyone here looks so tan and rested. Their lives must be one big extravagant party and here I am without pants.

"What do you think?" he says, looking at my reflection in the mirror. "Would you like to be a gorgeous, honey blonde?"

Would I?

"I think that would be much better for you. Your color is too harsh for your face. A woman in your condition should be glowing all the time." He holds out his arms as though he's preparing to conduct an orchestra.

The orchestra that is my new life. I hear our imaginary champagne glasses clinking together, in honor of the fact that I will soon be a gorgeous, glowing, honey blond.

From this day forward I'm going to live my life differently. I'm going to become more like Leonardo and Eduardo. Every moment will be a celebration. I'm tired of being such a grouch.

I look over at Alex being ushered into the room on the other side of the reception area by a man who has Jennifer Aniston's original *Friends* haircut, and who's just offered to wash her hair and give her "a blow." She's motioning to me with her head that something is happening a few feet in front of her. I lean forward to see what it is, and right before my eyes are Blaire and Sloane in all their tall, magnificently leggy splendor. As hard as it is to fathom, they look even more stunning and imposing here than they do in the office. Leonardo rushes to greet them knowing full well that their presence gives his salon an aura of coolness that money alone can't buy. I can only imagine that he'll detain them for as long as possible in hope that they'll take pity on him and let him do their hair for free.

As much as I regret that I will soon have to have a conversation with them I've already mentally calculated the rungs on Leonardo's preferred-client ladder I'll leap as soon as they acknowledge my existence.

"Zoe? Is that you? I can't believe it," Blaire says.

"In the flesh," I answer.

"Oh my God. What are you doing here?" Sloane asks.

"I'm getting extensions."

"So are we," Blaire says.

"I've been meaning to ask you why you cut your hair so short in the first place," Sloane says.

"I didn't cut it on purpose. I used a hair clip that I found in my drawer that oddly enough doubled as a razor."

"Are you serious? I thought they confiscated all of those clips," Sloane says.

"I'm afraid there was one left."

"I can't imagine what I'd do if that ever happened to me. I think I'd probably kill myself," Blaire says matter-of-factly.

"Oh, I totally would too," Sloane agrees, confirming once again that they are of one mind, particularly concerning matters of life and death.

"Well, let's not get carried away. It's only hair," I say.

"If it's only hair, what are you doing here?" Sloane asks.

"I'm fixing a problem."

"But you just said it's not that big of a deal. So why bother fixing it?" she asks, folding her arms.

"I fix a lot of things that I wouldn't kill myself over. For example, when my shower drain gets clogged, I call a plumber. If he's late for some reason, I don't exactly swallow a bottle of pills."

"Well, at least you won't have to worry about clogging your drain anymore." They link arms and instinctively walk away on cue. Leonardo is still standing there listening. He calls out to one of his assistants to set Blaire and Sloane up at the sink to get them washed. Then he slowly walks toward me. He turns my chair around so we are both facing the mirror and he whispers in my ear. "Don't worry. Don't worry about anything. We're going to make you a star," he says.

Clink.

Leonardo says he'll be right back and sure enough, he returns a few minutes later with a tray of hair in a full array of colors. I immediately spot the red sections and ask him if he plans to use any of those.

"Those? No! Those are red," he says. "We don't want any red."

I adore him.

Then he points with the back of his long-tipped comb to three colors he has personally selected for my extensions. Light honey brown, honey blond and golden blond.

"Now the question is how do you want to wear your extensions today? Because I can make them stick straight, wavy, or very curly," he says and wisks off my hat.

"Look at those gorgeous curls," he says. "Why do you wear them so short?" he asks.

"It's a long, sad story," I say, and then proceed to tell him the whole thing, beginning with the outfit I wore to kindergarten.

"How about if we transform you into an enchanting mermaid?" he suggests.

"You mean curly?"

"Of course. I will work with your own natural beauty."

"But I'm getting fake hair. Why bother with natural beauty at a time like this? This might be the only chance I ever get in my entire life to have long straight hair. I want the straight ones," I say.

"Listen to me. Let me make them curly and then you can always straighten them at home." Some little man walks over to me with my milkshake and I reach out to grab it from him before he has a chance to put it down. I take a huge gulp and punch my chest a few times to help it down.

"Forget that whole enchanted mermaid thing for now, okay? I want straight blond hair." There. I've said it. Talk about closure.

"I understand, my darling, straight it is. Whatever will make you smile, I will do."

"Thank you," I belch.

A few minutes later Blaire and Sloane appear with their wet hair combed out. Leonardo motions for them to be seated several seats away from me, but I can still hear everything they're saying.

He snaps his fingers and two little Mexican women appear from behind the sinks. He calls out some numbers that I assume refer to various extension colors and tells them to get to work on Blaire and Sloane. Within seconds both stylists appear at their sides and begin parting both girls' hair into twelve perfectly symmetrical sections. I imagine these two little women painstakingly working with tiny strands of hair for ten hours a day, six days a week and I can't help wondering how meagerly the Blaires and Sloanes tip them when they're done.

As the stylist begins weaving the extensions into Blaire's hair, Sloane announces to *her* stylist that she'd like something a little more spiky because she's tired of looking perfect all the time. "You can't imagine how boring it is," she says to the tiny woman who will be laboring at her roots for the next four hours, to earn what I hope is at least minimum wage. Somehow I doubt she gives a shit how it feels to be Sloane.

I can hear Blaire telling Sloane about Alex's brother's beach house and how incredible it felt to step outside the door only to find herself only a few yards away from the water. And how she had the best sex of her life the next morning on said private beach; and if she ever drinks another glass of champagne again, she'll just die. And the whole time, Sloane is interrupting her with the details of *her own boyfriend's* plans to build a bridge across the Hudson River with her name on it and how she can't wait to be invited to dine with the Trumps at Mar-A-Lago.

I feel myself dozing off as Leonardo begins working his comb through my curls, attempting to separate them in some sort of organized fashion. Every time he slides the comb down my scalp, I feel my unruly hairs spring back. I stare intently in the mirror, willing them to relax, but they just stare back at me, mocking me with their stubborn, willful pride. I finally give up and let myself doze off. I'm no match for them. I never was. Perhaps they'll listen to Leonardo.

When I wake up, I'm still sitting in the same chair, but I'm facing away from the mirror. It takes me a few seconds to realize where I am. I look down at my phone, which is in my lap. It's six o'clock at night. How is this possible? I look around. Blaire and Sloane are gone but I immediately spot Alex chatting away with the handsome guy who offered to blow her.

But something is different.

"Alex! What did you do?" I call over to her.

"I know. I can't believe it either. What do you think?" she says, rushing over to me.

"Wow. You're a blonde!" I say.

"So are you," she says, and turns my chair around to face the mirror. And there I am, with perfectly straight, honey blond hair down to my waist.

"I look like Lady Godiva," I say.

"You look fantastic!" Alex's new hairdresser says. No wonder she warmed up so quickly over there.

"What's your name?" I ask him.

Ten bucks it's Antonio.

"I'm Claudio, and you have just changed your life."

He air kisses me somewhere near both cheeks.

"Where's Leonardo?" I ask.

"He is in the back room with a client. You've been done for a while, but he refused to let us wake you."

"I missed everything."

"There's my sleeping beauty. What do you think of your hair?" Leonardo comes running over. Someone should make a ballet out of this place.

"How did you get my hair so straight? Did you chemically straighten it?"

"No, of course not, my love. I wouldn't do that without your permission. I used a hot iron."

He takes one of the hot irons from its little holster and begins wrapping the cord around its base. "Take this. It's my gift to you. You're going to need it," he says. "Now you are my most beautiful pregnant woman. Next we must give you a small trim, and you can go outside and show the world your beauty."

"A trim?"

"Just a little one, I promise, to make the ends more healthy looking."

"No, please. Don't touch it. I want every inch of it," I say, flinging it across my back."

Alex and I meet Eduardo at the reception area and he hands us our bills. Mine has three zeros but Alex's only has two. There must be some mistake.

"I think there's an extra zero here," I say. Eduardo takes the receipt from me to check it. "No, no my dear. Leonardo inseested that choo get two sets of extensions so next time, the second set wheel be washed and waiting. He only does theese for his most *especial* clients." He winks.

"I can't tell you how flattered I am," I say and show Alex

the bill. She covers her mouth and mumbles, "I'd suggest making a run for it, but I know you'd get caught."

"I hope you understand eat took three processes to get chore hair to match theese extensions," Eduardo continues, as I rummage through my bag.

"The amazing thing is that I slept through all three thousand dollars of them." The other amazing thing is that I can't find my checkbook. I look at Alex and whisper, "I forgot money."

She hands Eduardo her credit card and says, "Consider this your first mother's day present."

"I'm totally going to pay you back," I say.

"Don't be ridiculous. It's the least I can do for you."

"Three thousand dollars worth of fake hair is the least you can do for me?"

"Look at us, Zoe. When was the last time you felt like this? I never would have come here without you. Believe me, it's worth every penny," she says.

When we get outside it's pouring. I want to take my shirt off and put it over my head, but Alex is afraid I'll get arrested. Instead, she takes her jacket off and holds it over me, and I quickly stuff the hot iron into my panty hose. Nothing happens to her hair when it gets wet so she doesn't bother to cover it. By the time we get a taxi, we're both soaked.

Once we're seated in the cab, I look down at my wet, straight extensions and marvel at their beauty. Alex gives the driver our addresses while I feel around the top of my head.

Naturally my own hair is already showing its true character by wriggling itself as far away from the new hair as possible while blowing up like an angry balloon.

"How do I look now?" I ask Alex.

"Like a jelly fish."

Chapter 20

By the time I get in my apartment and run to the mirror, I have a mullet. I take the hot iron and plug it in. It heats up in a few seconds as I mentally prepare myself for the long tedious process of trying to straighten each one of these little curls. But as soon as I press the first little curl in between the hot plates, it singes into a million split ends. I call Chloe to ask her what the hell just happened.

She explains that I have to dry my hair first or else it's no different than sticking my head into an open fire.

I blow-dry my whole head and begin the straightening process all over again. It's like a miracle. Each little piece is coming out perfectly straight and laying down absolutely flat against my head. This is the most amazing thing I've ever experienced.

Once my original head of hair blends in with my extensions, I reach into the shower and get a bottle of shampoo so I can do a shampoo commercial in the mirror.

I turn and face the wall and then whip my head around and say, "Don't hate me because I'm beautiful! Just use what I use." Then I take a second to look at the bottle to see what shampoo Michael's been buying these days. And then I pick up where I left off, "Use Head and Shoulders."

I hear the door slam so I quickly throw the shampoo bottle in the shower and walk out to show Michael my new hair.

"Holy Fucking Shit!" he says. "You look like a porn star with that hair. What the hell did you do?"

"A porn star?"

"Yeah, come over here, you little hottie," he says, imitating what I can only assume he thinks sounds like a *male* porn star.

Well, I guess it's safe to say Michael has always had the same fantasy about me being a blonde that I had. But at least I feel ambivalent and guilty and hypocritical and weird about it. He's just blatantly into it. But as much as I resent him for liking the way I look, we end up having sex on a half-crushed carton of old paint brushes and somehow, afterwards, I forgive him. I mean it's only hair. I should try to at least enjoy it, or what's the point?

I take a quick bath and come out of the bathroom in a robe with my hair down.

"You left that hair thing on? I thought you went into the bathroom to take it off," Michael says.

"What do you mean, take it off? This hair is fusioned into my own hair."

"Permanently?"

"No, but for a long time, why?"

"No reason."

"I thought you liked it."

"Of course I like it. I just didn't realize it was stuck on there, that's all."

"So what you're saying is you liked it to have sex with, but now you'd like it to go away."

"NO, I didn't say that, did I? I just don't think it's you. That's all."

★　　★　　★

I walk into the bedroom and put on the grossest T-shirt I can find so he won't think I'm still trying to look good. I'm contemplating whether or not I should put my hat back on when the doorbell rings. I knew I wouldn't last long as a full-fledged girl. Who was I kidding?

"Nice outfit," he says as I walk right by him and look through the peephole. It's Chloe!

I open the door and her hands fly right to her mouth.

"Please don't scream," I beg.

"Are you kidding? Why would I scream? You look amazing as a blonde! I can't believe it. What a transformation. Oh my God, Zoe, you look exactly like Mom."

"Seriously?"

"Dan, Anita, come on in. Come see Zoe's new hair," she yells down the hall.

"You brought Anita?"

"I had to. It's a long story. I'll tell you later."

"Why didn't you call to warn me?" I whisper.

"Please act like you don't care," she says.

"And go put pants on," Michael says.

I go into my room and slip on a pair of sweatpants, but I'm totally disoriented now. I can't believe that horrible woman is in my apartment. The whole night is ruined, and for the first time in my life, I was sort of hoping Chloe would beg me to play beauty parlor.

Dan and Anita walk in right behind her. Dan looks exhausted, but Anita looks smashing as always in her little linen outfit and pearl earrings. I hate her.

"Zoe, your apartment is marvelous," she says. We both attempt an awkward greeting ritual that involves a half-hearted kiss on the cheek, but we're both so repelled, we're like two pimply high school kids who have been forced to go to the prom together for lack of any other options. She awkwardly hands me the gift she's holding.

"What's this for?" I ask.

"You're going to have a baby, are you not?" she asks.

"Oh that. Yeah, thanks."

"It's funny, I was just telling Dan and Chloe, you never really looked pregnant until a few weeks ago. I mean, obviously you were gaining weight but I never would have guessed. I mean, not that marriage is the end all for everyone, I just thought—"

"Well, it just so happens, Anita, Zoe and I will be getting married very soon," Michael says, slipping his arm around what was once my waist.

"Is that so?" she asks.

"That's right," Michael assures her with a flirtatious little wink.

Kiss-ass.

I could kill him for even talking to her. It's amazing that he could possibly think we're getting married.

"Well, as long as the two of you are happy, who am I to judge? It's okay, go ahead and open your gift, Zoe," she says, as though I'm standing here jumping up and down over it.

"I feel terrible the way we dropped in without any notice, but we ran into a situation this evening because I had to watch my grandchildren unexpectedly for a few hours, and my driver was detained when I needed a ride home. I called Dan assuming he wouldn't mind swinging by to get me. But of course I had no idea Chloe had plans this evening.

"And between the three of us, we couldn't muster up so much as one fully charged cell phone to tell you we'd be coming."

Why didn't you just call from Dan's sister's apartment before you left, and why the hell can't you take a taxi anywhere?

"Once they came to get me, I didn't want to insist that Dan take me all the way home because Chloe was so anxious to see your hair, which is lovely by the way—Leonardo, I assume?—but I can tell you that I'm never one to just drop in. I just thought, under the circumstances, I might as well tag along."

Since all of that was just one big confusing lie, I ignore it and begin tearing the paper off the gift box. I let the paper fall to the floor and then rest the box on my bent knee while I try to open it standing on one leg. Michael tries to help me but I turn away from him as best I can without dropping the box. I reach in and pull out a glass turtle.

"I hope you like it. I couldn't possibly imagine what style you'd chosen to decorate," she says, looking around, "And so I thought Steuben! because, after all, it does go with everything."

"Yes, it certainly does," I say, looking at the turtle. "Especially since you can see right through it."

Dan coughs and takes his mother by the arm. "Let's have a look around, shall we?" he suggests.

"Michael, why don't you give them a tour while I find a place to put our new frog," I say.

"Sure, honey," he says. "But just so you know, that's a turtle."

Chloe walks with me into the kitchen and I immediately turn to hug her.

"Zoe, you look so pretty. I can't stop looking at you. How does it feel? I wish Anita wasn't here so we could play with it."

Me too.

"What is she doing here, by the way? I couldn't understand a word of that story she was telling," I ask, while attempting to hoist myself up onto the kitchen island. Chloe gives me a little boost and hops up next to me. She starts explaining to me that Dan's sister suddenly had to go to some meeting at the school and so she needed Anita to watch the children until the nanny came back.

"As soon as the nanny arrived, Anita called Dan to see if he could stop by and say hello to the kids and then bring her home. Of course Dan agreed, but then as soon as the kids saw Dan they started to beg him to take them with him and then Anita insisted on coming with us, so it just became this whole big family outing. The kids were so excited. The next thing I knew, we all ended up here. I was going to call you but I wanted Anita to think you're the type of person who enjoys company."

"Why?"

"I don't know. And besides, the kids were so happy to see Dan; and I get the feeling they don't go out much. This is a huge night out for them."

"Where are they?"

"They're still downstairs with the nanny. She wanted to spruce them up a bit before sending them upstairs."

"Are you serious? The nanny is here too?"

"Yes, but she won't stay. She's just here to make sure they're presentable. Then she'll leave."

"Presentable for what?"

"Dan's sister and the nanny are very strict about their appearance."

"Did you mention to the nanny that there was no need to concern herself with their appearance for this particular outing?"

"The nanny has strict instructions, that's all I can tell you."

At that moment there's a knock on the door. I attempt to hop down off the counter, but I'm not sure how to balance my

weight. If I lean the wrong way, I could very well end up splat-
tered all over the floor.

Chloe helps me down by way of a piggyback ride, but then
she can't bend her knees to put me down so she gives me a
ride over to the door.

"Wow, you must have gained about twenty pounds already," she says, staggering all over the place.

"Thirty."

Chloe opens the door and the nanny pushes the two small
children through the opening and then backs away as though
she's part of a backstage crew. We greet the children and then
open the door a little more to tell the nanny to come in. But
she's already gone.

"How'd she get away so fast?" I ask the kids.

"I bet she took the stairs," Chloe says and turns us around
to look at the children for information. But neither of them
say anything. They just stare up at us as though there's something very wrong with the idea of me being on Chloe's back.

"She's my sister," I say to clear things up.

Nothing.

"Do you guys ever give each other piggy backs?" I ask.

Nothing.

"Put me down," I whisper to Chloe. "We're scaring them."

Chloe puts me down and I kneel down so I'm eye to eye
with the children.

I've never seen two people who so closely resemble Jane
and Michael Banks. They even have those same little stiff
coats.

"Can either of you bend?" I ask.

They just stand there with their bowed arms by their sides
until Anita comes over.

"There you are, my darlings. You both look wonderful. Why don't you go run along now?"

"Where would you like them to run along to?" I ask Anita.

"Set them up in that area over there," she says, waving her hand toward the other side of the loft.

"You mean the bedroom? There's nothing in there. Can't they stay out here with us?" I ask.

"They can be quite a nuisance, believe me," Anita whispers to me. "Go on children," she says. "Run along now."

The girl Banks takes the boy Banks's hand and slowly they begin to walk toward my bedroom until Dan intercepts them. They immediately put their arms up to him. He picks them both up and turns them upside down while they squeal and kick, almost like regular children.

"Dan, put the children down this instant!" Anita says.

"Why?" Dan asks, holding each of them by one leg.

"The last thing I need is to get them all worked up before bed."

"It's eight o'clock," Dan says. "I thought this was supposed to be their special night out?"

"Exactly my point. They'll be up way past their bedtime so it's best to keep them calm."

I walk over to the two dangling children and ask them if they'd like a sugary snack, but neither of them acknowledge me. They really have no personality at all. Maybe if I try a little harder.

"How does a great big bag of candy strike you?" I ask, and look over at Anita. Still nothing.

"Don't you remember meeting me at your Grandma Anita's dinner party before Chloe and Dan got married? Remember I gave you both pickles?" I ask, begging for recognition.

Dan puts them down and the boy whispers something to the girl.

"What was that?" I say, cupping my hand to my ear.

"He said that you only gave *me* a pickle," Girl Banks says. "And he also said he wants to touch your hair to see if it's real."

"Why? Does it look fake?" I ask him.

No answer. This has got to be the worst conversation I've ever had.

"Ask him if it looks fake," I command Girl Banks.

She whispers something to him. He looks up at me and then puts three of his little fingers right in his mouth.

"Go ahead and touch it," I say.

The boy takes his hand out of his mouth, touches my hair with one little, wet finger, and then puts it back in his mouth. Oddly enough his tiny germs don't even bother me.

"Ask him if it felt fake," I say, but she can't bring herself to do it.

"What's your favorite color?" I ask the boy.

Nothing.

"How do you make this kid talk?" I ask the sister.

That makes the boy and the girl laugh. Sensing I'm finally winning them over, I'm just about to lift up my shirt to show them the baby when Anita spots me and yells, "Children, I thought I told you to go to the other room."

They ignore her for a second, but as she walks toward them, they instantly scurry away like little white mice.

I feel my chest tighten at the sight of them running away from their own grandmother in their uncomfortable clothes, so I follow behind them. When we reach my bedroom I ask them if they want to play on the computer, but they both shake their head no. "How about pencil and paper?" No.

"Want to play hide and seek in my closet? It's empty." They look at each other and telepathically decide against that too.

"Which one of you is smarter?" I ask. The boy points to the girl.

"Prove it," I say.

Finally, the little boy speaks. "Chee can count to infimity."

I can see why he avoids talking. He has such a vast array of speech impediments.

"That would probably take, what, forever?" I say. "So let's play a game instead."

The girl is so excited by this she loses herself entirely and slightly bends her knees with joy.

The boy immediately imitates her and does a much deeper, more athletic knee bend.

"What kind of game?" the girl asks.

"Want to steal stuff out of your grandmother's pocketbook?"

"How old are you?" the girl asks.

"Almost thirty. Why do you ask? Are you suggesting thirty is too old to steal?"

"I think you're pretending."

"You're right, I was just kidding about the stealing thing. Never steal. You'll go to children's jail where they'll torture you."

"There's no such thing as children's jail," she says, twisting her dress around.

"Are you kidding? I know tons of kids in jail."

"What do they do in jail?" she asks, putting her hands on her hips.

"I already told you. They get tortured," I say.

"How does they get tortered?" the boy asks, imitating his sister by putting his hands on his hips.

"Don't stand like that," I tell him. "Kids are cruel. They'll call you a fag. Anyway, I don't want to tell you what really happens in jail because you'll have nightmares. Just remember this: Never steal and never kill anyone. That's really all you need to know except for one more thing."

"What?" the girl asks.

"Never make fun of short kids with red hair."

"We don't know any red hairs," the boy says.

"You really need to work on your grammar," I tell him.

"He's too little, that's why he never talks right," the girl whispers in my ear.

"What did she said to you?" he asks.

I almost can't talk to him anymore until I teach him how to speak properly.

"Are you sure you guys don't want to play a game or something?"

They both wrinkle their noses and shrug.

"Don't children play games anymore?" I ask.

"Do you have any gum?" the girl asks.

"You want to play *gum?*" I ask.

She walks over to me and whispers in my ear, "No, we want to *chew* gum."

"That's it? That's all you want to do with your life? Chew gum?"

"Yeah, we both want to chew gummed," the boys says.

"I don't have gum. How about some papaya pills? I chew on those when I feel like I'm going to throw up. Would you like some of those?"

They both shake their heads.

"Do you ever jump on your bed?" the girl asks.

"Not that often anymore," I say. "I don't want to make the baby dizzy. But you guys can, unless one of you is pregnant."

At that moment Anita tiptoes in.

"Well, isn't this nice? Honestly, Zoe, don't feel as though you have to entertain the children. They are perfectly accustomed to occupying themselves when the grown-ups are socializing. Isn't that right children?"

"I wasn't occupying them. We were just hanging out."

"Remember, you are to touch nothing in this room. Is that understood?" she says. "We are guests here and that means we respect other people's property at all times."

"There's really nothing fun for them to touch in here, Anita, or even play with," I say, looking around hopelessly.

"They'll be just fine," she says and escorts me out of my own room.

I feel terrible. There's not even a picture of a puppy or a box of old jewelry for the little boy Banks to play with. As we're almost out the door, I turn to look at them. They're both sitting on the edge of the bed with their hands folded and little frowns on their faces.

"As soon as we leave, start jumping," I say.

"No, thank you," the little girl says, knowing her grandmother would have her immediately arrested for something like that.

I don't want to leave them all alone, which is weird, because I don't even like kids.

As Anita and I walk back to the main area of the loft, everyone is sort of standing around not knowing what to do.

"This place is really fantastic," Dan says for the hundredth time.

"You know, just the other day I saw this fabulous antique pharmacist's cabinet that would be absolutely perfect for the entrance to your powder room," Anita says.

"I have an entrance to my powder room?" I ask.

"I was referring to that little nook over there."

"Oh, that. Yes, an antique of some kind would be great but I've decided not to fill up this place with arbitrary overpriced objects that were once owned by someone else, simply to make it appear as though I've led some sort of interesting life myself, because I haven't. I'm just a girl from New Jersey, so how would I possibly come to own an antique medicine cabinet? I mean, as far as I know our great grandfather wasn't a pharmacist or anything."

"Actually he was," Chloe says.

"NO, he wasn't," I contradict her.

Was he?

"Grandma said he was."

"Grandma was a liar," I remind her.

"Oh yeah," Chloe says.

"I hate to change the subject," Anita interrupts, shaking her head in disbelief, "but are you suggesting there's something inherently wrong with antique furniture?"

"You heard what I was suggesting. And yes, I believe there is something inherently wrong with antique furniture, for me. For you, it may be fine. I simply prefer not to lie about who I am by attempting to project a false image through my possessions."

"That's the spirit!" Chloe interjects cheerily. "Everyone is different. For instance, some people can't wear red."

"Exactly," I say. "And some people would rather not try to pass themselves off as something they're not."

"Is that why you're wearing someone else's hair?" Anita asks.

"Actually no. The reason I'm wearing someone else's hair is because my own hair was mysteriously cut off by a hair clip that I found in my desk. I would much prefer to wear my own hair." *Lie.* "Unfortunately, it's no longer available. The fact that I chose to go blond, however, has nothing to do with trying to pass myself off as something I'm not. It's because Leonardo ran out of brown extensions." *Look at that, another lie.* "It was either blond or nothing. I had no choice."

Dan walks over and puts his arm around me. "You're right, Zoe, most of the stuff we buy to fill up our homes is a total waste. Meaningless filler."

His intention is to get me off the hook, but the term *we* just ends up sounding like, "We *normal people.*"

Having said that, he walks over to the wall and leans against it, I guess to prove that a wall, in and of itself, is sometimes enough. Then Chloe walks over to me and says a few words about checking on something in the kitchen and together we pretend we have a very important matter to attend to in there, despite the fact that it doesn't contain any food.

She walks right over to the refrigerator, opens it up, and stares.

"What's the baking soda for?" she asks.

"Michael bought it. I guess he's waiting for me to buy something that will eventually smell."

She picks off a chunk of lettuce that's stuck to the shelf and hands it to me.

"Just leave that there," I say.

"But it's probably teaming with bacteria."

"So?"

"Since when aren't you afraid of bacteria?"

"I don't know. I haven't thought about bacteria all day, or sudden death, or rare blood disorders, or even athlete's foot for that matter. It's like I'm numb. I think it's the hair."

"I wish I didn't care about bacteria."

"Dye your hair. It worked for me. I don't care about anything now. Did you hear me lying out there? I never could have done that before. It was so freeing. It was like I could say whatever the hell I wanted. And what's the worst thing that could happen?"

"Someone might call you a liar?"

"Exactly!"

Just then Anita drifts into the kitchen and asks if I need help with anything.

"Like what?" I ask.

"Oh, I'm sorry. I thought you were preparing something," she says.

"I am. Dinner will be right out."

"Oh, how wonderful. I'm absolutely starved," she says, snooping around for signs of food. "May I be so bold as to ask what you've got on the menu?" she asks.

"It's a big surprise," I say.

"And lettuce," Chloe says.

Anita's probably really excited about the lettuce. What a great way to finally go off her diet.

"What's the surprise?" Chloe asks as soon as Anita leaves the room.

"I'm not sure. I guess I'll order in or something. Whatever. Que sera sera. Let's check on the kids," I say.

"They won't even talk to me," Chloe says.

"I know. They're not great conversationalists but we can't leave them in there all night."

Chloe and I walk over to the bedroom and poke our heads in. They're both asleep on the bed in their unmovable little coats. You can see that they've tried to avoid crumpling whatever papers were on the bed, so they've curled themselves up into two tiny unobtrusive balls.

"Why are they sleeping?" Chloe asks.

"It's very boring in my room," I say.

"Anita isn't very good with them, is she?" Chloe says.

"It's hard for me to believe she's Dan's mother."

"Yeah, he's *so* much taller than her," Chloe says and we tiptoe away and join the group.

"What do you say we get some dinner going?" Michael suggests.

"Fine with me," I say. "What's everybody in the mood for?"

After a few moments of silence, Michael asks, "Anyone feel like Chinese?"

Just once I'd like him to suggest something else.

"I think Zoe already prepared something," Anita says.

"Nah, I was just pullin' your leg there, Anita."

Everyone agrees on Chinese so I take everyone's order. Michael calls the restaurant and then we all just stand around way too far away from one another. We can't get any kind of real conversation going at this distance so we mull about silently and collectively pray that the food will come soon, and that its arrival will somehow make us all more friendly.

Michael and Dan are sitting on window ledges, Anita is leaning against the adjoining wall, and Chloe and I are sitting on one of the two steps that separate the living area from what will one day be the dining room.

"You should really get started decorating, regardless of your distaste for furniture," Anita says. "This place has tremendous potential."

"Oh, Anita, you're so gullible. I was just joking about that whole *furniture thing.* To be honest, I've been racking my brain for months trying to get this place decorated. I've been to the D&D building so many times, I could probably find my way around blindfolded. I just can't seem to settle on the right theme. I don't know whether to go Bohemian, Traditional, Contemporary, Neo-Classical or just plain, good ole Early American. What are your thoughts?"

"I didn't realize you've been so busy trying to fix this place up," Michael says. "Although we did have one chair in here for awhile, didn't we, Zoe?"

"We sure did. But that's my whole point. It was totally the wrong theme and I'm just so afraid to make that same mistake again."

"That's because it was an Adirondack chair, which is typically used for an outdoor theme."

"Whatever, at least I'm trying *everything*. That's the only way to really get it right. Don't you agree, Anita? Maybe I'll just go to Crate and Barrel tomorrow and furnish the whole place in one day. I can't believe I didn't think of that before. I mean, look at us. There's no place to sit. And, boy, do we need a table."

"This is some turnaround. I was under the impression that you thought furniture was just another bourgeois conspiracy to oppress other less fortunate apartment dwellers, like cockroaches and mice, because they can't buy things like chairs. It's that whole human dominance thing that she just refuses to buy into," Michael says, hugging me.

"He would think something like that, wouldn't he?" I say to Chloe.

"You have mice and cockroaches in this place?" Chloe asks.

"NO, he's just being sarcastic."

"You know what I just realized? Bugs never sit down," Chloe says.

"Actually, birds sit down," I rebound, knowing she probably thinks birds are bugs.

Dan walks over to Chloe and puts his arms around her. Anita shivers and says she's going to check on the children.

"They're sleeping," I say, but she walks out anyway. I guess she'd be willing to do almost anything to avoid seeing her son show affection toward another human being—even check on her grandchildren.

As soon as she leaves the room, we all sort of huddle together and talk normally for a second.

"What exactly is going on here?" Michael asks me. "I mean I'm willing to go along with it—especially if it means we'll be able to finally get some furniture in here. I'm just wondering what the hell you're doing?"

"I don't know. I just feel like lying. I guess it's the hair. I think I'm coming across as a much nicer person, don't you?"

"It's more like someone who's completely lost her mind."

"It's like the hair found its way into her brain. Hair can totally affect your mood," Chloe explains.

"I can assure you that's not what happened. She's just using the hair thing as an excuse to mess with Anita."

Anita walks back in the room, holding something that's caused a dreadful expression to take over the part of her face that still moves.

"May I ask where you got these photographs?" she asks me. Her hands are shaking. She walks over to me and hands me the pictures of Chloe and the man in the suit lying on the bed.

I can't very well tell her that Alex's brother stole them from Ruth's apartment so I do the next best thing. "Oh those? Someone mailed them to me."

"Is that so?" Anita asks, squinting at me.

"Yes-siree," I say, and take them right out of her hand. "Aren't they great? Look at this one of Chloe jumping. She's quite a little jumper, isn't she?"

Chloe takes the pictures from me and begins examining them. "Oh my God! I'm having an affair!"

"It sure seems that way, doesn't it?" Anita says accusingly. She takes the photos out of Chloe's hand and gives them to Dan.

He takes one look at them and laughs. "This is the worst retouching job I've ever seen. The guy looks like a poster lying on that bed. What the hell is this?"

"Wait a minute!" Chloe says, grabbing the pictures out of Dan's hand. "I know this guy. He's the mattress salesman at Sleepy's, but I don't remember him lying down next to me."

"That's because he never did. Some fool spliced his picture next to yours and reshot it," Dan says, tossing the pictures into the nearest open carton.

I think it's pretty safe to assume Anita was in on this little trick photography stunt. Nothing could be more obvious. She's so agitated and confused, when the doorbell rings she nearly jumps out of her skin. It's nice to watch Anita squirm as she tries to figure out how I got the photographs. I wonder when she was planning to present them to Dan and how disappointed she must be that her plan to frame my sister didn't work.

I walk over and answer the door and to my surprise it's Harold!

"What are you doing here?" I whisper to him.

"What the hell did you do to your hair?" he asks and steps back holding his chest, like he's having a heart attack looking at me.

"I thought you only delivered pizzas."

"I've got two jobs now," he says, moving in a little too closely and keeping the bag just out of my reach.

"Harold, I have a house filled with guests. Just give me the bag."

"You only want one?" he says, thinking we're going to play our little game.

"Harold, cut it out," I say.

"What's the matter? You're not in the mood?" he asks.

But Michael is behind me with his wallet out before I have the chance to answer.

"What seems to be the problem?" he asks, taking the bag right out of Harold's hands.

"This is Harold," I tell Michael.

"Hey, how's it goin'?"

"It's a pleasure to meet you, Harold."

"Oh wait, I want to meet Harold," Chloe says, running over.

Harold leans against the door in anticipation of meeting Chloe, but as soon as she sees him she just says, "Oh, hi" and walks away.

Michael gives Harold a fifty-dollar tip, tells him to forget where we live, and slams the door.

"Harold has a terrible skin problem," Chloe says. "He's not what I was expecting at all."

He does have a lot of lesions.

Michael takes me into the kitchen and asks me why Harold isn't what Chloe was expecting.

"Look, last month was very bad for me. I was extremely hungry and I may have led Harold on a bit to get some extra pizzas."

"Please tell me you're kidding."

"Of course I am," I say and punch Michael in the arm.

"Then tell me what's really going on," he says. And for the first time in my life, I don't have an answer.

"It was obvious that guy felt a little too comfortable here."

"I was starving!" I say, hoping this is a somewhat reasonable defense for seducing a very unappealing pizza boy.

Michael starts taking everything out of the bag and going

on and on about how I need to start thinking and acting more responsibly, and how he misses the old Zoe. Once all the food is out on the counter, we both look at each other.

"Any serving suggestions, Martha?" he asks.

He's really mad. I can't blame him. Harold is repulsive by anyone's standards, and it was wrong of me to try to trick him for food.

"I totally never did anything," I say.

"Zoe, there's not a doubt in my mind about that," he says, looking down at my rotundness. "The whole thing is just incredibly dangerous, that's all. Just don't ever do anything like that again. You also might want to try keeping some food in the refrigerator for emergencies."

"I'm totally going to start shopping," I say and flip my hair.

"And stop saying 'totally' and stop with the hair."

"I told you. I can't help it. I keep falling into character."

"Well, fall out of character, please."

Just then Chloe comes into the kitchen with a serving idea: "How about if I put a big beach towel on the bed and we all sit around it like it's a table?"

"The children are sleeping on the bed," I remind her.

"Okay, then let's just bring all of this over to your neighbor's apartment and, you know, invite them to share our food in exchange for a place to sit."

"We can't do that," Dan says, walking into the kitchen.

"Why not?" Chloe asks.

"Well, for one thing it's incredibly rude, and for another, the children are asleep in the other room. We can't just leave them here alone."

"Oh yeah, I keep forgetting about them."

"We'll be fine right here," Dan says as he starts to open the cartons. Zoe can sit on the counter and the rest of us can stand around the island. This is great, actually." He's sticking a set of chopsticks in each carton.

"Believe it or not we do have plates and silverware if anyone is interested," Michael offers, as he opens the cabinets.

"Oh, don't pull out those old plates," I say. "They look like they belong to someone's dead grandmother. Let's just eat out of the cartons."

"That's because they belonged to my grandmother. Before she died," Michael says, slowly pulling out a few plates.

"Oh God, Michael, I'm so sorry. I thought you bought them. I never would have called your grandmother dead if I'd known."

"Relax, Zoe. I know she's dead. I'm not insulted by it," he says, lifting me up onto the counter. I must weigh a ton. His face is turning bright red.

"Can we talk about something else?" Chloe asks.

"I couldn't agree more," Anita says. She's being awfully quiet. I bet she doesn't want to eat the food and she's trying to figure out how to get out of it.

"What would you like to talk about Anita?" I say and smile at her with every single one of my teeth. I am so enjoying being nice to people. It's so refreshing. I pick up a carton and start eating out of it.

"Let's talk about how Chloe is enjoying her vacation time, shall we?"

"Oh, I'm not on vacation," Chloe says, covering her mouth with one hand. So far she hasn't picked up one single kernel of rice without dropping it first and saying "oopsy!" "I'm on sabbatical. And technically, I'm not really on sabbatical either because I keep getting these amazing article ideas every time I try a new sport. Which reminds me, Zoe, I brought my Gore-Tex article for you to read."

"Dan's going to run it," she says to Anita.

"Oh, isn't that fantastic?"

"I'm so glad you brought it. I can't wait to read it," I say, licking my fingers. Michael hands me a napkin and I give him the same grin I just gave Anita.

"I did a little test run of Chloe's article with our focus group and it was a huge hit. Alex showed it to several shoe advertisers and they're already clamoring for position alongside the article. I think we've got a winner on our hands," Dan says, looking at Chloe.

"And you, Zoe? Are you planning to go on maternity leave for a few months?" Anita asks.

"Not really."

"That's too bad. I was hoping we'd have some time to rethink our editorial and perhaps recoup some of our advertisers. I mean, let's face it, we showed a total lack of discretion by running that article on witches, or whatever the hell that was, and what was that other dreadful one you wrote? 'Why girls fall in love with their best friend's bald, fat fiancés—that was just atrocious."

"How about that one I wrote about aging rich women who think they can buy back their youth with plastic surgery?" I say, tossing my chopsticks into the empty dumpling container.

"I don't recall any such article," Anita says.

It's amazing. I'd say she's immune to at least eighty-five percent of my insults.

All of the cartons are now empty except for the chicken and broccoli I saved for the Banks children in case they ever wake up. Anita barely put a morsel of food in her mouth, and Chloe only ate rice because she's carbohydrate loading for her white water rafting trip next weekend.

How could we run out of food so quickly? *I hope I didn't eat more than my share.* That would certainly put a damper on an otherwise perfect evening.

Michael helps me down off the counter and we begin stacking the empty cartons, while Chloe goes and gets a plastic garbage bag from under the sink. We each throw a few empty cartons in the bag while Anita sways back and forth with her hands behind her back. Dan takes the garbage out of Chloe's hand and ties a knot.

"Is there a garbage can for this or should we just ask one of the neighbors if we can throw it out in their apartment?" he asks.

The thing about Dan's sarcasm is that it's meant to alleviate tension and that's why it never feels mean in any way.

"I'll take that," Michael says, and then he just stands there not knowing what to do with it.

"Is this the first garbage you've had here?" Chloe asks.

"No, it's just that we prefer to visit the incinerator every time we have something to throw away," he says, looking at me as though I should have purchased a garbage can.

"Oh, you have an incinerator here too?" Chloe asks. "Zoe and I used to love ours when we lived together. We threw everything away immediately. We never had one bug."

"We did have fun, didn't we?" I say, and then I take the bag from Michael. "Let's take the garbage out together for old time's sake," I say to Chloe. But as soon as I take it from him, I can see that it's dripping and it's much heavier than I expected and my back is starting to hurt from standing up.

"I'll take it," Michael says reaching for it.

"But it's dripping," I say.

"Don't worry, I won't let it stain the rug," he says and walks out the door.

"You know, I think I'll go with him," Dan says, which leaves Chloe and me alone with Anita. I guess this is as good a time for a showdown as any. And the fact that I now know for sure, by the expression on Anita's face, that she was somehow involved with those photos, just makes it all that more interesting.

I go and search around for some teabags even though I know we don't have any. I'm trying to brace myself for a fight, but suddenly I don't feel well anymore. I've been standing up too much. I lean against the wall and let myself slide down until I'm sitting on the floor. I could go to sleep right here.

"As I was saying," Anita picks up right where she left off. "I couldn't possibly expect either of you to concern yourselves with the magazine's financial situation when you have so many other loftier matters to attend to. After all, money is such an ugly business, isn't it?"

"It depends on whose money it is," I say.

"Well, regardless if it's mine or some other publisher's, your lifestyle will certainly never be affected. You'll always have your wonderful boyfriend to support you, but what about your sister?" she asks me.

"I support myself. I still have a job," I correct her. "And he's not my boyfriend, he's my fiancé."

"Better yet, but did it ever occur to you when you were writing articles asking our readers to guess and circle the picture of which little girl in your kindergarten class grew up to be a gold-digging trophy wife, who was arrested twice for shoplifting, that no one, other than yourself, found your antics amusing?

"And did it also ever occur to you how drastically our whole family's lifestyle could change if we continue to lose our readership and advertisers? Have you no respect whatsoever for the Princely empire, or is it enough for you to entertain yourself with irreverent, meaningless articles about girls who eat their moisturizer?"

"I don't think you should blame everything on Zoe," Chloe says.

"Really? And why not?" Anita asks, amused.

"If you really cared about the magazine as much as you say you do, you wouldn't just pop in every now and then, in between your *appointments*. Zoe is working so hard at that magazine she can hardly move. She's devoted her entire life to that place and look how fat she is.

"No one else would dare work in her condition. It's easy for you to criticize what's going on because you're not really a part of it. You just sort of breeze in and out whenever you feel like it. A lot of the problems with the magazine are not Zoe's fault. You would know that if you were there more often. The other editors have made terrible mistakes that have caused ten times more damage than the stuff Zoe did."

"I can assure you that Anita knows a lot more about what the editors have done than she'd like us to believe."

"How dare you two tell me what I should do or what I know and don't know? You're on borrowed time, Miss Chloe; are you aware of that? The day I tell my son you're out, you're out. And don't you forget it. From now on the two of you will play by my rules, not Dan's. Our entire reputation is at stake and so is our family fortune, and if you think I'm going to sit back and let you destroy what took generations to build with your articles on girl behavior and hiking boots, you're very mistaken. And don't you even think about blaming any of what's happened on my girls."

"Your *girls?* I hate to break it to you, Anita, but your girls are grown women, and the fact that they work for you does not make them yours. However, if there was any doubt in my mind that most of what they've done to me, as well as the damage they've done to the magazine, was under your jurisdiction, it's perfectly clear to me now.

"The way you defend them is a dead giveaway and it makes me wonder if, in fact, the magazine is really as much your priority as you say, or even think it is. If you really cared about it, as much as you claim you do, you'd be grateful that someone came along and gave it a conscience after all these years. You were this close to becoming another *Cosmo*.

"I may not have hit the nail exactly on the head just yet, but you now own a magazine with a brain and some integrity. How about a little thank you?"

"Apparently, neither of you have any business sense at all." She's yelling now and, I guess you could say, stomping her feet.

"The only thing that matters when you're running a business is keeping it alive and prosperous. Is that so hard for you to grasp, or aren't you capable of thinking about anything other than what you're going to wear tomorrow?" That last question was obviously directed at Chloe, but I decide to answer it anyway.

"On the contrary, I rarely think about what I'm going to wear."

"And it shows," Anita says. "I was talking to your sister."

"I'm doing everything in my power to make the magazine a success with the new editorial, but change takes time and we'll eventually replace all of the advertisers we've lost with new advertisers. But I can't get a whole lot done when every time I turn around, one of your *girls* is pulling the rug out from under me. The truth is I underestimated how far you and your editors were willing to go to see that I got eaten alive at that place.

"And although I take full responsibility for all of my mistakes, you need to face up to the fact that you played a huge role in your own demise. Whether you agreed with me or not, we'd have been a lot better off if we worked as a team. You're only spiting yourself, Anita, and it's because of girls like you that I came to work at this magazine in the first place. You sacrificed your own success to undermine me.

"What does that tell you about girl behavior, Anita? If you want the magazine to work, work with me, not against me, because I'm not going anywhere.

"The way that magazine operates personifies everything I'm fighting against and yet it's worse than anything I could have ever imagined. Under normal circumstances, I could have risen to the occasion, but this pregnancy just put me over the edge. Fortunately, I won't be pregnant much longer. So don't fight me, Anita, because you stand to benefit the most from my efforts."

"Well, aren't you just as tough as nails. Who the hell do you think you are telling me to back off? You couldn't possibly know whom you're dealing with, Zoe, but you're about to find out. You're right about one thing, though. I will continue to do everything in my power to see that you go down and your sister is going with you, and if the magazine suffers temporarily, then so be it. Because, in the end, my own survival depends on it.

"You may think I don't work, but I work very, very hard. It's not easy being married to a man who despises me—a man who's been having an affair with another woman since the day we were married. But I'll never let him divorce me. I'll fight it to the end. Otherwise, do you know where I'd be? I'd be working like you two common girls, with bosses telling me what to do, worrying each and every day that I might get fired. I'll never go back to that. I know what it's like to do what you do, believe me, I know. But I managed to rise above it, and I'll be damned if I'm going to let you two put my lifestyle at risk for your so-called ideas."

"Working isn't that bad, Anita," Chloe says. "You make it sound like you'd rather lose your dignity than work. If you know Mr. Princely is having an affair, why don't you confront him or leave him? At least you'll be able to hold your head up. That's even more dignified, don't you think?"

"I think now that you and Dan are married, you can stop calling Dan's father Mr. Princely," I say to Chloe.

"I only met him a couple of times, though," she says.

"What do you know about dignity? I'm the only Mrs. Princely that means anything around here. Do you understand me? I earned that title. And to see you waltz in and grab it makes me sick. My son could have married an heiress, but somehow you roped him in. I'll never understand it.

"You think I wanted to get pregnant at nineteen? And be stuck at home with a baby at twenty? Of course I didn't, but I was damned if I was going to model until the age of twenty-five and then let them put me out on the street and tell me to go get a real job because I was too old. I didn't have rich parents to fall back on. I knew Dan's father would take full responsibility if he knew he fathered a child, and so I got him good and drunk, and the rest is history. I had to survive in this world. I had no other alternative. And now I live with a man who's never home, and my life depends on staying married to him. If that's not work, I don't know what is. But what other choice do I have?"

"How about secretarial work?" Chloe asks.

"I wouldn't lower myself to that if my life depended on it."

"But your life does depend on it. As of now, you don't have

a life because you were always so afraid of lowering yourself to make one. So you just latched on to someone else's life. You're nothing but a parasite. Don't you see that? And you expect us to feel sorry for you, Anita?

"It's not the end of the world to work, you were just looking for an easy way out, and you got it. Now you have to live with yourself. This is what you wanted. The sad thing is that you haven't learned anything from your mistakes. You've always been driven by money, and where did it get you? And now that you have an opportunity to do something good for a change and perhaps make a difference in the world, you refuse, because all it ever comes down to for you is dollars and cents.

"What I want for this magazine could change the lives of women like you before it's too late—before they become accustomed to being afraid to stand on their own two feet. Why can't you see the value in that?"

"Perhaps I'm not making myself clear. Your ideas don't work for women like me. I'm not about to go out there in a man's world and try to compete. Women who think they can conquer the world are fools. Only one in a million succeeds. I know exactly where my talents lie. My goal is to keep my world intact. Nothing more and nothing less. And I'm willing to go to great lengths to make sure neither of you get in my way. I may seem harmless and insignificant to you, but so far you've only seen my good side.

"Chloe, you can stay, because as far as I'm concerned, although Dan used very poor judgment in choosing you as a wife, you're completely innocuous in an office setting. But the day you cross that line is the day you're out, do you understand?

"However, as far as you're concerned, Zoe, I want you to

resign immediately and I want you to do it graciously. Use your pregnancy as an excuse if you have to, but make sure your resignation is effective immediately. Is that clear?"

I'm about to answer her when Dan and Michael come back in, laughing and clapping each other on the back. They always bond whenever Chloe and I aren't around. A simple trip to the incinerator and you'd think they spent the night in a strip club.

"So what'd we miss?" Dan asks.

"Not much," I say. "Anita and Chloe and I were just getting to know each other a little better."

Chapter 21

In honor of Chloe's first day back at work, we've decided to commute together, like we used to. We didn't exactly make it in to work the day after my so-called dinner party, because I broke out in a full body rash the next morning and thought I had shingles. But I'm fully recovered now and there's no way I'm quitting until this baby pops out, whether Anita likes it or not.

Now that I'm coming to the end of my ninth month, I've gained another twenty pounds, which brings me to a grand total of fifty, and I'm not even done. That's quite a bit of baggage when you're under five feet, but somehow I manage to roll from one place to the other.

It's a great time to be going back to work, though. Zoe's article "*Let Performance Footwear Be Your Life Coach*" set off a shoe-buying frenzy that had our advertisers lining up in droves. Leave it to my sister. Who would have ever thought she'd really be able to turn this magazine around. Our last issue broke all records in terms of both readership and advertising. Although I still can't believe the focus of our new editorial will actually be "Shoes! A Metaphor for Life," I can't deny the fact that Dan's decision to reconsider Chloe's original idea turned our magazine into the talk of the town. I'm so proud of her, I can't allow myself to think about what I'd hoped this magazine would become. It was my dream but it wasn't meant to be—at least not for now.

You'd think Anita would be singing in the streets and finally embracing Chloe after the success she's made of this magazine, but she's been meaner to Chloe than ever. I guess the success of the magazine has never really been Anita's main concern. Although she thinks it is. It's all about maintaining her position and Chloe has clearly moved into the number one spot. Unfortunately for Anita, Dan is more in love with Chloe than ever, and she's become the most important person in this company. Sadly, the more Anita realizes this, the meaner she'll become.

But now that I understand her, and how far she's willing to go to maintain the status quo, I intend to take care of everything, the only way I know how.

"Are you ready to face the girls?" Chloe asks.

"As ready as I'll ever be," I say, adjusting my gas mask. You can never be too careful when you're expecting. I wasn't planning to wear my mask to work, but lately I've become totally obsessed with airborne microbes. The effect of my extensions has officially worn off and my carefree days are over, I'm afraid.

"I guess this is it," she says and hops out of the cab. She walks around to my side and opens the door, expecting me to get out.

"Do you need a hand?" she asks when nothing happens.

"I think so," I say, trying to locate my seat belt by my sense of touch. It could be anywhere.

After groping around for a little too long, I somehow manage to find it and even unclick it, but I still can't move.

"You're not even trying," Chloe says. I can tell she's still a little annoyed with me about the gas mask.

"I am so," I protest.

"Well, then, how come you're not moving?" she asks.

"I'm moving, believe me. It's just happening slowly."

"Take my hand," she says.

She grabs my hand and attempts to pull me out with all of her strength. I can almost feel myself budge. But then I realize it was just because the driver took his foot off the brake for a second and Chloe let go.

"Take those latex gloves off," she says. "I can't get a good grip."

"I can't. They're stuck. I think my hands might have swelled up." She's trying to pull me out by my wrists now with both of her hands, but still, something about the way my weight is distributed is making this an impossible situation. Finally the cab driver puts the car in park and gets out. He tells Chloe to get out of the way and grabs both of my arms and yanks me out. I thank him, but all he does is bat me away like I'm some kind of a nut.

What's wrong with people? It's only a little mask.

As soon as we enter the building, I get that old familiar nervous feeling in my stomach—and then a new nervous feeling. It was probably just one of those Braxton-Hicks contractions. I get them all the time, except that last one had a little more kick to it. Chloe rushes ahead of me and I try to waddle as quickly as possible to keep up with her, but she's really in a hurry. I didn't even get a chance to ask her if she wanted to meet for lunch later. It's almost like she's embarrassed to be seen with me or something.

Everyone is staring at me. I knew I shouldn't have worn this T-shirt. You can see my belly button popping out, which is incredibly disgusting, I admit, but I can't fit into any of my cute maternity clothes anymore—especially since I never bothered to purchase any.

When I get out of the elevator the receptionist stands up and screams.

"What's the matter?" I yell, but she can hardly hear me through the mask. You have to be right next to me to really hear what I'm saying.

"Why are you wearing that? What's going on?" she cries. She must be a temp.

I walk right up to her and say, "There's nothing to worry about. I'm just very pregnant and very afraid of germs."

I walk through the halls without causing any other disturbances because it's still pretty early and no one's around.

When I walk into my office, I see Amanda is sitting at my desk. She stands up and screams, much in the same way that the receptionist did. Except this time I feel a huge jolt to my stomach that forces me to sit down immediately.

"Help me get this thing off!" I call to her, motioning for her to come closer. "I can't take any more screaming! It's scaring the baby!"

"How do you get it off?" she asks, afraid to touch it.

I point to the clip in the back and she releases it and pulls it right off, but then I immediately sense something else is wrong by the expression on her face. Oh no. I bet I have hat hair.

"What? Why are you making that face?"

"No, it's just that I wasn't expecting you to be a blonde."

"Oh, right. I forgot. You haven't seen me since I got my extensions."

"Well, it's great to have you back," she says and, for some reason, sits right back down in my chair.

"Um, Amanda, you're still sitting in my chair," I say.

"Well, actually, it's my seat now. Anita told me to move in here while you were gone."

"But I'm back now."

"I know, but someone else has my office now, so I have nowhere else to sit."

"How about over here?" I ask, pointing to the chair I'm sitting in.

"Oh. Okay, fine. I'll just move over there, then," she says. I don't believe this. Now I have to be with Amanda every second of the day. This is awful.

I call upstairs to Alex to say hello, but I know she's not in. She's been away on business and I'm pretty sure she's not due back until tomorrow. I let it ring about fifty times anyway, just for the hell of it, but there's no answer, so I call Chloe.

"Hello?"

"It's me. I just want you to know I took the mask off."

"Oh good. That was embarrassing."

"So, goodbye."

"That's it?"

"Yeah, I have to go because AMANDA is in my office," I say.

"Okay then," she says. "Bye."

"NO! Wait! Maybe you didn't hear me. *Amanda* is in my office permanently," I mumble.

"Why?"

"It seems to be her office now too," I say, hoping she'll call someone in particular.

"Why?"

"I don't know. I was wondering if *Dan* would know," I hint.

I wonder if this conversation is as awkward for Amanda as it is for me. There's no way to tell because she refuses to look up from the little pad and pencil she's holding.

"Gotcha," Chloe says, and hangs up.

A few minutes later Dan walks in. It's a miracle. Chloe understood me and did what I needed her to do.

"Dan, were you aware that Amanda and I now share an office?" I ask.

"No, I wasn't. What's going on?"

"This is actually my office now, Dan," Amanda says.

"I realize you were told to use this office while Zoe was gone, but she's back now so you're free to return to your own office."

"I can't. It's being used."

"Then come with me and we'll find you a temporary place to put your things until we can set you up in a new office."

"Well, I'm sorry but Mrs. Princely gave me strict instructions not to leave this office under any circumstances."

"Well, I'm telling you that the right thing to do is to come with me," Dan says.

"I can't do that," Amanda says.

"I don't think you understand, Amanda, this is no longer your office."

"Yes it is. I'm the new deputy editor."

"Amanda, I'm sorry to disappoint you, but that's just not so. I appoint the editors here, and Zoe is deputy editor."

"I think you need to check with Human Resources then because—"

"Amanda, come with me now or you'll lose your position in this company entirely. Is that understood?" Dan says.

Amanda finally leaves, but, at this point, I'm so worked up, I can't even think straight and I seem to have left my notes home for the article I wanted to write. I'll just have to try to remember everything. I roll my chair over to the computer and kick the other chair away.

I turn to face the screen, which shows an interoffice e-mail from Anita, and it seems someone has been sending an awful lot of e-mails from my screen name while I've been gone. I click on a few of them to see what I've supposedly been sending.

Oh my God, they're all porn!

What the hell is going on here?

I click back to the e-mail from Anita to see if it's something important.

To: Editorial
From: Anita Princely
Re: Staff Changes

I'd like to inform you all that Amanda Cummings will be acting as our new Deputy Editor in place of Zoe Rose, who will soon be leaving the company permanently to pursue full-time motherhood. Although we are all sad to see her go, I would like to advise you not to share any information with her if you happen to see her wandering around our offices. She is very mentally unstable, and I want to make sure no one here is at risk for personal injury. She could be dangerous.

Thank you for your cooperation.

Anita Princely

I forward Anita's e-mail to Dan, who, interestingly enough, is not on the recipient list. Neither is Alex, Chloe, or Rhonda. I guess Anita thought somehow none of them would notice that Amanda replaced me and that I would suddenly just quit when I found out. Apparently Anita still doesn't understand me very well. I send the following note to Dan with Anita's e-mail:

Dan,

Perhaps this e-mail that your mother sent around to almost everyone in the office will explain why Amanda felt she had replaced me as Deputy Editor. I'm sorry to say that I think it might not be a bad idea as it has also come to my attention that I may be addicted to pornography. At least it looks that way from the e-mails someone has been sending from my screen name.

Regardless of the fact that I may very well be mentally unstable, I'd like to submit this article for you to consider for our next issue. It's not exactly in keeping with our new shoe theme; but I'm hoping we'll be able to at least devote a section at the very end of the magazine to girl behavior, and use this article as our first piece.

Anyway, I've been meaning to write this for a long time. And I believe now is an excellent time to publish it.

Let's discuss.

Speak soon.

Zoe

Your Mother-in-law

Even if she tried to kill you with a poisonous dart, try to be understanding. She truly believes you kidnapped her son. She pictures you pulling up in your sleazy convertible, lowering your dark sunglasses, enticing him with a sultry wink and lurid photographs, and because he is weak, he went with you—even though he knew it was wrong.

Although she is furious with you—you know, for the abduction—she is even more mad at him. He's old enough to know better. She warned him about girls like you. Girls with breasts. Now he has left her with no other choice. She must prepare her case against you. She must convince him and herself that you are not worthy of him. In her mind, she has the right to win him back and she will use the most peculiar of all girlish tactics. She will go so far as to try to make her own son unhappy because she feels he has disobeyed her. She must punish him. After all, she is his mother. And she knows what is best for him.

I know you must be wondering, "Could she possibly have expected him to stay single forever? Is that what she wants for him?"

Well, yeah.

Here's the thing most girls don't understand, the whole time she was raising him, she was getting him ready for her, not you.

Why else would she care if he learned to pick up his clothes? He was like her little fiancé in training. You just broke off the longest-running engagement ever.

If you thought she was going to just hand him over without a fight, then you obviously don't remember how many armless dolls every little girl has in her toy chest. Girls don't let go. Even at the risk of dismembering loved ones.

You must learn to accept her cruelty as an offshoot of her pain. I know it's hard, but it's the only way.

Picture this. Force yourself. I promise it will help.

It's twenty-five years ago. There she is, in the laundry room, doing his laundry. See her coughing? That's because she has bronchitis. And still, she's doing his laundry.

See his little pants there in the dirty clothes pile? See how cute they are? Let's take a look inside his tiny pocket. A crumpled up leaf, a rock and one teensy Lego. What's he got in the other pocket? It's a picture that he drew for her.

As she is about to put the last article of toy-size clothing into the washing machine she looks at his drawing . It's a picture of the two of them. He drew his arm the length of a fire hose so it would reach hers. They are holding hands.

He drew a picture of them holding hands.

On the back it says, "Me and My Mo." She is welling up with tears. She's so proud of him. Despite the fact that he's a poor speller.

8:00 THAT SAME NIGHT.

HE IS BATHED AND IN HIS SUPERMAN PAJAMAS.

She has just tucked him into bed and he is begging her to stay. "Don't leave yet, okay?" he whispers.

"I'll never leave you," she whispers back, and she puts one hand on his head. She can hear him breathing. She waits for him to fall asleep and then she tiptoes out of his room. She turns to look at him one more time. He is perfect and, no, she will never leave him. She promised.

As the years went by, she couldn't help but notice the subtle changes. His feet were starting to grow at an enormous rate and he started lying to her about just about everything. The Lego was replaced by a condom, and she had to face the fact that her little boy was no longer hers. As much as she knows it's time to let go, part of her will never be able to. After all, she promised.

I told you it would help.

You could at least give her some of the wedding gifts.

Sometimes I think we should all just give our husbands back to their mothers. Boys don't really like being married anyway; and I don't think they enjoy seeing their mothers treat them like they just broke up.

The whole concept of marriage is just loaded with opportunities to hurt loved ones, but that's a whole other story.

There's nothing more beautiful than the sight of a mother-in-law with her daughter-in-law laughing and hugging as though they are the best of friends. That's what happens when you get a mother-in-law who's a woman, not a girl. She's not competing. She's taking on another child. A daughter. If you get a chance to witness this type of mother/daughter-in-law relationship, remember it, and try to re-create it when you become a mother-in-law someday.

You can't change your mother-in-law, but you can try to understand her. And more importantly, we can all learn from the girls who grew up to be the kind of women we ought to be.

As soon as I finish writing the mother-in-law article, I quickly send it to Dan and write the following e-mail to Anita.

To: Anita Princely
From: Your Deputy Editor
Re: Dan & Chloe

Zoe came back today but I don't think she'll be here much longer. She's ready to pop any minute. And I'm afraid you're right about her being mentally unstable. She showed up here today wearing a gas mask. Poor thing.

The reason I'm sending you this long e-mail is because I've been racking my brain to come up with a way to repay you for making me Deputy Editor and I just thought of the perfect thank you gift. Dan!

That's right, Anita Princely, I'm going to help you get your son back. It's true what they say, Chloe does have Dan wrapped around her little finger, but trust me, not for long. I have three brothers, and believe me, my mom was not about to give them up for anything. She got all three of them back. I was just a young girl at the time, but I witnessed all three takeovers. She chose a different plan each time, but the good news is they all worked. All you have to do is choose the one that's best for you, and poor Chloe won't know what hit her.

Plan A

For this particular method, I recommend a housedress and a pair of old ratty slippers. I know you typically prefer to dress elegantly and sophisticatedly and that you're particular about fabrics and cut (I am too), but unfortunately, what works in the office may not be working for you with your family. I hope you won't take this the wrong way, but you may be coming across as a bit chilly and unattainable. I hope you don't mind me saying that. I'm just trying to help you.

True, you always look beautiful, incredibly beautiful actually, but you just don't look enough like a sweet old grandma. You look much too young and pretty. According to my mom, when a man gets married, he doesn't want to think of his mother as a glamorous ice princess. He wants her to look like the kind of person his children will one day feel comfortable enough to spit up on. You know how it is. Everyone loves a comfy old granny. They're so down to earth and approachable.

Of course you can wear your normal clothes when Dan's not around, but one of the best ways to convince him that you weren't trying to ruin things for him and Chloe is to immediately switch into pajama mode. No one looks like they have an ulterior motive in a nightgown. A little crazy maybe, but certainly not cold and calculating. In fact, the more you mess yourself up, the better.

I can just hear Dan saying, "How could you possibly accuse my mom of being unfriendly? Look at her in that silly ole housedress with the cookie dough smeared all over her face. The poor thing is so gone, why it's impossible not to love her." He'll say those words with tears in his eyes and that Chloe won't have a chance. If you can't stand the idea of having food on your face, try walking around with only one slipper.

If you just can't bring yourself to dress down for family occasions, there is always Plan B.

Plan B

Start buying Chloe tons of stuff. I mean everything you can think of—watches, luggage, a diamond bracelet, stationery, new towels, plasma TVs—and keep in mind, big-ticket items work best.

Every time you find yourself churning inside over something she's said or done that just drives you crazy, head for the nearest shopping mall. Plan B works on the same principal as "kill 'em with kindness," but my mom likes to call it retail revenge. She used this technique on my oldest brother's wife because that one had a bit of a shopping problem, and boy did it work wonders. Just buy, buy, buy. It will make you look like an angel.

Start traveling to Paris and Milan on a regular basis and make sure you buy her things that aren't in our New York City stores yet.

You get double points for European goods. This option has a whole department store full of benefits. And the most important one is that you're saving your son from spending all of his money! Can you imagine how much he'll finally appreciate you when he sees how happy Chloe is? And just think of the opportunities for control! You'll look so powerful in his eyes, almost God like.

Of course, if neither of these ideas sound appealing, there is always Plan C.

Plan C is the high road

This one involves a good deal of self-introspection, self-discipline, and maturity. Knowing you, you will choose Plan C, because I know you are a person with integrity and pride. You do run the risk of giving up some of your power with Plan C, but I'm sure you'll agree that that's a small price to pay to regain the love and trust of your son.

With Plan C, the first thing you will have to do is apologize to Chloe for treating her poorly. I know it's degrading, and she certainly doesn't deserve it, but it's for a good cause.

Plan C produces a different result than Plan A or Plan B because if you decide to admit you've been playing dirty, the dynamics of your relationship with Dan will never again be based on your desire to control him and make choices for him. This is definitely one of the downsides of Plan C, but I still think the benefits totally outweigh the risks.

The result of Plan C is that your relationship with Dan will improve almost immediately, but unfortunately on his terms, not yours. Your approval or disapproval will no longer affect him. Another downside, I agree. He will continue to feel entitled to his own emotions even if they're not the same exact emotions you'd like him to feel. He'll also continue to want to make his own choices and accept his own failures and his own successes. In fact, he'll feel even more entitled to love and protect his wife once you've empowered him to let go of your judgment of his behavior.

He may even start saying things to you that prove he's tired of dealing with your ownership issues and he might even tell you to stop making yourself the enemy. I know this is the case because my mom had this same experience with one of my very own brothers, and although it was hard for her, she chose Plan C anyway. Of course she's in a psychiatric facility full-time now, but I know, in her heart, she feels she did the right thing for her son.

Although Plan C can be frustrating, it will help you find happiness and peace. Before you know it, you'll realize there are a lot more important things to do with your time than worrying about what Chloe and Dan are doing.

Like my mom always says, examine your intentions. Do you want to be loved or do you want to be in control?

Once little children realize that the world does not revolve around them, they become enjoyable to be around. And the last thing we want is for our children to think we're behaving like children, right? At least that's what my mom always used to say, before, you know, the breakdown.

Try to think of Chloe as your own daughter and understand that all she ever wanted was your approval and love. Give it to her. If you let her trust you, you might be amazed at how much closer you'll be with your son than you ever thought possible. If you can find it in your heart to be both of their mothers, then you will have an even bigger place in his heart. And you'll soon realize that your son has what you've always wanted for him. He has someone who cherishes your greatest accomplishment . . . him.

Whichever plan you choose, I'm sure you will choose wisely. Of course, Plan C is the one that seems to deliver a much more realistic and fulfilling relationship between mothers and sons, but it's your decision. I wish you the best of luck and I know you will do the right thing.

Best,
Your new Deputy Editor and Friend
Amanda Cummings

I forward my article to Anita from Amanda's screen name and head to the ladies' room. As I'm leaving my office, I spot Trai and oddly enough, he's got the exact same extensions as I do—except his are curly. *They look pretty good curly. Maybe Leonardo was right.* Wait a minute.

"Trai, what did you do to your hair?"

"You don't even say hello?" he asks, with far too much emphasis on the *s* in *say*.

I give him a quick hug and feel him recoil. I can't blame him. I don't look my best.

"Nice dreads," he says.

"Dreads? What's that supposed to mean?" I quickly grab a big chunk of my hair. I wouldn't exactly call them dreads, but they are a bit matted. I never should have crushed them under my mask.

"Listen, I gotta run, sweetie. Are you back for good?" he asks.

"Are you gay for good, or are you faking?"

He hits me on the arm and makes the phone motion up to his ear.

"Call me," he says and dashes off.

I really have to get to the bathroom now. I keep walking, hoping to make it there in time and that I don't run into anyone else—except there's Blaire and Sloane, walking down the hall bickering with their newly elongated hair. I never got to see how they looked after they got their extensions. Sloane must be devastated. Hard as she tried, they still came out perfect. And Blaire has fashioned hers into an elaborate up-do with tiny braids swirling in and out. I pull on my disheveled sticks and make a quick attempt to turn in the other direction, but it's too late.

"Is that you, Zoe? I thought so. Boy, you look like you're ready to blow any minute. I never got to see your hair all done," Blaire says, coming closer.

"I know. I never got to see yours either. They came out great," I say.

"Did Leonardo give you yours on sale? There seems to be something wrong with them."

"Actually I specifically asked to have mine mangled. And more importantly, according to Anita's e-mail, you girls aren't supposed to be talking to me, so I suggest you run along and continue fighting somewhere else," I say and keep walking as fast as I can. It's really difficult, though, because my thighs are ramming up against one another and it's making it almost impossible.

I'm no more than three steps away when I hear Blaire and Sloane going at it again. I guess Alex's brother completed his assignment as planned. They're at each other's throats and as much as they deserve it, I can't stand by and listen to them do the very thing I came to this magazine to change. I know I'm going to hate myself for this, but I turn around and walk toward them.

"You couldn't possibly NOT have known I was already seeing him," Blaire says.

"Well, I *didn't* know, and how could you call him after you knew damn well I had just spent the night with him?"

"Because I love him, that's why. And for your information

he never loved you. He told me straight out. He thought you had thick calves."

"Blaire and Sloane, can you both come here? I need to talk to you for a moment. I'd come to you but I'm conserving my energy. There's something I need to tell you." They both turn in their tracks, hands immediately on hips.

"Listen, I couldn't help but overhear you fighting. And I know you don't agree with anything I tried to do here, but keep in mind that my goal was to prevent the very thing you two are doing at this very moment. Think about what you're fighting over. I mean really think about it. Is he so worth it?

"Are you willing to give up that thing you two have, that bond, that incredible *revolting* closeness, for some imbecile who doesn't really know either of you? Don't you think you're worth more to each other than him?" They're both carefully considering what I'm saying, but they're also both still hanging on to the idea that if they play their cards right, things could work out with him.

"Look, the truth is I can't stand either of you. You've done everything in your power to make my life miserable and destroy what I tried to accomplish here. But I came here for a reason and it was to help girls like you become better people."

"Why, Zoe? So we'd learn to accept girls like you?"

"Believe me, I've asked myself that question many times and I'm no longer afraid to consider the possibility that it might have been true at one time. But now I know better. And as disappointing as it is not to have been able to teach you anything, I can't let you ruin what you have over some guy who doesn't want either of you. There, now you know. He's not in love with either of you. He's been seeing Courtney. And he's going to break up with both of you. In fact, he's more than seeing her. He's in love with her. That's it. You both lost.

Courtney won. It's over. The guy was a jerk anyway. Trust me. I've known him for a long time."

They were going to find out eventually. All I did was pull the plug a little sooner.

They immediately turn toward one another as allies, and I know I did the best I could, considering what I'm working with. They need each other again. I'll warn Courtney of their realignment later. But for now, Courtney's the one who got the guy. So I'm sure she'll be fine with it.

As I'm just about to open the door to the ladies' room, Rhonda slips out. I don't believe it. Alex wasn't kidding when she said they all made appointments with Leonardo. You'd think he could have pulled at least one other hair color out of his sleeve. We're all clones.

"Well, look who's back and look at that! We're practically twins. Leonardo, right?" she asks. "Something's wrong with yours, though. What happened?"

"They got mauled," I say. "I was wearing this mask before, because, you know, the baby and germs and everything."

"I understand, believe me. I'm a fanatic about germs too," she says and licks her finger to wipe something off my face. The thought of someone else's saliva on my skin makes my stomach turn in a way that I've never quite felt it turn before. In fact, I think I actually *heard* it turn this time.

"Anyway, when's the baby due? Oh my God! What are you doing? Are you peeing in your pants?"

I look down. Water is pouring out of me like a gusher.

It's amazing that I'm not flying around the room with the release of all this pressure.

"Oh my God! Oh my God! Don't panic but you're gonna have a baby. Come with me," she's screaming. "Somebody call nine-one-one! Never mind. I will!"

"I can't come with you. I have to go right to the hospital," I say, sounding oddly cool and collected.

"Wait!" she screams. "I have to call an ambulance, and you have to stop walking around. You're still peeing or watering or whatever it's called."

"Call Chloe and Michael and my mom and dad and Alex, okay? I have to go have the baby now. It was nice seeing you again," I mumble.

"Zoe, please don't go anywhere. I'm calling right now, see?" She walks over to some girl's cubicle and pulls the phone out of her hand. "Hang up and call nine-one-one!" she screams at her.

The poor girl dials as fast as she can and Rhonda says, "Now get up off that chair and take her down to the lobby, this is an emergency. Move!" The girl, who I've actually never seen before, walks over to me and takes my arm. Water is still dripping, and for some reason I'm finding it very hard to breathe. I think I'm finally having a real asthma attack. And yet, I'm not worried. I know I won't die. I can't die. I'm going to be somebody's mother.

"Can we take the stairs?" I ask her. "I'm afraid I won't be able to breathe in the elevator."

"Sure, okay, but the elevator will be faster."

"I know, but breathing's more important."

"Whatever you want," she says. "Let's go."

"I'll meet you in the lobby!" Rhonda screams out to us. "Whatever you do, don't leave without me!!"

"Okay then," I say. "See you downstairs." It's almost like I'm talking in my sleep.

The girl opens the door to the stairway and holds it open for me. As soon as I take my first step through the door, I spot the back of Ruth's head. And it looks like she's leaning up against someone—almost like they're making out. And then the other person steps aside, and it's Anita. Anita and Ruth are making out. This can't be happening, but it's all coming back to me now. All that stuff in Ruth's apartment. It was all Anita's. Ruth and Anita are a couple. Oh my God.

No wonder Ruth never got fired. She's dating the boss.

"Let's take the elevator instead," I say to the new girl, as I slowly back away. What a time for me to go into shock. I've got to stay focused. I see Ruth run down the stairs like a bat out of hell. She can really hustle when she wants to.

Anita comes after me and grabs my arm.

"Zoe, I know you're upset by what you just saw, but try to control yourself. You're peeing everywhere," she says.

"I know, what a mess. I hope you can forgive me. I was going to ask your permission first, but since you were making out with Ruth, I didn't want to disturb you."

"If you dare breathe a word of this, I will ruin you. Do you hear me? I will ruin you!"

"Take it easy, Anita. You can't possibly ruin me, and your love life is your business. And I won't tell a soul what I just saw . . . under one condition."

UGH!! I'm getting my first contraction! I always thought all those women were faking, but it actually hurts worse than anything I ever imagined. I just want to punch someone.

"Be nice to my sister, okay? That's all I have to say." I'm leaning against the wall, waiting for another contraction. Anita better not get too close.

"What do you mean? Be nice?"

"Figure it out for yourself and figure it out fast or I'll be on the phone with your husband and every gossip columnist in the country."

Oh my God! Here comes another one! I gasp and hurl myself toward the elevator.

Chapter 22

Every time someone new comes to see me, the nurse finds it necessary to tell me. Like I care. All I want is to get this monstrous thing out of me. I've already bitten the nurse twice and threatened to kill her.

So far she's announced the arrival of Rhonda, Michael, Chloe, my mom, my dad, Alex, and Dan, as though I'm expecting them for cocktails.

"Why do you keep telling me who's out there?" I scream at her.

"Well, it's just that some mothers like to invite their relatives in to share in the birthing experience."

"Do I strike you as someone who likes to share?" I scream in her face.

"Well, it's just that—"

"Shut up! JUST SHUT THE HELL UP!"

The door opens and it's Michael.

"I told you not to let anyone in, goddamn it. Look at me. What did I tell you? Do you even understand English?" I holler at her.

"I'm so sorry, Mrs. Rose. It's just that your husband—"

"He's not my husband. I don't believe in marriage. How

many times do I have to tell you! You're probably not even a real nurse."

Michael grabs both of my arms and tells me to calm down and breathe and to stop calling my doctor a nurse.

"I can't breathe! I'm too busy yelling and screaming!" I cry. And then he takes my head and presses it against his chest and I'm not yelling anymore. I'm not really breathing that well either, but at least I stopped screaming. Now I'm just crying and not too horribly either, I must say. He might have actually calmed me down. And I can't help thinking how much I want someone like that for my baby. And then he brings his face right up to mine and he's looking right at me, and it hurts so badly but he's right here and I can almost get through it. He's crying now too, and he keeps telling me he loves me and I tell him I love him too, and then he goes and asks me if I'll marry him again.

And out of nowhere I scream, "Yes! Yes! Yes!" And then suddenly it's over. The pain stops and I look down and I can't believe it. I see my baby. "It's a girl!" Michael yells, even louder than I was yelling before, and then he's kissing me and kissing me and then he's holding our little baby and then he hands her to me. And I don't even care that they're both covered in blood and some sort of white, filmy glue. That's how much I love him and how badly I just want to hold her.

"When did you have time to go out and buy a blanket and this little skater hat?" Michael asks the baby.

"Check her fingers and toes," my surprisingly beautiful doctor says with a big smile on her face. I guess she's used to forgiving people quickly in her line of work.

"What happened to Dr. Luden?" I ask.

"She's giving birth today too."

I count everything and it's all there. And then I look at her face and she looks right back at me. No, it's more like she's looking right through me, and I get chills all over my body because it's like nothing I've ever imagined. She looked right *into* me, as though she knew me, as if she loves me already and I love her so much I don't know what to do. Her lips are like tiny cherry blossoms and her skin looks like she's been bathed in a river of pearls and her eyes are like two little emerald dewdrops. She's the most beautiful baby I've ever seen and not just because she's mine. I'd be totally objective about something like that. Michael takes her hat off and we both look at each other for a second. "I thought babies were supposed to be bald," Michael says. "It looks like we've got ourselves a little pumpkin here," he says and kisses her on the head.

"Don't ever call her a pumpkin," I say.

"Why not? I have a thing for redheads. Didn't you know that?" And then the baby looks up at him, almost the way she looked at me a moment ago, *but not quite the same,* and one by one everyone starts walking in to see our little girl.

A few minutes later, I'm sitting up and nursing my baby as though it's the most natural thing in the world. Except I've managed to cover my fully engorged mammoth breast so as not to frighten my father who's just been crying the whole time and not talking to anyone.

I hope my breast doesn't suffocate her. I press it away from her nose so she can breathe and she looks up at me for a second as if to say thank you. I can't believe we're already talking to each other like this.

"Look at my wife. Isn't she beautiful? Look at her," Michael says.

"I don't know, to me she looks a little swollen. What do you think, Chloe?" Rhonda asks.

Chloe and Dan come around to hug me and then Chloe starts feeling all around my head.

"What happened to your extensions?" she asks.

"I pulled a lot of them out while I was in labor."

"Is that them?" Dan asks, pointing to a clump of hair in the garbage. "Because if it's not, they gave that little baby quite a haircut."

Chloe peeks into the garbage and says, "Those aren't Chloe's extensions. That hair is brown."

"That must be the doctor's hair," I say.

"You pulled her hair out too?"

"Not all of it, but she was really bothering me at one point."

"I'm so glad I never let my mother talk me into going to medical school. I was this close," Rhonda says.

My mother comes around to sit next to me and the two of us look down at my perfect baby.

"She looks exactly like you," she says. "I'll never forget the moment I first saw you and the way you looked back at me. It was like you already had so many questions."

I look down at my little girl's pink cheeks and her tiny out-stretched hands and tell her, "Don't you worry. I'm going to protect you and take care of you forever. One day you'll grow up to be a beautiful princess and I'll never, ever, ever, leave you. Do you know why? I'll tell you why. It's because grandma is going to give me one of her special pills. That's right. Aunt Chloe will tell you all about them."

"I knew it," my mother says. "You're already worse than me. At least I never said anything about you becoming a princess."

"Well, you told me *I* was going to be a princess," Chloe says.

"That's different. You'll believe anything," my mother says and the two of them lock arms.

"Let's take a walk," she says to Chloe. "It's time we have a little talk."

"Mom," I say. "Do you really think now is the right time? I mean, what's the rush?"

"She walks over to me and whispers in my ear, "I'm not going to tell her about the pills, I just need to tell her she's pregnant. That's all."

They start walking out together but then I call my mom back in again.

"Now what?" she asks.

"Tell her it doesn't hurt, okay?"

"I'm way ahead of you," she says and kisses me and walks out.

After everybody leaves and Michael goes to get us something to eat, I hear a faint knock on the door. It's Alex.

She walks in slowly and sits by the side of the bed. "Look at that! You really went and had a baby."

I turn to show her my little girl and she immediately fills up with tears.

"I never saw you cry before," I say.

"Me neither. I think it's because I can't believe how much that kid looks like you, and just seeing that hair again," she sniffs. And before you know it we're both sitting here crying like a couple of girls.

"And speaking of when we were little, I brought you know who, over here a little present. She hands me a big gift-wrapped box and I ask her to open it for me because my hands are full.

Alex carefully unseals the tape and gently pulls off the wrapping paper as though she's afraid to even scratch the box. She refolds the wrapping paper and puts it on my nightstand. I've never seen her handle anything so delicately. Then she takes off the top of the box and reaches in and pulls out a tiny pink-and-white polka dot dress, and holds it up against the baby.

"What's that supposed to be?" I ask, "The world's cutest dress or something?"

"It's just like mine," she says. "Only incredibly small."

She turns it around to show me the bow in the back and then she sort of twirls it back and forth to show me how it works.

"I hope she has better luck with this than I did," she says, wiping her eyes.

"How could she not?" I ask. "She has you and me on her side."

"True. And besides, this is a much nicer dress."

She's right about that. This dress is beautiful and sweet and simple. It's exactly the kind of dress I want my little girl to wear.

I want to hug Alex but she's not really the type. But then she puts the dress back in its box and comes over and hugs the baby and me. "Oh, wait. I have something else, too. I almost forgot. It's magazine-related, so you might not want to deal with it now," she says and hands me a manila envelope. She's right, I'm too exhausted to open it, but we end up talking about the magazine anyway.

She asks me how I'm dealing with the new editorial and I try to explain that I'm disappointed that I couldn't get my message out there, but at the same time, I'm happy for Chloe and I know I'll find another way, somehow.

I look down at my baby, knowing this is my chance to get this girl thing right—once and for all—from the very beginning.

"Now that there are two of us, who knows what we'll be able to accomplish," I say, yawning and looking down at her.

"Three," Alex corrects me. I put my head back and a moment later I feel myself dozing off. After a little while, I feel Alex slip the envelope under my blanket. I open my eyes slightly as she takes the baby out of my arms and places her gently in her little portable bed. I whisper, "Thank you," and close my eyes again. I hear her footsteps and the door closing. It's just me and my little girl now.

Chapter 23

I'm looking in the mirror for what may be the eightieth time this morning and I've come to the conclusion that I have to do something about my hair. I can't keep dying the roots blond with my home hair color kits.

It would be great if I could just go back to *Leonardo & You,* but I could never show my face there again. Not after the way I ripped all those extensions right out of my head with my bare hands. The man will think I'm an animal.

I finally resign myself to call a new salon but I have to do it quickly, while the baby is still sleeping.

Chloe keeps insisting I go see this woman Louise Galvin at the John Barrett Salon, so I call and make an appointment.

They tell me I can come in today because they just got a cancellation, which is perfect, because there's no way I could possibly forget that. Unfortunately, I have no one to watch the baby.

I try on a couple of outfits, but the baby keeps shaking her head no. She keeps insisting that I wear the pink-and-white polka dot dress Alex bought for her. She wants me to wear it whenever she's not wearing it, and for some reason I can't make her understand that I can't fit into a size 18-months. Although I'm getting there. Fortunately all that weight just fell right off. By the time she's five or six, we might actually be able to share a few things.

I finally put on the only other outfit that she likes: Chloe's old corduroy skirt, a white T-shirt, and the new black boots she and Chloe forced me to buy. They're not really "me," but what do I know.

When I'm all dressed, she says, "Look at me." That's our little signal that I look okay. Actually, that's her signal for everything. And now that she's officially picking out my clothes, I think it's time I stop referring to her as The Baby. It's such a derogatory term.

Louise Galvin, just as I imagined, is absolutely gorgeous and she's dressed to perfection. I'm not surprised to learn that she has her own line of products, some of which she's carrying as she walks toward me.

The woman has everything. Her salon is based in London, but she flies to New York every few months for special clients and people like me, whose hair is hopeless. I've already mentally committed myself to buying all of her products because she represents everything I believe in.

She's strong, independent, not afraid to take on a traditionally male-dominated industry, and she's already made quite a name for herself. Not to mention her long, blond perfectly straight hair, which I'm hoping comes in one of those bottles she's carrying.

Louise agrees to look after the baby for me while I go change. When I come back out, I can see that my daughter is walking around stealing brushes and combs from each of the stylists and sticking them in the waistband of her skirt saying, "Look at me." I should really teach her to say something else when she's stealing.

As soon as she's seated on my lap in front of the mirror, my daughter's whole demeanor changes. We're both staring at ourselves completely mesmerized. She points to my reflection in the mirror and says, "Look at me."

"I am," I answer her. The resemblance is uncanny in this light.

"So, what are you thinking?" Louise asks me.

"I'm thinking that I can't believe how much my daughter looks like me and I also can't believe the condition of my hair. What do you think?"

"Well, I was thinking the same thing and also that you have a strikingly beautiful daughter."

I look down at her to see if she heard Louise, but she's too busy staring at herself, with her big green eyes wide as saucers.

It must be great to be a little kid. You can look at yourself in the mirror for hours without anyone thinking you're being conceited.

"I also think that part of the reason your daughter is so beautiful is because her hair color compliments her eyes and skin tone."

"So what are you suggesting?" I ask, afraid that I'm about to have to politely leave.

"I'm not ready to suggest anything specific just yet. I'm just saying that if I were you, and I'd been born with your hair color, I'd have been very grateful. That's all. Being a redhead is somewhat unique, don't you think? Sort of a gift. And it's my absolute favorite color. I've done at least six redheads today. But I could never match yours or your daughter's color. There's nothing I could offer any of my clients that comes close to the beauty of absolutely, totally natural, red hair." And then she leans closer to me and says, "And what I wouldn't give for those incredible curls."

Fool that I am, I'm totally buying it. The whole thing. I look at my daughter still staring at herself in the mirror totally astonished by her own appearance, and I suddenly want to kick myself for wanting to change the very thing that makes us so much alike.

About an hour later my hair is dry and very curly and it actually looks a little longer than before. And she seems to have matched my natural hair color perfectly.

I can't remember the last time I looked in the mirror and didn't wish I had darker skin. I'm a redhead and that's all there is to it. My daughter kisses Louise goodbye, and as much as I hate to admit it, I want to kiss her too. She has no idea what she did for me.

Chapter 24

"You really need to come over soon and see all these packages I've been getting from Anita lately," Chloe says.

"Have you opened any of them?" I ask, holding the phone between my shoulder and my ear while I put the finishing touches on my most recent painting of my daughter. The apartment is filled with them. Every inch of wall space is taken up. We might have to get a bigger place if she keeps coming up with new poses.

"Are you kidding? Of course! I got a Mulberry bag on Monday, a Cartier watch on Tuesday, and a tiny pair of diamond-and-pink sapphire earrings on Wednesday. The UPS man and I are, like, best friends now. Sometimes he even hangs out for a few minutes while I open my package. I never would have guessed Anita would suddenly start liking me so much. I asked her why she keeps sending me gifts out of nowhere, and she said it's her way of showing me how important I am to her. Dan told me to give them back, but I don't think that would be very polite, do you?"

"Absolutely not! Don't listen to Dan. The last thing you want to do is get on her bad side again while she's trying so hard to show you how much she cares." Especially since it took her so long to get with the program.

"Exactly. I mean I feel terrible about all this, but what can I do? Oh wait! Here he comes again. I have to run!! Come visit soon so we can try on all the new clothes she keeps sending me. And when you talk to Dan, make sure you tell him you talked me out of giving everything back, okay?"

"I'm totally with you on this one, believe me," I say and we hang up.

Who would have ever thought Anita would go for Plan B?

Chapter 25

Michael has been waiting downstairs for at least twenty minutes, but I can't seem to get anything organized. We're going to visit Chloe and Dan and we were supposed to leave an hour ago, but a certain someone keeps pulling everything I'm packing out of the bag. I'm almost regretting the fact that I encouraged her to learn how to walk. And she keeps eyeing the stairs up to the loft as though she's devising some sort of a plan. I'm sure I'm just being paranoid; she'd never be able to figure out how to open that gate.

Still, I can't leave her alone for a second without her wandering off to change her clothes, and, for some reason, I can't find her pearls. If she finds out I lost them again, she'll kill me.

"Look at me," she yells from the other side of the room. The versatility of that one phrase is just astounding. No wonder she doesn't bother to learn anything else. I'm a little worried, though. I think I was reading at her age.

She's trying on my new bra now. Anyone can see she's got an eye for fashion, particularly in the area of which bras should be worn over which dresses.

I tear open my bag to throw in a box of pretzels and check

one more time for those damn pearls. I grab her favorite blush brush and her pink sponge curlers and zip them in a plastic bag. Then I grab a handful of the pamphlets I just had printed up for my latest project. I never go anywhere without them. And she never goes anywhere without her curlers. You'd think she would have realized by now that she's preaching to the choir with those things in her curly hair.

I'm trying to get a group of mothers together for my new self-defense workshop, which demonstrates how to render an attacker unconscious with nothing but a few distracting hand motions and a stroller. But so far no one has showed up for any of the meetings. And surprisingly I haven't gotten any names on my sign-up sheet for: MOTHERS AGAINST EVERY-THING either. Funny, I had that one pegged for standing room only.

I grab a few more pamphlets and a handful of diapers and toss them in the bag, which knocks over her juice cup, which spills out all over everything. I take everything out and run to the coat closet to get my old baby bag down from the top shelf. I haven't used this bag since I brought her home from the hospital.

I transfer everything to the new bag and just as I'm about to zip it up, I spot something coming out of the side zipper. It's the envelope Alex brought me in the hospital. I never got a chance to read it. It's been in this bag all this time. I take it out of the bag and slip it under my arm so I'll remember to open it in the car.

Then I look down and see that she found her pearls, "Look at me," she says, and points to herself and runs away, which means she's going to hide.

"Good. Go hide. But make sure you stay somewhere in this room."

Once I'm all packed up, I zip up the bag and take my keys off the hook, and run out the door. I take the stairs instead of the elevator to save time and run out to the curb waving to Michael.

"See, I told you we'd only be a few more minutes."

"I think you forgot something," he says.

"Right," I say and open the back door to throw in the bag and the envelope from Alex. I slam the door and run back into the building. I run back up the stairs and then I remember I threw the apartment key in the bag. So I run back downstairs, open the back car door, get the keys out of the bag, and run back in and up the stairs. I unlock the door and yell, "Okay, you can come out now, we're leaving," but she doesn't answer me. I start frantically calling her and searching everywhere until I hear, "Look at me."

I look up and there she is, standing at the top of the loft stairs, wearing a pair of high heels that my mom gave her to play with a few weeks ago. And then I relive my worst nightmare as she comes tumbling down the steps, hitting her head on each and every one. I run over to her, but I can't speak. I pick her up in my arms, and hold her so tight, she lets out a little squeal.

And then she looks up at me and points to herself and says, "I love mommy." Just like that. Like it was no big deal. And then she wriggles away from me and turns around to go back up the stairs. She's not even crying. She doesn't care that she just fell down a flight of stairs or that she just reached into my chest and grabbed my heart and ran up the stairs with it, or that there's an excellent chance I'll never get over what she just said to me.

"No, stop!" I scream. But she just looks at me, and points upstairs, and says, "New shoes!"

I'm so glad I wasn't playing with a Tonka truck this time.

I pick her up and run up the stairs with her. I tell her to pick out another pair of shoes to try on in the car but apparently none of my shoes qualify as a toy, so I let her bring my mom's high heels. Then I run back down the steps holding on to her for dear life, letting the tears run right down my face. I can't wait to tell Michael what she just said.

She loves me.

Once we're settled and on our way, I turn around and reach for the envelope in the backseat. I open it up and start reading.

Dear Editor,

I've never written to a magazine before. I've always worked until at least nine o'clock every night and my husband and I have always traveled quite a bit, which leaves me very little time for idle correspondence.

Throughout our marriage, my husband and I appeared to have a perfect life. We had an amazing apartment in the city, a spectacular beach house, tons of parties, great friends, an enormous amount of "stuff." Just to give you an idea of how much stuff we had, we had to buy the apartment next door to ours to use exclusively for closet space. I've always been considered beautiful and my husband and I both modeled quite a bit before he became an actor and then a director. I also owned my own cosmetic company for five years and eventually launched my own packaging company. We were the couple I'd always dreamed of becoming. We had absolutely everything we were supposed to have.

So why was I so unhappy?

I'll tell you why. It's because all my life, I've been hurting people. I hurt people to get the money I needed to buy my company. I hurt friends who no longer interested me when a more socially interesting or better connected friend came along, and I seduced my husband into falling in love with me—even though he was dating my best friend at the time we met. I've always chosen my friends for all the wrong reasons and I only associated with people who I'd be proud to introduce. And what made me proud? Looks and money. I still have no idea, to this day, what qualities I'm supposed to look for in a friend. I was brought up to only surround myself with people of influence. My mother gave me very explicit instructions to marry money and I never, ever disobeyed my mother. Her life exemplified everything I was supposed to want and I was determined to live that life.

I've never really had a friend, in the true sense of the word, now that I look back. I was always the most popular girl in school, but spent most of my time making sure my friends never got too close to one another and that their boyfriends liked me more than they liked them. I had this incredibly intoxicating power over everyone because I looked exactly the way they wanted to look and I had everything everyone wanted. Deep down, we all hated each other. We thrived on envy. And yet, I thought this was normal. As long as people admired me, why should it matter that I was miserable?

I've contributed nothing to this world unless I knew it could benefit me somehow. I never thought about this before. Never. I was just living my life the way I thought I was supposed to live it. And then one day, about a year ago, I picked up a copy of your magazine on a plane and read a letter from an editor about a girl whose best friend in second grade only had one dress and how everyone made fun of that little girl because she was dirty and poor and different. And I cried for the first time in twenty years, because I once knew a little girl just like that.

I remember her perfectly because I teased her more than anyone and I wasn't happy until I made sure everyone else was making fun of her too. And yet, she never cried. She held her head up high as she walked into school, day in and day out, in that same pathetic, torn dress. And I wondered how she dared keep coming back. But now I understand. She knew she wasn't hurting anyone and so she had nothing to be ashamed of. But I, who had everything, live with shame every day of my life because of the way I've always treated people like her.

It took me a long time to bring myself to write this letter. I realize it may never get read, but I couldn't live with myself if I didn't at least try.

The day I read that letter, I became a different person. I made the decision to sell my company, I told my husband, who I couldn't even look at anymore, that I wanted to leave him and I walked right out of my *perfect* life. I walked away from my fabulous water views, my precious antiques, my beautiful cars, and my so-called friends. I no longer need the right address, to obsess about my looks, my weight or my possessions because I have something to live for now that has nothing to do with appearances. I am trying to get my soul back each and every day. It's a struggle, I can't deny that. I have to retrain my thinking in every possible way. I have to try to look for qualities in people that I know I should value even though I don't quite feel it yet. I have to sit there and really think before I buy something because, until now, I never even knew what I liked. I only bought what I was taught was in good taste. I have no idea what my own taste is. Of course I'm afraid that once I discover what I really like, it might very well be in bad taste, but at least I'll know who I am.

I've now gone back to school to study what I've always wanted to study and I'm raising myself all over again, this time with my own values, not my mother's. And for the first time in my life, I can walk with my head held high, just like that little girl in the dirty pink dress. Because, for once in my life, I know I'm not hurting anyone. So if you're out there, Ali, I just want to say, I'm sorry. I hope you can find it in your heart to forgive me.

Sincerely,
Caren Westman

Want More?

Turn the page to enter
Avon's Little Black Book —

the dish, the scoop and the
cherry on top from
STEPHANIE LESSING

Best Friends

The truth is I, too, had a best friend in second grade who wore a pink party dress to school on her first day and I loved her as much as Zoe loved Ali. My best friend's name was Lisa, and I loved her despite the fact that the other girls made fun of her dress. I loved her because she was funny and smart and because, between you and me, I liked the dress. But then again, having been sterilized on a daily basis for most of my childhood, I thought being dirty was extremely cool.

When Lisa moved away, I thought I'd never have another best friend for the rest of my life. Of course, by the time the new school year started, I had turned that corner that forces us to rethink the criteria we use to select our best friends. That was the year I'd made up my mind to become a serious student. I was tired of messing around with slackers and I made a promise to myself that by the end of the year I would have improved my handwriting by one hundred percent. Yes, by third grade, my life was all about penmanship, and that's when I discovered Andrea Blackwell.

Andrea deserved those awards she won for best handwriting. She certainly was a *marvelous* child. Andrea, whose name was pronounced Ondrea, unlike all the other Andreas, used that word a lot. *Marvelous.* It's a word I hadn't stumbled upon quite yet, seeing as how we were eight, but once I got used to it, I could no longer imagine how I ever managed without it. As soon as I started hanging out with Ondrea, I became utterly ashamed of myself for spending so much time with my other friends, those barbarians. Ondrea was the only truly refined child in the class, and I was quick to follow in her well-heeled footsteps.

I wore a skirt to school every day of the first two weeks of our new friendship. I was as neat as a pin for the full fourteen days. I'll never forget my mother's face when I told her I was no longer satisfied with my hosiery.

"I'll be needing new knee socks, Barbara. Mine are pilled," I told her.

She had to fan herself. It was a startling recovery. Before I became friends with Ondrea, my mother was always yelling at me for climbing trees and digging in the mud. It was bad enough that my fingernails were always caked with dirt, but I had a habit of eating the mud as well. Perhaps all of her hard work was finally paying off. Her little girl was finally behaving like a lady. Her pride knew no bounds as she watched me pull lint off my cuffs with my nose in the air.

I'm not sure when my obsession with other people's handwriting began, but Ondrea's was the best I'd seen at that point in my life and I wondered if it had something to do with the shape of her hands. They were marvelous hands, no doubt, but that handwriting of hers was something else.

I began to observe her more closely, to record her habits, to get inside the mind of the girl with perfect penmanship. I studied her day and night.

By week three she was really starting to get on my nerves.

She was also starting to get very curious about what I was writing in my notebook all the time. If she had managed to get a look at it she would have seen that it contained a very elaborate description of the shape of her thumb, a finger which most people underestimate in relation to the art of lettering. She would have also seen that I was completely incapable of writing in a straight line, despite the lined paper. Like most children with a lot on their minds, my handwriting started off on the right road but then it had the tendency to get distracted and wander off somewhere high on a hill until it suddenly realized it was lost and had to meander its way back down. It looked a lot like the polygraph test results of a pathological liar. Ondrea would also have discovered that I couldn't stand this weird habit that she had of letting her mouth hang open with her tongue resting visibly on her bottom lip, while she sat mindlessly staring into space. Somehow I managed to overlook it, though, and continued pursing her on a steady basis. Superior penmanship can be very intoxicating and I was delighted the first time she invited me to go to her house after school.

I had no idea we would spend the evening doing homework. Sure I was ready to begin my career as an academic, but only in theory. What I really wanted to do after school was sit around and watch TV or run around screaming.

I was also shocked to find out that Ondrea's house was actually cleaner than mine. I didn't think it was possible, but there it was. White, chilly, clean. The carpeting, flat and austere. The dark wood polished and quiet. And there was her mother. Pale, translucent, and painfully thin. Little blue veins accented her milky antiseptic skin.

Ondrea and her mom called the housekeeper Miss Lilly. We called our housekeeper Pat, and Pat called my mom Bobbie. Miss Lilly asked me for my shoes when I came in. When I handed them to her, she lifted each one with two fingers, as though they were a pair of dead rats.

Ondrea's mother told Miss Lilly that we would have steak on the grill at six o'clock P.M. and that we would be dining outside.

I imagined Miss Lilly saying, "I'll have mine rare, Babs!" But instead she said, "Yes, Ma'am. Promptly at six."

I was excited for the steak.

Ondrea said that she already knew that she wouldn't be hungry. Miss Lilly gave her a stern look and Ondrea and I went back to our homework. What a waste of a perfectly good afternoon.

At that point, the only reason I stayed at her house was to see if she would go into one of her catatonic stares. The waiting was unbearable and I knew the *Flintstones* were on, but I didn't bother to bring it up.

After homework, we played a nice game of cards while I tried not to fall asleep. The house was so still, we were whispering, and then we heard Miss Lilly ring the bell. Ondrea looked at me and said, "It's time for dinner." I nodded politely, trying not to scream out, "Glory fucking hallelujah!"

I couldn't help noticing that our picnic had been laid out rather elegantly.

Everything was white.

The tablecloth, the plates, the white peonies that had been carefully lifted from the garden with no trace of ever having lived in dirt, the beautiful white vase that held the peonies, and the napkins, which were each adorned with one single, delicately embroidered sage green leaf. It was dinner art.

No wonder Ondrea was perfect.

Ondrea, her mother and I took our seats in silence and, then, out of nowhere, Ondrea's tall father entered the room without so much as a footstep of warning. He just appeared like a quiet ceiling spider.

"Where did he come from?" I wondered, looking around.

At my house, when my father walked through the door, I screamed, "Daddy!" and jumped up and down as though he had just returned from war. I think I jumped up and down like that every time he walked by.

This man was like a stranger in his own home. A forgotten human balloon drifting from room to room, completely ignored.

I tried to make him feel welcome so I said, "Hello, Mr. Blackwell!"

It was a very ballsy move on my part, but I didn't want him to think I was on their side.

At first I thought he might ignore me, but he very politely answered, "Hello, young lady."

I looked up enthusiastically to see if Ondrea and her mom were surprised to see what a nice person he was.

I was hoping they would give him another chance, but neither one of them was the least bit interested in this guy. He was like an extra. He sat down at the charming, well-appointed picnic table and then he just seemed to dissipate like steam. At one point, he asked if there was butter on the table and Ondrea's mother answered, "No." Clearly, he was not permitted to talk about butter.

Nevertheless, I heartily dove into my steak and began to cut and chew with gusto. I was determined not to let the tension of their strained relationships interfere with my appreciation of good food presented in a tasteful setting.

We were all just clinking along with our melodious knives and glasses chiming in on cue to fill up the empty silence when all at once I realized that Ondrea's mother had put down her fork and had repositioned her body to face Ondrea head on.

Mrs. Blackwell just sat there glaring at my poor friend with her blue veins bulging out of her forehead. Ondrea was not responding. The silence was deafening.

This went on for what seemed like an eternity but it was probably a full minute, which is a long time when it's too quiet to continue chewing what's already in your mouth. I was so tempted to just blurt out, "What'd she do?" with a mouth full of meat, just to kill the suspense, but Ondrea's mother spoke first, "Ondrea, dear, if you cannot swallow properly, you will have to leave the table. We've discussed this several times."

What on earth was she talking about? Is there more than one way down?

Ondrea put her fork down on her plate and never took another bite. She put her hands in her lap and looked at them for the remainder of the meal. It was obvious she was used to this sort of scrutiny and that it was senseless for her to defend herself. So she just sat there and accepted it. I couldn't believe she was going to let a perfectly good Porterhouse just sit there and rot all because her mom was some kind of a pharynx control freak.

I let my eyes shift over to Ondrea and I tried to give a few encouraging head tilts toward her plate, but she just turned to me and glared, exactly like her mother. . . . And then she did it. She went into the open-mouthed trance. Just then, I felt my own esophagus constrict and I began to cough. I coughed and coughed myself into a violent fit while everyone around me just froze. Somehow I managed to gulp down a little water and I attempted to make a little joke out of it.

"Excuse me, I must have swallowed a huge piece of meat without chewing it first," I jested, punching myself in the chest a few times.

I thought this would be a real ice-breaker, but it just made me look like an insensitive, happy pig. I should have stabbed myself. That would have been more in keeping with the flavor of the evening. Ondrea's mother finally stood up, indicating that the meal had come to an end. What a shame.

I never went back to Ondrea's house. Once I knew why Ondrea had perfect handwriting, it no longer seemed like something I wanted to work toward and I realized, after seeing her life close-up, that we had nothing in common. But I couldn't just forget about her. The more I thought about it, the more I realized she needed me more than I needed her, and I became determined to show her what she'd been missing while perfecting herself all those years.

I taught her how to dig for worms and climb the tree behind my house. I taught her how to eat with her hands and swallow without caring. I taught her how to do a handspring from one couch onto the other and how to sit around and do nothing. I invited her to my house after school almost every day. I wanted my house to be her house, but mostly, I wanted my mother to be her mother.

Ondrea made progress, but it was hard for her to loosen up and she was very hot and cold. I knew not to take it personally when she glared at me for purposely trying to get milk to come out of my nose, or when I demonstrated for our entire lunch table how many Oreos I could fit in my mouth at one time. I didn't take it personally because I understood her.

Every now and then she'd try to get me to come over to her house again, but I just couldn't do it. I couldn't take the frozen silence or the thought of seeing her mother humiliate her, and I wasn't that fond of Miss Lilly either, but mostly I feared choking to death in front of an almost live audience.

At first she didn't care and we played only at my house, but eventually she began to feel insulted by the fact that it was my house or nothing, and she began to protest. I refused to give in and she started coming over less and less. I tried to stay friendly with her, but it was only out of obligation and she knew it. When I sensed that she was becoming closer with Natalie Livingston, the girl who could spell every single word in the dictionary, I knew it was safe for me to move on.

When fourth grade rolled around, I discovered Claudine, who had such an impressive overbite, she could stick her pinky so far up into the space where her teeth were supposed to meet that you couldn't see any of her nail at all. That was the year I was forced to get braces. Naturally, as soon as Claudine demonstrated this talent of hers, I was completely taken in.

Claudine's mom was never home so we had the full run of her house every day. The house was filled with antiques, but Claudine and her brothers played kickball right there in the living room without a care in the world. I remember trying to picture Ondrea playing kickball in Claudine's house and how much fun it would have been for her to stand on top of a piano just once in her life, but she had a new best friend, and so did I.

STEPHANIE LESSING

Anthony Cella / European Studio

STEPHANIE LESSING is the author of *She's Got Issues* and a freelance writer who lives in Demarest, New Jersey, with her husband Dan and two children, Kim and Jesse. Stephanie was formerly the Promotion Copy Chief for *Mademoiselle* magazine and traveled with *Mademoiselle* to co-host fashion and beauty events, going on to freelance for magazines such as *Vogue, Glamour, Vanity Fair, Conde Nast Traveler, Self,* and *Women's Wear Daily.* Most recently, her work appeared in *New York Moves Magazine.* While attending the American College in Paris, she interned for the *Herald Tribune* and then graduated from Boston University with a B.S. degree from the School of Public Communications. *Miss Understanding* is her second novel.